THE LINDISFARNE SERIES

Books 4 - 5

THE LINDISFARNE SERIES

BOOKS 4-5

JOHANNA CRAVEN

Book Four:

The Rising Tide (Prequel)

HOLY ISLAND OF LINDISFARNE

ENGLAND

DECEMBER 31ST 1694

CHAPTER ONE

This house is not haunted.

Footsteps, though—yes. Tapping and crunching, somehow both inside the house and out.

But this house is not haunted. The past does not linger here, at least not outside of imagination.

Abigail Blake is thinking of the past tonight, feeling it swell and pulse around her. Echoes of her husband's voice, so loud inside her head it might well be coming from the halls of Highfield House. But her husband Samuel is lying in his grave now, buried in the churchyard of Saint Aidan's, across the water in Bamburgh.

Is that why her thoughts have gone here, to a terror of her own making?

Little wonder: fuming pots are still smoking on side tables, thickening the air with cinnamon and rosemary—forever more the smell of death. Windows cracked open to let the frigid air in and keep the smallpox at bay. More than a month since Samuel had fallen ill; since that dreadful morning he had woken dizzy with fever. In little more than a week, he was gone.

Has enough time passed to be certain none of the children will suffer the same fate?

Abigail had kept them all out of their father's sickroom, had stood firm against their protests—mostly from Nathan, who had been particularly close to his father. But she herself had been in and out of that room, ferrying water and cloths and colourless soups, praying at her husband's bedside. Speaking gentle words to keep his spirits high, until the fever closed in and stole him away.

This would be the worst of things, if her sons and daughter were to fall ill on account of her and her unheard prayers. Unheard? Undeserved, perhaps.

But she is weary of these thoughts now, this fear. Doesn't have the strength, or the will, to keep carrying it. In this whisky-tainted half-light, she is ready to turn their lives over to chance. If the illness is to come for them, let it come. She is too exhausted to fight it any longer.

A sound comes from outside the parlour window. The crunch of footsteps in snow. Glass still in hand, Abigail goes to the window and lifts the curtain. Peers out at the silver-white landscape.

Snowflakes patter silently against the dark glass, the dunes of Emmanuel Head transformed into moonlit white rises. The silence is profound now. Surely the footsteps were nothing but imagination. It's a sound that does not belong out there, not on a night like this.

Tonight, those north of the border will celebrate the coming of the new year. They will be sweeping their hearths and hanging holly to welcome the Hogmanay night. Here in England, with their antiquated calendar, the new year will not arrive for another three months. Here, they are still languishing in the year she buried her husband. A year she can't quite grasp the edges of in order to see it clearly.

Abigail closes her eyes. Lifts the glass to her lips. Her husband's whisky. Remnants of him.

The liquor slides hot down her throat. Does little to lighten the weight of her grief, or of this shadowed, creaking manor. Highfield House seems to have come alive in the four weeks she has been a widow. Become filled with more empty places, more echoes, more memories. It had not felt quite so big or haunted when Samuel was here.

In any case, she had stopped believing in ghosts many years ago. Stopped believing out of necessity when she had moved up here to Lindisfarne, to become the mistress of this monolith. And now what is she? Caretaker, she supposes. The house is hers but not hers. A roof over her head, yes, but she has no rights to sell this place. When he comes of age, her eldest son Oliver will be king of this castle, lord of these un-haunted, haunted halls.

The clock on the mantel chimes. Midnight. A new month, at least. To those north of the border: a new year.

When the twelfth chime falls silent, Abigail hears the footsteps outside again.

She sets her glass on the side table and takes the lamp from the mantel; tries to take her courage with her. She needs courage now, doesn't she, widow and caretaker that she is.

She goes first to the upstairs hallway to check on her children. Opens one door, the next, the next. Nathan and Eva are both sleeping deeply, small bodies rising and falling with breath, undisturbed by the pale beam of her lantern.

Oliver's blankets are tossed messily across the mattress and the curtains are parted, letting a stream of moonlight shaft across the empty bed. She is not surprised to find him missing. Her oldest child is an eternal challenge. Eleven years old, and razor sharp.

There is no way he ought to have made it out of his room without her being aware of it. Her sleep has been fragmented since her husband's death—no doubt fatigue is beginning to cloud her mind. Still, this old, groaning house makes late-night escapes difficult, at least from up here on the second storey. The window is too high, the stone wall unscalable. To have made it to any of the downstairs exits, he would have had to come down the only staircase. She had not heard him do so.

She peers through the curtains. At once, she knows the footsteps outside the house belong to Oliver. Because out in the dark bay beyond the house, lamps light up the shape of a ship. She has no idea who owns the vessel, or why it is here. But Oliver will have been fascinated by the sight of it from his bedroom window. Will have gone outside for a closer look.

She hurries downstairs, snatching her cloak from the hook beside the door and stepping out into the night. Her breath plumes out in front of her, silver against the black of the cloud-banked sky. Snowflakes glitter in the globe of lamplight, the moonscape of snow giving the dunes an otherworldly glow. The sea sighs as it pulls the pebbles of the embankment below the surface.

She calls Oliver's name, her voice disappearing, unanswered. Intrusive in the snow-hushed stillness. A distant wooden clatter floats across the water from the ship.

Abigail steps carefully down the path in front of the house, her feet sinking into the snow, dampening her stockings at her ankles. She steps out on the dunes, skirts and cloak sighing. Tiny steps, so as not to lose her balance on the ice. She calls for her son again. Pans her lamp through darkness. It's answered, suddenly, by another shaft of lamplight.

"Madam?" The voice that comes back is not her son's. It's smooth and deep, tinged faintly with the rolling vowels of the north. Similar to the way her husband had spoken. "Is everything all right?"

She lifts her lamp. The light picks out a tall man wrapped in a long black cloak, face half hidden by a cocked hat pulled low.

Shock rattles through her at the sight of him. There is no good explanation for any man to be out here on these dark dunes, whether he came from that ship in the bay or not. This wild top end of Holy Island is empty but for her and her children and their unquiet house.

"Stay away from me," she hisses, charging further onto the dunes and panning her lamp around in a wild arc. She calls Oliver's name again.

For several minutes, she loses sight of the man as she rounds the house. Snowflakes sting her cheeks, obscuring her vision. She squints into the darkness beyond the reach of her lamp, searching for her son.

She turns the corner of the house and meets a fresh flare of lamplight. There is Oliver, the man from the ship with a firm grip on his wrist. Abigail thrashes through the snow towards them. She grabs her son's wrist and yanks him out of the man's grip.

"How dare you lay a hand on my son?"

"Forgive me," the man says. "I was only trying to keep him safe. His lamp had blown out, and he was far too close to the edge of the headland." The clouds part slightly, and a sliver of moonlight lets her glimpse a little more of his face. He is close to her age, she guesses—a few years past thirty. But there's a searing aliveness in his eyes that Abigail does not remember feeling for years.

"Stay away from us," she hisses. She turns away and begins to march back to the house, tugging Oliver along beside her. An unlit lantern dangles from his free hand.

"There's no need to act so hysterical, Mama," he says casually. "I just came out to look at the ship." As though it is the most normal thing in the world for an eleven-year-old boy to be prowling through the snow so far past midnight.

"How did you get out of the house?"

He doesn't answer. Not that she expected him to. When it comes to Oliver, there is a time and a place for truth telling, and it is not here or now.

As they reach the front door, she finds herself looking back over her shoulder. Back towards the man with the cocked black hat. Back towards the ship.

Nothing, now. No footsteps, no voices, and they are alone on the headland once again.

Abigail slides her key into the front door of the house and shoves it open. Tries to convince herself that this silence, this emptiness, is what she has been seeking all along.

CHAPTER TWO

Sometimes, when he wakes, Nathan forgets his father is no longer here. Sometimes, when his mind is still bleary with sleep, he expects Da to come striding down the hall, throw open the bedroom door and say *Up you get, my lad, it's a bright morning for living.*

Other times, he dreams he is standing at his father's grave, watching his coffin being lowered into the earth. It's a dream that comes in vivid colours; a dream in which he is wearing his mourning clothes—tight-buckled breeches and the silk band that itched at his throat, the too-big black justacorps hanging off his shoulders. On the nights he has that dream, he wakes with the knowledge that Da is gone, fresh and clear and aching, and he wonders how he could ever have forgotten.

This morning, the knowledge of his father's death is sitting dully at the back of his mind the moment he opens his eyes. Da won't come in here to make sure he is awake in time for breakfast. Won't come in smelling of rosewater and tobacco, or with the cold sea air clinging to him.

Pale pink light is creeping through the gap in the curtain. Nathan remembers suddenly that it had been snowing last night, and the knowledge softens the edges of his grief. He scrambles out of bed to look at the freshly coated landscape. The snow reaches right up to the edge of the embankment, where it has been bitten into by the in and out of the sea. Everything is clean and vivid again, the bleak mud-streaked snow of yesterday now dazzling white.

A creak of the floorboards from Oliver's room next door draws

Nathan's attention away from the window. He tiptoes out of his room and presses his eye to the keyhole of his brother's bedroom door. Oliver pulls out the chair at his writing desk and sits. Dips a quill into ink and begins to scrawl something down on a piece of paper, his blond head hunched over the page.

Nathan wonders what he's writing. Copying something from a book, maybe—he has seen Oliver do that plenty of times. Pieces of information he finds most fascinating, wants to store away and never forget. Oliver knows so much about everything, especially the Viking raids that happened here on Lindisfarne more than nine hundred years ago. Oliver knows all the details: about the great famine that came before the raid, and the lightning and whirlwinds and dragons that the chronicles say came before the attack. Nathan loves hearing the stories of the Viking raids. At least until the part where the monks' blood is splattered on the walls of Saint Cuthbert's church.

"I can hear you out there, Nathan," Oliver says, not looking up from the desk.

Nathan backs away from the keyhole. He hears footsteps come towards the door. Feels the quickening of his heart. Oliver throws the door open and stands leaning against the thick wooden frame, arms folded across his chest.

Nathan dares to look up at him. He is never quite sure which version of his older brother he is going to get. Sometimes, Oliver dishes out a look that says he wants Nathan gone; other times, he's welcoming, like when he has a new game to play, or a new story to tell. Today, there's a look of bored indifference on his face.

"Have you come to see the hole in the wall again?" he asks.

Nathan nods. It's not entirely true; he's more intrigued by his brother than he is by the hole in the wall—but only by a little. The hole in the wall is definitely worth his fascination.

Oliver had shown it to him a few days ago. Nathan had had the sense that his brother had known about it for some time; had only just decided to share this piece of knowledge with him, for some hidden purpose of his own. But he didn't care. Oliver had let him into the secret now, and that was all that mattered.

Oliver steps aside, letting Nathan into the bedroom. "Do you remember where it is?"

"Yes." Nathan pushes on the panel to the right-hand side of the fireplace. The panel swivels beneath his hand to reveal the small, dark hiding place behind. He peers into it curiously. He has no desire to go inside; the last time he had done that, Oliver had insisted on coming with him, and closing the panel behind them. They had sat side by side in the tiny space, enclosed by a darkness so thick Nathan could not see his hand in front of his face. Oliver didn't speak, just sat there listening to their breathing. Nathan's shoulder pushed hard against the brick wall and he could feel his lungs growing tight. Could feel the warm, earthy air gathering in his throat. He had felt a very pressing need to get out of that hole in the wall—not that he would ever let his brother know that, of course. He had been more than a little relieved when Oliver had grown bored with whatever it was he was doing, and had pushed the panel in the wall open again.

A thrill in small doses, maybe.

Like he does each time he sees the hiding place, Nathan wonders why it is there. It's a deliberate hole, he knows that much. Not like the time he and Oliver had been playing in the cart shed and had accidentally rammed Da's caulking mallet through the wall. This is a different kind of thing altogether.

The day Oliver had first shown him the hole, Nathan had asked him if he knew who had put it there and why, but Oliver had just stood silently behind him. Then he'd said, "You're not to tell anyone about this, do you understand? Not Mama, or Eva, or Mrs Calloway."

Nathan had promised—not a word. He liked the thrill of keeping his older brother's secrets. When Mrs Calloway, their nurse, had asked him what he had been doing that afternoon, Nathan had said, *Nothing much, just keeping to myself,* as casual as you like, and had been proud of himself all evening.

Oliver had made him promise not to say a word about the knife he'd found in the water off Saint Cuthbert's island either. A Viking knife, he'd said. Left behind after the raids. Nathan had believed him then, back when he had just turned seven. But now he's almost eight, he's starting to wonder if that might not be so true.

"Come and look at this," Oliver says suddenly. Somehow, he's at the window—Nathan had not even heard him move from behind him. He's pulling back the curtain and peering out over the water.

Nathan joins him at the glass. There's a ship out on the water. Not a herring boat—much bigger, like a merchant ship or a pirate galleon. Nathan has seen plenty of ships like this: in the Lindisfarne anchorage, and out in Beadle Bay, but he's never seen one moored outside his house before. He wonders how he had missed it when he had looked out his bedroom window earlier. He supposes he had been too entranced by the fresh snow. Or the thought of Da being gone.

"Came in last night," says Oliver. "I went to have a look."

Nathan can't wait to be like his older brother. To think to himself, *I'm going to go have a look at that ship*, and just off and do it, without a care in the world. Nathan knows that if he tried such a thing, Mama or Mrs Calloway would catch him before he even made it down the staircase.

"Is it a navy ship?" he asks. "Or a supply ship? Or are they pirates?"

Oliver shrugs airily. He moves from the window and takes the page sitting on his desk. Shoves it into his pocket. "We'll find out."

Last night feels strangely dreamlike, the edges of his memories frayed by the dark, by snow, by the long, slow and sleepless voyage up the coast of England.

When he had returned to his ship last night, after rescuing the boy from the headland, Henry Ward had fallen into the deepest sleep he had had in weeks, a dram of Hogmanay whisky pushing against the edges of his dreams.

It had been a fleeting, instinctual decision to moor his ship on the far north side of Holy Island, rather than in the village anchorage. Instinct, perhaps. Six years as a privateer, and fifteen years on merchant vessels before that, and Henry Ward has relied on instinct a lot. More often than not, it serves him well.

There is no action to be had here on Lindisfarne, of course—he is here to sell the cargo he had taken from his latest seizure—an uneventful haul of sugar, molasses and coffee. But a habit for secrecy had taken over and directed him to moor the ship in the darkness beyond the uninhabited north side of the island.

At least, he had assumed it uninhabited. He had not expected to see a house on the headland. It was old and wind-pressed—he guessed it had been standing there for decades.

Ward had seen the boy's lantern moving through the dunes, and suspicion had drawn him out into his longboat to see who was moving through the darkness. His distrustful mind had imagined thieves and pirates and Frenchmen, and anyone else who might see fit to take a piece out of the cargo he has brought up here to sell. Distrustful, yes, but Ward can't deny he was glad to have gone out there. The boy's lamp had burned out while he was climbing the rugged scarp of the headland, and Ward had only just made it to him in time to light his way back down to the dunes. A few seconds later and he could well have been searching for the child in the cold black-ink water of the high tide.

This morning, he has taken the longboat to the village to face the questioning of the harbour master, and collect the deposit for the cargo. Once the money is in his hands, he will have his men deliver the shipment. His young cabin boy is with him to show him the way to the street housing his buyer's new office.

Finn is quiet as they climb up the beach from the anchorage into the village. He has been this way since Ward had told him they'd be visiting Lindisfarne. Eyes constantly drifting out towards the shadow of the Farne Islands.

Ward follows his gaze across the leathery grey water. "Your father still over there, lad?"

"I think so." Finn looks up at Ward, his brown eyes wide. "You're not going to send me back there are you?"

"No. Unless that's what you want?"

Finn shakes his head, looking at his feet. "No, sir."

"Good. I've no desire to look for another cabin boy."

Ward feels the eyes on him as they turn into the cobbled warren of the village. Reluctant though he might be to be here, Finn has done a good job of directing him straight towards the main street, where their buyer is located. Not that there are all that many wrong turns for him to have taken.

Ward knows himself an anomaly in this small village. A child of

Newcastle, he had been out to Lindisfarne a few times in his youth. His buyer has since moved from the mainland to the island—and is willing to pay a good enough price to make the journey up here worth it. Ward can't deny there's something faintly pleasant about returning to the county in which he grew up. Not that that familiarity makes him feel like any less of a stranger here on Holy Island.

Beside him, Finn is walking with his head down, woollen cap pulled low to hide his face. He watches his feet, shoulders rounded. Afraid to be recognised, no doubt, by anyone who might tell his father they have seen him. Ward walks close, doing his best to shield him.

Ward halts in his step as a tall, blond-haired boy appears at the end of the street. In spite of the darkness last night, he has no doubt it is the same boy he had seen roaming the dunes at midnight.

Oliver—the son of the woman who had appeared from the house with an admonishment on her tongue.

The woman who, inexplicably, has lodged herself in Ward's thoughts and is refusing to be relinquished. He can't quite make sense of why. Pity? Perhaps. But he has never really been one for pity. More likely, a sense of being drawn to a woman who had dared to scold him. Because he has never really been one for getting scolded by women either. Usually they are far more accommodating.

Oliver catches sight of him and quickens his pace in their direction.

"Wait here," Ward tells Finn.

Finn glances at Oliver, then nods silently. Steps back to hide himself in the narrow gap between two houses.

As Ward approaches, Oliver stops walking. "Are you to stay moored in the bay tonight?" he asks, not bothering with a greeting. "Outside our house?"

"Yes." Ward folds his arms across his chest, feeling inexplicably defensive. "I trust I'll not find you running about the dunes in the middle of the night again. You could have got yourself killed."

"What kind of ship is it?" Oliver asks. "Are you a merchant? A pirate? I assume you're not navy. Why are you moored at Emmanuel Head, instead of in the anchorage?"

Ward raises his eyebrows, taken aback by the child's boldness. Who is he to ask such questions? He guesses Oliver to be no more than ten or eleven—Finn's age. If his cabin boy ever spoke with such audacity, he'd thrash him into tomorrow.

"I'm glad I finally found you," Oliver continues, when he realises Ward is not going to answer his barrage of questions. "I've been looking for you for hours." He reaches into his pocket and produces a folded page. Holds it out. "This is from my mother."

Ward takes the page curiously, aware of a faint flicker in his chest. He unfolds the paper to find a few lines of small, neat lettering:

Please forgive my behaviour last night. I regret my outburst and hope you can accept my apology.

I would very much like to make it up to you. I do hope you and your officers will accept my hospitality at Highfield House this evening.

Yours faithfully,

Abigail Blake

Ward stares down at the words, caught off guard by the invitation.

He realises the boy is staring up at him, waiting for an answer. Ward clears his throat, in an attempt to buy himself a little time. He cannot accept, surely. It is not the done thing. Given the way Abigail Blake had been striding alone across the dunes last night, he can only assume she does not have a husband with her in that vast hulk of a house. Or at least, if she does, that he is severely incapacitated.

Then again, would it be rude to turn down her attempt at making things up to him? Ward would hate for her to think he sees her behaviour as unforgiveable. He cannot tell if this line of thought is valid, or if comes only from the way this woman has worked her way into his thoughts.

"Tell your mother I shall consider her offer," he says finally, feeling a need to extract himself from the boy's rigid gaze.

Oliver hovers for a moment, as though not entirely happy with the response. His lips part, and for a fleeting moment, Ward feels uneasy. Cannot make sense of why.

"Very good, sir," the boy says finally. "I hope my mother will see you this evening."

CHAPTER THREE

Abigail has not told her mother about Samuel's death. She does not want her pity. Does not want her assistance. And she does not want to open the door of Highfield House and find her mother on the doorstep.

Abigail's mother, Susanna, had always kept a tight hold on her. Abigail is not sure if that had caused the problem, or if it had been a result of the problem. All she knows for certain is that once, she had been just as troublesome as her eldest son.

Susanna had been aware of that false-hearted streak inside her daughter long before Abigail herself could truly make sense of it. That unplaceable *something* that made her look at the world through a warped and tinted lens; through distorted eyes that saw only darkness in the world. Made her act accordingly. Made her lie. Speak in sharp, spiteful words— directed, almost exclusively, towards her mother. Broken glass and torn dresses in an attempt to shake loose that restlessness inside her.

It's a part of herself she never wanted; a part she has always tried to keep hidden, tried to fight. The desire to hurt another, to deceive, to be cruel—these days, Abigail can see these things as separate from herself. Can see them as unwanted thorns that blow in—and will blow out again just as quickly, if she just closes her eyes and allows herself to breathe.

Abigail had not had close friends as a child. Susanna had kept her on a tight leash, in an attempt to tamp down the aggressiveness, the deceit, the destructiveness. Or at least to keep it hidden from prying eyes.

Abigail had kept her dark side hidden from her husband too. Had kept it locked away inside her for more than a decade of marriage, carefully filtering everything that came out of her mouth—impossibly challenging at first, but easier with time—in an attempt to make herself a more decent person.

Now, she has buried that troublesome part of herself so deeply it could almost have ceased to exist—at least it would feel that way if she couldn't see the same darkness in her eldest child.

Abigail was nineteen when her mother had pursued the match with Samuel Blake, a kind and hardworking merchant who had sold some fine imported housewares to her closest friend. To this day, Abigail is not sure if Susanna's enthusiasm over the marriage had come from the thought of her daughter marrying a wealthy and well-respected gentleman, or at the prospect of her being carted off to somewhere as distant and inaccessible as Lindisfarne.

It was a part of the world that was barely in Abigail's consciousness. A part of the world she had no desire to make home. But Samuel Blake was a kind and decent man who brought out the best in her where her mother brought out the worst. She would become mistress of a grand house, he had told her—a wild and windswept place he had unexpectedly inherited after his cousin's untimely death.

Abigail had not wanted to leave London. Had not wanted a life on this sometimes-island, in a house that felt heavy with other people's footsteps. But she had seen an escape from the suffocating life beneath her mother's wing. And leaving London, or sometimes-island, or echoing house or not—she had taken it.

Perhaps, she had thought, she might even outrun the parts of herself she did not wish to take with her. The parts that seemed far more glaring when she was in her mother's company.

When she had left London twelve years ago, Samuel's ring freshly on her finger, Abigail had promised her mother she would keep in touch; she was Susanna's only child, after all, and her father had been gone for many years. And for a while, she had. Weekly letters detailing the children's progress, her attempts at turning Highfield House into her home, lengthy descriptions of the island, crafted at her husband's desk, with her gaze turned out to sea.

But the weekly letters had dwindled to monthly, and then once or twice a year. And visits? Well, Abigail has not been back to London since she left more than a decade ago, and it's been years since her mother ventured up here. She's not seen the boys since Nathan was in leading strings; has never laid eyes on Eva.

Abigail knows her mother's distance has a lot to do with Oliver. The last time her mother had been around her son, Abigail had seen Susanna's unease. Had seen the fear in her mother's eyes that Abigail might have passed her cruel streak onto her son. Well. There is no *might* about it.

Nonetheless, Samuel's death is something Susanna ought to know about.

Abigail takes a deep breath and settles into the chair at the desk. Around her, the house is quiet; Nathan and Eva long asleep, and Oliver's footsteps sounding quietly in his bedroom. Rain is pattering against the windows, settling silent against the snow.

The room feels intensely inhabited by her dead husband; his quills still standing in a pot beside the ink, the smell of his tobacco still emanating from the drawer. Desk chair indented with his weight, leaving his ghostly imprint. Abigail closes her eyes. Inhales the fading presence of him. How long will it be, she wonders, until there is no trace of Samuel Blake left in here at all?

A sudden wave of grief surges up on her, tightening her throat and stinging her eyes. In so many ways, theirs had been a good marriage. A strong marriage. Though they had never had the kind of dizzying lust for one another she had read about in histoires, he had always treated her kindly, fairly. Looked upon her as a dear friend; a partner to navigate life with. They had not married for love, but a genuine and natural love had grown out of it. And as Samuel's wife, she had found an anchor, a solidity, that she had never felt before. A solidity that grounded her, made it easier to fight off the unwanted parts of herself. Samuel Blake had been an achingly decent man, and that had made her want to be a good wife to him. He, and later, their children, had been a reason to fight against the restlessness, the darkness inside her. She prays that one day, Oliver will find a similar reason.

Abigail closes her eyes, trying to find the will to write this cursed letter.

When she opens her eyes, her gaze is drawn through the open curtains, alighting on the faint rose of lamplight coming from the ship in the bay.

And suddenly her thoughts are back in the dark whisky haze of last night. The man with the cocked hat. The sudden appearance of the ship. Oliver's escape from the house. How he had managed to do so is a question she has not yet found the strength to linger on. But she needs answers from him. Needs the truth.

She shoves aside the blank pages and goes down the hall to her son's room. Opens the door without knocking.

"Get your books," she says. "We're to have a lesson."

Oliver is sitting cross-legged on his bed, whittling away at a piece of wood with the sharp end of a quill. He looks up at her through a thatch of thick ice-blonde hair, a faint smile flickering in the corner of his lips. He does not protest at having a lesson so late at night. No doubt he knows as well as she does that this is not really about his education. It's about hers.

These lessons with Oliver, these times when it's just the two of them, feel like the only times she can ever truly get through to her son. His lessons have become the time in which she pries out the answers she needs. When they are in company, even with just his brother and sister, Oliver is aloof and secretive. But when it is just the two of them, Abigail manages, sometimes, to crack through his façade.

It's a skill no one else has ever had. Not the children's nurse, or Oliver's teachers; certainly not his father.

Abigail tells herself it's because she's his mother.

She knows that really, it's because she and Oliver are so frighteningly similar.

He gets up off the bed without speaking and slides into his desk chair. Abigail drags the armchair over from the corner of the room and perches on the edge.

She reaches for the mathematics text from the pile of books on his desk. Opens to a page scrawled with algebraic symbols she has no idea how to decipher. She turns backwards through the book until she finds a page of simple arithmetic. "This page," she tells him.

She has taught him little. In the three months since he was expelled from the grammar school in Berwick they have covered little beyond basic

Latin phrases and arithmetic Abigail dug up from her own lessons some twenty years ago.

Oliver begins to work through the sums. Numbers and symbols flow easily from his quill; she knows he finds this less than challenging.

She ought to seek out a tutor for him. He is far too intelligent to be scrawling down childish sums with his mother. Abigail is well aware of his passion for knowledge—has seen him willingly studying algebra, reading Balfour's philosophy, Latin poetry and prose, and his favourite of all: history. His love for knowledge had just not extended to abiding by the grammar school's rules.

Heaven knows he could have a fine profession ahead of him; a finer profession than his merchant father. Medicine, perhaps, or the law. If only he could find a little discipline. Perhaps this dull arithmetic will remind him of the value of what he had thrown away.

Then again, this is not about arithmetic at all.

"How did you get out of the house last night?" she asks.

Oliver dips his quill in the ink. "Through the front door, of course."

Abigail keeps her face passive. Knows that this is Oliver; knows she has to sift through lies—sometimes veiled, other times deliberately blatant, like this one—before she reaches the truth. "I see." She nods towards the next row of sums. "Continue."

This is their unspoken arrangement: a lie leads to more schoolwork; the truth leads to the end of the class. Oliver will get to the truth, she knows. He always does. It's another of their unspoken arrangements. He will be honest with her—eventually—as long as she is honest with him.

His quill scratches across the page, a frown of concentration creasing the bridge of his nose. A log breaks open in the fireplace, sending a volley of sparks up the chimney. Outside, the rain has intensified, throwing itself against the windows and drumming against the roof.

Abigail fixes her eyes on her son, tension crackling between them. She feels an intense sense of connection to him; far more than she feels to her other children. A connection that both scares and comforts her. Nathan and Eva, gentle and compliant, are both entirely their father's children. Oliver is entirely hers.

"There's a passage," he says suddenly. "In the wall."

"What?" It ought to be a lie. Sounds like a lie. But there's a look in

Oliver's eyes that she recognises as honesty.

"Behind the priest hole."

"There's a priest hole in this house?"

"You didn't know?" By his tone, she can tell he knew she was completely unaware.

"Where?" she asks.

"In here."

Her thoughts begin to race. Samuel had grown up visiting this house— the house of his uncle. Had he known about this? She thinks of him and his cousin tearing through these passages as boys. It seems impossible that they would not have known of such a thing. But surely if he had, Samuel would not have put their troublesome eldest son in this bedroom. It's possible, she realises, that her husband might not have known of this. Possible this might have been a dressing room, or his aunt's bedroom, forbidden to the boys.

Oliver puts his quill down neatly in the centre fold of his book. "Would you like to see it?"

Abigail nods.

He goes to the fireplace and pushes on one of the dark wooden panels to the right of the grate. The panel twists open beneath his palm, revealing a small dark room tucked into the stone of the fireplace.

At once, Abigail is imagining all that might have happened in this house. Her windblown manor shielding Catholic priests within its walls. She imagines the terror that might have infused this place as priest hunters strode from room to room, hunting for their prey. Little wonder she sometimes finds herself so on edge in here, with so much fear and suffering trapped in the fabric of the house.

She cranes her neck so she is looking deep into the hole. Thick, hot blackness, barely touched by the lamp on the mantel, or the flames simmering in the grate beside them. "I don't see the passage," she says.

Oliver reaches into the back of the hole and pushes against the far wall. This is another wood panel, she realises then; not the unyielding stone of the wall. It turns beneath Oliver's hand, revealing a second, slightly larger brick-lined room. And in its far corner, a dark opening that leads down into blackness. Into the walls of the house, Abigail realises. The sight of it makes something twist in her stomach.

The smell of cold earth rises up to meet them. Abigail can just make out the top rungs of a ladder poking up through the hole.

"It's a double priest hole," Oliver tells her. "We learnt about them at school. The first room remained empty to trick the priest hunters, and the priest stayed hidden in the second room behind the first. And whoever built this one made it so a priest that's hiding could escape the house too. Quite genius, don't you think?"

Abigail swallows heavily. "Where does the passage lead?"

"It comes out right beneath Nathan's window."

Abigail stares into the dark chasm, thoughts racing. She wants to tell Oliver not to use the priest hole anymore. Knows that will only encourage him to do so more regularly. Perhaps she could have Mr Emmett from the village come and board the hole up at both ends.

She can only imagine what Oliver might do in retaliation.

A knock at the front door startles her.

No one ever comes out here—at least, they don't since her husband died.

Abigail stays motionless for a moment. Her daily, Ruth, has long left the house, and it is up to her to answer the door. Perhaps she ought to ignore it. Hope that whoever it is will go away. It's far too late for visitors.

"Are you not going to answer the door, Mama?" Oliver says finally. "What if it's someone in need of help in this bad weather?"

She peers at him curiously, trying to see behind his eyes. It's not like him to care about another person's plight. But he is right—someone could be in trouble out there. And she will not let herself be that person who does not care about others. She has fought too hard to keep that selfish and spiteful woman at bay.

Abigail makes her way down the stairs.

She turns the key and pulls the door open to a bloom of gold lamplight. Finds the man from the ship standing on her doorstep in the rain, with three other men behind him.

CHAPTER FOUR

At the sight of her, Ward feels an unexpected jolt in his chest. He takes her in in the lamplight; chestnut coloured hair pulled back from her face, bundled in a low knot at her neck. Pale cheeks and an even, symmetrical face that ought to be unremarkable, but somehow is anything but. Shadows underline clear blue eyes that carry an expression Ward cannot quite make out. Suspicion? Not quite. Surprise? This is closer.

No doubt she had not expected him to accept her invitation.

He can hardly blame her—Ward himself had not expected to accept it either. And yet somehow, once dark had fallen thick across the island, he had found himself drawn out here with his officers in tow, just as she had requested.

Abigail Blake is dressed in simple black skirts and a house jacket, devoid of embroidery or embellishments. Mourning clothing? Perhaps coming here was an enormous mistake. Still, too late for such thoughts. He can hardly walk away without a word now, not even if he wanted to.

"Good evening," he says.

The surprise in her eyes gives way to the same searing anger he saw from her on the dunes last night. "What do you want? Who are all these men?" It's not just anger in her eyes, he realises then. It's panic.

He also realises she is not about to let them in from this torrential downpour. "I'm sorry," he garbles. "I…" Rain runs down the back of his neck, soaks his shirt. Lost for words, Ward holds out the note Oliver had given him that morning. The note, he sees now, that most certainly was not written by his mother.

Abigail snatches the sodden page. Unfolds it and reads it quickly. She presses her lips into a thin line.

"And you imagined this to be genuine, I assume?" she says icily. "You imagined I might willingly invite a group of strangers into my home while my children are sleeping?" She looks at him for a long second. He can feel her scrutinising him; and beyond that, a faint curiosity. He feels suddenly, intensely vulnerable. A foreign sensation, but not, he realises, an unpleasant one. And that in itself feels unmooring.

Ward hears a poorly hidden chuckle from one of his officers. He clears his throat, feeling embarrassment flush the back of his neck. His sudden vulnerability might not be entirely unpleasant, but he does not like looking a fool in front of his men. And he knows he looks a fool now.

"It was a mistake," he admits. "I apologise, Mrs Blake."

"Yes," she says sharply, thrusting the note back into his hand. "That it was. Goodnight. I trust you can all find your way back to your ship without difficulty."

And the door swings closed, the thud echoing out across the rain-soaked dunes.

Abigail stands for a moment in the silence of the entrance hall. Her heart is fast and her entire body feels inexplicably hot. She looks up the stairs, searching for Oliver. She cannot see him, but she is certain he has found some hidden corner of the house to peek out from. Some corner she herself is completely unaware of. Like the passage that weaves through the walls of the house. How many more secrets is this place hiding?

The house feels suddenly monstrous, its emptiness heightened by the sudden disappearance of the men's voices. The hollow makes her grief suddenly acute, the fresh holes in her life gaping. She has never felt so breathtakingly lonely.

Before she knows what she is doing, she is pulling her cloak from the hook on the wall of the foyer and swinging open the front door. Striding down the path at the front of the house and out onto the dunes. Rain slaps at her cheeks, running down the back of her neck and soaking into her skirts.

"Wait," she hears herself call. She can see the men up ahead: tall, dark shadows lit only by the faint glow of their lamps. They stop walking almost as one. Turn back to face her.

The man with the cocked hat approaches her, boots sighing through the wet sludge of the snow. She imagines he is the captain of the ship.

"What's your name?" she asks.

He holds out a hand. "Henry Ward." He nods to the men behind him. "And my officers. Mr Graveney, Mr Hunter, Mr Cook."

She accepts his hand. "Well, Mr Ward. For all his trickery, I suppose my son is right. I owe you a debt of gratitude." She feels not a scrap of gratitude towards him, no. But she cannot spend one more sleepless night walking the halls alone in Highfield House. She doesn't care who is filling that silence. "You and your officers had best come in."

And she hurries back towards the house before she can change her mind.

She is the worst of mothers, Abigail has no doubt. Inviting these men here to assuage her loneliness, it comes from that selfish, spiteful part of herself that makes bad and dangerous choices. With Samuel in the earth, it seem to be tearing itself free.

She takes the men's cloaks and hangs them on the hooks beside the front door. A strange thing, she thinks distantly, to have men's clothes hanging here in the entrance hall again. Feels like a betrayal. Which, she supposes, it is. They're Samuel's children she is putting in danger, after all.

She glances up the staircase in search of Oliver. She ought to be furious with him, of course. But she cannot quite make herself feel the rage she ought to.

Why did Oliver do this? Why invite these men here? For all his disobedience, she knows he never does anything without reason. Never does anything just for the sake of being bad. He's far too intelligent. Far too calculating.

He's enthralled by Henry Ward, she supposes. Wants him at the house, perhaps. Or wants to punish her for the callous way he had spoken to the man last night.

Or perhaps he knows how much she does not want to spend another night in this house with no adult company to speak of.

She hurries into the kitchen, fetching a cloth for the men to dry themselves with. When she returns to the foyer, the smell of wet wool and men has thickened the air.

She leads the sailors into the parlour, trailing her fingertips along the dark wood panels of the wall in a vain attempt to steady herself. Her thoughts are racing. Does she have anything to offer her guests? She has little idea what Ruth has hiding in the pantries. This suddenly feels like the greatest of impositions, for Henry Ward and his men to have inserted themselves into her life like this. Never mind that she had been the one to call them back. Right now, she needs to blame someone other than herself for all this madness. Needs to direct her anger somewhere other than at her own terrible choices.

In the handful of hours since her housekeeper left, she and the children have managed to turn the parlour into a minor chaos. Abigail has left a poetry book face down on the tea table; Oliver's gloves are on the floor beneath the settle; Eva's doll lying beside the hearth. Abigail closes the book and kicks the gloves under the settle. Swoops down to rescue the doll from an officer's stray boot.

Ward's men migrate towards the fireplace, far more interested in the blaze roaring in the grate than in the state of her parlour.

"Please," she manages, "sit." Her polite invitation comes out barbed and coarse, as the two warring parts of herself clash on her tongue. Ward hesitates for the briefest of moments before lowering himself into the embroidered blue armchair beside the tea table. He is looking at her with a look of deep curiosity, the firelight intensifying the sharp contours of his face. His presence seems to suck all the air from the room, forcing Abigail to turn away.

Is it pity that has brought him here? This suddenly seems far more likely than his need for a blazing fire. Abigail suspects she is the kind of woman who ought to be pitied.

She goes to Samuel's liquor cabinet in the corner of the room. Takes out a bottle of brandy and five funnel bowl glasses.

Part of her wants to send these men back out into the night. Wants to return to the quiet stillness of the house. But something nameless, formless, is preventing her from doing that. Preventing her from doing what she knows is right.

The officers are already chatting between mouthfuls of brandy, joking about *better conditions than the tavern* and jibes at their captain's leaky ship. Abigail cannot tell if they are oblivious to the awkwardness of the situation, or simply doing their best to ignore it. Ward gives a half-hearted chuckle that doesn't light his eyes. His gaze follows her around the room.

She garbles something about food, and heads off into the gloom of the house, a strange mix of unease and thrill simmering beneath her anger.

Taking a lamp from its hook in the hallway, she bumbles around the kitchen, finding jars of salted meats and pickled oysters and a bowl of fragrant candied apples. A strange, cobbled-together offering, she knows, but when she takes the bowls of food back to the parlour, the men attack them eagerly.

She takes a shallow sip from the brandy glass one of the men have left on the table in wait for her. It's enough to settle the tirade of nerves. A small enough mouthful to keep her thoughts sharp. She perches on the edge of the empty armchair opposite Henry Ward.

He is still watching her, a look of uncertainty in his eyes. "This is very kind of you, Mrs Blake," he says. "But you must tell us if we are unwanted guests. The last thing I wish to do is impose on you."

She doesn't look at him. Can't look at him. "You're here now," she says tautly. "You may as well stay." And this anger, she knows well, it's not anger at the men. It's anger at herself. At her weakness for allowing these men into her home while her children are sleeping. While she is still in mourning clothes, with the grief over her husband still so fresh and raw inside her. Anger at her inability to face another night alone in this house. It's foolishness, she tells herself sharply. This is her home. She cannot be afraid of it. Besides, she is never alone in this house. She has three children keeping her company.

Three children she is now entirely and wholly responsible for. What a fine job she is doing.

She takes another mouthful of brandy. And just for now, she thinks, just for now, she is going to push aside the chaos and self-loathing inside her head. And she is going to listen to this chorus of masculine voices that is filtering through her house for the first time in weeks, bringing these midnight hours back from the dead.

"What brings you to Lindisfarne?" she asks, when the men's chatter lulls.

"We've cargo to sell," says Henry Ward. "I've a buyer up here in Northumberland who pays a very decent price. Makes the journey north worth the time and money."

"Cargo? You're a merchant sailor?"

A crooked smile lifts the corner of his lips. "Not entirely. The cargo came from a French vessel returning from the Caribbean."

"A privateer then."

"Indeed."

She is glad of it. For a moment, she had feared *pirate*. And then there would have been no way she could have justified this barely justifiable impulse soiree. But at this sea captain's words, some hidden part of her sparks to life. His words prick at some long-buried fascination with the sea; with lands beyond this one; with lives more than the one she is living. Since she was a young child, she has been intrigued by the lives of seafarers, by tales of Arctic islands and the great south land. In the rigid confinement of childhood under her mother's wing, reading about faraway worlds had made her feel less hemmed-in. Had given her a much-needed gasp of freedom.

It's a fascination she had never spoken of to Samuel. In spite of her desire to do so, she has never learnt to sail, as a number of the womenfolk of Lindisfarne have—has never even learnt to handle that rickety old rowboat that sits on the embankment in front of the house. When the tide rises, turning Lindisfarne back into an island, she is utterly at the mercy of others, if she ever needs to leave.

When Abigail was a child, Susanna had let her know, in no uncertain terms, that seafaring was not a fitting interest for a young lady. An interest a man would not be pleased to hear of in his wife. And so Abigail had tucked it away with the other parts of her that were not fit for a husband's eyes. Had filled that fresh hollow with poetry, and needlework, and a fierce determination to rear a garden on the windblown grounds of Highfield House.

But now these seamen are here—and her husband is not—Abigail wants suddenly to immerse herself in these vast and unreachable places. This world of Caribbean journeys and stolen cargo and privateering fleets tracing the coasts of other lands. Life on Holy Island can feel almost unbearably oppressive sometimes, cut off from the mainland for so many hours of each day. And since Oliver was born, she has been so preoccupied with being a mother—with being *Oliver's* mother—that she has had little time to contemplate what might be going on outside the confines of this island. It is oddly blissful to hear stories of the outside world.

The wooden beams above their heads creak loudly as the house shifts in the coldness of the night. Abigail thinks suddenly of her children. Heaven knows Oliver could be traipsing across the dunes right now.

Unlikely, she supposes, given how enthralled he is likely to be by the fact these men are here. Unless he had brought them here so he could disappear without her noticing…

She is rushing towards the staircase as the thought comes to her. Lets out a breath when she spots her son crouched at one end of the hallway, trying to catch a word from the parlour. She pins him with hard eyes. "Go to bed."

A smile flickers on Oliver's lips. A smile that lets her know he has won. The men from the ship are here, just as he intended. Although oddly, right now, Abigail does not feel as though she has lost.

She herds Oliver upstairs and stands in the doorway of his bedroom, watching as he climbs into bed. She peeks into Nathan and Eva's rooms, then hovers at the top of the staircase for a moment to gather herself against the tumult that is Henry Ward.

When she arrives at the bottom of the staircase, he steps out of the parlour to meet her. Lamplight flickers over his shorn cheeks.

"I'm sorry for appearing on your doorstep," he says, voice low. "It was foolish. I ought to have known your son was behind it."

"And what would have made you think that?"

He hesitates, as though caught off guard by her brittle response.

"My son is a challenging child," she says, before he can find an answer. "He takes some work to get to know."

"I see." Ward catches her eye. He's a strikingly beautiful man, with hooded blue eyes and a sharp jaw. A strong, aquiline nose. Coils of pale, unpowdered hair hang in a long queue down his back. Up so close to him, she feels immensely on edge, her skin heating beneath her mourning gown. She feels that simmering anger bubble up higher in response to her body's treachery.

"He's fascinated by you, I assume," she says. The words come out sounding like more of an insult than she intended. "We don't see many ships like yours here."

"I'm rather grateful to have had cause to visit," he says, sidestepping her sharpness. "Lindisfarne is a beautiful place."

"It is a beautiful place," Abigail admits.

"But not home for you?"

She smiles wryly. "Is it so obvious?"

The corner of his lips turn up, but he doesn't speak. What does he see when he looks at her, Abigail wonders? Can he sense that war inside her: anger and annoyance mixing with the confusing need to keep him here?

"I tried to make it home," she says, hearing her voice soften. "But I still feel like an outsider. They're a tight-knit bunch here. Not so willing to welcome a Londoner, especially one hiding away in such an unsightly beast of a house." She wonders why she is telling all this to a near stranger. She senses some unplaceable danger to Henry Ward—some innate sense that she would be better off keeping her distance from him. But right now, that feels oddly difficult to do.

"This was your husband's home?" he asks, a little tentatively.

"Yes. It was." She nods towards the vast expanse of the house. "This place has been in his family for generations. Samuel was a Northumberland native, but he did not grow up in this house. It belonged to his cousin, and his uncle before that. His cousin died shortly before we married, and the house passed into Samuel's hands."

Henry Ward nods slowly. He has noticed, surely, the way she speaks of her husband in the past tense. Would he be here otherwise? Surely not.

Ward drifts through the foyer, taking in the polished newel posts Samuel had carved by hand, the two portraits beside the front door, the vast painted seascape. He nods towards the artwork. "A Dutch artist?" he asks.

Abigail's cheeks flush. "I don't know," she admits. "The paintings were here when we arrived in the house. I admit I've paid little attention to them."

Ward steps closer, trying to inspect the painting in the dim light. "My mother was very inspired by the Dutch landscape artists. She would have loved this piece."

"Your mother was a painter?"

"Yes. She was very talented. Not that her work ever saw the outside of her workroom. My father had very firm ideas about where a woman's place was, and it certainly was not in an artist's salon." He glances over his shoulder at Abigail. "I'm sure I cannot blame him for having such an opinion. Although I did always think it a great shame that more people did not get to see her work." He turns to look at her squarely. "We shall be gone before dawn," he says. "I will make sure none of the villagers see us here."

She nods faintly. Knows that come the dawn, Donald Macauley and his son will be out on the dunes with hunting rifles; herring fishermen dotting the sea beyond Henry Ward's ship. Abigail can only imagine the stories they would tell if they saw a band of privateers leaving Highfield House.

He is true to his word. At the first hint of light in the sky, he and his men return to their ship. The officers thank her, stumbling bleary-eyed into the pre-dawn chill. Mist hangs over the water, the dawn chorus of birds beginning to reach across the island. Henry Ward lingers on the doorstep. In the pearly half-light, his eyes are almost violently blue.

"Thank you," he says. "For your hospitality. And for seeing past my foolishness."

His foolishness. Abigail had been far too fixated on her own foolishness to be bothered about his.

Still, she supposes, no real harm has been done. She can release her anger now, and her guilt. Because the men are off back to their ship, her children are safe, and no one from the village shall be any wiser.

And perhaps, she thinks, this single night of company might give her the strength to face the silent nights of Highfield House for a little longer yet.

CHAPTER FIVE

The *Eagle* comes to life slowly the next day. The men are sluggish returning from the tavern, or wherever else they had spent the night—these days, Ward knows better than to ask. He watches the trail of longboats crawl back to the ship as he leans up against the gunwale and brings a cup of watery ale to his lips.

The morning is bitterly cold, but Ward prefers the icy air over the stuffiness of the great cabin. His gaze is fixed on the house, a lonely grey figure against the eternal roll of the dunes. Thin lines of smoke are rising from the chimneys now, and he can just make out glimmers of light behind several of the windows.

When he thinks of last night, he feels a gnawing unease at having turned up on Abigail Blake's doorstep like a fool. No doubt if she had truly wanted his company, she would have made the invitation herself, rather than sending a note into town with her son, on the off chance they crossed each other's paths. Ward knows he had not thought about the issue hard enough, because he had wanted the message to be from Abigail. Had wanted that invitation. Wanted that chance to dig a little deeper into the mystery of her.

In any case, the night is over and done, and he needs to turn his eyes forward to far more important matters. He has learnt the hard way that a man can either commit his life to a woman or the sea—never both.

He tosses back the last of his ale and strides to the helm where Finn is on anchor watch. He is wrapped up in a tarred coat and thrum cap, his youthful alertness a stark contrast to the rest of the bleary-faced crew.

"Did you go to the post house like I asked?" Ward asks.

"Aye sir. There was a letter for you. I think it was from Scotland. It's on your desk."

"Thank you." Ward glances at him. Sees that hollow look behind his eyes. "All right, lad?"

Finn nods, then looks up at Ward, arms wrapped around his chest. "Are we leaving soon, sir?" He's on edge so close to home, Ward knows.

Almost two years ago, he had found Finn sailing alone in Beadle Bay. Had taken him on as a cabin boy with little thought to the consequences. Little thought to who might miss him.

Ward had been in need of a cabin boy, and Finn Murray had been there, guiding his skiff gracefully around the *Eagle*, a look of wonder in his eyes.

Ward had asked cursory questions that Finn had given equally vague answers to. *Aye, sir, I can take orders. No, there's nothing keeping me from coming with you. Aye, I can read and write a little.*

Answers Ward did not care to dig into at the time. Finn had seemed desperate to take up the cabin boy's post. Desperate to escape whatever life he had come from. Ward had assumed him an orphan. Convinced himself he was doing a good thing by taking the boy to sea and giving him a solid life.

It was not until several months later that Ward had learnt Finn had a father living out on the tiny island of Longstone, setting the shipping beacon alight each night. A father he had left without a word, after a trivial argument. Finn had let the information slip during a sailing lesson one day. Ward heard guilt in the boy's voice. Tried to ignore his own.

Ward knows now it was wrong to take this child to sea with him, at least without asking more questions. He wonders, sometimes, what Finn's father must be going through. The story Finn has painted for him of his life on Longstone is not a happy one. Constant arguments with his father, the two of them prone to flying into a rage. But Ward wonders how much of that is tainted with a childish need to overembellish.

Sometimes, he thinks about doing the right thing and depositing Finn back on his father's island. And then he realises how much he does not want to do that.

Ward tells himself it's because he has no desire to train another cabin boy. He's poured countless hours into teaching Finn the lines and sails of the barque, to navigate by starlight, to write in a legible hand. But he knows there's more to it than that. Knows he has grown too attached to the boy. Begun to see him, sometimes, as the son he never had.

Ward knows how dangerous that is. Apart from anything else, he knows how fragile this life is; how easily Finn could meet his end in a flare of French cannon fire.

Ward leaves the boy on watch and makes his way to the great cabin. The letter is waiting for him in the middle of his desk. He looks down at the seal. Lewis McGowan, Earl of Dunmore. Ward had sailed with McGowan on an East India Company post when they were little more than boys. The Earl had been a skilled sailor—Ward would happily take him into his privateering crew if the man had any desire to leave his life of luxury for the sea.

Lord Dunmore is cunning and charismatic enough to tease Jacobite knowledge out of his fellow Scottish noblemen. Pass it on subtly to men like Henry Ward, who are fighting the Jacobites and their French allies. He's also wise enough to recognise a failing cause when he sees one and privately back the government side.

Ward snaps the seal.

We ought to meet urgently, Henry, the letter begins, in the Earl's ornamental hand. Ward smiles to himself. Just like McGowan to approach everything with a sense of drama. *There are important things I feel you would like to know. Things too dangerous to commit to writing.*

I can just imagine you rolling your eyes at my flair for drama—Ward chuckles to himself at the accuracy of the statement—*but I assure you the pieces of knowledge I have gathered from the Jacobites are worthy of a little drama.*

A morsel of information to whet your appetite: Lord Haver, prominent Whig party politician, is harbouring Jacobite tendencies.

Ward lowers the page, blowing out a breath. All right, so the drama is justified. McGowan has caught him off guard. This is a precious piece of information. And accurate, most likely. Ward knows Lord Haver is a relative of McGowan's—although he imagines there is little love lost between the cousins.

The letter continues, with one sensation after another. Lord Haver's father is not his father at all, but rather, he is the son of a Highlander—*can you imagine such a thing?* in wild, curling letters of excitement. Haver is funnelling Williamite knowledge towards the Jacobites. Too fixated on the promise of power to step away from a political party on the rise, despite his conflicting beliefs.

Damaging information, Ward thinks, if it were to fall into the wrong hands. Lord Haver would no doubt pay a handsome sum to see that this knowledge never made it into the public eye. And what of the Whig party? If they knew such a thing, they would rid themselves of Haver, certainly. But the information could be fatal for a party with grand ambitions. No doubt they too would pay well to keep it from finding its way out.

And if this is merely the titbit McGowan is dangling in front of him to get his attention, Ward hardly dares imagine what else it is the Earl has to say about the Jacobites and their French allies.

He had planned to return to the Channel once he had completed the sale of the latest cargo. But the need to make the journey up to Edinburgh is suddenly pressing. Finn will just have to deal with being so close to home for a little while longer.

At the bottom of the page, McGowan instructs in dramatic, oversized letters: *Burn this once you have read it.*

Ward laughs at the Earl's theatrics. Folds the letter and tucks it in his desk drawer.

CHAPTER SIX

Abigail traipses through the snow towards the village, with her two youngest children running across the dunes ahead of her. She has left Oliver back at the house, with instructions to remove the dead ivy from the outside walls of the manor and feed it into the parlour fireplace for burning. She has no idea if he—or the ivy—will still be there when she returns.

She has said nothing to Oliver about Ward's visit. He has not asked her about it either. The unspoken questions hang in the air between them, thick and heavy. Abigail is grateful not to be in his presence this morning.

Nathan and Eva are barrelling ahead of her in their thick winter cloaks, their giggling rising in the cold air. They follow the trails of deer prints over the dunes, scrambling over the icy rises on hands and knees.

"Be careful," Abigail calls on instinct. She knows there's little need. Knows her children, island natives, are far more sure-footed on the snowy dunes than their mother.

Flushed and breathless, the children slow to a walk as they reach the village. A horde of fishermen barrels past and Eva hangs back to take her mother's hand, her laughter evaporating. She has become too used to the isolation of the house, Abigail thinks dully. A kitten frozen by the sight of a crowd.

They walk Nathan to the petty school run by the vicar's wife. Watch at the vicarage gate as he heads inside the building with the other young boys. He's the tallest of the bunch now, her long-legged son. He seems a grown-up figure in his breeches and buckled shoes, many of the boys still tottering in snow-dampened gowns. In a few months' time, he will finish his preliminary lessons here; Abigail prays the grammar school that had expelled Oliver will not change their mind about accepting his younger brother.

When the boys have all disappeared inside the vicarage, she and Eva begin the long walk back towards Emmanuel Head.

"Mama," says Eva, watching her feet, "what's your third favourite bird?"

Abigail smiles. "My third favourite bird?"

"Yes."

"Hmm." Abigail takes her daughter's hand. "Maybe a goose."

Eva's forehead crumples as she frowns in concentration. "If you followed a goose, where would you end up?"

Eva is still months from her fourth birthday, but sometimes there's a seriousness to her that makes Abigail wonder at the depth of her thoughts. She wonders how much of her father's death Eva has taken in. How much grief her delicate body is carrying. Like her brothers, she has an innate intelligence; churns out a constant stream of questions. Speaks with her mother's polished London vowels, completely devoid of the Northumberland roll that surrounds her. But Eva is every inch an island child, entranced by rockpools and wildflowers and the changing hues of the sea. Fearless in the gloomy halls of Highfield House.

Abigail hears someone call her name. She whirls around.

Mairi Mitchell is bundled into a faded tartan cloak, strands of pale hair escaping out the side of a blue knitted bonnet. Her youngest son, just weeks old, is strapped to her front in a woollen cloth.

"I'm sorry," Mairi smiles, "I didn't mean to startle you." Her green eyes take on a sudden seriousness. "Just wanted to see how you were faring. I've not seen you much since Samuel…"

Abigail manages a faint smile. "I'm managing," she says. "Thank you."

Mairi nods in the direction of the vicarage. "Nathan off for his lessons?"

"Yes. He'll be off to the grammar in a few months, God willing." Abigail regrets the words the moment they are out—regrets speaking of such a privileged thing to Mairi. She knows the Mitchells can only dream of sending their sons across the water to the Berwick grammar school.

But the smile Mairi gives her shows no hint of judgement or bitterness. "Do you have some time?" she asks. "Why don't you come back to my cottage a while?"

"Thank you, but I'd best get back," Abigail says. "I've left Oliver alone." The words are instinctive, impulsive. Wrought by the surprise of the invitation. In twelve years, Mairi Mitchell has never once invited Abigail back to her cottage.

"Of course," says Mairi. "I'll walk back to the house with you." Her words leave no room for protest. Abigail realises she is glad for it. Since Samuel's death, adult conversations have begun to feel exceedingly rare.

Then again, her conversations with Oliver often feel far too mature for her liking. Seem to dig further beneath the surface of things than her discussions with Samuel ever had.

She and Samuel had had a strong relationship. But there had always been a limit to how deep their conversations went. Abigail had made sure to keep it that way. Had been ashamed of the cruel thoughts that often came unbidden to her; ashamed of how regularly she had to hold herself back from lying purely for the sake of it, or from thinking unpleasant thoughts about anyone who looked at her the wrong way. She had hated the prospect of her husband seeing that side of her. Had not wanted him to feel as though he had made a mistake by marrying her.

Had not wanted him to know that their son's dark streak came from her.

They leave the village behind, following the path through stretches of snow-patched farmland. Eva trots ahead, stopping to poke at some unseen curiosity in the underbrush. Abigail hopes it's more interesting rock and less dead animal.

"How are the children managing?" Mairi asks.

Abigail digs her hands into her cloak to warm them. "It's been difficult for them," she admits. "Nathan has taken it especially hard. He and Samuel were very close."

Mairi nods. There's empathy in her eyes, if not understanding.

Abigail had met Mairi Mitchell in her first days on Lindisfarne. They have always gotten along, always spoken kindly to each other. But that warmth has never had the space to grow into a true friendship.

Samuel had always been wary of Mairi and her husband, Elias. Wary of the Mitchells' Jacobite leanings; their belief that the Stuarts belonged on the throne—an undercurrent that ran through much of Lindisfarne society.

When the Jacobites had first risen six years ago, in the months after William had taken the throne, Abigail had become aware of a fracturing of the Lindisfarne community. Unspoken, but undeniable. A sense of people becoming more closed off. More suspicious. More divided.

Us against them.

An unexpressed rift in which the Blakes and the Mitchells had always been on different sides. While Samuel had never forbidden her from spending time with Mairi, Abigail had always been able to sense a tension in his eyes, his words, his expression, whenever he saw the two of them together. Ever wary of upturning that precious solidarity she shared with her husband, Abigail had largely stayed away from Mairi. Their friendship has always been a thing of mere pleasantries and passing comments. Conversations that do little to scratch the surface.

Has she ever made anything of a true friendship on Holy Island, Abigail finds herself wondering? Acquaintances, certainly. But she has always had a sense of people keeping their distance. She has always told herself it's because of her eldest son; because of his sharp tongue, his light fingers, his probing eyes. She's lost count of how many times villagers have either cornered her and Samuel in the streets, or turned up on the doorstep of Highfield House, with a list of grievances against their child.

But when she thinks on it now, Abigail realises Samuel had never had the same difficulty in forming friendships that she has had. Samuel, with his booming laugh and welcoming smile, had always been the life of the harvest festivals, the fairs, the parties, the card games. Constantly stopped in the street for a chat; always off for an ale with this person or that. When Abigail had gone along to such social occasions, she had always had the sense she was only accepted because of whose wife she was.

Oliver is Samuel's son too. Had the village just been less judgmental of his father than his mother? Or is there something else about Abigail that has prevented people from getting closer? An understanding, perhaps, that Oliver might get his delinquent nature from his mother. Or some innate knowledge of how hard she has had to train herself in order to be kind.

Abigail nods towards the baby strapped to Mairi's chest. "How is the little one?"

"An angel," she says. "Can't believe my luck. Even lets me out to work for the cause." She gives a faintly wry smile, running a hand over the baby's woollen bonnet. "Elias says Angus must know in his blood he's a supporter of the true king."

Her words pique Abigail's curiosity. Mairi and her husband have never hidden their Jacobite alliance, even back during the Glorious Revolution when they could have found themselves hanging for treason. Mairi's husband Elias had fought in the lost battle of Dunkeld and had returned to Lindisfarne a broken and unhappy man.

None of this has ever been a secret. But it has been some years since Abigail has heard either of the Mitchells speak so openly of the movement. With her limited knowledge of the situation, she had assumed it had died out several years ago. "The Jacobite movement," she begins carefully. "It's still active?"

"Of course," Mairi says simply. "The Jacobites are passionate men and women. They'd not give up so easily."

They exchange glances, and Abigail reads the unspoken words there: that Mairi knows exactly why their friendship has never grown deeper; that she knows exactly what Samuel Blake had thought of her and her husband.

Abigail imagines, suddenly, a different life; one in which Mairi has always been a far closer friend. A life in which she has never felt that faint hint of scrutiny from the villagers. A life in which Highfield House does not feel quite so isolating and haunted. She imagines Oliver being friends with the Mitchells' eldest son, Hugh, instead of trading insults with him when they cross paths. Imagines Mairi's daughter, Julia, halfway in age between Nathan and Eva, running the halls of the house. How much easier this grief, this sudden forced independence would be for her and her children if they had close friends to lean on.

"What do you do?" she asks Mairi curiously. "When you go out working for the cause?"

"Raising funds," Mairi says. "Calling on wealthy donors around the county. Encouraging them to open their pockets to support the cause.

Funding weapons and training and the like." She wraps her arms around the baby. Gives a short laugh. "Elias volunteered me for the position. Says I've a knack for making people do as I please."

Abigail glances back over her shoulder at Eva, who is still fossicking through the snow on the edge of the path. "It must be quite something," she hears herself say, "to be a part of such a movement. To be a part of something bigger. Something beyond yourself."

Her own words surprise her. She had not been aware that such desires were floating around her own head. But they're an extension of her earlier thoughts, she sees now. The need for someone to lean on. The need to care for something bigger, wider, more all-encompassing than her cloistered life, drowning in the echoes of Highfield House.

Mairi's pale eyebrows quirk, and Abigail knows her comment has surprised her too. Mairi looks out towards the clog of clouds on the horizon. "It is something, aye. Certainly. To know you've done your part in putting the world to right. Spreading the word to others."

Abigail glances sideways at her. Was that meant as an invitation? An invitation to further questions, at the very least—if not to more? She doesn't speak, uncertain of how to reply.

The house is upon them now anyway, the pale morning sunlight washing the walls the colour of a stormy sky. Oliver is inspecting the hull of his father's rowboat, which is beached high up on the embankment by the low tide. A small pile of dead ivy sits in coils by the corner of the house, most of it still clinging to the walls. At least, Abigail supposes, her son is still on the island.

Eva breaks into a run to catch up with Abigail, her apron pockets now bulging with pebbles. She takes a fistful of her mother's skirts as she walks down the front path. Stares over her shoulder at her brother, but he doesn't look her way.

Mairi turns her gaze up to the house. "It's been an age since I've been out to this part of the island."

"Most people have little cause to do so." Abigail unlocks the front door, letting Eva scurry inside with her apron clattering. "Thank you for walking with me," she tells Mairi. "I enjoyed the company."

"Of course." Mairi meets her eyes, and there's a depth in them that Abigail had not picked up earlier. "There's no need to isolate yourself out here," she says. "I hope you know you're not alone." She offers a tentative smile. "Perhaps we've been too long in letting our husbands speak for us."

CHAPTER SEVEN

Nathan is lying in bed, staring up at the darkness that has swallowed the ceiling. Something had woken him from a deep sleep, and now he can hear Oliver moving around inside his bedroom. The fire opposite Nathan's bed has almost burned out, leaving a faint orange glow in the grate. The rest of the house is quiet; just the creaks and groans of the place moving in the night.

Once upon a time, those noises had scared him. Made him think of fairy dogs and redcaps, and all the other terrible creatures from Mrs Calloway's stories. But Da had told him the noises were just the house growing and shrinking as the weather turned hotter and colder. Now, he's not afraid. He likes to think of it as the house breathing.

The floorboards outside his room creak. This is not the house breathing, Nathan knows. This is his brother. The door opens and a faint glimmer of lamplight enters his room.

"Let's play a game," Oliver says.

Nathan scrambles out of bed. "What game?"

"Quiet. You'll wake Mama."

"What game?" Voice softer this time.

"It's called the Viking Game." Oliver is standing in the middle of the room with one arm folded behind his back. Lamplight flickers over his face, turning his cheeks into shadows. "One of us will be a monk from the priory. And the other will be a Viking come to gut him like a pig."

Nathan hesitates. Can't quite determine whether what he's feeling is fear or exhilaration.

"You be the monk," says Oliver. "Go and hide, like they hid in the monastery when the Vikings were attacking. And I'll come looking for you."

Nathan chews his lip. "What happens if you find me?"

Oliver hesitates for a moment. "You have to tell me a secret."

"But you won't hurt me?"

"Of course I won't."

"All right," Nathan says.

"I'll count to twenty," Oliver tells him. "And then I'm coming to look for you." He shifts his hand from behind his back and Nathan sees a flicker of silver in the lamplight. His stomach tightens. "Why do you have the knife?"

"Because it's a Viking knife, obviously. And this is the Viking Game."

Nathan swallows heavily. He doesn't like that knife. But he's sure Oliver is not going to gut him like a pig. At least, he's fairly sure.

His brother turns away and starts counting quietly.

Nathan hurries down the stairs on silent feet. The ground floor of the house is almost completely black, with only faint threads of lamplight from the upstairs hallway straining down into its depths. Nathan reaches out into the darkness, trailing a hand down the wall to keep his bearings. He passes the hallway that leads towards the parlour and dining room. Takes the narrow passage leading to the old servants' quarters.

The blackness is like ink in this corridor, and it smells of dust and forgotten days and nights. The air is freezing, like it's been a hundred years or more since a fire was lit down here. Nathan can't remember a time when these rooms were lived in—as far as he can remember, Mrs Calloway and Miss Ruth have always left the house before night-time. To avoid having to walk back to the village in the dark, Mama had said. Maybe that's true. Maybe they're scared of the redcaps.

Nathan can't help but think of ghosts and goblins and redcaps as he pushes open the door of the first servant's room. Perhaps he'd be better hidden if he went all the way to the back of the passage, where the dark is thickest. But he really, really does not want to do that.

The door creaks as it opens, letting out a breath of air even more cold and stale than the air in the passageway. An icy draught circles his bare legs, his feet frozen against the flagstones. A thin crescent moon is shining in through the uncovered window, and in its fragile light, Nathan can see the outline of a single bed, a wardrobe pushed up against one wall. Considering his options, he creeps over to the wardrobe. Pulls open the door and steps inside.

The faint noises of the house are swallowed, and for long minutes, it's soundless inside the empty wardrobe. How many minutes? Five? Ten? Longer? Nathan isn't sure. He only knows it's freezing in here, and he would very much like to be back under the covers of his bed. But he also knows that that is not an option. He has agreed to Oliver's game, and he must see it through the to end. That's just the way things are. Have always been.

Finally, there's a sound so faint Nathan is not sure if he's imagining it. Footsteps? Maybe. A line of lamplight shines through the gap at the bottom of the wardrobe door.

He holds his breath. As much as he'd like to go back to bed, he knows this is a good hiding place, and he doesn't want Oliver to find him yet. He wants him to have to search and search for him, and be forced to go down to that blackest part of the corridor. Wants him to think, *well that was a damn good hiding place.*

Footsteps come towards the wardrobe. Nathan sees his brother's eye at the keyhole.

"Found you, monk," Oliver says in a low, slow voice. "Come out and face your maker."

The door flies open, and before Nathan can make sense of what is happening, Oliver has a hold of his wrist and is tugging him forward, out of the wardrobe. He clatters to the floor, knees crashing against stone. Oliver rolls him onto his back and leaps on top of him, knees on either side of his chest. He presses a firm hand to the centre of Nathan's chest and holds the knife to his throat.

Nathan's heart is pounding in a jagged, uncomfortable rhythm, his skin prickling. His knees are throbbing, his breath coming short and strained. Every muscle in his body feels tense, and to his horror, he feels tears threaten behind his eyes. He forces them away. Holds his breath until his brother lifts the knife from his throat.

Nathan feels his body go limp.

Oliver stays looming over him. "Now tell me a secret."

Nathan stares up at his brother's lamplit face. Behind him, blackness swallows the house. He forces his voice to come out steady. "I saw Miss Ruth eating some of our sweetmeats."

Oliver makes a noise in his throat that suggests he's not all that impressed with that secret. "I've got a better secret than that."

"What is it?" Nathan knows the rules to this game: he has to find his brother's hiding place before he gets to hear the secret. But he also knows there is no way Oliver is going to hand over the knife and pretend to be a monk about to be slaughtered. And he can tell from his brother's boasting that, whatever this secret is, he really wants to share it. "Tell me," Nathan pushes. "I found a good hiding place, didn't I? So you should tell me the secret."

Oliver tilts his head for a moment, considering. "All right," he says finally. He clambers to his feet, letting Nathan scramble into sitting. "The captain of the ship was at our house. With some of his crewmen. He was talking to Mama. Sitting in Da's armchair."

"Really? When?"

"Two nights ago."

Nathan is hideously disappointed that he had slept through this. Men from the ship were at the house? What were they talking with Mama about? Did they tell her stories about faraway places and cannon fire? He wants desperately to ask her—secret or no. But he doesn't like the thought of the captain being in Da's armchair. Doesn't like it at all.

"Let's play again," says Oliver.

"I don't want to." The thrill of the game—if that's what it ever was—has been thoroughly washed away by this news. Nathan doesn't care about the Viking Game anymore. All he can think about is the men from the ship. And Da's armchair, with the loose threads on the embroidery and the seat that smells of pipe smoke, positioned just right so you can see out the window and look at the stars.

Besides, he hated the feel of that knife at his throat. Hated the feel of being pinned to the floor, with the air being squeezed from his lungs. His skin feels hot and prickly, and something is crawling inside his belly.

"*I* want to play again," says Oliver. "Go and hide."

"No. I want to go to bed." Nathan dares to look squarely at his brother, and his firmness seems to catch Oliver off guard. Nathan even manages to surprise himself—he knows he is breaking the rules. The game ends when Oliver says so. But he stares his brother down, their eyes meeting, Nathan's heart ratcheting against his chest. Finally Oliver takes the lamp and disappears deeper into the house, leaving Nathan sitting alone in the ocean of dark.

CHAPTER EIGHT

Edinburgh is grey and noisy and crammed with bodies, a stench rising from Nor Loch that makes Ward think of dying things. Shadows of the high-rises in the Royal Mile hang heavy over clamouring streets. Hooves and voices and clattering wheels.

Ward shoulders his way through a throng of people towards McGowan's home behind Lawnmarket. Chimney smoke and breath meeting cold air bathes the city in an eternal cloud.

Ward has not been up here in years. Can't make sense of why McGowan feels the need to plant himself in such a humming and overcrowded blot on the map. Auld Reekie seems to have only gotten madder since William took the throne. He's glad when he wrangles his way through the Earl's front gates and escapes the madness of the street.

McGowan's butler leads him into an elaborate chaos of a parlour, white walls trimmed in gold, and every piece of furniture, from the tea table to the liquor cabinet, festooned with carvings of cherubs and scrolls and delicate chains of flowers.

"Good God, man," Ward blurts, when the Earl comes striding into the room. "What fresh hell is this place?"

McGowan laughs. "Your displeasure breaks my heart." He goes to the liquor cabinet and tugs on a cherubic hand to open the glossy wooden door. "I knew it wouldn't take you long to be on my doorstep, Henry." He gestures towards a plush red-velvet armchair. "Sit down. I've a fine malt whisky that's been awaiting your arrival."

Ward smiles. "With luck it'll make me forget the hideousness of your parlour."

The Earl chuckles. He fills two glasses and hands one to his guest. "*Slàinte mhath*," he says. "To your health."

Ward raises his glass in thanks.

McGowan sinks into the chair opposite his guest, crossing one leg over the other. He's dressed in a royal blue justacorps with gold trimming, large buckles on his breeches and shoes. Long dark wig tied with a black bow. He looks as overdone as his parlour. "How has your journey north been?" he asks. "Did you make the cargo sales as planned?"

Ward chuckles, sipping at the whisky. "Let's not bother with small talk."

"I'd take that personally if I didn't know you better." McGowan goes to the writing desk in the corner of the room and picks up a copy of the *Edinburgh Gazette*. "Heard the news from London?"

Ward takes the paper, the headline catching him by surprise.

The much-lamented death of our late gracious sovereign Queen Mary…

He blows out a breath. "Seems news is slow to reach Lindisfarne." At once, his mind is racing, grappling at what the death of the queen will mean for the war effort. He knows there's every chance the Jacobite movement might see Mary's death as cause for a new rising. "How long have you known of this?" he asks McGowan. "Is it why you sent for me?"

"No. The news only reached us yesterday. But it makes what I'm about to tell you even more pressing."

Ward sets the paper on the tea table. "Talk of a new Jacobite plot?"

"Indeed. Led by one of Parker's men, who fought at the Boyne a few years back."

Ward taps his fingers against his glass. This plot must have been simmering in the background long before the queen had fallen ill. He nods for McGowan to continue.

"He's raising forces around London with a plan to kidnap King William and take him to France."

Ward leans back in his chair, absorbing the information. "'Kidnap.' I assume that to mean 'assassinate'."

McGowan smiles crookedly. "That I can neither confirm nor deny. But I imagine you do not need me to." He brings his glass to his lips. "I'm sure I need not tell you that if the plot succeeds, especially while the nation is in mourning, the monarchy and the government will be out for blood. Mainland France will likely see action again."

Ward nods slowly. "How trustworthy are your sources?"

"I'd not share anything with you I did not believe was entirely accurate."

A broadside of shouting floats in from the street. "How do you know all this information about Lord Haver?" Ward asks. "Did he tell you directly?"

"Not quite. But news finds its way across the family tree."

Ward sips his whisky, enjoying its rich smokiness. "That letter you wrote me about Haver, you know it's damn valuable, don't you. That information gets out and the Whig party would be in disarray. They'd pay a handsome sum to make sure that didn't happen. As would your cousin."

"Aye," says the Earl. "I know it's valuable. That's why I told you to burn it once you'd read the damn thing."

"Surely you know me better than that."

The Scotsman sighs, but there's light in his eyes. "Aye, I do. For all your talk of honour and decency, I know you're not above a little blackmail."

Ward grins. "Only if the circumstances call for it."

Abigail pulls a jar of ink from the desk drawer and uncorks it, hoping the morning sunlight will bring her some resoluteness. Just write this cursed letter, she thinks. Get the damn thing over with. She will tell her mother honestly and succinctly of Samuel's sudden illness and passing; will assure her she and the children are well taken care of by his settlement—a settlement supplemented by the income from the tenants of his house in London. Hopefully that knowledge will convince Susanna not to climb into a carriage and come hurtling up here to Northumberland on some ill-advised rescue mission. Dealing with her mother right now is the last thing Abigail needs.

She starts to write. But somehow, the words that spill from her quill are not to her mother. They are to the privateering captain she had found prowling across the dunes last week. The privateering captain she had welcomed into her home. Well, perhaps *welcomed* is not the right word for what she had done. But he had ended up in her home nonetheless.

She does not think as she writes; just lets the words spill from her quill as though they have their own being. They're trite, meaningless words she scribbles down on the page: long, badly formed sentences about the warblers outside her window, and the recent heavy snowfalls, and the roses she managed, against all odds, to grow in the windswept coastal soil of Emmanuel Head. And then, not so trite and meaningless: Samuel's death and the cloud of grief she has been submerged under for the past month. The fragrant smoke of the fuming pots that had filled Highfield House, as she lived in fear of her children following their father, one by one, to the grave. Giving voice, she realises, to the chaos of thought and emotion that has been swirling around her head since her husband has been gone, with no place to put it. She cannot speak to the staff about such personal things as her fears for her children. Is fairly sure Mairi Mitchell has too busy a life to be bothered by birds outside the window.

When she gives a coherent thought to what she is doing, Abigail almost laughs at her foolishness. She tells herself writing to Henry Ward is just an excuse not to write to her mother. But there's something cathartic about putting these words down on the page. Henry Ward will never read them, of course. No one ever will. And that allows her a modicum of honesty that she rarely permits herself.

I fear what the villagers would think of me if they knew of these dreadful thoughts that come and go…

A knock at the door. Abigail drops the quill, splattering ink over the page, glad for the interruption to this most foolish of exercises. She hears Ruth answer the door. Hears the soft bell-like voice of the visitor, too quiet to make out the words.

Abigail makes her way down the hallway, stopping outside Oliver's bedroom to peek through the keyhole. She is relieved to find him sitting on his bed, hunched over a book. When she can do so without her son catching onto it, she will go to the village and ask Mr Emmett for his help to close up the priest hole. Board up the tunnel that leads out onto the dunes.

Ruth ushers Mairi Mitchell into the foyer as Abigail makes her way downstairs. Mairi is bundled into her cloak and bonnet, her baby squirming in the crook of her arm. Her face is flushed with cold, making the freckles on her cheeks look more pronounced.

Mairi looks about the cavernous foyer of Highfield House, locking eyes briefly with one of Samuel's painted ancestors that looks down from upon the wall. Has Mairi ever been inside the place before? Abigail doubts it.

Mairi smiles at her as she approaches, waving aside the offer of tea. "I'll not stay long." She jiggles the baby gently. "It may be out of place of me to ask. But I wondered if perhaps you might wish to come with me tomorrow when I go visiting."

Abigail raises her eyebrows. Drops her voice. "When you go visiting? You mean, for the Jacobite cause?"

"Aye." Mairi looks suddenly regretful. "I'm sorry. It was foolish of me to ask. I shouldn't have—"

"Don't be sorry."

Mairi dares a tentative smile. "It's certainly not my intention to force you into anything you don't care to involve yourself with. But if you wish to know what it's like to be a part of something bigger… Or if you just wish for some company…" She shakes her head. "It's mad of me to suggest such a thing, I'm sure. You've the children, and—"

"The children have their nurse." Abigail hesitates, surprised at the voice in the back of her mind that is nudging her to accept Mairi's invitation. That part of her that makes foolish choices seems to be making all her decisions of late.

But this does not have to be a foolish decision. Does not have to be something rooted in darkness and deceit. She is a recently widowed woman in desperate need of friendship. There is nothing dark about that. Heaven knows she could use a little more light in her life.

She takes Mairi's elbow and guides her back through the front door, out of earshot of the housekeeper. Cold wind swirls up off the sea, making Abigail shiver. "You're not putting yourself in danger are you?"

"The movement has been quiet for years. We've been lying low since that dreadful business at Glencoe. These days we can operate safely enough in the shadows."

"And the death of the queen?" asks Abigail tentatively. "Is that likely to change things?"

Mairi hesitates a moment. "I'll understand, of course, if you don't wish to be anywhere near such a thing," she says, gliding past the question. She gives Abigail a bright smile. "I shall leave you to think it over. If you wish to join me, I'll be leaving from the Pilgrims' Way at nine tomorrow morning."

CHAPTER NINE

The next morning, Abigail finds herself striding across the island towards the Pilgrims' Way. She traces the rugged scarps of the northern coast, watching the last of the water drain across the sand connecting Lindisfarne to the mainland. In the low tide, the land feels vast and open, the white sky endless.

Mairi smiles when she sees her. It's an almost conspiratorial look—or perhaps just made that way by the thump of Abigail's heart. In spite of her attempts to convince herself otherwise, she can't shake the thought that she is doing something incredibly foolish. Something that could see her imprisoned. Hanged. See her children growing up as orphans.

She's overreacting, of course. As Mairi said, the movement is quiet these days. There is little chance of being caught. And besides, she's not a Jacobite. Just a woman in need of something to fill the chasm left by her husband's death.

Better this way than with a house full of top-heavy privateers.

A wagon is waiting at the edge of the path. Ordered and arranged by the Lindisfarne Jacobites? Abigail does not recognise the coachman.

She accepts his hand and climbs into the wagon, Mairi scrambling up behind her and setting the baby's basket on the floor at their feet.

"Will it just be the two of us?" Abigail asks. She is relieved when Mairi nods.

"For today, aye. There are not so many of us working for the cause these days. Only a few of us left on the island."

"Your husband and Donald Macauley?"

"Aye. And a few others."

"Do they know you brought me with you?" For not the first time, Abigail wonders at Mairi's reasons for inviting her along today. Is this an attempt to repopulate the Jacobite cause? Or just an invitation for a little company? An attempt by Mairi to reach out now Samuel is not standing between them.

"They don't know," Mairi admits, lowering her eyes. "I didn't see any reason to tell them."

It feels like a hollow statement. Abigail can tell it was not apathy that had caused Mairi not to say anything to her husband, but rather the knowledge that he would not approve of the situation. Between Samuel's rigid anti-Jacobite beliefs, and Oliver's disobedience, Elias Mitchell has had few good words to say about the Blakes.

"Why am I here?" she asks. "Because your cause needs more people? More support?"

Mairi looks out across the leathery sand of the Pilgrims' Way. A flotilla of gulls shoots skyward as they pass. "The cause does need more support," she admits. "But I..." She shakes her head as though to straighten her thoughts. "Elias was a shadow of himself when he returned from Dunkeld. He barely spoke, didn't sleep, turned to the drink. Barely gave a passing glance to the children. Really, he's not been the same man since." She tugs at a loose thread on her woollen gloves. "I know it's not the same as what you're going through. But I do understand what it's like to feel so lonely. And I thought, if I could take a little of that away for you..."

Abigail manages a faint smile of thanks. She blinks away the tears that threaten behind her eyes. When she trusts herself to speak, she asks, "Where are we going?"

"We'll go south today. Work our way down the coast near Bamburgh. There're wealthy families in the area that have supported us in the past. Some of them fought with Elias at Dunkeld. With luck they'll be willing to open their pockets again today. You needn't have any part of that if you don't wish to," she tells Abigail gently. "You're welcome to just keep me company. Heaven knows I could use a decent conversation."

Abigail returns her smile. "I know the feeling."

The wagon jolts as they leave the sand of the Pilgrims' Way and begin to rattle down the coastal road of the mainland. There is something steadying about the rhythmic clop of hooves, about the innate warmth that Mairi exudes, about the gentle sighs and gurgles of the baby in the basket. Abigail allows herself to sink back against the rough-hewn seats of the wagon. Allows her body to settle into the up-and-down rhythm of the journey.

The sea disappears as the road winds across snow-patched green farmland, the water re-appearing at the foot of Bamburgh Castle. A dull knot lodges in Abigail's stomach as they approach the village. The last time she had made this journey, it had been to bury her husband.

Without any instruction from Mairi, the coachman continues through the village and rattles the wagon through the iron gates of a property set a few hundred yards back from the coastal road. A large stone manor stands ahead of them; a three-storey palace of glittering windows and polished marquetry that makes Highfield House seem like a windblown relic. Trees grow in neat rows behind the property, their branches skeletal and snow-flecked.

Mairi takes the coachman's hand and steps from the wagon. "Do you wish to wait behind?" she asks. "I'll not be too long."

And Abigail realises she has no desire to sit back and watch. She feels as though she has done that for the past decade, tucked away on Emmanuel Head, peering out at the rest of the world from the salt-stained walls of her tower. In Mairi Mitchell, she sees the tentative beginnings of a friendship. A raft out of her ocean of grief and loneliness. She has no intention of letting that slide away. She says, "I shall come with you."

CHAPTER TEN

Standing on the yardarms of the *Eagle* usually makes Finn feel as though he has climbed to the top of the sky. Makes it feel as though the ocean could go on forever, and as though there is so much of the world to see, he will never manage every piece of it.

Today, he feels none of that. Today, he can't shake the gnawing in his stomach.

He edges along the yardarm, the lines rough against his bare feet and a cold wind howling through his hair. Up here, with the deck laid out beneath him like a tapestry, each roll of the ship feels magnified.

This patch of sea is far too familiar.

Finn hadn't been entirely truthful when Captain Ward had asked him if he wanted to be taken back to Longstone. *No,* he'd said. *No, no, no.* But there's a part of him that longs for it.

Not that he could ever do it, of course. What would Da do if he ever saw him again? Give him the thrashing of a lifetime, probably, then lock him in the cottage so he'd never get out again.

Finn supposes he can't blame him. Because once the thrill of leaving Longstone, of starting this new life with Captain Ward, had worn off enough to become commonplace, guilt had taken root inside him.

His da had never been a worrier—that was his ma's thing. But he is sure that now, two years since Finn has been home, his da is sick with worry for him. Maybe he thinks he's dead.

Sometimes Finn tells himself he and Da are better off without each other. And perhaps there's some truth to that. After all, when it was just the two of them in that cottage, after his ma died, things had been near unbearable. He and Da had barely been able to go a day without one of them erupting at the other over something stupid. Arguments over what they'd eat for supper, over whose turn it was to restoke the firebasket, over the shoes left in the doorway to trip over. Like they took it in turns to blame each other for losing Ma, and the only way to deal with that grief was anger.

Finn reminds himself of the yelling and the anger, and the way the tiny cottage had felt so stifling, on the days he feels most guilty. The days when he most misses his father.

"You half asleep or something, lad?" His crewmate's shout yanks him out of his thoughts. He looks down the yardarm to see the watch leader glaring. Finn curls his body over the broad branch of the yard to fasten the gaskets around the newly furled sail. Tries to focus on the task at hand. Wasn't that the first thing Captain Ward had taught him about climbing aloft? Focus, focus, focus. All too easy to lose your footing and end up splattered across the foredeck like poor old Johnny Greentree had. Then again, according to Captain Ward, poor old Johnny Greentree had also fallen from the bowsprit and drowned, taken a bullet for sloppy marksmanship, and been hanged for attempted mutiny. These days, Finn is fairly certain Johnny Greentree is just a figment of Captain Ward's imagination, made up to scare his cabin boy into acting right.

 Finn knows he's thinking of Da right now because of where they're sailing. When they're out in the North Atlantic and he's scrubbing pots and carrying powder and running messages between the officers, he never thinks of Longstone and the firebasket. Or hardly ever, anyway. He wishes they were out in the North Atlantic now.

But no, they are crawling down the English coast from Scotland, and Holy Island is an ink blot on the horizon.

Finn wonders if they're headed for the big house on the head again. He knows the captain and the officers spent the night there last week. Finn is insanely jealous. He's wanted to set foot inside that house for as long as he can remember.

Captain Ward had seemed surprised when he'd first seen the house on the headland, the day they had come in to Lindisfarne to sell the cargo.

Like he'd not expected to find anyone living out there in a place so lashed by sea.

Finn was not surprised. He doesn't remember when he first saw that house, but he remembers asking his da to take him out to see it, again and again. Sometimes Da would grumble and complain he was too tired, or too busy, or that asking to go and see someone else's house was a brainless thing to do. But most of the time, he would take him in the sloop, across the water from the Farnes to that wild top corner of Holy Island where some well-to-do family had made their home.

The Big House, they used to call it. *Da, will you take me to look at the Big House?* Those were the days before he and Da would throttle each other if one looked at the other the wrong way.

When they were back in the cottage on Longstone, Finn would sit around the table with his parents and think about who might live in the Big House with all the chimneys and windows and plants growing over the walls like a runaway forest. *Maybe it's a king and queen*, said his ma. *A pirate that found treasure*, said Finn. Da would just snort and shovel stew into his mouth. He never liked guessing games, or make-believe. Said there was no point to it. *Why pretend the world is anything other than it is?* he would say.

Finn had always found that hard to accept. Maybe because his ma's imagination was so colourful and alive. Back when he was a little child, she would sit on the edge of his bed and tell him stories from the Highlands where she had grown up. Tales of giants and fairies and ghostly pipers, all lit up by the flickering light of the firebasket. She had made life in that little cottage a magical thing—the howling of the wind was the mournful cry of water kelpies, the flitting of seals in the shallows a glimpse of a selkie.

Maybe it was because of all that that Finn didn't want to accept the way Da saw the world. Or maybe because he didn't want to accept that there was only one way to life, one way that things could ever be. That felt far too limiting. Felt like a trap.

Even before Captain Ward had found him that day in Beadle Bay, some part of Finn had always known his life would not be confined to Longstone like his father's was. He had always known he would push and pull, and scrap and fight until the world was something more.

Really, if he thinks about it—and these days, he tries hard not to—he knows it was this that had been at the centre of most of his arguments with his da. Finn had wanted more for his life. Da had believed their sole purpose was to keep the firebasket burning. Stop others from losing their lives in the Farne Islands, the way his brothers had.

Holy Island is so close now, he can see the jagged silhouette of the castle. Beyond it, the dark shapes of the Farnes are dotted on the horizon. If the ship got just a little closer, he would be able to make out the shape of the firebasket from up here. The cottage where Da will be filling his barrow with coal and peat and rattling it over the rocks towards the beacon.

Finn reaches for the ratlines and steps onto the shrouds, doing his best to pull his eyes away.

Ward tells himself it makes sense to stop here at the house. He is travelling south, after all. Passing right by Holy Island.

Makes sense—no, that's not right. Not a part of this makes sense. But there's a pull to return to the house that he can almost manage to justify.

What is it that's drawing him here? Concern for her? Partially, yes. But he knows there's more to it. Much more. She intrigues him because she unbalances him, he realises. At the helm of his ship, he is confident; a natural leader. Around her, he is uncertain. Ward realises he likes the challenge of her.

And that, he reminds himself, is all Abigail Blake can be: an intellectual challenge. The woman is still in mourning clothes, after all. Whatever this restlessness inside him is that comes to life when he's around her, he cannot let it turn into anything at all.

He climbs from the longboat, boots crunching against the shingle on the embankment. A brief visit, he tells himself. For no other purpose than to ensure Abigail Blake and her children are safe and well. He has given the men instructions to prepare for a return to sea immediately—primarily to ensure he has no time to linger in Abigail's company.

He slows his pace as he approaches the house. Oliver Blake is standing in the garden, tearing trails of withered brown ivy from the wall. Behind him, fragile green stalks are straining through a snow-patched garden bed.

Oliver turns at the sound of Ward's footsteps. Watches him with that same shrewd and severe look he had given him in the village last week. The day he had handed over that forged letter from his mother.

Ward strides towards him, ready to scold him for his deception. Before he can speak, Oliver says, "You again." A thread of withered ivy dangles from his gloved hand.

Ward blinks.

"Did my mother invite you here?"

"That's no concern of yours."

Oliver tilts his head. "Are you a pirate?" he asks.

"No. A privateer. Do you know the difference?"

"Of course. Privateers operate legally to supplement the navy's strength. You operate with a letter of marque, signed by the king. You must give a percentage of your earnings back to the monarchy, to help fund the war effort. And you may only operate with a commission. Otherwise your actions are classified as piracy."

"Indeed." The response catches him off guard. Oliver Blake is intelligent and well spoken. It surprises him. Ward cannot imagine this boy paying too much attention during his schooling. An innate intelligence, perhaps. And if this is the case, it would be a great shame for him to be led down the wrong path.

"Do you operate in the Caribbean?" Oliver asks.

"On occasion. I prefer to remain in the Channel or Northern Atlantic. Intercept the French merchants on their way back to Europe. It's a far more lucrative business than venturing halfway across the world."

Oliver nods. "I should like to see the Caribbean," he says. "And many other places besides."

"You wish to be a sailor?"

"I wish to see the world. There's no life to be had here."

Ward chuckles. "That's a definitive statement from such a young man."

Oliver shrugs. "I know what I want."

And Ward believes him.

"All the other boys in the village are earning money already," says Oliver. "It's not fair that I'm forced to endure so many mindless lessons.

There are far more exciting things I'd like to be doing."

"You ought to be grateful you come from a family that can afford to educate you. Most are not so lucky."

Oliver snorts. "My mother thinks I ought to be a physician or a lawyer. But I think that all sounds dreadfully dull."

Ward gives him a short smile. "My father wanted those things for me too."

Oliver's pale eyebrows rise. "Really? But you did not want such a life either? You wished to go to sea? Like I do?"

Ward smiles wryly. "I did not have the brains for such an undertaking. My father was most disappointed." Even after twenty years, speaking of it still stings. "He was a seaman himself. Wanted better for me. But he did not get it."

Oliver tilts his head, as though caught off guard by Ward's admission. Ward is caught off guard a little too—it's a thorn he rarely speaks of. But he has some sense—or at least, some hope—that this piece of his past might be of value to Oliver Blake. Might help nudge him in the right direction.

"But you're very successful now," Oliver says. "A privateering captain."

"Yes. I had a lot to prove." The last comment feels too indulgent, and Ward instantly regrets it. Oliver says:

"Will you take me to sea with you? As a part of your crew?"

Ward gives a short smile. "I already have a cabin boy."

Instead of the disappointment he was expecting, something lights behind Oliver's eyes. "So you do take crewmen my age."

Ward folds his arms. "What makes you think you have what it takes to be a member of my crew?"

"I'm smart. Brave. And I'll work hard."

"You are also sharp-tongued and rude. And you knowingly deceived both your mother and me by giving me that forged letter."

Oliver's lips part. His eyes drop downward for a fraction of a second before he looks back up at Ward with a fresh confidence. "Well. If I was on your ship, things would be different."

"Is that so?"

Before Oliver can answer, the front door of the house groans open and Abigail steps off the doorstep. Surprise flickers across her face at the sight of him.

"I hope I'm not intruding, Mrs Blake," Ward says quickly. "I just wished to call on you before we made our journey south again."

Abigail holds his gaze for a moment. He can read the indecision in her face; almost as though she is trying to determine if she ought to be angry with him. Or her son. Or, perhaps, herself.

"Inside, Oliver," she says finally. "Leave Mr Ward alone."

"*Captain* Ward, Mama."

She doesn't respond, just stares him down, unflinching. Ward watches the boy hesitate, as though debating whether to obey his mother. Then he seems to remember Ward's own presence, and the request he had made about going to sea. He drops the piece of ivy and steps inside without another word.

Abigail watches him disappear into the house. Then she looks back at Ward. "What did he say to you?" she asks, toying edgily with the hem of her dark shawl. A loose strand of hair blows across her face.

Ward fights the urge to touch it. "He was sharing his knowledge about privateering and the war effort. We had quite an interesting conversation. You did not tell me your son wishes to have a life at sea."

Her dark eyebrows rise. "A life at sea?"

"He asked if I would take him in my crew."

Abigail blows out a breath. "My son is not going to sea," she says sharply. There's a cold rigidity to her today, as though she is doing her best not to let him in. As though she regrets the moments of openness she had given him the night he had come to the house.

Ward clears his throat. "I'll not inconvenience you. I just came to thank you again for your hospitality last week. I'm very grateful. As are Mr Graveney and the other men, I'm sure."

Abigail raises her eyebrows—no doubt she can see the flimsiness of his reasoning. Of this detour out to Emmanuel Head merely to thank her for something he has already thanked her for.

"Are you returning to sea?" she asks after a moment.

"Yes. We're to leave this evening."

"Please be careful." The soft-hearted words seem to come from nowhere.

Inexplicably, Ward feels something shift in his chest. Because it does not feel like a throwaway line. It feel as though Abigail Blake truly cares if he lives or dies.

He nods faintly. "I shall."

"Will you be returning to Northumberland?" Abigail asks.

"Yes, God willing. I have a deal in place with our buyer."

She gives him a faint smile. Her face lightens, and for a second, he sees behind her eyes. "Then perhaps we will see each other again."

CHAPTER ELEVEN

The second time she goes out visiting with Mairi Mitchell—*visiting* because this is the only way she can put words to what she is doing—they go straight for the village of Bamburgh. February now, and the winter is deep and harsh, with a glacial wind billowing off the ocean and black cloud palling the town.

Abigail and Mairi stride through the empty streets, holding tight to their bonnets as the wind tries to whip them off their heads. Mairi keeps her cloak pulled tight around her body, shielding her baby from the weather.

They rush past the narrow throat of Castle Wynd, where Samuel had grown up. Past Saint Aidan's, where his grave now lies. Abigail is glad to have cause to hurry.

She can just imagine the displeasure she'd see in Samuel's eyes if he knew what she was doing—and who she was doing it with. He had always seen the Jacobites as criminals; troublemaking rebels who sought to upturn the balance of society.

A few hundred yards from the church, they reach a large stone manor house that opens out onto forested land. The seat of the wealthy Headingly family, Abigail remembers her husband telling her.

"Your husband was a Bamburgh native, wasn't he?" asks Mairi, as they hurry up the narrow stone stairs at the front of the property.

"He was." Abigail wonders if Mairi can see the vague unease behind her eyes; that thought that she might be recognised here. Certainly not in a house like this—Samuel's merchant business had never been successful enough for him to rub shoulders with men like Sir Headingly—but she does not know how far down the social ladder Mairi plans on going with her visits.

The baronet is welcoming, and clearly expecting Mairi. He and his wife herd the two of them into the parlour and ply them with tea and honey cake.

"Do sit down and rest a moment," Lady Headingly is saying. "Warm yourselves from that dreadful wind." She ushers them towards the fire roaring in the grate. "I'm sure you've a very busy day ahead of you. And with the little one in tow and all…"

"Indeed," her husband cuts in. "We're so pleased you could make it. I know there are still plenty of us out here willing to give to a meaningful cause." He goes to a shelf and swings down a narrow sword with a flourish. "Have I shown you this before, Mrs Mitchell? My father passed it on to me before he died. Dish-hilted rapier. Quite a fine piece of work. Father used it on several occasions as a duelling weapon but he carried it with him—"

The baby at Mairi's chest lets out a sudden wail. She mouths an apology to Abigail and disappears out of the parlour. Sir Headingly barely breaks his stride. "He carried it with him while defending Blair Castle. He was far too old to be fighting by that point, of course—as was the sword, no doubt. But he was too passionate a man to be persuaded. He said if he could do his part to see James returned the throne, he would happily die for the cause. Didn't die for it mind you. Heart gave out a few months after he returned to England…"

"I see," Abigail says, at appropriate points in the conversation. And, "Yes, how interesting."

She feels exposed without Mairi's presence to hide behind, but if this couple have any idea that she is the widow of a Bamburgh native—with anti-Jacobite tendencies—they show no sign of it.

She's fascinated that all this might be going on beneath the surface. That all around the country, there might be whispered meetings and stories told, and coins changing hands in wait for the next opportunity for the Jacobites to rise. At least, she hopes coins will be changing hands here. Right now, she's beginning to lose faith that the baronet will ever stop talking.

"Sir Headingly," she says sweetly, when he pauses for breath. "What a wonderful story. I wonder if you might be willing to part with a little of your hard-earned fortune so the Jacobites might one day rise again?"

When Abigail finally emerges from the house, Mairi is walking slowly back and forth along the street, bouncing on her toes to soothe the bleating baby. A cloth pacifier dangles from her free hand. The wind has eased, but there is still a fierce chill in the air, and Abigail pulls her cloak around her tightly.

"I thought you'd never make it out of there," Mairi says with a smile. "Was about to send in a search party."

Abigail laughs. "I'm quite certain you gave Angus a poke to set him off on purpose." She passes Mairi the coin pouch the baronet had given her. It's a ridiculous sum—far more than she collects each month from the rent of Samuel's London townhouse. Almost makes the ordeal of the dish-hilted rapier worth it. "The man can certainly talk," she says. "But he also has deep pockets."

Mairi tucks the pouch into her pocket. "It's the only reason we put up with him." She plugs the knotted pacifier into the baby's mouth. "Must have heard about that damn sword at least six times by now."

Abigail smiles. "Have we other visits to make today?"

"We've three others expecting us, but my Angus seems determined to make things as hard as possible today," Mairi says, running a soft hand over the baby's head. She looks up at Abigail hopefully. "Do you think you might go to Lord Milgate? He's most welcoming. Generous too. And I'll call on the others."

"Of course. If I can handle Sir Headingly, I can handle anyone, surely."

Mairi laughs. She presses a gentle hand to Abigail's elbow. "Thank you. I'll meet you back at the wagon."

Abigail makes her way deeper into the village, following Mairi's instructions to the Milgates' home. It's an uplifting feeling, she realises, to be a part of this. The connection, the sense of involvement; they feel precious. Feel like things she has been craving for longer than she has been aware of. It's far too easy to ignore the danger at the edges.

The exchange is straightforward—Lord Milgate has clearly been expecting her; or rather, someone from the Jacobite movement. She tucks the coins deep into her pocket and begins to stride back towards the wagon, squinting in the pale winter sunlight that has broken suddenly through the clouds. She lifts her face skyward, enjoying the rare feeling of warmth on her cheeks.

A hand reaches out and snatches Abigail's wrist. She whirls around, heart jumping into her throat. In front of her stands a girl of no more than thirteen or fourteen. She holds a thin blade out in front of her.

Abigail feels a flush of rage clashing against her panic. She yanks out of the girl's grip. "What do you want?" she hisses.

"I want the money in your pocket, of course," says the girl. Dirty brown hair hangs loose down her back, falling over her face and obscuring one eye. A birth mark the shape of an apple darkens one cheek. "I thought that was obvious."

It's a bold move, Abigail thinks, for the girl to attack her out in the open street like this. But the girl is standing close, her body angled to hide the blade from any passers-by. She clearly knows what she is doing.

"I have no money," Abigail tries.

The girl's lips quirk, as though she can see the utter untruth of the statement. If she had seen her leaving Lord Milgate's house, Abigail realises, she would know well enough she is not a penniless pauper. And even if she hadn't, her velvet-lined cloak makes it clear she is no peasant.

The girl doesn't speak again; just raises the knife slightly. Enough to make her meaning clear.

In her head, Abigail plays out the events that might unfold. She could run, could call for help, but there is every chance the girl would catch her before she found anyone willing to assist. Every chance she might hurt her.

She could swing a fist; catch the girl by surprise. No. She will not be that person. Will not give in to the rage simmering beneath her sense of reason.

She could empty Lord Milgate's coins into the girl's hand. Admit to Mairi what happened.

This is the most sensible course of action, surely.

But something stops her.

If she returns to the wagon with empty pockets, will Mairi believe she has been robbed? Or will she think Abigail lying? Accuse her of taking the money for herself? It's a believable thing, she knows—the new widow, with three children and an enormous old house to wrangle into some kind of order. And in spite of the tentative friendship the two women have been able to cobble together these past few weeks, Abigail knows there is enough lingering distrust between their two families for Mairi to doubt her.

Abigail takes out her coin pouch, heavy with the sum Lord Milgate had handed over. She doesn't take her eyes off the girl's knife. "I shall give you half of what I have," she says. "And in return, I'll not tell the constable I saw at the harbour where you're hiding. Or what you look like."

The girl considers her. Abigail can almost see her thoughts turning over, trying to determine if she is telling the truth about having seen the constable.

"All right then," she decides. "Half. But you keep your mouth shut. You don't tell a single soul you saw me. And you come back here at the same time next month and give me the same amount again."

Abigail almost laughs at the girl's foolishness. Does she truly imagine she might just come strolling back down the Wynd at the same time next month to empty her coin pouch into this child's hands? "Very well," she says evenly. "As you wish."

The girl reaches into her pocket and produces a grimy hessian bag. She opens it out in front of Abigail, nodding expectantly. Abigail pulls out half the coins from the pouch and tosses them into the bag. Rage flickers under her skin. And a hot pull of embarrassment. Never in her thirty-two years has she been robbed before. Has always considered herself too wise for that. And now, in her first months without her husband, here she is handing over a small fortune to a child barely older than her son.

She clenches her hands into fists, forcing her anger down. She has gotten away with only giving the girl a fraction of the money, at least. She has to consider that a victory. Not to mention the fact that she has come away from this unharmed.

That knowledge does nothing to slow the thud of her heart, or the anger blurring her vision. Teeth clenched, Abigail turns and begins to walk away. The thing is done now. Over and gone. Walk away.

"You're Oliver's ma, aren't you," the girl says suddenly.

Abigail's whirls back around, stomach diving. "How do you know my son's name?"

The corner of the girl's mouth turns up. "See you next month, Mrs Blake." She turns and disappears into the shadowy snarl of the Wynd before Abigail can question her again.

CHAPTER TWELVE

Mairi is waiting inside the wagon, Angus now fast asleep against her chest.

Abigail stops walking for a moment before Mairi sees her. Draws in a breath to steady herself. To remove any lingering anger and panic from her face.

She cannot say a word to Mairi about what just happened. She had promised the girl her silence. Half the coins in the pouch in exchange for keeping her mouth shut. And while there's a part of her that wants to believe one girl with a knife is nothing to be afraid of, Abigail knows she cannot take the risk. Because that one girl with the knife knows her name. Knows her son. And that means there is every chance she knows how to find her family.

Her and her sons and daughter, in their vast, fatherless house.

There is every chance the girl with the knife could appear on the doorstep of Highfield House, demanding payment, when Abigail does not return next month to give her the rest of the money she had promised.

And she will come back—Abigail sees that now. She will stand at the corner of the Wynd where the street narrows and darkens, and she will wait for the girl with the apple-shaped birthmark. She will drink noblemen's tea and eat honey cake, and put more of the Jacobite funds in this child's hands. How can she risk doing anything else?

Mairi's face breaks into a smile as Abigail climbs into the wagon. "How did you get on?"

Abigail reaches into her pocket and hands over the coin pouch, mumbling some garbled response she herself can barely make sense of.

She holds her breath, waiting for Mairi to question it. *Oh, Lord Milgate usually gives far more.* But she just tucks the money into her pocket and smiles. "Well done, Abigail. You've a knack for this. We're lucky to have you."

"I'd like to come with you again," Abigail blurts. "If you'll have me?"

"Of course."

"The same time next month?"

Mairi smiles. The wagon jolts forward and begins to rattle over the cobbles. "I'll look forward to it."

The reprieve feels all too fragile when Abigail is sitting around the dining table with the children that night, bowls of pottage steaming in the candlelight and sleet tapping against the glass. The fire roaring in the grate fails to reach the far corners of the dining room, and they are all bundled into padded house jackets, scarves and shawls at their throats.

Abigail's eyes dart constantly to Oliver. She knows she needs to ask him about the girl with the knife. But of course, she cannot do so now; not with Eva and Nathan here.

This tree-trunk of a dining table feels so empty without Samuel's chair filled. As though he had taken up far more than just that one place at the head of the table. With just her and the children here, their small bodies dwarfed by the high-backed chairs, the dining room feels cavernous and hollow. The four of them sit at one end of the table; the boys side by side opposite Abigail, Eva sitting up on her knees beside her mother.

"What did you learn at school today, Nathan?" Abigail tries to keep her voice level. Tries to make it seem as though there is nothing untoward going on here. Never mind about the girl with the knife.

Nathan shrugs, dragging his spoon mindlessly through his pottage. "Some things."

"What things?"

"Please may I have more bread?" Eva cuts in before her brother can speak.

Oliver leans over and whispers something in Nathan's ear. Abigail's eyes dart between them as she cuts a slice of bread in half and places it on

Eva's plate.

Nathan presses his lips together. Sinks lower into his chair.

"Are you all right, Nathan?" Abigail reaches out to cover his hand with hers.

He nods, eyes down. Slides his hand out from under hers and clenches his fingers around his spoon.

Something has passed between him and Oliver, Abigail is certain. She is also certain Nathan will not tell her what. He is fiercely loyal to his older brother, for reasons she cannot quite make out. She is certain Oliver has never done anything to deserve such devotion.

When she had returned to the house that afternoon, the boys had been up in Oliver's room. *Playing a game*, Mrs Calloway had said. Abigail regrets not digging deeper.

"You can tell Mama about our game, Nathan," Oliver says, shovelling a spoonful of pottage into his mouth. "We were just playing hide and seek. Weren't we."

"I can play hide and seek," Eva says brightly.

Oliver glances at her, as though he had forgotten she was there.

Nathan says, "Not hide and seek. The Viking Game."

Abigail feels a pull of unease. "What is the Viking Game?"

The boys eye each other. Neither respond.

Abigail tries, "Did you enjoy that game, Nathan?" Her thoughts go to the priest hole in Oliver's bedroom wall. To that ink-black passage that leads down into the walls of the house. She hopes with every inch of her that the boys have not been playing in there. For not the first time, she tells herself to have someone come and board the damn thing up.

"Nathan?" she presses, when he doesn't speak. "Did you enjoy playing with your brother today?"

"Yes." He doesn't look at her. Doesn't look at Oliver.

Abigail doesn't push the issue. She takes a sip of her wine; closes her eyes for a moment. Yes, she thinks, she can convince herself that Oliver was a caring older brother today, just as she can convince herself there is nothing untoward about the fact that he knows the girl with the knife. Right now, she needs to convince herself of these things. Cannot find the space for anything else.

After supper, she takes Nathan and Eva upstairs to bed. Her saving graces, she thinks, these two almost painfully innocent children. It would do her good to remember that from time to time. Remember that she has three children—not just one.

She goes out of her way to be doting. Sits on the edge of Eva's bed with her daughter's tiny fingers folded through her own. Tells her a half-remembered childhood story she mostly makes up as she goes along. Eva falls asleep quickly, her dark hair messy on the pillow, leaving her mother's voice sounding loud and lonely in the quiet room.

Abigail finds Nathan sitting up in bed, the star maps he and Samuel had always pored over spread out across his blankets. At the sight of her, he folds them carefully and slips them beneath his pillow.

Abigail blows out the lamp. She sits on the edge of his bed in the fresh darkness, the last glow of the fire giving the room a soft rusty light. She knows she needs to ask again. Nathan deserves more than her silence.

"What is the Viking Game?"

Nathan fiddles with the stitching on the hem of his blanket. "Just hide and seek. That's all."

Abigail hesitates. "Did Oliver show you the hole in the wall?" she asks carefully.

For long moments, Nathan doesn't speak. She can sense him deliberating about whether telling the truth will get his brother in trouble. Finally, he says, "Yes."

Abigail considers her next words. She suspects that Oliver will not have told Nathan about the hidden passage. The pieces of knowledge Oliver shares with his brother are for his benefit alone. And Abigail knows he will not share such a precious secret as a way to escape the house. "Did he do anything you did not want him to do?"

"No." This time there is no hesitation. The blankets sigh as Nathan rolls onto his side to face her. His blue eyes are dark and wide in the firelight. "Why is it there?" he asks. "The hole in the wall. Who put it there?"

"The people who built the house put it there, I imagine," she says. "Your great-great grandfather and the builders he worked with."

"Why?"

She hesitates, debating how much of the troubling history to share with him. "It's a priest hole. A hundred years ago, people were hunting down the Catholic priests because of their views on God. But there were people who wanted to save them too. They hid them in their houses. In priest holes like the one Oliver showed you." Abigail had known nothing about the threads of Catholicism in her husband's family. She wonders if Samuel had been aware of it. Wonders how many generations ago the papistry had died out. Wonders if anyone in his family had lost their life upon the gallows for it.

"A priest hole," Nathan says carefully.

"Yes." Abigail pauses. "You know you can tell me, don't you," she says finally, "if your brother does anything to you that you don't want him to do. Anything to hurt you." She puts a soft hand to Nathan's shoulder. Feels him flinch slightly beneath her touch.

When she emerges into the lamplit hallway, Oliver is waiting for her, leaning up against the wall. He holds her gaze, and for a strange, fleeting moment, she sees Samuel. It catches her by surprise. She's never seen more than a flicker of his father in him before.

"Something happened to you today," he says. "I can tell."

"Everything is fine." Abigail doesn't look at him as she strides down the hallway to the staircase. She's not surprised, really, that Oliver has picked up on her unease. Her encounter with the girl in the alley has left her with a restlessness beneath her skin that she has been unable to shake.

Oliver hurries after her. There's a faint look of hurt in his eyes that she might be refusing to answer him truthfully. Because this is not what they do, is it? An unspoken agreement. A truth for a truth.

But right now, she cannot honour that agreement. Because she does not want to face Oliver's truth. Does not want to know how the girl with the knife had known she was his mother.

She is adept at this; at pushing aside pieces of her son's life. She knows she cannot ignore it forever. But she will wait until they are next sitting face to face over his Latin texts, and the morning light has strengthened her enough to carry the truth upon her shoulders.

CHAPTER THIRTEEN

"Thank you so much for your support, Mr McBain," says Abigail, in a voice that does not sound like her own. "But as I'm sure you know, the Jacobite cause is reliant on the generosity of men like you to find its feet again. If you could spare a little more, we would be ever so grateful. As would the true king." She flashes him her warmest smile. Hopes he cannot see the unease behind her eyes. Or hear the lack of authenticity in her words. Can he tell she is here on account of her own safety, rather than any belief in the true king?

McBain, a round-shouldered old man with intense grey eyes, hesitates for a moment. Abigail doesn't blame him—he's already handed over enough to feed a small country. He digs back into his pouch and passes over another handful of coin. She thanks him profusely, promises him his money will be well spent, and flies out the door in case he changes his mind.

She strides into the village with her eyes down and her hood pulled up high. Her heart quickens as she approaches the end of the Wynd.

Before she had left the house, she had filled a pouch with her own coins, in case she had not succeeded in wrangling money from the donors today. Now such a thing seems foolish. What if the girl with the knife searches her? Takes more than the sum they had agreed upon? Abigail is fairly certain she cannot rely on her to keep her word.

Handing over the money intended for the Jacobites is bad enough. Handing over her own precious funds is unbearable. She is no penniless

73

widow; Samuel had left her a decent settlement. Enough to give their sons and daughter a good home, a good education, a good life. She cannot risk losing the money intended for her children's future.

When Abigail rounds the corner, she finds the girl with the apple-shaped birthmark waiting. In spite of the sum she had handed over to her last month, the girl is still dressed in the same tattered brown skirts and kerchief, the same dirty coif pulled low on her head. "I'm glad you came," she says airily. "I didn't fancy traipsing all the way out to Lindisfarne to fetch the money you owed me."

"How do you know my son?" Abigail snaps. "How do you know where we live?"

The girl gives a warmthless smile, but doesn't respond.

Abigail realises suddenly that they are not alone. An older woman is watching them from outside a cottage a little further down the lane. She comes striding towards them. She is close to Abigail's age, with the same brown hair and storm-grey eyes as the girl—her mother, no doubt. The woman takes the money and shoves it into the pocket of her apron.

"Well done, Lizzie," she says to her daughter, though her eyes are fixed on Abigail. And then: "When will we be seeing you again, Mrs Blake? Same time next month?"

Abigail tightens her hands into fists. "Why are you targeting me?" she hisses. "Is it because of Oliver? Did he do something to you?"

Lizzie glances at her mother, and for a moment, neither of them speak. "You're a wealthy woman with a pocket full of coin," says the mother. "Why else would we be targeting you?"

It feels like a lie. Doesn't it? Then again, this is the simplest explanation. Perhaps she is looking for entanglements where there are none. Perhaps she has just been unlucky enough to be in the wrong place at the wrong time.

Abigail tells herself she will not stay powerless. But this is a game that needs to be played with care. She is afraid of how much these people might know about her family. Afraid of what they might do if she does not give them the money they are demanding.

And then, suddenly, frighteningly, it sparks inside her, that aggressiveness at her edges. Her body is suddenly hot and pulsing. She snatches the front of Lizzie's bodice, shoving her backwards. Presses her up against the stone wall of the nearest house. Lizzie cries out in shock, and it's seconds before her mother has magicked a knife from within her apron. She holds the tarnished blade to Abigail's throat.

"Let go of her."

Abigail's fingers shake as she tightens them around Lizzie's bodice. "How do you know my son?" she hisses. "How do you know where we live?" She feels the blade push harder against her neck. A fraction more and her blood will spill. She hears her heart ratcheting in her ears.

"Let go of her," Lizzie's mother says again.

Abigail swallows a gasp of pain as the knife digs harder into her skin. She releases her grip on the girl. Tries to find gratitude for the fact she is still breathing.

Abigail is in a daze as they rattle back onto Holy Island, the wheels of the wagon sighing over shimmering grey mudflats. She sits opposite Mairi, her black shawl bundled tight around her neck, hiding what she is sure is a red welt left by Lizzie's mother's knife. Her thoughts swing between telling Mairi about the thieves and keeping silent. She knows she has little choice but to turn up here next month and fill Lizzie's pockets again. It feels as though it will only be a matter of time before Mairi begins to ask questions.

Perhaps she is being foolish by thinking Mairi will doubt her if she tells her about the thieves. Perhaps Mairi has even had her own run-in with them while out raising funds for the Jacobites. And if she pulls down her shawl to reveal the angry red mark on her neck, surely this will go some way to proving she is telling the truth. Proving she has not taken the money for her own purposes.

But speaking of the thieves feels too dangerous. She had promised Lizzie her silence. She is afraid of what might happen if she opens her mouth, even in the privacy of the wagon.

Once again, Mairi had not questioned the limited amount Abigail had handed over, and yes, a part of her is grateful. A bigger part of her is thinking about how Lizzie might know Oliver.

It reminds her that there is so much she does not know about her son. So much he does not tell her. Such as his desire to make a life at sea.

Once upon a time, he had told her everything. An impossible stream of chatter had flowed from his lips, as he had narrated every inch of his day-to-day life to her: the seals he had seen off Saint Cuthbert's Island, the prayers he had learnt at the petty school, the way the he could hear mice in the roof when he lay very still at night. She cannot make sense of when that had changed. It had not been a sudden thing; of that she is certain. Just a secrecy that had seeped in almost without her being aware of it. These days, though there is honesty between them, it's a carefully cultivated thing, restricted to the confines of their lessons. Staged, almost. Honesty, but not openness.

Perhaps she cannot blame him. She had killed his dream of going to sea with a single sentence to Henry Ward.

She hates the idea, of course. Too many men who go to sea never return. But she cannot deny there is a part of her that knows it would be good for her son. The discipline. The hard work. The adventure. Perhaps a stint as Henry Ward's cabin boy would help turn him into a more decent young man.

She shakes the thought away. She cannot allow herself to think it, in case it grows legs and runs away. Oliver belongs here with her. She is the only one who understands him. The only one who can keep him safe.

She is distantly aware that Mairi is speaking to her.

Abigail blinks, trying to force her attention back to the conversation. "Pardon?"

"I said, do you need to get home immediately?"

She ought to get back, of course. She has left Oliver at home with only Ruth at the house. But more and more these days, her worry over her eldest son has more to do with what horrors he will inflict on his siblings, rather than what he will get up to on his own. Right now, Nathan is away at school, Eva in the safe hands of the children's nurse. And that gives Abigail the space to admit to what she would rather deny: that she needs a little space from her son right now.

Before she can really make sense of it, they are back in the village and she is being led into the Mitchells' cottage.

The door opens straight into the single room of Mairi's cluttered home. A large fireplace of blackened bricks takes up much of one wall, large cooking pots and kettles on the hearth, shelves cluttered with jars, and piles of utensils on the wall above the wooden table. The other end of the cottage is a sea of sleeping pallets, and the blanket-lined drawer being used as Angus's cradle.

Two red-headed children come barrelling towards them—Mairi's daughter, and her second son, his wild curls escaping out the top of a pudding cap. Mairi shepherds them away from the fire, smiling up at an older girl Abigail recognises as the daughter of one of the fishermen.

"Thank you for watching them, Molly," Mairi says. "I hope they were no trouble."

Molly smiles. "Same time next month then?"

Mairi walks her to the door, nodding over her shoulder at Abigail. "Sit down," she says. She closes the door behind Molly and bustles back toward the kitchen. "I'll fetch us something to drink."

Abigail sits. Mairi settles Angus into the cradle and swings the boy in the pudding cap onto her hip. She tosses a fresh log into the fire, ushering her daughter away from the grate. Takes a bottle of ale from the shelf and uncorks it with her thumb.

The door groans open. Elias Mitchell and his eldest son stride inside, Donald Macauley behind them. The three of them have wind-reddened cheeks and wild hair, the smell of the sea on their skin. Surprise flashes across the men's faces at the sight of Abigail at the table.

Elias gives her a curt nod. "Mrs Blake." He strides over to the fireplace. Murmurs to his wife in words Abigail cannot quite make out. She hears a sharp, hissed response from Mairi. She presses their son into Elias's arms.

Donald Macauley lowers himself into the chair opposite Abigail, folding his gnarled brown hands on the table in front of him. He inspects her openly, his dark bushy brows poking out from beneath his worn woollen fishing cap. Knowing his stare is intended to rattle her, she forces herself to hold his gaze.

In the twelve years she has been on Lindisfarne, she has had little to do with Donald Macauley and his family. An unspoken rule that the family from the house on the head did not associate with penniless farmers. Or known Jacobites. Samuel had always been nervous that, if the Jacobites found their feet again and he and Abigail were seen in the wrong circles, it could have dangerous consequences for their family.

"Strange seeing you here, Mrs Blake," Macauley says finally. "Didn't think we were good enough for the likes of you."

Mairi slams the ale bottle on the table, her green eyes flashing. "That's enough, Donald," she hisses. "What are you thinking being so damn rude to a guest of mine?"

Abigail stands, almost without the thought entering her head. Perhaps Samuel had been right to be concerned. What has she been doing involving herself with the Jacobite cause? It was only ever going to lead to trouble.

"I'd best be getting back," she says. "The children…"

Mairi takes her wrist defiantly. "Just a moment now." Her words are not directed at Abigail, but at Donald Macauley's glare. "There's no need to leave, Abby. You're welcome here."

"I really think I…"

Mairi's grip on her wrist tightens. What is she playing at? Is she attempting to show the men that Samuel Blake's wife is trustworthy? That she will not turn them in, regardless of what her husband might have thought of their kind? Perhaps she is overthinking everything. Perhaps Mairi Mitchell just wants to feed her a cup of ale.

Mairi looks pointedly at her husband. "Tell Abigail she is welcome here." A barbed look passes between them.

A stiff smile appears on Elias's lips, but it doesn't reach his eyes. "Of course she is," he says thickly. "Please. Sit, Mrs Blake." He continues to glare at his wife.

Abigail feels pinned into a corner. Cannot tell if she is grateful or angry at Mairi.

She sits.

Mairi sets four tin cups on the table and fills them all from the ale bottle. Elias deposits his son on the floor and slides into a chair, stretching his long legs out in front of him. Abigail bundles her skirts tightly around her legs—an instinctive urge to make herself smaller.

Mairi sits opposite Elias, pinning him with fiery green eyes. "We had a productive afternoon in Bamburgh today," she says.

Abigail cannot help but feel as though she is caught in the middle of something between Mairi Mitchell and her husband. Cannot help but feel as though her presence here has been carefully cultivated. She knows Elias has always disliked her family. Is this an act of defiance on Mairi's part? Abigail can't help but fear what Elias might do to his wife once the visitors are gone.

She sees the looks pass between Elias and Donald Macauley. She knows there is nothing accidental about Mairi having dropped this piece of information into the conversation. Mairi wants the men to know that Abigail is involved in the Jacobite cause. Wants them to know she is trustworthy, perhaps?

Is she trustworthy? Even Abigail herself has no idea.

This is what she wanted, she reminds herself. To be a part of something bigger. To have her life expand beyond the walls of Highfield House. But as she brings her cup to her lips, she finds herself shrinking under the scrutiny of the two men. Can't finish her ale quick enough.

CHAPTER FOURTEEN

"You can wipe that sour look off your face now, lad," Ward says to Finn. "Lindisfarne is long behind us."

Finn is sitting at the table in the great cabin, his arithmetic text spread out in front of him and a scowl on his face like an infant who's tossed his rattle out of the cradle. "I don't like arithmetic, is all."

Ward snorts. "Rubbish. You've been out of sorts for weeks." He closes his logbook. Slides it back in his desk drawer and joins Finn at the table. "I know being in Northumberland has bothered you."

Finn keeps his eyes down. "Well, it's like you said, it's behind us now, aye?"

"Yes." If he's honest with himself, Ward has been out of sorts too, but more so for leaving the place. He can't help but think of her.

It's madness, he knows. He has learnt all too well that there is no place for a woman in the life he has made. At least not if he is to continue having the kind of success he is accustomed to. In any case, his crew had signed aboard his ship expecting action and good pay. Not to be languishing in some Northumbrian outpost while he attempts to pursue a woman still in her mourning clothes.

"What's it like?" Finn asks suddenly. "The house?"

Ward looks up, surprised at the question. "Old," he says. "But quite fine. If a little dark and gloomy."

Finn mumbles something into the pages of his book that Ward can't quite make out.

"Speak clearly, lad."

"I said, will we be going back? To Lindisfarne, I mean. To sell more cargo?"

Ward hesitates. Whatever the answer is, it's far too complicated to share with his eleven-year-old cabin boy. "Perhaps," he admits. "But things have changed of late. We need to be prepared to adapt our plans as necessary."

"Because of the queen's death."

"Indeed." Ward is grateful for an excuse to pull his thoughts away from the dangerous topic of Abigail Blake. "Why do you think the queen's death affects us so?"

Finn puts down his pencil, the bridge of his nose creasing in thought. "There's only one monarch now," he says. "Instead of two. Maybe the Jacobites will think the Williamite cause is weakened. They might act again. With their French allies."

Ward smiles. "Good." It's a thoughtful answer—brings him a swell of fatherly pride he is not sure he ought to be feeling. "We'll make a sea captain of you yet."

Finn looks up at him boldly. "If I was a sea captain, I'd have no need for arithmetic. I'd just make my navigator do all the calculations."

Ward lets out a short chuckle. Raps his knuckles against the pages of the arithmetic text. "Another chapter for your smart tongue."

Abigail sits on the stool in her dressing room, pulling a brush through the dark hair spilling over her shoulders.

Tonight she will ask him. Tonight she will seek answers. Whatever Oliver has got himself involved in, she needs to know.

Right now, she misses Samuel with an ache that feels almost unbearable. She wishes she did not have to carry this alone. But really, what would Samuel have done? He had had no control over their son. Had tried every approach, fluctuating between threats and beatings, to calm and logical explanations of why Oliver's actions were wrong, and heaping praise for the smallest of good deeds. Nothing seemed to make a difference. Far from the reverence a son was expected to give his father,

Oliver had paid Samuel nothing but coldness and disrespect. Abigail is the only one who has ever had a thread of control over their son.

Still, Samuel was the only person she has ever been able to speak to openly about Oliver. And right now, she would give anything to share this burden with her husband.

Movement in the mirror catches her eye. She sees Nathan huddling behind the doorframe, peeking into her dressing room. She flashes him a smile, too grateful for the sudden company to be irritated that he is out of bed. "All right, my love? There's no need to hide."

He emerges from behind the doorframe and perches on the edge of the chair in the corner of the room. He chews at the cuff of his nightgown, a habit he had left behind years ago.

Abigail puts down the brush and turns to face him. "All right?" she asks again. She slides off her stool and kneels in front of him so her eyes are level with his.

He nods, his thin fingers curling around the arm of the chair. Abigail covers his hand with her own. He pulls away sharply.

She frowns. "Did I hurt you?"

He looks away. "No."

A knot begins to tighten in her stomach. "Are you hurt?" she asks again. And then, with a growing sense of dread, "Did your brother do something to you?"

"No."

She had expected the response, of course. But she knows her younger son well enough to read beneath his words.

"Were you playing the Viking Game again?"

"No."

She puts her hands to his shoulders, preventing him from turning away from her. Feels him flinch, and then tense beneath the gentle curve of her hands. She pulls her hands away. "You don't want me to touch you?"

He squirms under her scrutiny.

"Are you angry with me?" she tries.

Nathan shakes his head, faint. Almost imperceptible.

Is it the loss of his father that has caused this behaviour, this need for distance? Perhaps. It's been four months since Samuel's death. Still, she knows how close Nathan was to his father. A delayed reaction, perhaps.

Or perhaps something else.

Just a phase, she tells herself. But her words of self-reassurance do nothing to placate her.

Once she has returned Nathan to bed, she hunts through the house for Oliver. She finds him on the floor in the parlour, hunched over a pile of knucklebones.

"Get your books," she says. "We're to have a lesson." She blurts out the words on a burst of courage, before she changes her mind. She could attempt a normal conversation, of course. A simple conversation between mother and son that does not involve Latin lessons and thinly veiled manipulation.

But she knows she would not get the answers she wants. Needs. This unspoken arrangement of theirs, it must be honoured if she is to get to the truth.

Oliver looks at her intently, but it is not with surprise. "It's late," he says.

Abigail stares him down. "Get your books."

She waits in the parlour as he disappears upstairs. Tracks his footsteps up the staircase, down the hallway to his bedroom. She half expects him to disappear out of the house through the passage, but no, here he is, returning to the parlour with his French text in his arms.

Abigail clenches her teeth. Oliver is far better at French than she is— and he knows it. She knows there's no accident to his having chosen this subject tonight.

He sits cross-legged on the floor beside the tea table. Abigail sets him to work copying down a page of conjugations. Watches him intently as his quill scratches across the page. Every few seconds, his gaze flicks up to her, but neither of them speak.

Finally, Abigail says, "There's a girl in Bamburgh who knows you. A thief. Her name is Lizzie."

He looks up at her; a passive, even look that gives nothing away.

"Do you know her?" she asks.

"I know Lizzie."

"How?"

Oliver sets down his quill, carefully, so as not to drip ink on the page.

"How do *you* know Lizzie?"

Abigail feels hot and unsteady. How can her eleven-year-old son always unbalance her like this? She leans forward, meeting his eyes. "No games," she says. "Not tonight. Just the truth."

"Just the truth."

She nods.

"I caught her trying to pick my pocket outside the church the day of Da's burial. I told her she was too sloppy. I told her the best way was to create a distraction, then adopt a little sleight of hand."

Abigail forces herself not to react. She knows this is what he wants. She ought to ask, of course; ask the question he has guided her towards: whether or not he too is a petty thief like Lizzie. She'll not give him the satisfaction. Not tonight, at least.

"She knew I was your mother. How?"

"She saw me with you in the churchyard," Oliver says airily. "You were talking to the vicar with Nathan and Eva. After I spoke with Lizzie about thieving techniques, she suggested we try it on you. I told her not to. I said you were my mother, and you had just buried Da." There's a look of expectancy in his eyes, as though he is waiting for her praise, her thanks for steering Lizzie away from her.

Abigail knows she ought to put an end to this, to make her son see right from wrong. Any decent mother would, surely. But Oliver needs a different approach. The only way to manage him, she knows, is to let him in. Make him feel willing to share.

"How do you know Lizzie?" he asks again.

Abigail hesitates.

"Mama. Just the truth, remember?"

Abigail fiddles with the silver ring on her finger. "She accosted me in Bamburgh one day last month. Tried to rob me of everything I was carrying. She agreed to take half, on the condition that I return the following month to give her the same sum."

Oliver snorts. "That was foolish. You ought to just have given her everything that first time. Then it would all be over and done."

Abigail forces down the rage-filled response that rises to her lips. Half this anger is at herself, she realises. Because she knows Oliver is right.

"You gave her Da's money?" He sounds indignant.

"No. Money that was meant for someone else. Something else."

Oliver tilts his head, taking her in. Suddenly, there's a look of concern in his eyes that seems utterly genuine. "Be careful," he says. "You can't tell anyone about Lizzie, Mama. She won't like it."

"She's just a petty thief. I'm not afraid of her." She cannot tell if this is a lie.

"You ought to be."

"Why?" Her anger flares, stoked by the look of smugness that suddenly overtakes his concern. "Why should I be afraid of her? Is that what you want? For me to be frightened?" She lets out her breath. "You dreadful boy."

Oliver stays sitting cross-legged beside the tea table, not rising to her outburst. "I shall tell you why," he says, "if you calm yourself first."

Abigail closes her eyes. Clenches her teeth until pain shoots through her jaw. Oliver has always been the one most able to bring her spiteful side to the surface. Tonight, with fear at her edges, it is far too difficult to keep her anger and frustration inside. But anger will not get them anywhere. Tonight, she needs answers.

She sits back in the chair, clasping her hands tightly in her lap. "Forgive me," she says tautly. The back of her neck feels hot and prickly, the coarse wool of her robe irritating her forearms. "Why should I be afraid of Lizzie?" she asks stiffly.

Oliver twirls his quill between his fingers. "Because Lizzie… she's not the only one…"

"I know," Abigail says tautly. "Her mother—"

"No," says Oliver. "It's bigger than that." He hesitates. "They're part of a thieving ring."

Abigail swallows heavily. "A thieving ring?" She wishes very desperately that she and Oliver were in a situation that would allow him to lie to her.

"Aye. They operate out of Bamburgh and target the nearby areas. Lizzie says she and her ma have been a part of it for years. She says there's maybe thirty or more people in it. They pool their takings and share it between them all. Her ma joined it after her da died at Killiecrankie."

"Killiecrankie? She's a Jacobite?"

"Not any more. Lizzie says they were all Jacobites once, all of them in the ring. But they turned against the cause after all it took from them."

Abigail's stomach rolls.

Why are you targeting me? she had asked Lizzie's mother. Does she have her answer? It seems too coincidental for Lizzie not to know she had been out raising funds for the Jacobites. But how could she know such a thing? Unless Mairi…

No. Abigail cuts off the thought before it can properly form. She will not let that deceitful, untrusting side of herself accuse Mairi Mitchell of delivering her into the hands of the thieves. In any case, the Mitchells are devoted to the Jacobite movement. Mairi is out raising money. It would not make sense for her to throw Abigail in the path of someone who is stealing from the cause. She curses herself for even allowing such a thought to enter her head.

"How do you know all this?" she asks Oliver.

"Lizzie told me. I think she was trying to impress me. Or frighten me. Or maybe she wanted me to join them because I know so much about pickpocketing. I don't know. Anyway, she told me everything." He leans back on his elbows. "Probably told me too much, really."

Abigail stares into the dancing light of the fire. She imagines the thieving ring growing in the years since those bloody battles at Dunkeld and Killiecrankie; since bodies littered the snow at Glencoe. Imagines widows and orphans and maimed men seeking a way to fight back against the life they had been handed.

She has no thought, of course, of how deep this runs. She only knows that by collecting coins from Jacobite supporters, she has made herself a target for the thieves.

What will happen now if she does not turn up next month with the money Lizzie had demanded? Thirty or more people involved, Oliver had said. Thirty or more people who would have little difficulty finding Highfield House if they chose to hunt her down.

And what choice does she have but to keep doing what she is doing? Skim the top from the Jacobite funds, and no one need be any the wiser.

CHAPTER FIFTEEN

Henry Ward is pleased to be breathing Northumbrian air again. Never mind that this drumming rain feels far closer to midwinter than the late spring the calendar claims it to be.

Ward's pockets are heavy from the sale of a captured French brig, sold at auction in London. He'd lingered around the capital for several weeks on Lord Dunmore's advice, but the pull to head north had been too strong to ignore. He's not missed the grumblings of the men who had signed on for another voyage into the Atlantic.

"This is foolish," his boatswain, John Graveney had said to him outright. "You'll find a buyer in London. This crew signed on expecting action."

"It would take me just as long to find a new buyer as it would to sail back to Holy Island. Besides, I've a deal in place with our Lindisfarne buyer. I've no intention of letting him down."

Graveney did not argue the point, but Ward suspects the man is not fooled. John Graveney had come to the house that first night—Ward suspects he knows exactly why his captain is insisting on returning to Northumberland. There's a faint pull of embarrassment there, yes. Henry Ward has always been able to offer his crew far more than an uneventful jaunt up the coast of England. It's why he never has trouble filling his ship. He would hate for his crew to find out he is making this journey based largely on the mirage of a woman. He hopes his officers have the good sense to keep their mouths shut about Abigail and their visits to the house.

And the house is upon them now, rows of dark windows looking out towards a gunmetal sea. Through the eye of his spying glass, Ward sees rain rolling down the windows and spraying off the tiles of the roof. Trails of smoke rise from the chimneys and melt into the grey afternoon sky.

He feels an odd unease that has little to do with the weather. A thrill, perhaps. He has no idea what kind of reception he is going to get from Abigail. He is dimly aware that that is part of the allure.

When the ship is moored in the bay beyond Emmanuel Head, Ward releases the men not on anchor watch. In spite of the downpour, the crew make for the longboats and disappear around the point towards the village. Ward pulls on a thick broadcloth cloak and cocked hat before making his own way ashore. Over the embankment to the house.

He knocks on the door. Waits in impatient anticipation as footsteps click on the other side, rain pummelling the back of his neck.

The housekeeper looks faintly surprised to see someone braving the terrible weather.

"I'm here to see Mrs Blake," Ward tells her.

The young woman looks him up and down, a frown of what looks like disapproval creasing her face.

Ward smiles inwardly to himself at his unease. After the life he has lived, there is certainly something humorous about feeling the scrutiny of Abigail Blake's housekeeper.

"She's just left for Bamburgh," calls a voice from behind him, before the woman can speak.

Ward whirls around to see Abigail's eldest son approaching from the direction of the outbuildings. He is wearing a dark cloak with the hood pulled up over his fair hair. He jogs up to the awnings of the house to shelter from the rain.

"Bamburgh," Ward repeats. He is dimly aware of the front door closing.

"Aye."

"Why would she go out in such dreadful weather?"

"She had pressing business," Oliver says. "Business that couldn't wait.

Besides, it wasn't raining like this when she left."

"What kind of business?"

Oliver pauses for a moment, seemingly aware that Ward is hanging on his every word. "It's not my place to say."

Ward swallows down his annoyance. "Do you know when she will be back?"

"I don't know. But if I were you, I'd go over there and find her. She could be in trouble."

Ward frowns. "What do you mean? Why is she in trouble?"

"She's caught up in some unpleasant things. Thievery."

Ward's thoughts begin to race. He had not imagined Abigail to be a lawbreaker. Wonders what could have driven her to do such a thing. A meagre settlement from her late husband, perhaps. The pressure of three growing children and an aged and groaning house. Or perhaps he has just completely misread her. He hardly knows this woman, after all. "Are you telling the truth?" he asks Oliver.

"Of course."

Ward knows, from his few dealings with Oliver Blake, that the boy is not to be easily trusted. But he cannot shake the nagging worry. If Oliver is telling the truth and Abigail is in trouble, he can hardly stand by and do nothing. And if he is lying? Well, then, what harm will a detour to Bamburgh do? Better to be safe, surely.

Ward turns his gaze back out to sea, where the ship is just visible behind sheets of silver rain. Most of his crew has just absconded to the tavern. But he can sail the barque with a handful of men.

"I told her I ought to go with her," Oliver continues. "To keep her safe. She wouldn't hear of it."

It's blatant, the boy's attempt to paint himself in a good light. Make himself into a loyal and obedient cabin boy. Ward is not swayed—but it does make him suspect Oliver is telling the truth about his mother being in Bamburgh. About his mother being in trouble.

Rain drips off the brim of his hat and pelts into the mud of the garden. "Whereabouts in Bamburgh can I find her?"

"I don't know for sure," says Oliver, "but perhaps you might try the harbour first. She paid one of the Lindisfarne fishermen to take her over there. No doubt she'll be looking for someone to bring her home when she's done."

Ward nurses the *Eagle* over to Bamburgh with the anchor watch. Moors her in the shadow of the castle and takes a longboat to shore.

In spite of the rain, the harbour is bustling, with a small army of ketches and sloops riding the choppy surface of the inlet. Wind skims across the water, making lines clatter noisily. Bodies swathed in dark cloaks and hats dart between the anchorage and the village, horses spraying up water as they clop across the cobbles. Ward leans up against the wall of the Rose Tavern, trying to huddle beneath the meagre awnings. Through the steamy window, he can see a fire raging in the grate. He briefly considers going inside to warm himself.

No, it's too risky. He won't have a clear view of the street from inside. Does not want to miss Abigail if she passes.

As he waits, wrapping his damp cloak around his body in a meagre attempt at warmth, he asks himself why he is doing this. Returning to Northumberland, sailing out here to Bamburgh, had not felt like a choice. It had felt like a necessity. Abigail Blake has been at the back of his thoughts—and more often than not, at the front of them too—since he had met her that Hogmanay night. He has found himself replaying their conversations in his head, found himself picturing her face when he closes his eyes. Found himself sifting through her guarded words, her unreadable looks, to determine whether she sees him as a welcome addition to her life, or as a hindrance.

Perhaps he will get the answer to that if she sees him here today.

In many ways, he feels like a fool—not least because he knows he has not kept this infatuation entirely hidden from his crew. He'd never speak of it openly, of course. Not even to himself. Once and only once he had allowed himself to care for—love—a woman.

Amelia was the daughter of the navigator on Ward's final East India post. Ward had just secured a ship and commission, and was about to embark on his first privateering voyage. He had assumed that Amelia being the daughter of a seaman gave her an insight into what their life together would be; assumed she understood that he would spend much of each year on the water, loving her from afar.

But in the opening months of the war, she had asked him to choose.

Her or a life as a privateer. Ward's one and only response had been anger. How could she pressure him into making such a choice? He had been trying to make a life as a privateer since the days of the Child's War. She knew all the details: long and tedious negotiations with ship-owners and potential sponsors, the challenge of filling his crew as a new and untried captain. Her ultimatum had been completely unexpected.

Ward had sailed into the Channel without dignifying her request with an answer. Had fully expected to find her waiting when he returned to London months later. Instead, it was a letter waiting, curt and succinct, notifying him of her marriage to another man.

The sight of Abigail jolts him out of his thoughts. She is walking briskly towards the anchorage with her hood pulled up and her cloak tight around her slender body. She looks up briefly to find her way and her eyes catch his, sending a frisson of energy through him.

She changes course to march towards him. "Are you here waiting for me?" Her voice is sharp and accusatory.

A hindrance, then.

"Yes." He dampens the urge to take her elbow and pull her into the shelter of the tavern's awnings.

Her eyes dart. "How did you know I was here?"

"I went to the house. Your son told me where I could find you. He said you might be in trouble."

Something passes across her eyes—something he can't quite read. For a moment, he hesitates. Has he been misled by Oliver Blake once again? Is his coming out here the last thing Abigail wants?

"I see," she says finally. She looks at him for a fleeting moment, and that look is enough to convince Ward to keep persisting. There's something beneath her eyes, something faint, that—what? Wants help? Wants to be open with him? Wants to tell him what she has entangled herself in? He cannot quite tell. But it is *something*.

He hesitates, debating whether to ask her about the thievery her son had claimed she was a part of. Instead, he says, "My ship is in the inlet. Perhaps I might take you back to Lindisfarne? When you're ready, of course."

Her eyes dart again and her lips part, her response hovering unspoken. Ward realises he is holding his breath. Finally, she gives the faintest of nods. Allows him to lead her back towards the water.

Abigail wishes she wasn't quite so pleased to see him. Wishes this didn't feel quite so much like a dashing rescue.

She does not want to be the kind of woman who has to be rescued.

Nonetheless, the sight of Henry Ward waiting outside the tavern had loosened a scrap of the unease that had come from handing over the money to Lizzie today.

That morning, Mairi had sent a message to Highfield House with her eldest son, telling Abigail she would be unable to make the trip out to Bamburgh today as they had planned.

Without Mairi, Abigail had not dared call on the donors, in case word got back to Elias Mitchell and the other Lindisfarne Jacobites, and she had resorted to handing Lizzie a pouch full of her own coin.

The exchange has left her even more angry and bitter than usual, and she is glad for at least the illusion of protection against the thieving ring that Henry Ward might provide.

Not that she has any intention of letting him know that.

The last thing she can afford to do is let her guard down around him. Allow herself to rely on him. She must keep him at a distance—not least because it has been mere months since her husband's death. Never mind that he makes her heart quicken—surely that's nothing more than a thoughtless reaction to the prospect of having a man in her life again. Because if there's one thing Abigail knows for certain about Henry Ward, it's that he will not always be here. She will blink, and he will be back out in the Channel, fighting the French and the Jacobites, and there is every chance he will never return. She will not allow herself to grow close to anyone else, only to lose them again. Will not put herself in a position to have the ground shaken beneath her once more.

But for all that, he is here now, helping her into the longboat lying on the sand of Bamburgh beach. Shoving the boat into the water. Pulling on the oars and drawing them both out towards the ship.

Away from Lizzie. Away from her mother. Away from the thieving ring hiding in Bamburgh, intent on tearing down the Jacobite movement from the shadows.

The oars sigh softly as Ward pulls them through the water. Abigail can feel his eyes on her. There's something oddly thrilling about being trapped beneath his gaze. She is not sure a man has ever looked at her this way before. And for all her feverish talk about not letting him beneath her skin, she knows he is already halfway there.

She is beginning to regret her decision to climb into this longboat. Because he is going to ask questions, surely, about what she has been doing in Bamburgh, and she can tell him none of it. Not a piece. She has not seen any evidence that Lizzie and her mother have an entire ring behind them—today, Lizzie had been waiting for her alone at the end of the Wynd, and the exchange had happened with barely a word. But it is not something Abigail wishes to test. She trusts what Oliver had told her about the ring. And she does not dare imagine what might happen if anyone from the thieving ring found out she had been speaking of them— especially to a privateer with a loaded pistol. How much had Oliver told Ward about what she was doing when they had spoken at the house earlier today?

Abigail shivers. The rain is beginning to ease, but water has soaked through to the velvet lining of her cloak and she feels waterlogged and frozen. A stilted silence hangs between her and Ward, and Abigail can tell he is waiting until they are aboard the ship before he asks his inevitable list of questions. Her mind struggles to cobble together a believable story.

She draws her eyes downward. His enormous presence seems to engulf her, unbalance her, tighten her lungs.

The longboat bumps into the hull of the ship, the vessel looking enormous above them. Ward hollers up to his men and two lines appear over the side of the ship. He hooks them to the bow and stern of the longboat. Abigail feels a strange sense of weightlessness as the boat is winched from the water.

Accepting Ward's outstretched hand, she steps carefully onto the deck. For a moment, her breath leaves her. For all her fascination with the sea, she has never set foot on a ship like this before. She is surprised by its solidity; surprised by how close the three masts seem to come to disappearing into the clouds. Surprised by how insignificant she feels standing beneath the broad branches of the yardarms. Out ahead of her, she sees the majestic wings of the eagle figurehead, hovering forever above the water. The ship is no monstrous galleon, but it feels powerful. Strong. And—naively, she knows—unbreakable.

Apart from the handful of men who had winched the longboat from the water, Abigail can see just one other man aboard. He is standing at the front of the ship with a spying glass in hand and an enormous tarred coat wrapped around his broad shoulders. He glances her way. Gives her a curt and curious nod. When was the last time a woman stepped aboard this ship, she wonders? Perhaps she is the first to do so.

Ward marches over to the man on watch and rattles out a murmured list of instructions. Then he leads Abigail through a narrow doorway into the saloon. Down a shallow staircase and through a long hallway with closed doors lining each side. Their footsteps echo, and a deep wooden groan comes from somewhere within the ship. Ward pulls a key from the pocket of his justacorps and unlocks the door at the end of the passage. Ushers Abigail inside.

The cabin is larger than she expected, with a wide bank of windows at the stern and a narrow bunk against one wall. A long wooden table takes up much of the centre of the room, the unlit lamp above swinging gently with the movement of the sea. A rolltop desk sits in one corner, quills and inkpots lined up in neat pots in the corner.

Ward locks the cabin door and turns, leaning his back against it, eyes meeting hers.

She wants to be angry. Angry at being led down here, at being entrapped in this cabin like an animal. But there's a thrill about being locked away with him like this. Her heart is thumping with something that is only fear at its edges.

"Are you safe?" asks Ward. And at this moment, there is nothing heated or predatory about his gaze. There is just concern. That look in itself manages to take away a fraction of the weight that has pressed down on her shoulders since her husband's death. It's a dangerously addictive feeling.

She nods. "I'm safe." She does not know if that's true. But right now, inexplicably, she feels safe. Feels, locked inside this cabin, that the rest of the world does not exist.

Ward takes a tinderbox from the drawer of the desk and lights the lantern above the table. A soft orange light lifts the gloom of the wet afternoon.

Abigail unhooks her waterlogged cloak and slides it off her shoulders. Though the air inside the cabin is stale and sea-soured, she is grateful for the warmth. Ward takes her cloak and hangs it over the back of his desk chair. He takes off his own, slinging it onto a hook beside the door. Passes her a cloth from beside the washbin.

"Here," he says. "Dry yourself. I'm afraid I cannot offer much in the way of a fire."

Abigail gives him a faint smile. "The worst enemy of a ship."

"Indeed."

She uses the cloth to dry her face and hands. She can smell him on the fabric—maleness and sea. She sets the damp cloth on the edge of the table. Nods her thanks.

Ward has removed his wet justacorps and stands before her in his shirtsleeves and waistcoat. He takes a step towards her and his hand closes daringly around her wrist. "Is there anything I can help with?" he asks. His eyes are probing, full of questions she can tell he is desperate to have answered.

"No," she says. "Thank you. There's nothing to concern yourself with. My son just tends to worry for me unnecessarily."

Ward raises his fair eyebrows, and she can tell he does not believe her.

She needs to give him something, she realises. A piece of the truth at least. After all, he has clearly come traipsing out here to save her. That should annoy her, but somehow it doesn't. And it's *that* which annoys her, she thinks dully.

"I…" she begins, then fades out, unsure of where to start. How much to share.

She realises suddenly that she wants to tell him everything. Wants to tell him about Lizzie, and her mother, and her father lost to the Jacobite cause. Wants to tell him about Oliver's warning that she has entangled herself in a thieving ring, with thirty or more souls who could appear on her doorstep if she tries to step away.

She knows it's dangerous to speak of such things. To risk anyone from the thieving ring turning out in retaliation. But somehow, it feels as though nothing she says or does in this cabin will ever find its way out into the light.

She slides onto the long bench at the table in the centre of the room. Curves her hands around her knees. Ward slides in beside her, close, his shoulder pressing softly against hers. She can smell rain and the ocean on his skin. Feels his knee brush against her fingers.

He nods faintly at her, encouraging her to speak.

"I've done something foolish," she says, trying to determine the best place to begin. "I'm not a Jacobite. I've never supported their cause, or even given more than a passing thought to who is sitting on the throne. But since my husband died, I've felt the need to be a part of something… more… Something bigger." The words feel too vulnerable, too foolish. They hang heavily in the stillness, punctuated by the groan of the ship as it begins to slide out of the harbour. "An acquaintance—a friend—of mine invited me to go with her to raise funds for the Jacobite cause." She catches a flicker of something in Henry Ward's eyes. Unease? She can't place it. "We've been calling on the homes of noblemen around the villages. Collecting money for the cause. But I've…" She draws in a breath, feeling herself creeping towards the edge of the precipice. "I've not been handing all the money I raise back to the Jacobites. I—"

"Abigail." Henry gets to his feet suddenly. He goes to his desk drawer, then stops abruptly. Looks back at her, indecision in his eyes. His fingers hover above the handle of the drawer. "There's a letter in here," he says finally. "I promised the man who wrote it that I would not show it to anyone." His eyes meet hers pointedly. "But if you were to find it yourself…" He fades out.

Abigail gets slowly to her feet, following Henry's gaze towards the desk drawer. Curiously, she pulls it open. There, at the top is a folded piece of paper. She can see a large crimson seal on the front, snapped open.

Henry nods at her. She takes the letter and sits back down beside him at the table. As she moves to open the page, his fingers come to rest lightly on her wrist. He says, "Nothing in this letter can leave this room."

Abigail nods faintly. She opens the page and reads slowly over the elaborate curls of handwriting. *A morsel of information to whet your appetite: Lord Haver, prominent Whig party politician, is harbouring Jacobite tendencies…*

Lord Haver's name is only vaguely familiar to her, but she can tell this accusation—connection with the Jacobites on account of being the illegitimate son of a Highlander—would be more than a little damaging to all concerned if it were to find the light of day.

The corner of Ward's lips turn up slightly. "Quite an accusation, wouldn't you say?"

She nods. "Is it true?"

"Lord Dunmore, who wrote the letter, is spying against the movement. He assures me the accusation against Haver is true. But that is far from the worst of it." His fingers tighten almost instinctively around her wrist. Unbidden, Abigail feels something flicker in her chest. "Lord Dunmore also tells me the London Jacobites have a plot underway that involves the kidnapping and possible assassination of King William. And if the plot to kill the king is successful, I'm sure I don't need to tell you that anyone involved in the Jacobite cause will be in great danger." He shifts on the bench to meet her eyes. "Whatever ties you have with the Jacobite movement, you must cut them immediately."

For long moments, Abigail says nothing. Does not allow herself to move, or barely, to breathe. She is intensely focused on the warmth, the weight of his hand against her own. Intensely focused on the drumbeat in her chest. Homing in on these things takes the focus away from this dangerous knowledge Henry Ward has just shared with her.

"This money," he continues, "that you have been pocketing from the Jacobite cause… Have you been doing such a thing out of financial necessity? Because of the pressures of being a new widow…" He hesitates, choosing his words carefully. "Perhaps my opinion is of little concern to you, but I just want you to know that I would not blame you for such a thing."

Abigail smiles inwardly to herself. She cannot be surprised at his jumping to conclusions, she supposes. Henry Ward seems like the type of man prone to conclusions. Assumptions. The kind of man who believes himself always right.

A part of her longs to correct him. Tell him that Samuel Blake had been a better man than to leave his wife with no choice but to steal. But this untruth, it feels safer. Feels believable. Pitiable, even. Not that she wants pity. But sometimes it can be advantageous. Besides, she can only imagine the chaos she would unleash if she set a crew of privateers upon the Bamburgh thieving ring.

She doesn't speak. Does not confirm or deny. But the look in Henry's eyes makes it clear he has decided this is the truth. He squeezes her fingers. "Promise me you'll not involve yourself in the cause any further."

She wants to promise him this, of course. Wants to walk away from the thieving ring and the Jacobite cause, and never look back—especially now, with this new information about the assassination plot. Perhaps such a thing would cost her her friendship with Mairi, and any chance of being accepted by the villagers—but she would rather spend every day and night haunting Highfield House than risk being locked up for treason. But how can she make such a promise? If she does not return to Bamburgh next month to hand over more Jacobite funds to Lizzie, there is every chance pieces of the thieving ring will turn up at her door.

"Abigail," Henry pushes. "Please. Promise me."

"Yes. I promise." The words fall out without further thought. And they are true, she realises. She will stay away from the Jacobite cause. She has seen what happens to people accused of Jacobite alliance. Imprisonment. Exile. Execution.

And somehow, she will find a way to extricate herself—and her son— from the Bamburgh thieving ring.

Somehow.

"Good," Ward says. Pauses. "And if you are in need of assistance… financially…" He pulls his eyes from hers awkwardly.

She cannot take the lie this far. She may have convinced herself she needs Henry Ward's pity. But she does not need his money. Samuel had made sure of that. "I shall manage," she assures him.

"Forgive my boldness," he says after a moment. "I should not have… It is not my place to speak of such things." He hesitates for a second, as though debating whether to speak further. Without saying more, he goes to the desk and pulls a bottle of dark amber liquid from a cupboard by the desk. He fills two glasses and sets one on the table in front of her. "Here. You look as though you could use this."

She smiles faintly. Takes a grateful sip of the whisky. It's rich and smoky; warms her throat as it glides down. With each mouthful, she feels the tension inside her unravel a little. Allows herself, just for now, not to think about the thieving ring and the way she is trapped in their net. Allows herself not to think of Oliver's friendship with Lizzie. The liquor in her blood unleashes a recklessness that feels almost painfully liberating.

Henry leans back against the desk as he brings his glass to his lips. She can feel him watching her. Through the bank of windows at the back of the cabin, she sees the sharp corners of Bamburgh Castle disappearing into the cloud.

"I'm sorry for my rudeness earlier," she says. "Today, and every other day before that."

A smile lights his face. "I enjoy the company of a woman who challenges me."

"Challenges you, or offends you?"

A chuckle. "I'm not that easily offended."

Abigail smiles. She gets to her feet and moves slowly towards the rain-streaked windows, allowing her body to adjust to the rhythmic up-and-down motion of the sea. She runs her finger over the delicately carved scrolls adorning the window frames.

"It's a beautiful ship," she says. "Is she yours?"

"Yes. I took her as a prize two years ago and kept her as my own. She was once a French merchant. *La Sainte Marie.*"

"Were you not afraid that changing her name would curse you?"

Henry's lips part. Abigail can tell her knowledge of such a thing has surprised him. She sips her whisky self-consciously.

"I had quite an interest in seafaring when I was younger," she admits. "Sailors' superstitions have always fascinated me."

"Just when you were younger?"

"Yes, well." She looks down. "It is not the kind of interest a husband wants in a wife. Not that my husband ever knew of my interest. Perhaps I am being too harsh on him. Perhaps he would have indulged me."

Henry moves towards her, his boots clicking softly against the floorboards. "How long has your husband been gone?" he asks. His voice comes out husky.

"Samuel passed a few weeks before Christmas," she tells him. "Smallpox. It was very sudden. An immense shock."

"You must miss him terribly."

"Of course." She can't look at him. Feels the skin on the back of her neck flush with guilt. Being so close to Henry Ward's sleeping quarters feels almost painfully intimate. Speaking of her husband here feels like a sin.

"And you?" she asks. "A wife? Children?"

"No. I've never felt the need for such a life."

It does not quite feel like the truth. But Abigail does not pry. It feels safest this way.

She picks up Lord Dunmore's letter from the table and reads over it again. She looks at Henry with a crooked smile on her lips. "I see you've not followed his instructions to burn the page after reading."

He chuckles. "That's because I'm not a fool."

"Does anyone else know about this information?" she asks. "Besides you and the man who wrote it?" She smiles crookedly. "And Lord Haver?"

"Hopefully not. The less people who know, the more valuable the letter. The more Haver and the Whigs will pay to keep the information secret."

"My mother likes to say that nothing stays a secret forever," Abigail says. "'Come midnight, all truths will be revealed,' she used to say." The lies she has just let Henry Ward believe prod at her. "I always thought that sounded terribly dire." Those words had always been a thinly veiled threat on Susanna's part; an attempt at scaring her daughter into honesty. Not that they'd done much good, Abigail thinks wryly. Midnight has long passed, and there any many truths her mother is yet to learn.

Henry smiles. "I suspect Lord Haver is doing all he can to prove your mother wrong."

"This letter must be worth a great deal," Abigail says.

Henry nods. "The information on its own is very valuable. But the letter, with Dunmore's seal, makes it even more so. Gives it legitimacy."

"Then surely it's not safe for you to be carrying it on your ship into conflict."

"Probably not, no."

"Have you no safer place to keep it? A home in London?" She smiles. "That does not float?"

He chuckles. "I've little need for a home that does not float at present. The war is keeping me far too busy."

"Then I can keep it safe for you. At the house." The moment the words are out, Abigail can't believe she has spoken them. This is too forward, surely.

Henry doesn't answer immediately. He meets her gaze. Holds it without speaking.

"I would like to make of copy of its contents first," he says. "Ensure I've a written record of the thing. But thank you. I think that would be a wise thing to do. I shall bring it to you later tonight."

CHAPTER SIXTEEN

The knock at the door comes far earlier than she expected. Evening sunlight is still spilling through the high windows of the dining room, and Abigail is sitting at the table with her children, dishes of bread and stew in front of them.

As the sound of doorknocker crashes through the house, Abigail throws down her spoon and leaps to her feet. Eva stares up at her in wide-eyed alarm.

"Stay here," Abigail tells the children. She hurries off to answer the door before any of them ask questions.

She is nervous tonight; inexplicably so. Why should she be nervous? This is not the first time she has had Henry Ward and his men in her home. She trusts—for better or for worse—that they will not do harm to her or her children.

It's not about trust, of course. It's about the undeniable attraction she had felt for Henry on his ship today. An attraction that had managed to blot out the fear and strain of the thieving ring—at least for a few hours. Those few hours have been enough for her crave the feeling.

She cannot let herself act on these thoughts, of course. Not so soon after Samuel's passing. Besides, tomorrow, Henry Ward will be gone; back out into the Atlantic to put himself in the line of cannon fire, and there is every chance he will never return.

Abigail pulls open the door. Silences the part of herself that is glad to see Henry alone.

She glances down at the small brass box in his hand. "What is in there?" she asks, voice low. She knows Oliver will be listening, trying to catch pieces of their conversation.

"The letter."

She raises her eyebrows. "You thought to lock it up?"

"It's very valuable. I would hate for it to fall into the wrong hands."

"Are you sure you trust me with it?"

"Of course."

He passes it to her, their eyes meeting. The box is small and plain; the size of her palm, fastened with a delicate lock that's tarnished at the edges. "Do you have somewhere safe you can keep it?" he asks.

"Yes. My nightstand. It will be safe there."

He nods. Smiles. "Thank you."

"Good evening, Captain Ward," says a voice from behind her.

Abigail whirls around. Oliver has appeared in the entrance hall, Nathan and Eva peeking out from behind him.

Henry looks taken aback for a moment, then his face shifts into an uneasy smile. "Good evening, children."

Abigail tries to hide the box in the folds of her skirts. She flashes hard eyes at her children. "Back to your supper at once."

They hover in the entrance hall for a moment, Oliver opening his mouth to speak, and then seeming to decide against it. Abigail keeps her eyes pinned to them until they have all disappeared back into the dining room.

Her thoughts knock together. Eva and Nathan will have questions, surely, about this man who has appeared on their doorstep. She has no thought of how much—if anything—Oliver has told them about who Henry Ward is. Will it be less damaging if she brings him inside to introduce them properly? Or should she let him disappear, and hope the children's curiosity vanishes with the morning?

In the end, it's not her children's curiosity that makes the decision for her. It's that treacherous part of herself that does not want Henry Ward to sail back into the Channel without a little more time spent in her company.

"Will you come in?" she asks, before the rational part of her brain can catch up with her. "I'm sure the children would like to meet you properly."

A look of uncertainty passes across his eyes. "Of course," he says finally. "I would very much like to meet them too." He sounds faintly terrified at the prospect.

She leads him down the passage and into the dining room. The children are silent in their seats, watching with wide-eyed expectancy, their spoons lying abandoned on the table and their stew growing cold.

Abigail gestures to Henry to sit, careful to guide him away from the chair at the head of the table—the chair left empty by Samuel's death. He sits beside her, opposite Oliver. Gives another gawpish nod to Nathan and Eva.

He is uncomfortable around children, Abigail notes. Awkward. Even if he had not shared as much with her already, she would have been able to tell, by the rigidity he shows around her youngest two, that Henry Ward is not a father. He seems to have managed Oliver well enough in their few interactions she has observed. But he seems more than a little unmoored by Eva and Nathan's open-mouthed stares.

Abigail takes a glass from the cabinet and fills it from the wine bottle in the centre of the table. She sets it in front of Henry and slides back into her chair beside him. Manages stifled introductions. My youngest son, Nathan. My daughter, Eva. And of course, you know Oliver.

She swallows heavily. "Say good evening to Captain Ward, children."

It's a dreadful thing to do, of course, to have this man sit down at the dinner table with her children, mere months after their father's death. She wonders if they are still too young to judge her.

Nathan mumbles a greeting, but his eyes are drawn quickly back to his plate. Eva is kneeling up in her chair, small hands curled around the edge of the table.

"Good evening," she says, her seriousness belied by the smear of stew on the side of her mouth. She inspects Ward with critical eyes. "Who are you and why are you in our house?"

Abigail hides a smile at the bug-eyed horror her three-year-old daughter manages to elicit from this privateering captain. "That's not polite, Evie," she says, fighting the urge to watch Henry try and wrangle out a response. She turns to him, mouthing an apology.

"Are you here on business, Captain Ward?" asks Oliver. "I didn't imagine there'd be much call for privateering in Northumberland."

Henry looks relieved at having escaped Eva's interrogation. "Usually not," he agrees. "But I sell much of our cargo to a Lindisfarne-based merchant." He answers a little too quickly. An answer rehearsed enough to make Abigail wonder at its truth. Wonder if Henry Ward might not have made the journey up here for other reasons.

For her.

The thought makes the back of her neck heat. Makes this far too dangerous. She pushes it away.

"I've been reading about Viking shipbuilding," Oliver says. "I was surprised to learn their longboats could travel at speeds close to your barque." He scoops a careful spoonful from the edge of his stew. "At least, at speeds close to what I estimate your barque to travel at. Given I've never been aboard myself."

A smile flickers in the corner of Henry's mouth. "And what is your estimate of my ship's speed?"

"I would assume nineteen or twenty knots under good conditions. Slightly faster than a fully manned Viking longboat."

"A very fair estimate," says Henry. Oliver looks pleased with himself. "I have some books on shipbuilding techniques you might enjoy. They make mention of the Vikings' superior maritime technology. I shall bring them for you next time I come to the house."

"People thought they saw dragons in the sky," Nathan says suddenly, "before the Vikings raided Lindisfarne. And whirlwinds."

Abigail turns to him in surprise. Where had that come from? She had no idea that Nathan had such knowledge. Had he heard of such things from his brother? His father? She is fairly certain dragon sightings and Viking raids are not general topics of teaching at the petty school.

Ward smiles. Sips his wine. "Is that so? How interesting. What do you think it was they were really seeing? Not dragons, certainly."

Nathan cowers slightly under Henry's attention, but there's a small self-satisfied smile on his face. In a soft voice, he says, "I don't know. Lightning maybe. And storm clouds."

"I would imagine that's very likely."

Nathan's blue eyes light as he reaches for his spoon again. He's just as entranced by Henry Ward as his brother is, Abigail realises. Is not sure if this makes her relieved or fearful.

When supper is finished, she sends the children upstairs. They thunder up the staircase and the ground floor of the house falls quiet. Seems to shift and widen around her and Henry. With her children's sudden absence, she is acutely aware of the fact they are alone together.

She walks him to the front door, a rapid thumping in her chest.

"They're fine children," Henry says. "Very intelligent."

"Thank you." Abigail smiles. "Nathan and Oliver both seem fascinated by all you have to say. And Eva is at that age where she is just clamouring for knowledge. I hope she did not offend you."

He laughs. "I told you, I'm not easily offended. She'll grow to be a very bright young lady, I'm sure. She's much like her mother."

Abigail's heart skips at the compliment. "She's her father's daughter."

"I see you in her also."

His eyes bore into hers, making heat flush the back of her neck. She opens the front door, letting sea-drenched air flood into the foyer. She can hear the tide sighing against the embankment. Out beyond the house, the sea shimmers in the pearly light.

Abigail reaches into her pocket and feels for the brass box. "When do you imagine you might need the letter?"

"Perhaps never. With luck the need for it will never arise. But it's reassuring to know it's safe here if ever I need it."

This feels too one-sided. Henry Ward has entrusted her with his most prized possession, and she has not even given him a scrap of truth about all that is going in her life. Has even allowed him to believe the lie he had created about her keeping the Jacobite funds for her own purposes.

She cannot tell him about the thieving ring. But she can give him something.

She looks up at him. "Will you wait here a moment?"

He nods. "Of course."

Abigail darts back inside the house, leaving Henry on the doorstep and the door wide open to let the island evening blow in. She climbs up to the study and pulls the bundle of letters from the desk drawer. Hurries back out to the doorstep and pushes them into Henry's hands before she can change her mind.

It feels like a bold and exposing move; she has filled these letters with so many personal thoughts. Each time she had sat down to tell her mother about Samuel's passing, she had found herself writing to Henry instead; speaking of her grief, her fears, even her regret at having willingly stepped into the Jacobite movement. Handing them over to him to read, as she had never intended, makes her feel intensely vulnerable. But there is no danger in it. She has not written a word about the thieving ring—has not dared to speak of it even within the safety of these private letters. And she wants to be vulnerable with him, she realises. Wants to be open, and honest, at least more than she has so far. Wants to give him more than lies.

He looks down at the bundle of papers. "What are these?"

"Letters." She swallows heavily, feeling her cheeks colour. "To you. I thought you might care to know about…" She hesitates. Care to know what? The challenge of growing roses in coastal soil?

A sudden wave of regret breaks over her.

But there's a new light in Henry's eyes. A light she hadn't expected. "You wrote to me?"

She can't look at him. "There's no need to read them if you don't wish. But I just felt as though…" She fades out. Feels foolish.

"I very much look forward to reading them. Thank you." He sounds taken aback. As though this is far more than he was expecting. His free hand rises almost instinctively to cup her cheek.

Abigail holds her breath, feeling her heart pounding in her ears. Feeling desire unfurling inside her. She is hot and restless beneath her mourning gown.

This is nothing, she tells herself. This pounding heart, this flush of her skin, it is not for Henry Ward. It is for the possibility he represents; it is a longing for that security, that safety, that solidity, she had felt as a wife. That sense of not having to face the world alone.

But she knows there is nothing safe, or secure about Henry Ward. He is a man who steals ships and cargo, a man who likely thinks little about taking another's life. A man who justifies it all with a letter of marque. Yes, she has enough knowledge of the situation to know that the line between *privateer* and *pirate* is a hazy one.

Henry Ward is not *safety* or *security* or *solidity*. He is something else entirely.

She ought to step away, yes. Honour her husband's memory. Her husband, who is lying lifeless in his grave. Her husband, who had brought her to live in this faraway house, where no one can see what happens on the doorstep. Her husband who, for all his goodness, had never set her body alight like this.

She feels herself drifting towards Henry, towards the unspoken invitation she can see in his eyes. Feels the tidal pull of him. How easy it would be to reach for him; feel him, taste him, breathe him in. Too easy, here on the doorstep with the great hulk of the house hiding them from the rest of the world.

No one would ever know.

But yes—too easy. This is the act of a woman who had not loved her husband. A woman who has found easiness in her new life as a widow. And Abigail is not that woman. Her head is suddenly full of Samuel. Her kind and decent husband, who had made her into a kind and decent wife. He deserves far better than this.

She steps away from Henry. "Good night," she says, on a breath that barely makes it from her lips. "Take care." And she closes the door before she loses her resolve.

CHAPTER SEVENTEEN

Abigail is at Mairi's door early the next morning. With the bright light of morning, last night's encounter with Henry Ward feels dreamlike and illusory. It has given way to the brutal reality of all he had told her on his ship yesterday. The reality that she has no choice but to step away from the Jacobite fundraising. What that will mean for her entanglement with the thieving ring, Abigail cannot quite yet make sense of.

What will happen when she does not appear at the end of the Wynd next month, to hand over the required funds to Lizzie and her mother? Abigail has no thought of how deep the ring goes—and how much effort they will put into finding her when she fails to appear at the promised hour.

Perhaps she is overplaying her own importance. Perhaps they will simply find another wealthy woman to rob, and they will never think of her again. Or perhaps the Bamburgh thieves will appear on her doorstep, demanding the Jacobite money they see as their owed right for all they have endured and lost. She has no thought of which scenario is the more likely. She only knows she cannot risk being arrested for treason.

Mairi opens the door of her cottage with the baby in the crook of her arm, and another son clinging to her skirts. Abigail shakes her head when Mairi tries to wave her inside. She does not want to drag this out any longer than necessary. Nor does she want to come face to face with Elias or Donald Macauley again.

Mairi steps out into the street with the baby warbling under her arm. She pulls the door closed behind her to pen her other children inside. "Is everything all right? You look bothered."

"I'm afraid I cannot come with you to fundraise any longer," Abigail blurts. In spite of all that has happened, the words are hard to get out. The past months she has spent in Mairi's company have shown her how precious their friendship is. The thought of spending every day and night in Highfield House with just the children and staff for company is a bleak and unswallowable prospect.

For the briefest of moments, the thought of returning to London flits across Abigail's mind. An escape from the thieving ring. From the Jacobites. From Highfield House. The wise option, surely. But that wise option is chased away by the knowledge of how desperately she does not want to be under her mother's influence again. Her mother, who does not yet even know her daughter is a widow.

Abigail knows being around Susanna again will bring out all the worst parts of herself. The anger. The bitterness. The lies, the short temper, the words spoken with the sole purpose of causing offence. These unwelcome parts of herself she can feel simmering too close to the surface after all the stress and sadness of the past months. And she has spent too long outrunning her old self to willingly turn around and embrace her. Abigail will not let her children have that woman for a mother. She does not dare imagine what that might do to Oliver.

Mairi shifts the baby to her other arm. "Is this because of how Donald and my husband spoke to you the day you came here to the house? Because—"

"It's not about that. I just…" Abigail had come to Mairi's cottage with her speech rehearsed. Had planned to blame her reluctance to go visiting on what her late husband would have wanted. Planned to rattle out a trite line about honouring Samuel's memory. But those words die on her lips. They feel far too hollow to be taken as truth. Especially after how close she had come to being pulled into Henry Ward's orbit last night. "I've heard rumours," she says instead, "that the Jacobites are planning something."

Mairi smiles crookedly. "The Jacobites are always planning something."

"Yes, I suppose." Abigail knows she needs to be careful. Cannot step too close to the contents of Henry's letter. She had promised him she would not share a word of it.

But she is worried about Mairi. She knows Henry is right—if the Jacobites succeed in their assassination plot, the redcoats will be on the hunt for traitors. Abigail knows the Mitchells are dedicated to the Jacobite cause. Knows she has little chance of convincing Mairi to step away. But she can at least warn her to be careful.

"I'm worried," Abigail says carefully. "If these rumours are true, the authorities will be hunting Jacobites with a new intensity. And I… Well, I'm all my children have now. I cannot risk anything happening to me. Especially for a cause I've never truly been aligned with."

Mairi doesn't speak at once. "I see. I'm sorry to hear it." Sorry why, Abigail finds herself wondering? Because she will miss her company? Miss her assistance in raising funds? Or because she will miss the sizeable sums she hands over to the thieving ring each month?

A blaze of suspicion comes up on her suddenly, taking her by surprise.

Mairi frowns. "Abby? Is everything all right?"

Walk away, Abigail thinks. She has no proof. Nothing but her own bitter notions that Mairi knows anything of the thieving ring. Notions that are completely unfounded. Mairi is dedicated to the Jacobite cause. Of course she is, of course she is.

But it's a suspicion she cannot shake. After all, Mairi had sent her to Lord Milgate's house that first day. Right into the path of Lizzie. And how else would the thieves possibly have known she was raising funds for the Jacobites? How else would Lizzie have known to specifically demand money on a monthly basis, to align with the schedule of the Jacobite fundraising?

"Do you know of them?" she blurts, unable to hold the words back. "The thieving ring?"

Mairi's pale eyebrows rise. "A thieving ring? What are you talking about?"

Abigail feels her skin prickling beneath her bodice. Regret gnaws at her. The sense that this was a mistake. But it's too late to turn back now. "In Bamburgh," she says tautly. "There's a ring of thieves targeting Jacobite fundraisers."

Mairi pries a strand of her hair from the baby's fist. "Is that why you don't wish to come with me anymore?" she asks calmly. "Because you had a run-in with thieves?" Her words are so logical, so innocent, they make Abigail doubt everything. Make her feel like a fool.

"Yes," she says, unable to cobble together a more adequate response. "I had a run-in with thieves. Who are seeking to steal from the Jacobite cause." She clenches her hands into fists. That gnawing regret turns into a gaping pit in her stomach. She has said too much, of course. Has said far too much. What had she been thinking, letting these baseless accusations come flying out of her mouth like this? She knows how dangerous it is to be speaking of this, even to a friend—although she is fairly certain these accusations have just put an end to her being able to call Mairi a friend.

Mairi lets out an incredulous laugh. "I'm sorry, are you accusing me of sending these thieves out to target you? Thieves that are out to steal from the Jacobite cause, no less." She shakes her head. "Why in heaven's name would I be working with thieves who are seeking to steal from the cause I'm raising funds for? Did you stop for a moment to think about the madness of what you're suggesting?"

Abigail says nothing. After all, what is there to say? Yes, she had stopped for a moment to think. And she had made these accusations anyway. And yes, she can see their utter foolishness. Sees the layers and layers of damage she has done.

"Elias and Donald had their doubts about you," Mairi says coldly. "I told them they were wrong. I told them you we could trust you. But they were right. I ought to have kept my distance." She slams the door and disappears before Abigail can respond.

"We need to make a deal," says Abigail that night. "Neither of us will go near the thieving ring again." She and Oliver are alone in the parlour, the rest of the house quiet around them. Rain is pattering softly against the windows, the remains of a fire popping in the grate.

Oliver eyes her, considering. He runs a hand over the book on the table in front of him. "Lizzie is my friend."

"I don't want you having friends like that."

"She's not a bad person, Mama. She just got caught up in things she didn't wish to. I'm sure you know what that's like."

Abigail inhales slowly, forcing herself not to react. His comment is far too all-seeing. Far too accurate. She shifts awkwardly in Samuel's armchair. "Neither of us will go near the thieving ring again," she repeats.

Oliver sits back on the rug, crossing his legs. He toys with the lacing at the neck of his shirt. "You cannot just walk away," he says. "That's not how this works. You ought to have known better than to fall for such a thing in the first place."

"If they want more money from me, they will have to come and take it," she tells him brusquely. Hopes he can't hear the unease in her voice.

"And you don't think they will do that?"

Abigail doesn't speak at once. She knows just how easy it would be for the thieves to find her. Even if Oliver has not already told Lizzie where he lives, anyone on Lindisfarne could point the thieves in the direction of Highfield House. She doubts there would be too many people in the village willing to put themselves in danger to protect her. Especially after the accusations she had thrown at Mairi today.

Oliver looks up at her, spearing her blue eyes with his. "I will stay away from the thieving ring," he says finally, "if the next time Captain Ward comes to the house, you tell him I would do well as his cabin boy."

Abigail hears her sharp exhalation. She ought to have expected some attempt at manipulation like this. But she cannot make this deal. Cannot condemn her son to a life in which he is unlikely to return home. With every fibre in her body, she knows she will never send her child away to sea with Henry Ward. But right now, she has few options other than to tell him what he wants to hear.

"All right. I will tell Captain Ward." She slides suddenly out of the armchair and kneels on the floor in front of him. Presses her palms to his cheeks. Dear God, she loves him so much, this first-born child of hers. It's an angry, suffocating love, so different from what she feels towards her other children. She loves Eva and Nathan desperately too, of course. But it feels as though Oliver needs something more. As though he needs her to love him as fiercely and violently as possible, to keep him from pulling adrift. "But you must promise me you will stay away from Lizzie," she says. "And everyone else in the thieving ring."

He nods, not breaking her gaze. "I promise."

Oliver stands, and her fingers brush against his hip. She feels something hard and metallic in the side pocket of his breeches.

"What's in your pocket?" she asks.

Without hesitation, Oliver reaches down and pulls out a small, narrow object. Sets it on the tea table in front of them. It's a silver fishing knife, tarnished and bent in places.

Abigail's stomach turns over. So many questions fly at her. The one that makes it out her lips first is: "Where did you get that?"

"I found it in the water when Nathan and I were playing on Saint Cuthbert's Island." The response feels almost painfully innocent. He smirks. "I told Nathan it was a Viking knife. I think he believed me."

"You are cruel to your brother."

"No I'm not." He holds her gaze. "Nathan loves spending time with me. Just ask him."

Abigail makes a noise in her throat. For better or for worse, she knows he is right. "What is the Viking Game?" she asks suddenly.

Oliver shrugs. "Just hide and seek. Nothing more."

Abigail stares down at the knife sitting beside them on the table beside Oliver's inkpot and Latin text. "Why have you been carrying this around with you?" She forces the question out. Is afraid of the answer.

He shrugs again. "It's useful."

"For what?"

"Making repairs to Da's boat. Cutting the ivy from the house. Other chores like that."

She swallows. Thinks of Nathan's new refusal to let anyone lay a finger on him. "Did you hurt your brother with this?"

"Of course not."

Abigail doesn't speak at once. She wants desperately to believe him.

"Did Nathan tell you I hurt him?" Oliver asks.

Abigail glances down, away from his eyes. She knows she needs to tread carefully. Does not want to give Oliver any reason to turn on his younger brother. Not that he has ever needed it.

And not, she realises now, that he even needs an answer to this question. She knows Oliver is well aware of the pull he has over his brother. Surely he knows Nathan would never speak out against him, or put him in any kind of trouble. It's no small part of her that wishes Nathan would learn to stand up for himself a little more. Not that he has ever really had a hope of doing so, with Oliver's shadow having loomed over him his entire life.

"What was in the box?" Oliver asks, veering abruptly away from the topic of his brother. "The box Captain Ward gave you when he came to the house last night."

Abigail knows there's little point feigning ignorance. "Nothing you need to concern yourself with." She slides back into the armchair, suddenly needing to put space between her and her son.

Oliver sits back on the floor beside the tea table and opens his book. "Is it something to do with the thieving ring?"

"Of course not."

He looks at her with intent blue eyes. "I thought we were sharing things with each other. I thought that was what we do."

Abigail reaches down and takes the knife from the tea table. She curls her hand around it, feeling an odd frisson of exhilaration. Power. But this is the kind of power that should not belong to a child. She will lock this cursed thing away. See that Oliver does not go near it again. "We do share things," she says. "But some things are not for you to know."

Oliver exhales loudly through his nose. He leans forward and turns the page of his text with far more force than is necessary. He picks up his quill and dips it in the pot. Is deliberate in spattering ink across the tabletop.

Abigail watches him for a long time, turning the knife over between her fingers. Finds herself rattling through possibilities of where she can hide the damn thing so he does not find it. Perhaps there's little point. He clearly knows the house and its hiding places far better than she does. And if he wants to carry around a knife, there are far too many other places he could find one.

She sets the blade back on the table.

"I told Mairi Mitchell about the thieving ring," she blurts.

Oliver looks up. "I don't think you ought to have done that."

"I know. It was a mistake."

"Why did you do it?" There's a genuineness in his face now. Concern. Kindness. Abigail is glad to see this side of him. It's unspeakably precious. And tonight, she needs it.

"I accused her of sending me into Lizzie's path. I was with her just before it happened."

Oliver frowns. "I don't think Lizzie knows Mrs Mitchell."

Abigail smiles wryly. "No. I'm sure she doesn't. It was a foolish thing to do. Mrs Mitchell was very upset at my accusations."

Oliver sits up on his knees. "What will you do?" he asks. "Will you ask her to stay quiet about what you told her?"

Abigail lets out a humourless laugh. "I think such a thing might only encourage her to do the opposite."

CHAPTER EIGHTEEN

The white flag droops at the top of the French ship's mainmast, barely lifted by the breeze. Surrender.

Ward feels a familiar humming beneath his skin. That acute sense of aliveness that comes with conflict; comes whenever the prospect of death draws a little closer.

It's an easy prize; the ship is far smaller than the *Eagle*. Eight guns at most. The warning shots the *Eagle* had fired across their bowsprit had been enough to send the white flag flying up the target's mast before they even managed to get any of their cannons clear.

The unfortunate *Fortune* is a naval ship, fitted en flute—less guns and more men. There'll be little in the way of cargo aboard, Ward knows, but he's sure they'll find provisions for the French sailors that he can commandeer for his own men.

Of course, they'll also find a crew of enemy navy. It will fetch a fine ransom from the French Government.

Ward stands at the gunwale beneath a thick bank of cloud. Watches as Hunter, his quartermaster, gathers the boarding party. The two vessels are roped together, grinding against each other with each roll of the sea. Half Ward's crew of eighty-five men will board the prize. Men to ferry her provisions back to the *Eagle*. Men to lock the French prisoners in the hold.

The other half will stay aboard. Keep their ship protected.

Murmurs of anticipation ripple through the boarding party. Pistols and cutlasses in their hands. Bands of red fabric knotted around their upper arms so they can be easily identified as allies should any trouble arise.

Ward keeps one hand curled around a loaded pistol. He watches as his men file over the gunwale and onto the prize ship. The sky splits open, and fat beads of rain begin to bounce off the deck. Ward waits, watches as his men disappear into the forecastle of the French ship. The *Fortune's* crew have retreated to closed quarters, and he listens intently for the sound of gunfire. Muffled shouts drift across the water. Orders. Not conflict. Above his head, the yardarms groan.

When the stillness thickens enough to convince Ward the *Fortune's* crew have not retaliated, he calls to Finn with instructions to send the navigator to the ward-robe. Ward climbs through the saloon and down into the ship, plans of ransoms and Northumbrian journeys beginning to take ship in his mind.

The navigator is leaving the ward-robe with instructions to plot a course for London when Hunter strides through the door, Graveney and Cook close behind. The three them smell of action: sweat and sea and the lingering punch of gunpowder that seems to have infused every corner of the ship.

Ward nods at the folded pages in Hunter's hands. "The ship's papers?"

"Aye sir. All look legitimate. A hundred and ten sailors returning to the Continent from Saint Kitts."

Ward takes the papers, reads carefully over their contents. "Good." He takes the wine bottle from the centre of the table and fills three cups for his officers. "She'll fetch a fine ransom from La Royale." He sinks into the leather-padded chair at the head of the ward-robe table. A pleasant exhaustion is weighing down his body. He sips his wine, stretching his long legs out in front of him.

"What of her crew, sir?" asks Graveney, sliding into a seat at the table.

Ward glances down at the papers. "A hundred and ten men. Are they all accounted for?"

"Aye sir," says Hunter. "All locked below."

Ward looks at Graveney pointedly. "Then they will fetch a fine ransom from La Royale."

Graveney rubs his narrow chin. Glances at Hunter, as though seeking support.

Ward leans forward in his chair. "Something to say, Mr Graveney?" He keeps his voice level, despite the irritation gnawing beneath his skin. He has always prided himself on being a fair captain. On letting his men have their say. And he wishes that, whatever it is John Graveney has to say, he'd just come out and say it.

His boatswain hesitates. Takes a gulp of wine, as though to fortify himself. "We've held vessels for ransom in the past, sir. Never seen the need to hold the whole damn crew hostage. Why not just hold the captain and master?"

"We've held merchant ships for ransom in the past," Ward says pointedly. "A naval crew will fetch far more."

"We're ransoming the vessel," Graveney says tautly. His dark eyes spark suddenly. "Since when do we barter with men's lives?"

Ward straightens, eyebrows rising. "Careful, John. That sounds a little too much like a pro-French sentiment to me."

Graveney's neck reddens beneath the dark bristles of his beard. "Pro-French?" he snorts. "You think I'd be sailing with you if I'd a pro-French bone in my body? This ain't about supporting the French. It's about common decency, and you know it." He tosses back another mouthful of wine. "You're heading a little too close to piracy if you ask me."

Ward tightens his fingers around his cup, inhaling to settle the anger simmering beneath his skin. *Heading too close to piracy* is a barbed insult— he has always been careful never to cross that line into lawlessness. This is wartime. Ransoming the crew of the *Fortune* is a privateering act of patriotism. Any man who steps onto a French naval vessel must do so knowing he is taking the risk of imprisonment. Who in hell does Graveney think he is, speaking to his captain in such a manner?

Nonetheless, Ward can't deny there's an uncomfortable gnawing beneath his skin. A quiet voice inside his head asking him if perhaps John Graveney is right. Perhaps this is not an act of war, but an act of greed. And it's this, Ward realises, that is irritating him most of all. He does not like being wrong.

"Your opinion is noted, Mr Graveney," he tells him sharply. "Thank you." He flashes his eyes at his boatswain, a heated look that makes it clear his company is no longer welcome. "I wish you a pleasant evening."

John Graveney strides up onto deck, glad to escape the tension of the ward-robe—and the captain. He draws down a long breath. The air smells of gunpowder and that hot, acrid stench of death. Just his imagination, surely—they had fired little more than a smattering of warning shots, and no one had been killed on either side. He puts it down to the uncomfortable stirring beneath his skin.

The French prisoners, yes. But that is not all of it. The French prisoners are just the tip of a far deeper thorn he's been doing his best to ignore.

He's always been an ardent supporter of his captain. Has been privateering with Ward for more than four years—has signed on with him for commission after commission. Graveney has always found him to be fair and decent—if not a man to leave much room for error. But in the past—how long? Months? Year?—John Graveney has been questioning his captain more and more.

No, that's not right. He's been questioning *himself*.

Coming of age as the son of a penniless bladesmith in London, Graveney had always agreed blindly with his father, his uncles, his friends. The French were bastards; the Jacobites hopeless fools. He'd never stopped to consider for himself what he really believed. Had only ever been towed along the path of those around him. Believed what he was told to believe.

And in these past months—year?—he has felt that begin to change.

No. The uncertainty about the timing of this is a lie. Because if he stops to think about it, which he is trying his best not to do, he can pinpoint exactly when and where this unease had taken root inside him.

A boarding of a merchant ship in the North Atlantic. She'd been carrying a French crew and a handful of Jacobites Graveney guessed had been exiled from England. The *Eagle* had come only for the French ship's cargo—Ward had had no interest in the old, slow merchant vessel, or the men on board.

Graveney and several others had held the crew at pistol-point while the rest of the boarding party had emptied the ship of its silks and spices. And as the men had looked down the barrel of Graveney's pistol, he'd seen fear in their eyes. Had heard a murmured prayer, spoken in English. He saw rosary beads pass through trembling fingers. And for a fleeting moment, Graveney was a child again, hearing his own mother speak these same forbidden prayers in their creaking Broad Street garret. Watching her pass those same forbidden beads through her own trembling fingers.

His mother had been gone for many years. Two decades and more. Her dangerous, lingering Catholic beliefs had not been spoken of by anyone in Graveney's family since her death. But suddenly those beliefs were at the forefront of his mind. The sound of the Catholic prayer, murmured by a frightened Jacobite on some plundered French ship in the rolling North Atlantic, seemed to reach down into a distant, unremembered part of him. Unbidden, he felt a sudden, unwelcome connection to these men; these enemies. Felt the pistol waver in his hand.

Graveney looks across the dark water to the slim figure of the *Fortune*. She is flying over the water in the hands of the men from the *Eagle* Hunter had instructed to stay aboard as a prize crew.

Perhaps even more unwelcome than the connection he'd felt to the Jacobite on that cursed French merchant brig, Graveney is feeling that same connection to these Frenchmen they locked into the hold of their own ship today. A flimsy connection, yes, but he can't deny it's there.

He wishes this was not a part of him; or at least that it was a part he could forget existed. Because these Catholic beliefs of his mother's, they are also the beliefs of the French enemy. The beliefs of the Jacobites.

And they're beliefs that don't align with a man paid to fire broadsides at those very same people.

Walk away. The thought comes to him suddenly. A laughable thought because he cannot walk away from this ship, either literally or figuratively. Never mind that they're out in the middle of the Atlantic; this is his only way of making a decent living. And Graveney has been in far too much debt for far too many years to pretend he does not need this commission. Owes almost fifty pounds to cursed Amos Sheffield alone, after far too many bad decision at the card tables.

Perhaps he could find a berth on a merchant ship, a vessel not so actively involved in the war. He'd put himself at the mercy of French privateers—and what a damn irony that would be after all this handwringing and foolishness. But more pressing than that: he'd throw away the chance of another promotion; a senior officer's position on Henry Ward's ship that would pay well enough to finally put his debts behind him. Live a better life than his drunkard of a father ever had. A life that, for the first time, has almost begun to feel within reach.

He's clambered his way up to boatswain. Knows he has the knowledge and skills—and the respect of the crew—to be quartermaster when withered old Abe Hunter finally falls off the perch.

He's just not sure he has the right thoughts in his head.

Graveney curls his hands around the railing and lifts his face to the sky. The last faint mist of rain dampens and cools his cheeks. He doesn't want to be thinking like this. He wants his old, predictable way of thinking—that black and white view of the world where there are good men and bad men and nothing in between.

The beliefs are inconvenient, irritating. And they're beliefs that need to be conquered if he's to have any future as a member of Henry Ward's crew.

CHAPTER NINETEEN

"May we speak a moment, Mrs Blake?" Mrs Calloway asks from the doorway of the parlour. The children's nurse, a small, rounded woman in her late thirties, is looking at Abigail with the same gentle, pitying expression she gives Eva and Nathan when they've tripped on the stairs or spilled their ale.

The request makes a too-familiar pull of dread tighten in Abigail's stomach. Usually, when the children's nurse seeks her out like this, it's to tell her of some godawful thing Oliver has done. Abigail has long given up expecting the nurse to exert any kind of control over her eldest son, but Oliver still manages to insert himself into her periphery from time to troubled time.

She puts down the letter from Samuel's accountant outlining the monthly funds from the tenants in the Chelsea house. Stands from the armchair and ushers the older woman into the room.

Mrs Calloway perches on the edge of the settle, folding her weathered hands in front of her. Seems to consider her words.

"Just tell me what he's done," Abigail blurts.

The nurse's eyes soften. "I'm not here about Oliver, Mrs Blake. I'm here because I'm concerned about you."

"Concerned about me? Why?" It's a foolish question, Abigail knows—comes out sounding forced.

She has kept to herself for weeks. Has stayed hidden from Mairi, from the rest of the village. Has had Mrs Calloway take Nathan to and from school. Relied on Ruth to keep them all fed and watered.

The first time she had not gone to Bamburgh to meet Lizzie at the appointed time, she had spent the day in abject terror, refusing to let her children do so much as peek through the curtains. Had kept Nathan home from the petty school; kept Oliver pinned beneath her gaze.

Lizzie had not come to the house. Her mother had not come to the house. Three weeks now, and no one from the thieving ring has shown their face on Lindisfarne. But feeling as though she has gotten away with something feels far too premature.

Abigail spends her days with one eye on the dunes, expecting thieves from Bamburgh; the other eye on the sea—hoping for Henry Ward. Around her, the house seems to hollow and widen, fraying the edges of the courage she has tried so hard to cultivate.

She keeps Eva penned inside, tucks Nathan away the moment he returns home from school. As for Oliver, she knows she has little hope of keeping him close; just has to hope the promise of her putting in a good word for him with Henry will be enough for him to stay away from Bamburgh and the thieving ring.

Mrs Calloway tilts her head, choosing her words carefully. "You seem to be spending more time than ever alone in the house," she says finally. Her gentle Scottish lilt makes her words sound like a lullaby. Abigail bites her tongue to force herself from snapping at the woman's over-the-top gentleness. She's less than a decade younger than Mrs Calloway. She does not need to be mothered. But, Abigail reminds herself, nor does the poor woman need to be snapped at for her kindness.

"Father Dering has been asking after you at church," Mrs Calloway continues, apparently oblivious to the war of good and evil going on inside Abigail's head. "And his wife was hoping to speak to you today at the school, given it was young Nathan's final day."

Abigail lets out her breath, struck with a barb of guilt. It had completely slipped her mind that Nathan was to finish at the petty school today. What kind of mother is she? "Of course," she says hurriedly. "Did he enjoy his last day?"

Mrs Calloway gives her a soft smile, but Abigail can sense— imagines?—a veiled criticism beneath. "I'm sure he will be eager to tell you all about it." The nurse leans forward, her brown eyes meeting

Abigail's. "If I might speak openly, Mrs Blake… I know how difficult it is to lose a husband. I know the way the grief can spring back up on you when you think you are past the worst of it. But I know that locking yourself away like this is not the way forward."

How she wishes this was all a simple matter of grief. How much easier that would be. She wishes, too, that she could tell Mrs Calloway the truth: that she is too scared to leave the safety of the house in case anyone from the thieving ring should catch her out on the open expanse of the island. That in a strange sort of way, Highfield House has come to feel like her protector.

Instead, she forces a smile. "You're right, of course." She wants this conversation over. "I shall be sure to venture into the village tomorrow. And I shall speak with Mrs Dering about how Nathan fared at school."

Mrs Calloway looks at her intently for a moment, clearly unconvinced. "Very good," she says, after a moment of hesitation. She stands. "I shall be off home for the evening then, if there's nothing else you need."

In pieces, she ventures out. An afternoon visit to speak with Mrs Dering. A walk with her children to the rockpools in the shadow of the castle. She chooses the brightest, sunniest days, when sunlight spills across the dunes and leaves few places to hide.

The garden flourishes as the days grow warmer and the summer stretches long and endless across the island. The day she had arrived on Lindisfarne, Abigail had decided to make this garden her project; had been determined to make something vivid and colourful from the jungle of native grasses she had found fringing her house. With an old shovel she had found in the stables, she had set about turning over the earth into garden beds, finding little more than sandy soil that left her first attempts withered and brown.

Now, after twelve years of practice, and countless hours reading up on the subject, the garden is the living, breathing wonder she had always hoped it would be. In the summer warmth, it's an explosion of colour; carefully cultivated lavender and roses, intertwined with native sea-thrift, among the green and gold grasses that run free across the dunes.

Of all things, she is grateful for this garden. Grateful for its colour; so stark a contrast to the dark wood and stone of the house. Grateful for the calmness she feels when she is here among these plants. For the fragrant scent of aliveness; for bees and birds and butterflies.

But this afternoon, it's not calmness she feels. Because there's a flash of movement in the dunes. Large and dark and solid. Abigail feels her lungs tighten like a fist. A roe deer, perhaps. This is the logical solution. But she cannot quite find the space for logic. Instead, she is picturing men with pistols and muskets, and Lizzie's dirt-streaked face with an apple-shaped birthmark.

Her eyes go instinctively to her daughter, who is half-buried in the lavender bush.

"Evie," she hisses. Louder. "Evie. Quickly. Inside."

Eva looks up from the garden, a slightly bewildered expression in her eyes. "Why are you yelling, Mama?"

Abigail tries to level her voice. "I'm not yelling. Inside now, please."

A look of seriousness falls across Eva's face and she trots inside the house.

Abigail follows, locking the door behind them. She hurries to the parlour and yanks closed the curtains. Can't help peeking through them onto the dunes. She sees nothing, no one. But she can see only a small fragment of the island surrounding her. Surrounding them. She feels painfully adrift inside the house.

Eva is watching from the doorway, chewing on the end of her plait, clearly infected by her mother's panic.

Abigail forces a smile. Kneels to take her daughter's soil-covered hands. She smells lavender and sea in Eva's hair. "Everything's all right, Evie. I'm sorry, I did not mean to scare you."

The pounding of the door knocker echoes through the entrance hall, making Abigail jump. She draws in a breath. "Nathan is upstairs in his bedroom," she tells Eva. "Go up and see what he's doing."

Eva's eyes light, her unease forgotten. She flies upstairs, leaving Abigail alone in the foyer.

Another knock at the door.

She hesitates. Answer? Or hide away and hope the house will keep them safe?

"Who's there?" she calls.

"Mrs Blake? We need to speak."

A woman's voice. It's a sharp and polished voice, her Northumbrian accent far softer than most of the villagers'. A stranger's voice.

Abigail feels suddenly, intensely alone.

But this is not who she wants to be. She will not condemn herself to a life lived in fear. She is stronger than that. At least, she wants to be.

She pulls open the door.

The woman on the doorstep is not a stranger. This woman on the doorstep had stood face to face with Abigail at the narrowest end of Church Wynd and held a knife to her throat.

After you attacked her daughter.

The thought does not bring her the self-loathing she suspects it ought to. It brings her a sudden burst of confidence. She will not let herself be afraid of this woman.

Abigail steps out of the house, pulling the door to behind her. "How did you find me?" she asks. She makes her voice taut and brusque, to match Lizzie's mother's. "Did one of the villagers tell you how to find the house? Or was it my son?"

The woman doesn't answer.

Lizzie's mother is dressed in patched and colourless skirts, the coif on her head pulled almost to her eyebrows. The look in her eyes is solemn and serious, but not as threatening as Abigail had expected. "You made a deal with my daughter," she says evenly. "And you have not kept your word."

"The only thing I promised Lizzie was that I would return the following month and give her the same amount as I did the first time." Abigail grits her teeth. "I did as I promised. Again and again." She lifts her chin. Injects as much forcefulness into her words as she can manage. "I'm sorry. But our arrangement is finished."

A faint smile flickers in the corner of the woman's mouth. "You are not the one who gets to decide that, Mrs Blake."

Abigail's fingers curl instinctively around the doorframe. "I cannot work for the Jacobites any longer," she says, pushing past the threatening edge to the woman's words. "It's too dangerous."

Surprise flickers across the woman's eyes. As though she is taken aback by Abigail speaking aloud of their connection to the Jacobites. Up until this point, it had been a silent undercurrent.

"Working for the Jacobites has always been too dangerous," Lizzie's mother says finally. "Nothing has changed."

Abigail doesn't answer. Lizzie's mother is not what she had expected. This woman is well-spoken and clear-eyed. Clearly comes from a well-off family. Has clearly made some terrible choices. Abigail tries not to focus on how much the woman reminds her of herself.

After several moments of silence, Lizzie's mother says, "If you won't go to the Jacobite donors again, there are other ways you can pay what you owe."

Abigail clenches her fists. "I don't owe you anything," she hisses. "Leave me alone. And tell your daughter to stay away from my son.

A wry smile crosses the woman's face. "Perhaps you ought to tell your son to stay away from my daughter. I don't believe the friendship was instigated by Lizzie." She swats at the bee circling her head. "In any case, we need money from you, Mrs Blake." The words are almost painfully casual.

"No," Abigail snaps. "You don't. I'm not working for the Jacobite cause any longer. I have nothing to give you."

The woman's gaze travels up to the broad ivy-streaked façade of the house. "I can see that's not true. Your husband clearly ensured you were taken care of before he died. Which is more than most of us can say. Most of us widows to the Jacobite battlefields have pennies to our names."

"So you think it your right to take what my husband left me?"

Lizzie's mother shrugs. "My right? Of course not. But people like us, we've stopped caring about what's right and what's wrong. The world has taken far too much from us to bother ourselves with that." She crosses her arms across her thick chest. "You made a deal with my daughter," she says again. "And you will pay us what is owed."

This time, Abigail hears the threat all too clearly beneath the woman's words. "I cannot give you any money," she says tautly. "I need everything I have for my children."

"Well. Like I said, there are other ways you can pay what you owe."

Abigail grits her teeth. "What ways?" she dares to ask.

"Take it from another's pocket. Just as you were doing before."

"Blatant thievery?" Abigail spits. "Join your ring? Do you truly think I will agree to such a thing?"

"I would imagine you might consider it. You're clearly on edge. As though you are expecting us to do something terrible to you and your family."

The accuracy of the words strike her, but Abigail does her best not to react. She will not dignify this outrageous request with anything more than silence.

She unlocks the front door and traps herself inside the house, half waiting for the door knocker to sound again. But there is quiet for a moment, and then the soft footsteps of Lizzie's mother crunching back down the path.

What will the woman do now? Is she returning to Bamburgh to collect the rest of the thieving ring? Are hordes of thieves about to turn up on her doorstep to punish her from stepping away from the ring? Surely Abigail is not that valuable. After all, it had taken Lizzie's mother three weeks to seek her out. Perhaps with time, the thieves will come to see that trying to squeeze money out of the family in Highfield House is a pointless endeavour.

Or perhaps Abigail is just being overly optimistic.

She looks up at the sound of footsteps on the staircase.

"Was that Lizzie's ma?" Oliver asks. "I thought she'd come eventually. I suspected she'd be angry when you didn't go to Bamburgh like you promised."

Abigail says nothing.

"Did you give her money?" Oliver asks coolly.

"Of course not. I'm not going to hand over your father's money to a pack of thieves."

"There are other ways you can pay what you owe."

Abigail's chest tightens at his use of the exact same words as Lizzie's mother. "We are not thieves," she hisses. "Do you understand?" She presses her hands down hard on his shoulders, forcing him to look at her. "We are going to stay away from Bamburgh and the thieving ring until they decide we are simply not worth the trouble."

Oliver doesn't speak. But the look on his face makes Abigail all too aware of the blind naivety of her plan.

"Flowers," says Eva. "'Flowers' starts with F."

"Very good," says Mrs Calloway as they follow the coast path back towards the house. "And Nathan, can you think of a word that ends with the letter F?"

Cliff, he thinks. *If*, *of* and *kerchief*. Usually, he likes the letter game. But today his attention is snatched by the sight of Oliver out on the embankment beyond the house. He's pushing Da's rowboat through the sand and pebbles on the edge of the beach.

Nathan bursts into a run. Pretends not to hear Mrs Calloway barking at him to get back here this instant and think of a word that ends in F. When he gets to the embankment, Oliver is standing in ankle-deep water, with Da's rowboat bobbing out ahead of him.

"Where are you going?" Nathan asks breathlessly.

"I've something to take care of," Oliver says. "It's very important."

"Can I come?"

"No." But he hovers in the water, one hand on the boat, as though waiting for more questions. Hoping for more questions, maybe.

"Are you going to the mainland?"

"Perhaps."

"To visit someone?"

"Can't say."

Nathan scuffs the toe of his shoe into the damp sand. "Does Mama know where you're going?"

A smile flickers on the edge of Oliver's lips, and Nathan can tell he has landed on the question his brother had been hoping for. "No," he says. "But even if she did, I don't think she would stop me."

CHAPTER TWENTY

This time, Ward knows there's little justification for a journey back to Lindisfarne. This time, he knows it's driven only by his need to see Abigail.

Information on the capture of the *Fortune* and her crew has been sent across the Channel to the Admiralty of La Royale. Ward knows he has at least another week before the letters of credit arrive in payment of his ransom demands.

Enough time for a journey north.

He has left the *Fortune* languishing in the Thames with the prize crew. Had briefly considered leaving the *Eagle* behind too, and making his way northward on a passenger ship without the rest of his men. But no, this crew still has another six months on their articles of agreement, and Ward knows they will not appreciate the lull in action. He'd taken just enough cargo from the hold of the *Fortune* to cobble together an excuse about calling on his Lindisfarne buyer.

At his request, his cook had loaded the ship with fresh meat and vegetables before they'd left London, and now the feast is spread out across the ward-robe table. Ward knows it's a thinly veiled attempt at buying his officers' approval. None of them had been in favour of another trip north.

Tonight though, with their plates wiped clean of even the last speck of gravy, and cards spread across the table in a game of Ruff and Honours, Hunter and Cook seem to have forgotten their grievances. John Graveney is still wearing that pinched expression he's had since they took the *Fortune*. Ward is beginning growing tired of it.

"I assume we'll be getting another night of luxury at the house, Captain," says Hunter, bringing his wine glass to his lips. There's a glint in his eyes that tells Ward he's under no illusions that this journey has anything to do with cargo.

"I'm sure Mrs Blake will welcome you." The words come out more clipped than Ward intended. It feels as though Hunter is encroaching on something private. Ward hates that his crew are aware of his infatuation with Abigail. A part of him despises himself for it. Has he learnt nothing after Amelia?

It's an argument he's had with himself over and over. Each time, he comes to the same glaring conclusion: Abigail is not Amelia.

He drops down the Queen of Spades and scoops up the trick. Draws in a breath before he speaks again, in an attempt to rein in his annoyance. His irritation is not being helped by the windless conditions and the infuriatingly slow creep up the coast of England. He's beginning to feel as though they'll never reach Northumberland. "And with luck we'll have a hefty pay day when we return to London."

Graveney snorts. "You think La Royale will pay to return a ship full of dead men?"

Ward looks at him pointedly. "There's been only three deaths among the prisoners." He nods down at the deck of cards. "Deal."

"Five men," Graveney corrects him, ignoring the cards. "And there'll be far more by the time the ransom money arrives. How quick do you think the fever'll take a crew locked in their own hold?"

"I—"

A knock at the door and Finn hurries inside, collecting their dinner plates from the table. Ward holds Graveney's hot stare. Feels irritation prickling under his skin. A faint nagging of his own conscience. He pushes it away. He did not find the success he has through sentimentality. A nagging voice inside his head reminds him that he did not find it by gallivanting up to Northumberland every time the wind changes either.

Finn clatters the last of the plates together. "Anything else you need, sir?"

"No. Thank you, lad." Ward waits for Finn to leave before turning back to Graveney. "Deal," he says again, rapping his fingers against the deck of cards. "I didn't invite you here tonight to rehash old arguments. The decision on the *Fortune* has long been made."

Graveney opens his mouth to speak again, then seems to change his mind. He picks up the deck and begins to shuffle.

When the game is over and the wine bottle is empty, Ward waits for the other officers to leave. He calls for Graveney to return at the table. His boatswain does not look surprised at the request. He sits opposite Ward, leaning back in his chair and folding his wiry arms across his chest.

Ward doesn't speak at once. He turns his empty cup around, choosing his words carefully. What he wants is to unleash his anger on Graveney. Curse him for his disrespect. For questioning him. For acting in such a petty, childish manner.

But he can also see that anger is going to get him nowhere.

He spears Graveney with hard eyes. "If you wish to be released from your articles of agreement, I'm willing to do so. I'll see to it that you receive your share of the payment from La Royale."

Graveney just sighs.

"I'd be sorry to lose you," Ward continues. "But I'm beginning to think that may be for the best."

Graveney rubs his narrow chin. "And why d'you think that would be for the best, Captain? Because I dared to disagree with you about taking the entire crew of the *Fortune* prisoner?" He gives a short, humourless laugh. "Because I certainly ain't the only person aboard who didn't believe you ought to have done that."

Ward rubs his eyes. "The thing is done, John. The letters have been sent. What point is there in going over and over all this?"

Graveney hesitates a moment. "Well," he says finally. "The situation might come up again, aye?"

"It might," Ward agrees. He toys with the edge of the deck of cards. Chooses his words carefully. "Men change, John. There's no shame in it. If something has caused you to alter your alliance, I will not question it. I just ask that you leave my crew."

"Alter my alliance?" Graveney repeats on a laugh. "Are you asking me if I'm about to jump ship and fight for the French?" He shakes his head incredulously. "I've given you four years of loyalty and these are the accusations I get in return? All for thinking you shouldn't have locked up all those men and left them to die like rabid dogs?"

Ward hesitates. Has he jumped to conclusions? Is he seeing French and Jacobites sympathies in John Graveney, when all that is there is a scrap of decency? He can't tell if Graveney's words are genuine. Can't tell if he's simply telling his captain what he wishes to hear. His instinct is failing him. Still, Graveney is right: he has given him four years of loyalty. Not to mention the fact he is an organised and thorough boatswain. The *Eagle* has been in fine shape since he had taken up the role two years ago. He would not be an easy man to replace.

"I'm not asking you to leave," Ward says finally. "I'm merely giving you the option. If what we do no longer aligns with who you are."

Graveney stands, making it clear the conversation is over. "I've no intention of leaving," he says. "I was simply making my opinion known. I've every intention of sailing with this crew until the war is over."

Ward is still thinking about *until the war is over* when he makes his way back to the great cabin that night. What he will do after the war is something he usually does his best not to think about. The thought of returning to merchant service, even as a captain, feels almost unbearably dull. And as for the other direction many privateers take in peacetime—piracy—well, that is simply not an option. He's worked too hard to make a name for himself to tumble into infamy. In any case, it's a decision for another day. He's seen little sign that peace is on the horizon.

Ward slides off his justacorps and unbuttons his waistcoat. Rids himself of his boots and shirt and climbs onto his bed in his breeches. Somehow, in the process of undressing, and contemplating the shape his life will take when the peace treaties are signed, he has gone to his desk drawer to collect the pile of Abigail's letters.

He leans back against the headboard, turning slowly through the pages. Lamplight flickers over the curls and scrawls of Abigail's handwriting, and the dimness makes the words blur.

This is far from the first time he has read these letters. Several parts of them, he knows from memory.

Her sentences are often clipped and fragmented, her thoughts often rambling and incoherent. Ward can tell the letters are a way for her to process what's going on in her head. Her fears, her grief, her eternal struggle with keeping the cruel and callous side of herself at bay. Each time he reads these lines, Ward finds himself smiling. Somehow, perhaps foolishly, he likes the dark side of Abigail Blake. Likes the challenge of her. The imperfection. Because that imperfection allows him to be imperfect too. Allows him to acknowledge his mistakes—like holding an entire crew ransom, instead of just her officers.

Abigail's letters, written more than four months ago, when he had last seen her, are interspersed with mentions of her fundraising visits, and her fears that the Lindisfarne Jacobites might discover she is not handing them the full amount that had been donated. How desperately Ward hopes she has done as she promised him and stayed away from the Jacobite cause.

He is well aware that she has not told him the full story. Not given him every piece of why she had ended up with Jacobite funds in her pocket. Not that he needs the full story. It's a common enough tale: a widow left with a miserly settlement and young children to raise. Perhaps he ought to have been more forward, more insistent in helping her financially. That way he would know for certain she has freed herself from the danger of being involved with the Jacobites.

Then again, it has been more than eight months since he had first heard of the kidnapping plot from Lord Dunmore. Perhaps, like so many of the Jacobites' plots, it has just petered out into nothingness.

Nonetheless, the desire to take Abigail's struggle away is immense. As is the desire to be more to her than just a fleeting figure on the edges of her life.

He folds the wad of paper and slips it beneath the mattress. Rolls onto his back, listening to the low groan of the ship on its windless slog northward. Once again, Ward asks himself what he wishes his life to look like once the war is over. And this time, he realises, he has an answer.

CHAPTER TWENTY-ONE

It's Sunday morning. She ought to be in church right now, instead of sitting here in the parlour rehemming her children's clothes. This is far from the first service Abigail has missed. Like she has done most Sundays since she had accused Mairi of being involved with the thieving ring, she has sent Eva and Nathan off to the service with Ruth and Mrs Calloway. Is not sure if her children's presence in her absence will reflect better or worse on her. At least if she is cast down into Hell, she will not take her children with her.

Samuel's rowboat is missing from the embankment this morning. She tells herself she does not know where Oliver has taken himself off to. Is doing her best to remain ignorant. But that is becoming harder and harder to do. Because since Lizzie's mother had appeared on the doorstep and demanded Abigail steal for the thieving ring, there have been no more visitors. No more threats. Abigail is doing her best not to consider why that might be. Doing her best not to consider what Oliver might have overheard. What he might have chosen to do on her behalf.

She ties off her sewing and folds Eva's rehemmed smock gown, setting it on the table in front of her. She takes the next piece from the pile, her attention drawn to movement outside the window. Mrs Calloway is herding Nathan and Eva towards the house, Ruth and Father Dering behind them.

Abigail grits her teeth. She supposes this was inevitable, this pity visit from the priest—or maybe *scolding visit* is more apt. No doubt he has more than a few words to say about her neglecting his sermons.

Abigail leaves the sewing on the tea table and goes down the passage to meet them in the foyer.

The children's faces light at the sight of their mother. She ignores Father Dering as Eva barrels into a frantic diatribe about a particularly terrifying seal she saw near Saint Cuthbert's Island this morning. Abigail can feel the priest's eyes on them. Wondering, perhaps, where Oliver is, and why he had not joined his brother and sister at church today.

When Eva runs out of breath, Abigail sends the children upstairs with the nurse and draws in her courage to face Father Dering.

She is expecting fire and brimstone. But his face holds a lingering kindness.

"I know it's a foolish question to ask you if you are all right," says Father Dering. "I know you've suffered a great loss. And I can only imagine the challenge of raising children on your own, especially in a place as isolated as this." She catches the hidden meaning behind his words. Not *raising children on your own*, but *raising Oliver on your own*.

Up close, she notices how lined and weathered the vicar's face is; notices it's a powdered wig on his head, clumsily slapped on over his own thinning hair. Deep folds of skin hang beneath his eyes. He looks older than Abigail assumes him to be. It does not seem that long ago he had been a young man in the pulpit.

She looks past him up the staircase. Nathan is scrambling up the stairs on his hands and knees, Eva copying her brother several paces behind. Abigail smiles faintly.

"Well," she says finally, turning back to the vicar, "of course it has not been easy. But we are managing. It's been many months since Samuel's death."

Father Dering hesitates. "Is there a reason we have not seen you in church for several weeks?" The question feels probing. As though he knows more than he ought to. Has Mairi Mitchell said something to him about Abigail's run-in with the thieves? About the accusations she had thrown about?

For not the first time, the thought of telling the truth about the thieving ring flits into her head. The pull of it is strong. She could return to the village. Attempt to rebuild her friendship with Mairi—or at least beg forgiveness and attempt some kind of civility.

No. It's too dangerous. Silence is the only way. Especially if Oliver has involved himself in thieving because—no, she is not going to think that thought.

"I hope everything is well with Oliver," Father Dering says carefully. "I hope he has not found himself in trouble."

"It's nothing to do with Oliver," she says, making the words sound almost truthful. She sighs. "I know he is a difficult boy. But there's a good side to him. He is very protective of me. Especially since his father has been gone."

Father Dering smiles faintly. "I'm glad if it. And yes, I firmly believe everyone has decency in them. It is up to us to draw it out."

Abigail's throat tightens suddenly.

"Whatever challenges you are facing, God can help you through them," says the vicar. "You are always welcome at my services." His voice hardens slightly. "Besides, I'm sure I need not tell you the importance of church attendance for the good of one's soul. A true relationship with the Lord is our only way to avoid condemning ourselves to eternal damnation."

Abigail lowers her eyes, biting back an angry retort. She is condemning herself quite enough, thank you very much, without adding the threat of eternal damnation to the pile.

The door knocker thumps, making her heart jolt. The knock sounds aggressive, dangerous—or perhaps just made that way by her sudden racing thoughts. She tries to tamp down her fear. It's just a knock at the door.

Then she hears: "Mama." Oliver's voice, on the other side of the door. He sounds panicked, distressed. Close to tears.

Abigail throws open the door and her son stumbles inside. One side of his face is red and swollen, a long tear in the shoulder of his jacket. The shirt beneath it is stained scarlet with blood. Ruth murmurs in shock as she hurries into the foyer. Abigail hisses out instructions to fetch cloths and water and the housekeeper hurries off towards the kitchen.

Blood has soaked through the sleeve of Oliver's coat, turning the blue wool black. The swelling on his chin is already beginning to darken to bruising.

"What happened?" Abigail demands. Her stomach is rolling. Not least because Father Dering is here to see this. She can feel his presence behind them. Cannot bring herself to look at him.

Nathan pokes his head down from the top of the stairwell, Eva in his shadow. Abigail barks at the nurse to get them out of sight.

"Oliver," Father Dering pushes, "did someone harm you?"

"No," he says shakily. "It was an accident. I slipped and fell on the rocks."

Abigail sees the priest's jaw clench, and she knows with certainty he has not bought the lie. She takes Oliver's uninjured arm and guides him towards the staircase. "Thank you for your visit, Father," she says brusquely. "But I've to tend to my son now."

For a moment, Father Dering hesitates, as though debating whether to argue. Whether to insist on staying. Insist on demanding more truthful answers. Abigail is relieved when he says, "Of course. I shall see myself out."

Abigail leads Oliver up the staircase. Ruth hurries up the stairs behind them with a fresh jug of water and clean cloths in her hand.

Abigail takes them from her, nodding her thanks to the housekeeper and closing Oliver's bedroom door behind her. She helps Oliver sit on the edge of his bed and gently slides off his coat. Eases his bloodstained shirt over his head. She is relieved to see that, though the slash on his arm is long, it does not appear to be deep. He sits shirtless on his bed with his head drooped, picking listlessly at his grimy thumbnail. Abigail can't help but let her eyes linger on him for a moment; on his narrow chest, his long, twig-like arms, the round slump of his shoulders. She cannot remember the last time she saw him even partially undressed. She is struck by just how young and childish he looks.

She empties the jug into the washbin and soaks a cloth. Squeezes it out and hands it to Oliver. "Hold this to your jaw."

He does so obediently. Abigail holds a second cloth to the cut on Oliver's arm, wiping at the dried blood that has trickled down towards his elbow. Focusing on the task at hand allows her, however momentarily, to push aside the questions she knows she must ask. The reality she must face, of what her son has involved himself in on her behalf.

"Who did this to you?" she asks at last. She hopes he will be honest with her, here and now. Hopes she won't have to go through the rigmarole of the lessons in order to get him to speak.

A tearful murmur escapes him. Abigail has not seen this vulnerability from him for many years. Had started to doubt it even still existed.

When he doesn't speak further, she says, "Have you been out picking pockets? Did someone attack you when you tried to steal from them?"

His silence is all the response she needs.

"You promised you'd not go near the thieving ring," she reminds him gently. Tries to keep the waver from her voice.

"I know," he murmurs. "But I was just doing what Lizzie's ma wanted you to do. I thought if I gave the ring what they wanted, they would stay away from you." He rubs his eyes with the back of his hand. "I thought you wouldn't have to lock yourself in the house anymore."

Abigail feels something lurch in her chest.

"I don't understand why they were coming after you in the first place, Mama. Was it because of me? Because I told Lizzie I was a better pickpocket than her?"

"No." She closes her eyes. How much should she share with him? Perhaps keeping things from him is doing more harm than good. "I went out raising funds for the Jacobites with Mrs Mitchell," she admits. "Lizzie caught me as I was leaving one of the donors' houses. She forced me to give her a cut of the money. They are against the Jacobite cause because it took so many of their husbands and fathers. And they knew I was raising money for the movement."

Oliver doesn't speak at once. Abigail wipes at the blood on his shoulder and wraps a clean cloth around his upper arm. She ties it tightly, feeling him wince.

"Why did you go fundraising with Mrs Mitchell?" he asks finally. "Da hated the Jacobites."

Abigail nods. "I know. But… your father is not here anymore." It's the most rational explanation she can manage. And perhaps closest to the truth. She closes her eyes. "I'm sorry," she hears herself say. "This is all my fault. I stepped away because it's not safe to work for the Jacobites anymore. But I should have kept giving the thieving ring what they wanted."

"It's not your fault, Mama."

Abigail sits beside him on the bed and laces her fingers through his. She feels like a failure. Feels weak. "Whether or not it is my fault," she begins carefully, "it is my problem. Do you understand? It is not for you to solve. You need to keep the promise you made to me and stay away from the thieving ring. I don't want you putting yourself in danger on my behalf."

"And in return, you will tell Captain Ward I will make a fine cabin boy?"

She traces a finger across his thumbnail. Thinks of the tearful waver in his voice when he told her of the attack. The fear in his eyes. She thinks of cannon fire and raging seas and the ever-present shadow of death. "Is that truly what you want, Oliver?" she asks. "Have you truly thought about what that life would be like? How much danger you would be in at times?"

A look of hot surprise flashes across his face. "Of course I have. And of course it's what I want." He pulls his hand from hers. "I'm not afraid," he snaps. "If that's what you think." He stands up and goes to his wardrobe for a clean shirt. He pulls it on over his head, doing his best to disguise a grimace of pain. "The letter," he says suddenly, "in your nightstand. Why is it so valuable it needs to be locked up in that box?"

Abigail's heart jolts. "How do you know it's a letter?" He shouldn't know that. No one should know that. No one except her and Henry.

Oliver doesn't answer. Abigail gets up from the bed and rushes across the passage to her bedroom. Pulls open the nightstand. There is the brass box Henry had given her, with its tarnished corners. Holding her breath, she lifts the lid. The clasp slides easily from the lock, revealing the letter inside.

She charges back to Oliver's room, the box in her hand. Shoves it under his nose. "How did you open this?"

He shrugs. "I've read a lot about lock picking. It wasn't difficult. Hardly worth locking in the first place. Honestly, I'm a little disappointed in Captain Ward." He looks at her squarely. "Why is it so valuable?" he asks again.

"This has nothing to do with you," she snaps. Turns away. For all his bravado, she knows the attack has rattled him. And she also knows that if she is to look at him right now, she will not be able to keep her anger under control. And a fight is the last thing either of them need.

She pulls in a long, steadying breath. It's all right, she tells herself. This is nothing to panic over. What does it matter that Oliver has looked into the box and read the letter? His questions show he knows nothing of the situation with Lord Haver, the Whig party dissenter. Of course he doesn't. He's eleven years old. She forgets that sometimes.

When he returns for the letter, Henry will see that the lock has been broken. Will see that his precious letter has not been as safe here as she promised him it would be. The prospect sits uncomfortably in her chest.

"Is the letter in the box valuable enough to bribe the thieving ring into leaving you be?" Oliver asks.

His words make Abigail whirl around to face him. "What?"

"If it's so valuable, perhaps we could make a deal with the thieving ring."

She grits her teeth. When had her son started using phrases like *make a deal* and *bribe the thieving ring*?

She hesitates for a fraction too long. Enough for him to grab hold of that hesitation. "It's not mine to do anything with," she says. "I'm just keeping it safe." And a fine job she has done of that, she thinks dully.

As much as she does not want to admit it, she knows Oliver is right. The letter would fetch a hefty price, and would be especially valuable to those in the anti-Jacobite movement. Perhaps it *would* allow her to make a deal with the ring. Perhaps it would be a way to keep her and her son safe. She pushes the thought away. The letter is not hers. She cannot let this line of thought progress any further.

As though reading her thoughts, Oliver says, "You don't think Captain Ward would want you to use the letter to get yourself out of trouble?"

How does he see so clearly, she wonders? How is he so all-seeing, so all-knowing?

"He would understand," he continues. "I'm sure he would. After all, I think he loves you."

And of all her son's precocious words, it is these that knock her most off kilter. She busies herself at the washstand, refusing to let him see how much he has unbalanced her. What has he seen, heard, to have jumped to this conclusion? And as for whether or not it is true, she cannot allow herself the space to consider that right now.

"The letter does not belong to me," she says firmly. "And that is all there is to the matter."

CHAPTER TWENTY-TWO

Mr Emmett trudges across the embankment, inspecting Samuel's rowboat that is being lapped at by the tide. "Are you sure you'll not keep it, Mrs Blake?" he asks. "You don't want a way off the island in case you need to leave for any reason when the tide is high?"

"I'm sure," she says. If she ever needs to leave, she will find someone at the anchorage to take her off the island. It's far more pressing to make sure Oliver cannot get to Bamburgh and the thieving ring again. He will be furious when he finds out the boat is gone, of course. But so be it.

"All right, then. As you wish." Emmett scratches his grey beard. And you don't want no payment?"

"No," Abigail says shortly. She doesn't care about the paltry pennies the damn thing will fetch. She just wants it gone. Wants her son to stay away from Bamburgh and its bleak undercurrent of thievery. "Just take the boat, please."

"I've a new game," says Oliver, appearing at Nathan's bedroom door. "It's called Plundering."

Nathan looks up from where he is sitting cross-legged on his bed. He crumples the star map in front of him, hiding its contents from his brother. "Plundering?"

"Aye. Like a pirate."

Nathan chews his lip. He can't deny there's a part of him that's afraid. He had not enjoyed the last game Oliver had invented. Every time he thinks of the Viking Game, he feels a prickling beneath his skin. The last time they had played it, Nathan had hidden in the priest hole. Oliver had taken an age to find him, and Nathan thought he had at last managed to trick his brother.

But then he had grown tired of the priest hole. Grown bored and sore, and a little afraid. Could feel the heat from the fire seeping through the bricks. When he had tried to wriggle out, he discovered Oliver had blocked the hole closed, trapping him inside. Finally, Oliver had pulled him out and murmured *Come out and face your maker*, and had pressed the knife into Nathan's neck so hard it had left a line of blood. The next day, Nathan had been careful to keep his neck cloth pulled up high so Mama and Mrs Calloway couldn't see the mark the knife had left.

They have not played the game since. Have not played anything since. But the Viking Game, and the priest hole, and the fear that swallowed him when Oliver held him down and pressed the knife to his neck have always been on the edge of Nathan's thoughts.

He wants to tell Oliver to go away. Wants to tell him he does not care about whatever stupid game he has invented this time. But the game is called *Plundering*. It makes him think of pirates and vast oceans, and the man at their dinner table who had come from the ship outside the window. And Nathan just has to know what this game is.

A candlestick, Oliver says. "Fetch it from the dining table. And we're going to pile up our haul here in the priest hole, like we're pirates hiding treasure."

"What are you going to plunder?" Nathan asks.

"The funnel bowl glasses," Oliver says. "From the liquor cabinet." The flickering lamplight makes the bruising on the side of his face look even darker. "Do you think that's a good treasure?"

Nathan nods.

"Good. Off you go."

A candlestick. He can do that. That's not frightening at all.

Nathan hurries out of the room, his stockings sighing against the floorboards. He can hear Mama and Eva chattering in the dressing room;

can't make out their words. He creeps past on silent feet. He's not entirely sure what Mama will do if she catches him taking a candlestick from the dining table, but he supposes that a pirate plundering treasure ought to do so quietly.

The fire has burned out in the dining room, and the dark is lit only by a sliver of moonlight that struggles through the high windows. Nathan tiptoes through the shadows. He has to kneel up on a chair to reach the candlestick in the middle of the big table. He hides it under his shirt and rushes back upstairs.

He slips breathlessly back into Oliver's room. Produces the candlestick with a flourish.

"Well done." Oliver nods towards the open priest hole. Nathan sees that he has already added the funnel bowl glasses to their collection. He puts the candlestick down beside them.

"What next?" he asks.

"The pounce pot from Da's study."

Obediently, Nathan races off through the house again. He pulls open the top drawer of Da's desk, ignoring the pull of sadness that arrives with the smell of his tobacco. He hurries back to the bedroom with the pounce pot. Sets it down inside the priest hole with the rest of their treasure.

"Next," says Oliver. "The brass box from Mama's nightstand."

Nathan frowns. "What brass box?"

"In the nightstand," Oliver repeats. "In the drawer." He folds his arms across his chest. "If it's too hard for you—"

"I can get it," Nathan says hurriedly. He rushes out into the passage, breathless, before Oliver can protest.

He slips into his mother's bedchamber. He needs to be very quiet now. He is right next door to the room with Mama and Eva in it. He tiptoes. Holds his breath as he gently tugs open the drawer of the nightstand. It makes a metallic clattering noise as he opens in. Nathan peers inside curiously. He sees a handkerchief scrunched into a ball. A few pieces of jewellery that he has not seen Mama wear in an age. An empty bottle of scent and a few loose coins. Right at the back, like Oliver had promised, is a small brass box.

Nathan grabs it, shaking it curiously. The box is light; doesn't make a sound. There's a lock on it that looks as though it might be broken. He wants to look inside, but is too afraid to open it in case he can't get it closed again. He slides the drawer shut carefully.

Only when he is back in Oliver's room does he let himself breathe. He holds the box out to his brother. "Is this the one? What's inside it?"

Oliver takes it. "That's the one." He opens the lid of the box and peers into it. "The game is over now." And he pushes closed the priest hole, trapping their treasures inside.

CHAPTER TWENTY-THREE

Nathan lies on his stomach on the floor and reaches his arm under the bed. There, at the back, hidden behind a stack of books, is Da's telescope. Well, *his* telescope. Da had given it to him just after his seventh birthday last year. Said he was old enough to take charge of it now. Keep it safe. And that is what Nathan intends to do.

Tonight, he is not interested in looking at the stars, or the sparkling silver eye of Venus that appears first in the sky. Because tonight he can see lights on the sea. It could be the navy, or merchants. It could be the man who had sat at their dinner table and talked about Viking boats and privateers.

He wriggles forward on his stomach and pushes aside the fortress of books until he can reach the wooden box containing the telescope. He pulls it out from under the bed and takes the lid off carefully. Sets the wooden stand up at the window, settling the telescope in the cradle like Da had taught him.

Nathan peers through the lens. At first, he sees only swirls of darkness, interrupted by pinpricks of light. He adjusts the lens until a glow appears in his view. There is the ship. Through the powerful eye of the telescope, he can make it out clearly, with its three masts lit by lamplight like trees under the moon. He can even make out figures moving back and forth across the deck. He wonders if any of them are Captain Ward.

Nathan wants to hate the captain of that ship. Wants to hate him because he comes into the house and sits in the armchair that used to belong to Da.

But he can't hate him. He can't hate him for so many reasons—firstly, that the man in the ship had made his mother smile. And he can't hate him because Captain Ward knows so much about ships and sailing and Vikings. But most of all, Nathan can't hate the man from the ship because he might take Oliver away.

"I'm going to be his cabin boy," Oliver had said at breakfast one day. "He's going to take me to fight the French and see the world."

Nathan pulls his eyes away from the telescope and glances over his shoulder into the darkness of his bedroom. There's a part of him that wants to tell Oliver the ship is here. He knows his brother will be excited. But he also doesn't want to share this with him; wants his own private excitement. Besides, Da had told him to keep the telescope away from Oliver. It's why he hides it underneath his bed at the very back, behind the books, so far away that his fingers barely reach it. Oliver says he doesn't care about the telescope—says he doesn't care that he can't find its hiding place. But Nathan knows he's just pretending.

He is buzzing at the sight of the ship. Can't tell if it's the thrill of having those sailors in the house again, or seeing the smile on his mother's face, or the glittering possibility that the man from the ship might take Oliver away. He can't keep it to himself.

He creeps down the hallway and opens his sister's bedroom door. "Evie," he whispers.

She rolls over, disoriented by the lamplight suddenly spilling in from the hallway. "What?"

"Come and look at the ship."

"What ship?" Her voice is thick with sleep.

"Just come."

She slips out of bed and follows him back down the hallway into his bedroom. At the sight of the telescope set up the window, she hurries towards it. Peers into the lens.

"Can you see the people moving around on the ship?" Nathan asks. "Can you see the lights?"

Eva murmurs noncommittally.

"The man from the ship might come to the house," Nathan tells her. "And he might take Oliver away."

Eva turns away from the glass, dark hair clouding messily around her face. "Why is he taking Oliver away? Where's he going to?"

"To be a cabin boy."

Footsteps make the staircase creak and Nathan herds his sister away from the telescope. Tries to get her out of his room before their mother catches them. They have barely made it to his door before Mama strides inside. She opens her mouth to scold them, but Nathan blurts:

"Captain Ward's ship is here, Mama."

Words die on her lips, and a complicated look falls over her face, as though she can't quite decide what to say. "Are you sure?" she asks finally.

He nods. Sees his mother's gaze drawn towards the telescope. She makes her way towards it. Looks through the window, then bends to peer into the lens.

When she straightens, there's a look in her eyes that Nathan can't read. "Back to bed at once," she says, her words thin and hollow. "Both of you."

The sight of Henry Ward's ship in the bay has her pacing back and forth across the study, a chaos of emotions rattling through her. Her heart is fast, and she feels more alive than she has in months.

I think he loves you… It's foolish, she knows, to let a child's words unbalance her so much. But as she peeks out of the study window at the lights of the ship, Abigail realises how desperately she wants them to be true. She also realises just how little she and Henry really know of one another. *Near strangers*, she thinks. He does not feel like a stranger.

She knows that, whether he loves her or not, Henry is going to come to the house. She is going to feel that same dizzying attraction she has felt for him since the beginning. And this time, with a certainty that reaches deep inside her, she knows she is not going to have the strength to stay away.

Or perhaps it's like this: she does not *want* to stay away. Because against every grain of sense in her body, Henry Ward has come to represent an escape from this isolated, dangerous life she has built; this life with fear at the edges. It's an escape she needs to take, if only for a night.

Abigail pulls the curtains closed in the study and goes to her dressing room. She's a chaos of nerves; can barely find a coherent thought in her head. She takes a deep breath. It's late; long past midnight. Surely he will not come to the house tonight. She has a little time to gather herself.

She opens the wardrobe. Finds herself pushing past the dark shapes of her mourning wear to a sky blue mantua hanging at the back. She cannot remember the last time she wore it. She only knows it makes her feel far more alive than the dark clothes she has been drowning in since that bleak, snow-flooded December.

She runs her fingers down the feather-soft silk of the blue gown. The bodice is front-lacing—she could wrangle herself into it without Ruth's help. Could avoid laying herself out to the judgement of her housekeeper. Ought she be judged for wearing something other than her mourning gown? It has been more than nine months since Samuel's death.

Abigail closes the wardrobe door. Henry will not come tonight, she tells herself again. Not so close to dawn, when the secret of them would be exposed to the daylight. The blue gown is a decision for tomorrow. And perhaps if she were to wear it, she could also wear the pearl necklace that has been sitting at the back of her nightstand… She almost laughs at herself. Since when is she the kind of woman so fixated on how she will look for a man? She had barely ever considered such things in the presence of her husband. At least not since they had moved to Lindisfarne and become windblown and wild. But there's a lightness to these thoughts that has been long forgotten. And so tonight, she will willingly allow herself this vanity.

Abigail goes to her bedroom and pulls open the drawer of her nightstand. Reaches in to feel for the necklace. Her fingers graze the delicate pearl strands. But something is missing.

Her stomach dives.

She flies across the hallway into Oliver's room. Tears the blankets from his bed. "Where is the letter?" she hisses, yanking him from sleep. "What have you done with it?"

He rubs his eyes, squinting to make out the shape of her. "I gave it to the thieving ring."

Abigail feels hot, then cold. "Please tell me you are lying."

"I'm not lying."

Abigail's heart thunders. "The letter does not belong to me. I told you, it is not mine to do as you wish with." She scrubs a hand across her eyes. "Who did you give it to? And why?"

"I gave it to Lizzie's ma. I made a deal with her."

"A deal?"

"Aye." Oliver sits up in bed and looks her in the eye. "I gave it to her on the promise that they would stay away from us, Mama. That they would not come after you or me again, or ask us to steal for them. I made her sign an agreement and everything."

Abigail lets out her breath. "Do you truly think they will honour that, Oliver? Do you truly think that's how people like that go about their business?"

He falters. Doesn't respond.

Abigail begins to pace across the dark bedroom. She wants to believe he has done this out of a naïve attempt to help her. But she cannot shake the thought that this is act of retaliation. Punishment for her giving away Samuel's boat. Punishment for her taking away that small piece of his freedom.

Punishment, perhaps, for suggesting he might not have the strength and courage to be Henry Ward's cabin boy.

"How did you get to Bamburgh?" she asks, her voice catching in her throat.

"I went at low tide, of course. I walked part of the way. Got a ride with a farmer part way." He shrugs.

Abigail goes to the window and lifts the curtain.

"What are you looking at? Is Captain Ward's ship here?" Oliver is out of bed in a second, racing to the window.

Abigail drops the curtain. Holds Oliver back. "Get back into bed," she snaps.

"Is the ship here?" he asks again.

"How can you be excited about such a thing?" she hisses. "I dare not think what Captain Ward will do when he finds out what you did with his letter."

Oliver's eyes flash. "No, Mama. You can't tell him what I did. He'll never let me join his crew!" He lurches forward, trying to grab at her hands. "Please. Just tell him you had no choice because the thieves were after us. Tell him how they were forcing us to steal for them. Tell him you were afraid they were going to come to the house. He'll forgive you. You know he will." He looks up at her with wide, imploring eyes. "I did this to help you."

You did it to punish me for giving away the boat. But no, she won't speak these doubts aloud. Won't give them any form, any life.

"Go back to sleep," she snaps, marching back towards the door. "I need to think about what to do."

Oliver stays sitting up in bed. In the glow of the lamp coming from the hallway, she sees the distress splashed across his face. "You're still going to tell him I would make a good cabin boy, aren't you?"

She doesn't reply.

"Mama? You promised!"

"I promised I would do so if you kept away from the thieving ring. Which you have failed to do. If you cannot keep your word, why should I keep mine?" She grits her teeth, fighting to keep her voice level. "Actions have consequences, Oliver. When are you going to accept that?"

She pulls the door closed angrily and strides back to her bedroom. Thoughts of the blue gown and the pearl necklace now seem painfully trivial. Because tomorrow, when Henry appears on the doorstep, she must tell him his letter is lost. And she must cross her fingers and hold her breath, and pray that his feelings for her, whether they are loving or something far more base and primal, extend as far as forgiveness.

CHAPTER TWENTY-FOUR

The children are lively around the breakfast table this morning; the boys chattering loudly at each other about the ship outside the window, and Eva interjecting with unrelated asides.

Though there is a part of her that wishes they were speaking of anything else—anything that might not cause such chaotic thoughts in her—Abigail is glad she is able to fall unnoticed into silence.

She takes a long, steadying mouthful of tea. After the discovery of the missing letter, she had barely slept, and she does not want Eva and Nathan to pick up on her unease.

Oliver is laughing, talking brashly, behaving as though their conversation last night had never happened. He seems oblivious to the chaos he has thrown her into. No, not oblivious. Just ignoring it. Because now he is looking her way. Catching her eye with a pointed look.

There's every chance he might not even have gone to the thieving ring with the letter, she thinks. Every chance this story about the agreement he had made Lizzie's mother sign is a complete fabrication. He might just have tossed that little brass box into the ocean, or left it lying in the street. She knows he is aware of the letter's value. But she also knows the depth of the deceitfulness inside her son.

After breakfast, she sends him upstairs with a long list of school work to complete, and strict instructions not to show his face until it's done. She takes Nathan and Eva into the parlour to wait for Mrs Calloway to arrive.

Abigail perches on the edge of the settle with her sewing, the children hunched over a game of knucklebones by the hearth. She finds herself looking towards the ceiling. Listening for any sound from Oliver's room. No doubt it will be mere minutes until he has crawled out through the passage again. *Good*, she finds herself thinking. She needs not to be around him today. Needs a moment to breathe. She realises that, somewhere beneath the love and the protectiveness, she is afraid of her son.

Eva lets out a wild shriek, making Abigail's heart jolt. She throws down her sewing and drops to the floor beside the children. Eva throws herself at her, arms cinching around Abigail's neck. Tears are rushing down her cheeks.

"I'm sorry," Nathan is saying beneath his sister's wailing. His own tears spill. "I'm sorry, Evie. I didn't mean to…"

Abigail wraps an arm around Eva's waist. "What happened?"

"She grabbed my shoulder," says Nathan, wiping at his tears with the back of his hand. "And I just… I just… I got scared and pushed her."

Abigail bends her head to meet his eyes, Eva still pressed into her. "You got scared. Why did you get scared? Tell me, Nathan."

He cries harder. "I don't know."

"Was it your brother? Has Oliver hurt you?" Her voice wavers. "Tell me, Nathan, please. Please. I promise I'll not be angry."

But even as she speaks, she knows this is not the time for interrogation. She doesn't need to hear it spoken to know that Nathan has gotten too entangled in this dark world that Oliver has built for him. Doesn't need the details.

It pains her that he will not let her near him. Will not let her hold him, comfort him. Attempt to make that world a little lighter. But she has let him down enough. Has let both him and Eva down enough.

She knows Oliver is getting worse. Whether a result of his father's death, or Henry Ward's appearance, or just his rapid approach toward adulthood, he is becoming more and more dangerous. Impossible to manage.

Her instinct has always been to keep him close. But perhaps that is just making things worse. Perhaps it's her stifling closeness that has caused him to be like this. Perhaps she has poisoned him with her own darkness.

Perhaps he would be better off on Henry Ward's ship.

She can hardly believe she has allowed herself to think it. What kind of mother is she?

The answer comes just as quickly: a mother who is desperately concerned for her two youngest children.

She knows she is guilty of neglecting Nathan and Eva. When Samuel was alive, it had not seemed quite so dire. They had had an unspoken agreement that she would tend towards Oliver and he would favour the other two. *Favour*—no, it's wrong. Because she does not favour Oliver over her other two children. Does she? No. Not favour—just a different kind of love.

She cannot deny there are moments she is grateful for the children's nurse, for the petty school, for taking Eva and Nathan off her hands. Not because she does not want to be around them, but because once she has given Oliver what he needs, she feels drained dry. Has nothing left to give.

The moment Mrs Calloway arrives, Abigail goes to the village. She has never sought Henry out before; has always waited patiently—or not so patiently—for him to come to her. But she cannot wait. She needs to do what must be done now, before she loses her nerve.

It has been weeks since she has shown her face in the village. She is wary of seeing Mairi and her husband. Wary of seeing Donald Macauley. Wary of Father Dering, and the barrage of questions he no doubt has for her after she had cast him out of the house with Oliver's blood beading on the foyer floor.

Abigail keeps to the edges of the village at first, skirting the farmland in the shadow of the castle. She looks out at the anchorage, searching the water, the jetty, for any longboats from the *Eagle*. When she sees none, she pulls her cloak tightly around her, puts her head down and enters the narrow coils of the village.

She cannot avoid familiar faces in a place this small. She hands out succinct and flimsy greetings to the vicar's wife, to Mrs Emmett. Pretends not to see Mairi's eldest son as he runs down Church Lane.

Once the boy's footsteps have disappeared, her eyes begin to dart again.

Henry will likely be speaking to his buyer this morning. Or wiping off the remains of a late-night visit to the tavern with his crew.

Or perhaps, more likely, he is still aboard his ship. Perhaps the wisest thing to do is return to the house and wait for him to show himself. She is not sure she can unearth that kind of patience today.

Abigail rounds the village; sees no sign of him. She returns to the anchorage and paces back and forth across the rafts of dried seaweed, the crunch of her shoes lulling her into something trancelike and necessary. He will come to the village, she tells herself. He will come to liaise with his buyer, as he always does when he is in this part of the world. And if he goes to the house to see her instead, Ruth or Mrs Calloway will tell him she is here in the village looking for him.

Finally, she sees him. He and several of his crewmen are seated in the longboat that is rounding around the point. She feels something flip in her chest.

Henry's eyes meet hers while he is still far out on the water, and the moment the longboat knocks against the jetty, he leaps out, striding down the worn wooden walkway towards her. There's a look of concern in his eyes that Abigail can tell is a reflection of her own.

"I need you to take him," she blurts. "Oliver. I need you to take him, before I change my mind."

Henry looks at her squarely. He dares to reach for her hand. She doesn't pull away as his fingers close around hers. "What's happened?"

She closes her eyes for a moment. "I'm scared for my other children," she admits. "And I'm scared for Oliver. I'm scared of where he will end up if nothing changes." Her blue eyes bore into his. "Please, Henry. I'm desperate."

He puts a hand to her shoulder, guiding her away from the jetty, and the eyes of his crew. They stand in the pale shadow of one of the fishermen's huts dotted along the sand. The wind carries a rhythmic wooden clattering across the water from the ships in the anchorage.

"I convinced myself I could manage him," Abigail says. "That I could keep him in line somewhat. But I see now that I've only been fooling myself. I've never had any control over him. I used to criticise his father for that. But I see now that I'm no better."

Henry doesn't speak at once, and a part of her is terrified he is going to refuse her request. A bigger part of her is terrified he is going to agree.

"Will you at least consider it?" she asks. "Please?"

"Of course." Almost imperceptibly, he tugs her closer. His hand slides up her arm. "Are you safe?" he murmurs. "You're not involving yourself with the Jacobite cause any longer are you?"

"No," she says. "I'm not." As for whether or not she is safe, that's a question she does not have room for right now. Because all she knows for certain is that Nathan is not safe. Eva is not safe. They will not be for as long as Oliver is in the house with them.

Henry's rough fingers tighten around her bare forearm, and in spite of the squall inside her, she feels a sudden aliveness beneath her skin. "Come to the house tonight," she says. "You and your officers. And perhaps you might speak with my son?"

CHAPTER TWENTY-FIVE

When Ward gets back to the ship, Finn is still slumped at the table of the great cabin with his head in his hand, and the map Ward had set him to copying spread out in front of him. As far as Ward can tell, he has made exactly zero progress on the work in the two hours he has been away on the island.

He stands over the boy with his arms folded across his chest. "I've had quite enough of this moodiness, lad. I know you don't like being up here in Northumberland, but I've not even asked you to come ashore. No one need know you're here." He had briefly considered leaving Finn in London with the *Fortune's* prize crew. He knows the boy would have preferred not to make the journey back up to this part of the country. But he feels too responsible for Finn to keep him out of sight for so long.

"I know, sir. Sorry." He lets out a hacking cough.

Ward raises his eyebrows. "You're unwell."

"No I'm not."

He chuckles. "What, you think I'm going to toss you overboard if you're ill?"

Finn looks up at him with watery eyes, then looks back down again quickly. "Maybe. If I have what the prisoners on the French ship had."

Ward feels a tug of unease. He forces a smile. "I don't think so. Just a bad head cold I'd say. I think I'll keep you around for a little longer yet." He nods towards the map. "Finish up what you're doing and go and rest."

Ward holds the door open for Finn, then tucks the map and pencils back in his desk drawer. He pushes open one of the windows at the far end of the cabin, letting a stream of cool air inside.

He thinks of Abigail. Is not sure what to make of her desperate plea for him to take her son to sea. When he had last raised the subject with her, she had been violently against it. He wonders what has changed.

One half of him had told him to refuse; told him he did not want a boy like Oliver in his crew. The other half told him to accept at once; told him to do blindly whatever Abigail asked of him.

And so, caught in the indecision she so often manages to wrangle from him, he had not given her an answer.

He is open to the idea of having another cabin boy in his crew. Less open to the idea of that boy being Oliver Blake. Still, perhaps Abigail is right. Perhaps such a thing will change him for the better.

In any case, if he were to agree, he would offer the boy no more than a brief initial agreement; a month or two at sea at most. Perhaps that would be enough to set Oliver's life on the right track.

As it has done for Finn? Ward is not sure how to answer that. He'd like to think so. For all this morning's moodiness, he's certainly managed to wrangle some discipline into the boy; stop him from ranting and raving in anger whenever things don't go his way. And he's certainly instilled plenty of nautical knowledge in him.

But Ward can't help but wonder if Finn wouldn't have been better off staying out on Longstone with his father. Safer, certainly. Happier? Maybe.

Ward wonders what Abigail's reaction would be if he took Finn to the house with him tonight. He has never told her that he already has a cabin boy; has always imagined that, as a mother of young boys, she might look down on such a thing. But her request suggests that maybe he is wrong about this. Or at least that she is desperate enough to acknowledge that not everything is black and white.

There's a chance, of course, that Abigail might recognise Finn as the Longstone lightkeeper's boy. A slim chance though, surely. He can't imagine Finn Murray has ever had any reason to associate with the family from the house on Emmanuel Head.

Finn will benefit, surely, from a night in a comfortable bed—a chance to sleep off his illness. More importantly, if he is to consider taking Oliver aboard his ship, he at least wants the two boys to cross into each other's territory beforehand.

It's a little past nine when the knock at the front door echoes through the house. Abigail has fed the children and sent Eva and Nathan up to bed. Exiled Oliver to his bedroom for now—she needs a little space from him to clear her thoughts. Determine if she is making the right decision in asking Henry to take him to sea. As of yet, she has said nothing to Oliver about the issue. Since he had told her about taking the letter, she has spoken to him in only brusque half-sentences that barely keep her anger at bay. But tonight she will bring him downstairs to speak to Henry properly about his going to sea. Assuming Henry agrees to it.

Assuming he does not fly out of the house in anger the moment she tells him the letter is gone.

Abigail toys with the pearls at her throat as she makes her way downstairs to answer the door. Smooths the soft blue folds of her gown. The coloured skirts give her a much-needed burst of confidence. Out of the dark clothing she has languished in for so many months, she feels more energised, more hopeful. Feels less like she is drowning under the weight of life.

At the back of her mind, she is also aware that the blue mantua is an invitation. A signal to Henry that tonight, if he is willing, she will put the loss of her husband behind her.

She has no idea if, after he hears about the letter, he will still be willing.

The group is a large one tonight. Six men stand on the doorstep, along with a boy who can be no older than Oliver. He's tall and broad-shouldered, but with a smooth, youthful face. Abigail ushers them into the foyer, unable to take her eyes off the boy.

"He's one of yours?" she asks Henry quietly. Knows he can hear the surprise in her voice.

Henry's eyes glide over her, taking in her gown, the jewels at her throat, the cerise powder on her cheeks. Her attempt at snaring his affections— or rather, outrunning her own uncertainties—suddenly feels far too overt. Henry gives her a faint but weighted smile. "He is," he says, as though suddenly remembering the question. He puts a hand to the boy's shoulder; a protective, fatherly gesture. "A hardworking cabin boy, fighting the last of a fever. He's in need of a warm bed for the night."

Abigail nods stiffly. The sight of this child has made her request all too real. This is the life she is sending her son towards. A hundred questions fly at her; questions she wants to ask the boy. Whether he is happy. Whether Henry Ward is a fair captain. Whether it was his own mother who had sent him off to sea as a punishment for not being the son she wanted him to be.

She wonders at Henry's rationale behind bringing the boy here tonight. She knows it's no coincidence that he has done so immediately after her asking him to take Oliver. Up until this moment, she had not even been aware that Henry had any children on his ship.

She gives the boy a thin smile she knows doesn't reach her eyes. "Of course," she tells him. "You can have my eldest son's room. He can share with his brother for the night."

Ward watches after Abigail as she glides up the staircase in a sea of blue silk. He can tell Finn's presence has rattled her. Caught her by surprise. He grips the boy's shoulder. "Behave yourself, lad. Do as Mrs Blake tells you."

Finn nods faintly. "Aye sir."

Ward sends one final glance up the stairs, then follows his officers towards the parlour, leaving Finn alone in the entrance hall.

The sight of Oliver pressed against the wall in the passageway makes him jump. The boy is shadowed, barely lit by the lamplight spilling from the wall. Ward can tell he has been waiting for him.

"Good evening, Captain Ward," he says evenly.

Ward waits until the parlour door has closed behind the rest of the men. "Good evening, Mr Blake. I'm glad to see you. There's something I'd like to discuss."

A look of hope appears in Oliver's eyes. "Yes?"

Ward tilts his head, considering the boy. Something has happened that has made Abigail desperate for him to take her son. He needs to know what it is.

He could ask her, of course. But perhaps it would be more valuable for him to ask Oliver directly. His willingness to answer—or lack thereof—will tell him plenty about the boy's character.

"You may know your mother has changed her mind about you becoming my cabin boy," he says. "She has asked me to discuss the matter with you."

The glow in Oliver's eyes intensifies. "Has she?" he sounds suddenly innocent, excited.

"Do you know what it was that made her change her mind?"

Oliver pauses. "I can't imagine, Captain. Perhaps she just knows how much it would mean to me."

Oliver Blake is well spoken, certainly. But his words lack genuineness. And, Ward imagines, truth. He stares him down. "I value honesty among my crewmen very highly, Mr Blake."

"What makes you think I'm being dishonest?"

The self-assured question catches Ward off guard.

"I'm very honest," says Oliver, before Ward can cobble together a response. "Just ask my mother. We always tell each other the truth."

Ward makes a noise in his throat, unconvinced. He has always prided himself on being able to trust his instinct. And his instinct is telling him to be wary of anything that comes out of this boy's mouth.

Oliver takes a step closer to Ward and something darkens behind his eyes. "I can also keep secrets," he says, voice low. "Such as Lord Haver's connection with the Jacobite movement."

Ward hears his own sharp inhalation. He forces himself not to react. "How do you know of that?" he asks evenly. "Did your mother tell you?"

"No. I read about it. In the letter. In her nightstand."

Inwardly, Ward panics. Has Oliver told anyone else of this? If he has, and this information is on its way to becoming common knowledge, the letter will become near worthless. He had kept it locked up for a reason. Has no idea how Oliver managed to read it. Surely Abigail would not have told him about it.

"I did not know who Lord Haver was at first," Oliver continues, too lightly. "I did not really understand why you deemed the letter so valuable. But I understand now. I can see why you would wish to keep that information to yourself until the time is right."

Why is the boy telling him this? To prove his knowledge? His intelligence? No. Ward sees it then.

Blackmail. He will keep the news of Haver's dissent a secret, in exchange for a berth on the *Eagle*. The outrage that comes up on him is hot and sharp. Ward forces himself to swallow it down. "I am not able to be extorted, Mr Blake," he says firmly. "You can attempt to spread the information you read in that letter, but I'm afraid it will not serve you well."

Panic flashes across the boy's face. "I'm not trying to extort you. I swear it." His façade falls away. "Please, Captain Ward. Give me a chance. I shall be the best cabin boy you have ever seen. And I shall never resort to such trickery again." He looks up at him with wide, desperate eyes. "Please."

Ward's thoughts turn over. He knows he is letting Abigail down. But he also knows he has made the only decision possible. Yes, he wants to help Abigail turn her son into a more decent young man. But he will not do so aboard his ship. There is little point dragging the issue on any further. "I'm afraid not, Mr Blake," he says. "A privateering life is a dangerous one. I cannot have anyone aboard my ship that I do not trust implicitly."

Oliver's face falls. His eyes flash and he opens his mouth to protest. Seems to decide against it. He turns on his heel and disappears down the hallway, without giving Ward another word.

Abigail rubs her eyes with impatience. She has laid a bed for Oliver on the floor of Nathan's room, but she cannot find her eldest son anywhere. The last time she had seen him, before the men arrived, he had been in his bedroom. She had made it clear that that was where she expected him to stay. But now the room is empty. So is the priest hole. Has Oliver gone downstairs to speak with Henry without her knowing? Is he out running wild across the dunes?

As she is making her way back down the hallway towards the staircase, she hears a thump coming from inside Oliver's bedroom. Footsteps on floorboards. She throws open the door to see him pushing closed the panel of the priest hole. His pale hair is windblown, and she can tell he has just climbed up through the passage inside the wall.

Abigail closes the bedroom door behind her. Lifts up the lamp in her hand to illuminate his face. "What were you doing out there?" she demands.

"Nothing."

She can practically see the anger radiating from him. She wonders what has caused it. All she knows is that she cannot send him down to speak with Henry while he is like this; so closed off and angry, with these hot, glowing eyes. If Henry sees this side of him, he will never take him as his cabin boy.

Let him sleep off his rage, at least for a few hours. She can always come and wake him before Henry and the other men leave.

Abigail thinks of the bed she has laid for him on the floor of Nathan's bedroom. No. She will not put him in with his brother. Not while he has this wild look in his eyes.

"You're to sleep in my dressing room tonight," she tells him firmly. "On the settle."

"Why? Why can't I sleep in my room?"

Abigail doesn't respond at once. She senses that Oliver will not take it well to learn that Henry's cabin boy will be sleeping in his bed. The boy who already has the position Oliver is craving. The boy who has already passed Henry Ward's test.

"Because I asked you to sleep on the settle," she says tautly. "And that is all there is to it." She plants her free hand on her hip. "Oliver? Do you have an issue with that?"

He holds her gaze for a moment. "No, Mama," he says resignedly. "I've no issue with that." He turns for her dressing room, without waiting for a response.

Abigail watches after him, trying to steady the unease inside her. She tightens her fingers around the handle of the lamp and makes her way back downstairs. Henry's cabin boy is hovering in the foyer, shifting his weight, his gaze drifting over the seascape and portraits hanging on the wall. He looks uncomfortable, out of place. As though he is waiting for the house to swallow him.

He turns to look up the staircase at the sound of her footsteps.

Abigail stops on the landing and gestures to him to join her. "This way."

Obediently, he scrambles up the stairs behind her. Down the passage. Abigail brings her finger to her lips as they pass Nathan and Eva's rooms, not wanting to wake them. Or is it Oliver she does not want to disturb?

She pushes open the door to Oliver's bedroom. "You can sleep in here."

The boy sniffs. "Thank you."

Abigail nods. Swallows heavily. "Sleep well," she manages. She pulls the door closed. Steps across the passage and peeks in to check that Oliver has obeyed her orders. He is curled up on the settle, the blankets pulled high, so that only his pale hair is visible. She can tell he's sulking.

She hovers in the doorway, debating whether to speak with him.

"Abigail." Henry's voice is gentle, quiet. Comes from the landing. He has never ventured up the staircase before. She senses that he is not allowing himself to venture all the way up, into this most private part of the house.

At the sight of him, the sound of him, she feels a chaos of emotions boil up inside her. She must tell him about the lost letter, of course. And she must talk to him about Oliver. But most of all, she wants to go back downstairs with him in her blue silk gown and her pearl necklace, and give in to herself. She is craving an escape from the pressures of the last months, the last weeks, the last days—never mind how fleeting and foolish.

She makes her way down onto the landing. Stands close to Henry. A coil of his pale hair has come loose from its queue, and hangs across the sharp plane of his jaw. She reaches out and lifts it lightly from his skin. Lets it trail over her fingers.

"I've sent Oliver to bed for now," she says. "He was not in the right frame of mind to speak with you about such a serious matter."

Ward reaches up to cover her hand with his own. Laces his fingers through hers. "Let's not speak of him now," he says. "There'll be time for that later." He lowers his voice slightly. A deep murmur that Abigail feels inside her. "I've been waiting months to see you. I can't tell you how much I've been longing to be alone with you again."

And it is exactly what she wishes to hear.

CHAPTER TWENTY-SIX

With her hand laced through his, Abigail leads Henry into the dining room. She can hear the murmur of voices coming from the parlour, and she is distantly aware that she is being a terrible host. She can't make herself care.

The room is dark, lit only by the lingering glow of the fire. Curtains pulled across windows, hiding the outside world. The air feels warm, pulsing, alive.

Henry tugs her towards him. Plants a tentative kiss on the edge of her lips. Abigail closes her eyes, enjoying the warmth of him. The gentle sigh of breath on her skin.

Voice low, he says, "I want to be more to you than just someone you see on occasion."

Abigail feels a smile on her lips. "I want that too."

He reaches out and tucks a strand of dark hair behind her ear. "I've also been thinking about your financial struggles," he says. "And what you've been forced to do since your husband's death."

Abigail swallows heavily. At once, her heart is pounding for an entirely different reason. She does not want her secrets and lies brought out into this half-light. Just for now, she wants to forget they exist at all.

"I've opened a bank safe in London," Henry tells her. "An account with the new Bank of England. If it is not too forward of me, I would like to put the safe in your name too. Or rather, your son's. That way, if you are ever in need…"

Abigail hears her exhalation. She cannot believe he would do such a thing for her. She wants to feel guilt—knows it is his belief that she is a penniless widow that has led him to do this. But she cannot quite make herself feel it. Because this gesture, it goes a long way to solidifying whatever this unnameable thing is that's simmering between them. Goes someway to solidifying a future without fear and loneliness and danger.

"Thank you," is all she can manage.

He meets her eye. Trails rough fingertips down the delicate line of her jaw. "I hope it will go some way to showing you how I feel about you. And showing you there is a place for you in my future." He swallows visibly. "If you wish it."

And in that future, she thinks, she will tell him everything. Will tell him every painful truth. And maybe, just maybe, it should not be guilt she is feeling right now, but rather gratitude for all this. For this man who cares for her. Wants to make a future with her. Loves her? Perhaps. But right now, even without the promise of love, it is enough.

There is a danger to Henry Ward, yes. He has harder edges than Samuel had had; has a life scented with gunpowder and defined by the laws of the sea. And perhaps that is why she is drawn to him in a way she never was to her husband. Because she has hard edges too.

But: "You are always at sea," she says.

"I do not have to be." He smiles at her. "I am not at sea right now."

He pulls her close, kisses her hard. His presence feels all-consuming, as though she might drown beneath his weight. It feels impossible that someone as striking, as compelling as him might want someone as plain— and as tainted—as her. Her body comes alive at his touch, and she moves towards him, hands sliding instinctively over his rigid contours.

"Your men are in the next room," she whispers. Her breath strains against her stays, heat unfurling inside her.

His hands grip her thighs and lift her onto the table as though she weighs nothing. He smiles against her lips. "We had best be quiet then."

His mouth is on hers again before she can protest; and nor does she want to. She wants everything this man is willing to give her, she realises. Security, pleasure… and yes, horribly, a life in which her eldest son is no longer her struggle.

He slides his hands up beneath her skirts, pushing reams of blue silk higher until she feels the outside world fall away.

Nathan knows it's very late—could even be midnight. He has not slept for a second.

He knows the privateers are here. Tonight, he had pointed his telescope at the ship and watched as they had climbed into their boats and come towards the house. He had watched the globes of lamplight come bouncing over the dunes like fairy dog eyes. And he had listened as Mama had let the men inside. Laughter and footsteps and voices.

Mama had come into his room soon afterwards, laying out blankets on the floor. For who, Nathan does not know. He had pretended to not be awake—had not even flinched when Mama had bent over to kiss his forehead. He knows she believed him to be asleep—she would not have touched him otherwise.

There have been lots of footsteps up and down the hallway, lots of shadows moving beneath his door. Mama and Oliver's voices, their words too soft to make out.

It's quiet for a while. Nathan hears the occasional burst of manly laughter floating up the staircase, which makes him think of Da. He wonders if the laughter belongs to Captain Ward, who is going to take Oliver away.

A door across the hallway groans as it opens. Nathan slips out of bed and peeks through the keyhole of his bedroom door. He sees his brother coming out of Mama's dressing room and tromping down the passage, back towards his own bedchamber.

Nathan hears mumbled voices. Someone else is in Oliver's room.

He opens the door to his bedroom as quietly as he can. Steps out into the passage and presses his eye to the keyhole of Oliver's room.

Oliver is standing eye to eye with another boy that Nathan doesn't recognise. The boy is dressed in only his shirt and breeches, his feet bare. His brown hair is all falling out of its queue; messy, like he's just gotten out of Oliver's bed. Does he come from the crew of sailors who are gathered downstairs? Does he, like Oliver, want to be Captain Ward's cabin boy? Perhaps he already is.

Oliver lifts the lamp in his hand, shining it into the other boy's eyes. "Why won't you speak to me?" he hisses. "Are you a half-wit? Or are you scared?"

The other boy is taller than Oliver, shoulders wider. Older? Maybe. It's hard to tell. "Leave me alone," the boy says huskily. "I just want to sleep. Your mother gave me this room."

Nathan feels a sudden, intense need to be a part of this—whatever this is. He wants to meet the boy who sails on the ship with Captain Ward. The boy who has clearly got under Oliver's skin.

Nathan can't bear the thought of staying out here in the hallway any longer. Holding his breath, he slips inside the room.

The boy from the ship turns to look at him, but Oliver gives him little more than a fleeting glance. Oliver sets the lamp on the floor and lifts his other hand, revealing the Viking knife he had hidden in his fist. Nathan feels his heart quicken. He takes a step back, his spine pressing hard against the wall.

Oliver holds the knife out in front of the boy. "Look at this," he says. "It's a Viking dagger. From the days when they raided the island."

The boy snorts. "A Viking dagger? It is not."

Oliver's eyes flash. "Are you calling me a liar?"

"You're lying, aye? Or are you just stupid?"

Nathan feels the air prickle. Feels the rage pouring off his brother. Oliver takes a step towards the boy from the ship. Turns the blade over slowly. Then he looks towards Nathan.

"Tell him, Nathan. Tell him it's from the Viking raids."

Nathan hesitates. He wants to please Oliver, of course. But he does not want to look foolish in front of one of Captain Ward's crewmen. "I think it's just a fishing knife," he says at last. He dares a glance at his brother. Can tell by Oliver's narrowed eyes that he is unimpressed with this answer. Nonetheless, Nathan knows they have something far more impressive to show the boy than some tarnished old blade from the sea. "But there's a real priest hole in this room," he announces. "Behind the panel in the fireplace." He begins to hurry towards it, but Oliver shoves him hard against the shoulder.

"Get out."

Nathan feels a fizzing blaze radiating across his shoulder where Oliver touched him. The rage in his brother's eyes makes something close in his chest and he hurries out into the hallway. Stands with his back against the wall, staring at the closed door. Perhaps he ought to go downstairs and fetch Mama. But what would Oliver and the boy from the ship think of him then?

He presses his eye back to the keyhole of Oliver's room. Swallows a murmur of fear. Oliver has the blade to the boy's throat. Now, his stomach. He is speaking low, threatening words that Nathan cannot quite make out. And then he catches, *Left them all to die.*

He is speaking of the Viking raids, Nathan knows. Speaking of the monks slaughtered in Saint Cuthbert's church. Whirlwinds and dragons and the blood that pooled across their island.

Come out to face your maker.

Nathan feels frozen in place, his breath rattling against his lungs. He cannot tear his eye away from the keyhole. Cannot go back inside that room. And he cannot run downstairs to find his mother. Even though he is becoming more and more certain that that is exactly what he ought to be doing.

Once, he and Oliver had found a baby bird lying on the ground beneath a tree on the edge of the Macauleys' farmland. Nathan had watched silently as Oliver had pelted it with rocks until it was nothing more than a bloody mess. That had frightened him; made him see the darkness in his brother went deeper than he had first imagined. But surely that darkness doesn't go so far as to cut the throat of the boy from the ship.

Nathan thinks of Oliver trapping him in the priest hole. Thinks of him holding the knife to his throat; hard, too hard. Thinks of that line of blood running down onto his collar, and of hiding the bloodstained shirt beneath his bed beside the telescope so that no one would ever know. And somehow, while he is thinking all these things, he is also not thinking at all. Because there is a part of him that is far too afraid to think. He feels as though, if he thinks the wrong thought, Oliver will push that knife into the cabin boy's neck.

He shifts his weight and the floor beneath him creaks.

"I can hear you out there, Nathan," says Oliver, not pulling his eyes away from the cabin boy's. He doesn't move the knife from his stomach. "Go to bed."

Go downstairs, the voice inside Nathan's head screams. *Get Mama*. But he can't bear to think what Oliver would do to him then. He does not want to be put back in that priest hole.

When he doesn't move, doesn't speak, Oliver turns slightly so Nathan can hear him clearly through the closed door. "Do you want to spend another night in the walls?"

The cabin boy shoves Oliver away. He darts towards the door, but Oliver grabs hold of him, yanking him back. Slashes the knife across his forearm.

Nathan hears himself murmur at the same time as the boy from the ship shouts in pain. He sees the flash of movement pass across the tiny window of the keyhole. Sees the crimson bloom of blood on the boy's arm, stark against the white of his shirt. And Nathan watches the boy from the ship swing a desperate fist. Watches it strike the side of Oliver's head. Oliver falls sideways, his head slamming into the thick wooden post at the foot of the bed. And Nathan is unable to stop his cry from escaping as he watches his brother fall.

CHAPTER TWENTY-SEVEN

Henry's forehead rests against hers, and she feels his body rise and fall with gradually slowing breath. "You are all I think about," he says. "When I'm at sea."

Abigail smiles. "I hope that's not true. That sounds very dangerous."

Henry laughs; a warm honey laugh that Abigail feels inside her. The idea that she might fill his every thought is an impossibly pleasant one. It dulls the ache of these past months, of the thought of losing Oliver to his ship—by her own making. And it gives her the courage to confess to that which has so far been a complete impossibility: that she no longer has the Jacobite letter. No, she is not going to think of that now. Almost, but not quite yet. She is going to let herself get lost in the pleasure of this moment. Enjoy the feel of his body close to hers, for just a little longer.

Loud laughter rises up from the parlour. Drunken laughter, like the men are steadily working their way through the bottles they brought with them.

"You ought to join your crew," she says. "They will be wondering where you have got to."

He chuckles. "I'm fairly certain they know exactly where I've got to. And it's far more pleasant being in here with you."

"Leave them aboard next time," she says, surprising herself with her boldness.

His blue eyes shine. "As you wish."

He is like an illusion, she thinks. She realises she is waiting for him to disappear. Waiting to wake one morning and find he was nothing more than a dream. Never mind that her body is still buzzing with pleasure, and there is a dull ache between her legs.

She hears a cry from upstairs.

Nathan.

She pushes herself from the table and straightens her skirts. Hurries out of the dining room and up the stairs, Henry's footsteps thumping behind her.

She sees Nathan in the passage. He has his eye pressed to the keyhole of Oliver's bedroom door, palms flat to the wall. Abigail can see his back rising and falling with rapid, panicked breath. She hurries to him. Impulsively, she takes his arm, cursing herself when he yanks away. "What's happened? Where's your brother?"

His look of white-faced dread is one she has never seen before. It's going to fell her, she thinks. Whatever is on the other side of this door is going to bring her to her knees.

Henry throws the door open and charges inside, before she can prepare herself.

She stops breathing. Stops thinking. Hears a strangled cry that could be her own. There is no other sound; no sense. The world contracts and there is nothing but her son sprawled across the floor beside his bed. A thick seam of blood runs from his temple, shining in the gold glow of the lamp. Trailing, disappearing, into the dark floorboards. Abigail falls to her knees beside him, and some part of her is present enough to feel desperately for a pulse. But the glassiness in his eyes; the cold, vacant stare. She has seen this often enough—recently enough—to know this is death. Lying on the floor beside him is the thin-bladed knife he had pulled from the sea. She hears a sound try to escape her throat. She pulls it back in as her lungs strain. Presses her hands to Oliver's cheeks. Shakes him. Wills him, blindly, to come back to her.

Henry rushes to the window and wrenches it open. He leans over the sill and peers into darkness. Sea-scented air billows inside. He hollers out into the night, bellowing his cabin boy's name. He whirls from the window. Throws open the wardrobe. Peers under the bed. "Where did he go, lad?"

Abigail is only distantly aware that Nathan is in the room with them.

At Henry's question, he edges towards his mother, but then backs away, as though afraid to approach his brother's body. He stumbles from the room and hovers against the wall in the hallway. Shakes his head.

"You don't know?" Henry demands. "How could you not know? Did you not see where he went?"

Nathan murmurs in fear.

"Henry, please," Abigail manages.

She knows, of course. She knows where the cabin boy is. The priest hole; the passage. There is no other explanation.

But something prevents her from speaking.

Ward thunders downstairs. She hears him speak to his men—curt, barked instructions to find his cabin boy. Distant, distorted sounds. The front door slams.

Abigail realises Nathan is no longer in the hallway behind her. She calls for him weakly, his name catching in her throat. She feels a deep cold taking over her body.

Nathan does not appear. Does not come to stand back here beside his brother's body. Does not come to join his mother in this breathless vigil as she sits in a pool of sky blue silk.

Find him.

Every cell in her body screams at her to stay here with Oliver, but she knows Nathan needs her. How many times in her children's lives has she chosen her firstborn over his siblings?

It's the deep quiet that pulls her to her feet; draws her out into the passage, and towards Nathan's bedchamber. Every inch of her is shaking, her vision swimming. The walls of the house feel as though they are tightening around her, forcing the air from her lungs. She stumbles into Nathan's room. Sifts through the shadows, finding the bed empty.

Down the hall to Eva's room. Abigail finds Nathan curled up at the bottom of his sister's bed. Eva is still sleeping, and Abigail is grateful.

Her chest is heaving. Grief is pressing down on her so heavily she can barely lift her head. But she cannot let it out now. Not here. Not around her children. She sits beside Nathan on the edge of the bed. Close. Letting him know she is here. No touching. Hopes the weight, the warmth, of her body beside his own will go some way towards comfort.

Ward pauses at the bottom of the staircase, staring up into the gloomy hallway. A part of him is desperate to go back to Abigail. Another part of him can't bear to face her.

But he knows staying down here is the height of cowardice.

He forces himself back up the stairs. Through the ajar door, he sees her sitting on her daughter's bed, her son curled up beside her. Ward hovers outside the room, feeling like an intruder. Less than an hour since he had imagined a life in which this family might become his own. Now, surely, that imagined future is in pieces.

He continues down the hallway. Dares to step inside Oliver's bedroom. At the sight of the boy's body, he feels a profound hollow yawning open inside him. A deep grief; if not for Oliver himself, then certainly for his mother, and those glittering possibilities that had come alive between them tonight.

He stares down at the knife beside the body, the trail of blood running towards it from gash in Oliver's head. What had happened here? He thinks of Oliver's deceitfulness. Thinks of the temper he has spent the past two years trying to purge from Finn. For a strange, fleeting moment, it feels as though bringing these two boys together was never destined to lead anywhere other than this. The regret is searing. Makes his body blaze.

He reaches down to close Oliver's eyes. The boy's skin is beginning to whiten. Body beginning to grow cold.

A door creaks in the room down the hall and Abigail appears at his shoulder.

"Help me move him," she murmurs. She crouches at Oliver's side, her eyes not leaving her son's face.

Ward bends, scoops Oliver's limp body into his arms. He takes a step towards the bed.

"No," says Abigail. "Take him to my room." She nods to the room across the hall.

Ward nods wordlessly. Carries him into his mother's room and lays him on the bed, his blood beading crimson across the pillow. He smooths the boy's shirt. Ties, pointlessly, the lacing at his neck. And then he turns back to Abigail. Does he hold her? Comfort her? He has no idea. He knows no words, no apology, will ever come close to being enough. But he cannot just give her silence.

"The boy will be punished," he says finally.

Abigail drifts over to the bed and curls up beside Oliver's body. She shows no inkling that she has even heard him.

"I've men out looking for him now," Ward continues anyway. "And at first light I'll go out to Longstone in case he's decided to return to his father."

His words seem to snap Abigail out of her daze. She sits up. "Your cabin boy is the lightkeeper's son? He's the one who did this to Oliver?"

Ward nods faintly. He knows he has done what he had promised Finn he never would—but how can he stay silent?

Abigail lets out a long, shaky breath and turns back to Oliver. Ward dares to press a hand to her shoulder. Feels her flinch beneath his touch.

"Leave," she says.

"Abigail, I…" He scrubs a hand across his face. "You shouldn't be here alone."

"I'm not alone."

"You know what I mean."

But he is not welcome here. That much is clear. He can see in her eyes that she holds him responsible for this.

And as much as he wants to stay; as much he hates the thought of leaving her here alone, he knows his presence is doing more harm than good right now.

"I'll go to the village," he says. "Send the vicar to the house."

He waits for a response that doesn't come. And he steps out of the house into cold spring darkness that feels impossibly weighted.

Abigail closes her eyes, Oliver's limp hand held tightly between both of hers. Keep him close, she thinks. Keep him close like she has always done. And somehow, she will change things.

The knock at the door echoes through the house, splintering the stillness. Abigail holds her breath, praying the sound won't wake Nathan or Eva.

The sound is swallowed quickly, the knocking disappearing into nothingness. Barely aware of herself, Abigail gets to her feet, makes her way downstairs. She is distantly surprised her legs have managed to hold her.

Father Dering stands on the doorstep, dressed in a dark cloak and cocked hat. "Mr Ward told me what happened."

She can't find a response; just steps aside to let him into the house. Leads him up the staircase and into her bedroom.

Father Dering approaches the bed. He kneels. Takes Oliver's hand in his and murmurs a prayer. Abigail lets his words wash over her. *Lord, forgive us our sins. Help us in our final hour.* Feels that grief pressing down on her, darkening her vision. No. Not now. She cannot let it out.

"Was this an accident?" Father Dering asks finally. "Mr Ward was unclear on the details. I can see Oliver has hit his head, but…"

He knows, Abigail is aware, of the kind of boy Oliver is. Was. Does not dare think of what questions are circling in his head.

She can only imagine the storm of gossip that will arise if the villagers learn Oliver died from a fight with the lightkeeper's son. It will engulf her house, her surviving children. And it will engulf that tiny spit of Longstone, where the firelight burns to keep men alive.

The truth will not bring her son back. It will only tarnish his memory.

"He fell," she manages. "The bedhead…" It sounds like a lie. Sounds like a story the villagers will poke holes in.

For a long time, Father Dering doesn't speak. Doesn't ask for the missing pieces of the story.

Is this, Abigail wonders distantly, why she had not told Henry of the priest hole, and the passage his cabin boy had used to escape the house? Because even in the depth of her shock and grief, there had been fear of what Oliver might have done in the last moments of his life? And perhaps she did not want the boy she had sent up here to Oliver's room to be hanged for his… what? Crime? Act of retaliation? Self-defence?

One child was dead already. Condemning another to death would not bring her son back.

Father Dering clears his throat. "You know better than anyone that smallpox is rampant in these parts. No one would question…"

Abigail nods wordlessly. Does her son deserve this—for his end to be tidied into something more palatable? She knows the truth will just lead to more questions—questions about what Oliver did to invoke the cabin boy's attack. She knows, because they are questions she cannot help but ask herself.

She knows she could ask Nathan.

Perhaps she ought to. Can't bear to. She does not want to know the answer. Nor will she force Nathan to relive such a thing. She does not want him to speak of his brother any more than he has to.

Perhaps she does not want him to speak of his brother any more, ever. Because she knows that being Oliver's younger brother has left a deep imprint on him.

Father Dering clears his throat. "The watching of the body," he says carefully. "Do you wish to undertake it yourself? Or would you rather he be taken to the church?"

Abigail hears a muffled sob come from her throat. When Samuel had died, she had sat with his body throughout the night with Ruth by her side. Watching over him. Confirming his death. Ensuring he would not mistakenly be sent to his coffin alive. Keeping vigil over her husband's body had taken almost every ounce of her strength. She cannot fathom doing so for her child.

"Take him," she manages. "Please."

Father Dering takes her arm to steady her. "Of course. Is there anyone from the village you would like me to send to the house? My wife? Or Mrs Mitchell, perhaps?"

"No," Abigail says quickly.

"Are you certain?"

She nods.

The rest happens in a haze: the priest wrapping her son's body. Placing him in the wagon to be taken to the church. Father Dering disappearing from the house, the soft sigh of wagon wheels against the path carved through the dunes. They have come to an unspoken agreement that her son has died of smallpox. Believable enough, Abigail supposes. She has barely shown her face in the village for weeks, months; easy for the villagers to believe she was nursing her ill son.

Abigail goes to her daughter's bedroom. Curls up between the shapes of her sleeping children. She presses herself against Eva's tiny body, inhaling her warmth, trying to settle her own breathing into the same steady rhythm as her daughter's. She cannot be alone in the vast expanse of her own bedchamber tonight, with Oliver's blood staining her pillow.

But nor can she close her eyes and let sleep take away this most unbearable of days. Do so, and she sees Oliver's lifeless body on the floor beside his bed. Sees his eyes, vacant and cold, fixed on nothing. Sees the look of dread on Nathan's face as he turned away from that keyhole.

Instead, she lies awake, staring through the gap in the curtains. Her eyes fixate on the tiny globe of firelight spilling from the shipping beacon on Longstone. And she feels the grief tear open inside her.

CHAPTER TWENTY-EIGHT

When dawn begins to lift the sky, Ward climbs into a longboat. He pulls slowly, steadily on the oars, feeling the pit inside him turn into something heavy and hollow. He shivers, a chill going through him that feels far beyond the effect of the cold dawn air.

The island of Longstone emerges from the cloud like ink in water. In the pale morning, the firebasket is still glowing, a gold glimmer against the sea of white. Ward can just make out the crooked jetty, the stone cottage on its raised foundations, bolstered against the sea.

Already, he is perhaps too close. He does not want to be seen. But he needs a glimpse of what is happening on that island.

He and the other officers have been hunting for Finn since they had left Highfield House last night. They had torn apart the island, searching the dunes and coves and the snarls of the village by lamplight. The tide had been high, and Ward had not imagined Finn had battled the ocean to get onto the mainland. But now he has to consider it a possibility. He knows the boy a capable swimmer.

He also knows there is a chance Finn might have found a boat unattended at the Lindisfarne anchorage and fled back here to Longstone. Unlikely, perhaps, given what Ward knows of the tension between Finn and his father. And perhaps more unlikely that he would not flee further afield. Somewhere the shadow of the *Eagle* cannot reach. Perhaps if Finn is to return to Longstone, to the father he had run from, he will do so once the ship has left these waters.

Ward pulls the oars from the oarlocks and settles them inside the longboat. The boat drifts on the water, caught in a deep stillness that the soft lash of the waves against the boat quickly becomes a part of.

Ward squints in the pale light. No movement from the island. He sees only one small sloop tied up at the jetty, suggesting Finn has not returned home.

Ward blows into his gloved hands to warm them. Is he going after Finn out of concern for his safety, or because he wants him punished? He can't tell. The rage in him, the disappointment, is almost unfathomable. But so, he realises, is his fear for the boy's wellbeing. Because when all is said and done, Finn is still just a child. And the thought of him running, afraid, penniless, makes Ward's stomach knot.

There is a part of him that does not want to find the boy. Because if he is to find him, he will have to make this terrible choice of what to do with him. By all rights, what Finn has done ought to be punished by death. The ship's articles say as much—a killing outside of battle or duel is punishable in kind, even if the death was unintentional. Ward cannot bring himself to even entertain the possibility that Oliver's death was anything other than an accident.

He is not sure he would have the strength to mete out the punishment his own articles say Finn deserves. The right thing? Perhaps. What Abigail would want? Surely. Surely if she got her hands on Finn Murray, she would tie the noose for him herself.

Throughout the sleepless night, Ward has been replaying that moment when he first burst into the room to find Oliver's body. The window was closed, he thinks. Jammed shut. He'd wrenched it open it to call out into the night for Finn. *The window was closed.* Which means Finn could not have used it to escape the house.

But what alternative is there? Had he somehow made it downstairs without anyone noticing? It seems so unlikely.

Or is he wrong about the window? The more Ward thinks on it, the more the memory blurs, and the less sure he is. But what does it matter? Oliver is gone. Finn is gone. And Ward cannot help but blame himself.

Over and over, he has been playing yesterday's choices in his head. His decision to take Finn to the house. His abrupt refusal to take Oliver to sea. His enticing Abigail downstairs when she had been busy tending to her children. How might things be different if, for just one of these instances, he had chosen a different path?

He had meant everything he had said to her about their building a future together. Last night, with her breath on his skin, that future had almost felt tangible. Now, everything has fallen away. Ward wonders if he will ever be welcome at Highfield House again.

He watches the island for a long time, a thousand thoughts colliding inside his head. The sky has lightened completely now, the beacon dwindling against the morning. Ward watches a man—Finn's father, no doubt—emerge from the cottage and trudge across the rocky island towards a small stone shed. As he returns to the house, he seems to catch sight of the longboat loitering on the sea. He strides out across the jetty. Lifts a hand to shade his eyes from the needles of rising sunlight.

He stands motionless for several moments, matching Ward's own inaction.

"Can I help you there?" he calls gruffly. Ward can't tell if the offer is genuine, or a veiled threat.

Ward opens his mouth to call back. To ask about Finn. But something stops him.

Finn is not on the island; this is clear enough. And he has nothing of any use to share with this father who has lost his son. Days ago, yes. He could have told him his boy was safe and well, could have admitted he was the one who had drawn Finn into a life of privateering. But now he has nothing of use to offer his father.

You are a coward, Ward thinks to himself, and the thought is followed by thick pull of self-loathing. But he lifts the oars and settles them back into the sea as silently as possible. Pulls away, averting his eyes from the man standing alone on the edge of that lonely, windblown island.

Which village is this? Finn tries to rattle though the hazy map inside his head. He had passed through Beal after he had swum across from the island, then followed the road north until it vanished into the dark. When dawn had come, he had kept moving. So maybe this cluster of houses is Ancroft or… He doesn't know. All he's sure of is that he has never been so cold in his life.

After he had found the priest hole, and the passage that led out of the house, he'd run across the island without his jacket or boots and leapt into the sea to escape Holy Island. Had spent the night shivering in his wet shirt and breeches. It's a cold that reaches his bones; that makes his thoughts sluggish and tangled. His throat is burning and every muscle in his body aches. The cut on his arm is pulsing. It's stopped bleeding now, but it's left a battlefield of blood on the sleeve of his shirt.

Finn crouches behind a low stone fence, staring at the washing line behind a cottage on a bend in the street. He knows he needs to keep moving. Keep heading north, where Captain Ward will not find him. But he also knows that to do that, he needs boots. Dry clothes. Food.

There's a pair of breeches on the washing line. Shirts flapping in the breeze. In his fevered state, he thinks of the ghosts of pipers, and sails luffing on the mainmast of the *Eagle*. It's a coat he is craving more than anything, but a dry shirt and breeches will be a welcome start.

Finn's eyes dart. He can see smoke puffing from the chimney of the cottage; sees flickers of movement through the cloth window. Over the fence, in and out, he thinks. And no one will be any the wiser.

He is nervous. He's never stolen anything in his life—not if you don't count the French ships and cargo he had been a part of taking. But Captain Ward always said that was patriotism, not theft, because they had a letter of marque.

Captain Ward would thrash him silly if he knew what he was about to do. So would Da. The thought makes his chest ache. Because Finn knows he will never see Da or Captain Ward again. How can he? He can never go home to Longstone now. Captain Ward will be looking for him, waiting to string him up for killing Mrs Blake's son and running away from his crime.

He wonders if all the men he had sailed with feel like this after they fire the cannons and pull the triggers on their pistols. Do they feel this same dark and heavy weight in their bellies at the thought of the lives they have taken? When they lift their tankards to celebrate a victory, are they thinking of men who will never celebrate again?

All Finn knows is that he will carry this on his shoulders for the rest of his life. When he is falling asleep, he will feel that blade pressed to his belly. When he closes his eyes, he will see the boy's head cracking against the bed. And he will feel, always, always, always, that terrible guilt and regret that had broken over him when he had seen the boy's lifeless eyes staring up at his. That desperate need for time to reverse. For that impossible chance to do things differently.

And what is a stolen shirt compared to all this? What point is there trying to be a decent person now? The thought makes him dart over the fence and yank the shirt and breeches from the washing line without another second of hesitation. He runs down the street, his bare feet muddy and sore. Hides behind a tree and wrestles off his damp, bloodstained shirt. Changes into the stolen clothes. A man's clothing—the shirt hangs loose on his shoulders and he has to cinch the lacing of the breeches tight to keep them from sliding over his hips. But they are dry and clean, and that is all that matters.

What now? A coat and boots and food, yes, but after that? How does he go about surviving when he has no place to go and not a penny in his pocket? Finn supposes he will just keep walking. If he keeps going north he will reach Berwick, and that is a town that is big enough to hide in. Perhaps even big enough to find another ship to sail on, or a farmer looking for workers.

He knows Captain Ward has taught him a lot of useful things. Things most lads with his upbringing would never know. Reading and writing, yes, but more than that too: navigation and ship handling and many other things besides. Like how to take orders. And that, Finn thinks, might be the most valuable thing of all.

He puts his head down and starts to walk, his wet clothes bundled up beneath his arm. Just keep walking, he tells himself. Keep walking, and he can put it all behind him: Lindisfarne and Longstone, and his time on the *Eagle*. But the harder he tries to stop the thoughts, the more violently they fly at him, until his mind is full of his father, of Captain Ward, of the boy he had killed. Full of the woman whose son he had taken, and those invisible, sleeping children behind the doors of the house with the passage inside the wall.

CHAPTER TWENTY-NINE

Nathan is wearing his mourning clothes again. They don't hang off his body as much as they did when he was standing at Da's coffin last winter. He can feel his toes pressing into the ends of his shoes now, and his jacket is tighter around his shoulders.

He stands on the edge of the grave with Mama and Eva, just as he had when they had buried Da. Today, though, it does not feel like a mountain is pressing down on his shoulders, or like all the air has gone from his lungs. He wonders if that makes him a bad person. His brother is dead. And yes, he feels a strange hollow, the sense that something has been gouged from his life, never to return. But shouldn't he feel like a mountain is pressing down on his shoulders?

His gaze drifts along the rows of villagers gathered in the churchyard. There are Mr and Mrs Emmett, and Mrs Dering, who had taught him at the petty school. Mrs Calloway is here, dabbing at her eyes with a handkerchief, even though Nathan knows she never liked Oliver. There is Mr and Mrs Mitchell, and Hugh, who would yell insults at Oliver whenever he saw him.

Does Hugh Mitchell feel like something has been gouged out of his life too, now he has no one to yell at in the street? Does he too feel this strange hollow inside him?

Hugh's little sister is standing beside him, winding a piece of red hair around her finger and staring hard at the stamped metal patterns adorning the fabric on the lid of Oliver's coffin. Nathan wonders what she is thinking. She looks up, as though feeling his eyes on her, and Nathan turns away quickly.

Father Dering's robes billow in the wind and make him look like a giant bat. He says, "May God watch over this dear child, taken too soon by a cursed illness."

But Nathan knows it wasn't the illness that had killed his brother. It was the boy from the ship. Oliver had put the Viking knife to the cabin boy's throat, and the cabin boy had swung a fist. Oliver's head had hit the bedpost and—the thought comes before Nathan can catch it—maybe he deserved it. And that, Nathan thinks, definitely, *definitely* makes him a bad person.

Before they had come out here today, Mama had sat him on his bed and pressed her hands down on the mattress beside his, like she was holding his hands but not holding his hands. She was not dressed in the same black gown she had worn for so many days after Da's death. Instead, she was wearing white, because Oliver was an innocent child, or a child at least, and white was the colour you wore when an innocent child was sent back to God.

"Nathan," Mama said, "no one needs to know what you saw the night Oliver…"

Died—he finished the sentence in his head; the sentence she couldn't say.

He just nodded. Did not want to tell anyone what he had seen. The things he saw through the keyhole have been going around and around in his head since that night, and he feels as though speaking about it will give them even more power. He has not spoken about them to anyone. Even Mama has never asked for details of what happened, and Nathan is grateful.

"When people ask, we will tell them Oliver caught the smallpox like Da." Mama's voice was thin and rattly. "Do you understand?"

Yes, he understood. Understood he was to breathe in this lie so much it became the truth. Understood they would not have a wake in the house for Oliver, for people to pray over his body and lay flowers, in case people saw the gash in his head and came to learn how he really died. They would just bury Oliver in the churchyard and the bells would toll, and then he and Mama and Evie would go back to the house to hide away.

Mama tugs him and Eva forward to the edge of the grave. Nods at them to take a handful of the freshly dug earth. Nathan does so obediently, feeling a pull of reminiscence from Da's burial. He looks down at the coffin holding his brother's body. Tries to imagine Oliver inside it. Like being inside the priest hole, he thinks. But forever. That hollowness in his stomach yawns open, and he releases the handful of earth. Watches it flutter down. And as it lands on the lid of the coffin, it seems to make a thud far louder than could ever be possible.

John Graveney leans back against the *Eagle's* saloon and stretches his long legs out in front of him. Blows a slow, steady line of pipe smoke into the sky. A heavy grey is pressing down on the island, and he can't tell if the dampness in the air is trying to be cloud or rain.

He looks up at the sound of approaching footsteps. Quartermaster Hunter grunts like a long-suffering donkey as he lowers himself down beside Graveney, dropping the last few inches with a dull thud.

Graveney chuckles. "All right there, old man?" He takes another quick draw on the pipe before passing it to Hunter.

The quartermaster snorts in response.

Graveney closes his eyes, blowing out the smoke. Tries to let the exhalation settle him.

He's aching to leave Lindisfarne. They've been here more than a week, the ship languishing in the bay beyond the anchorage—keeping their distance from the house, no doubt, after what happened between the two boys. Time is standing still. There's a restless frustration burning under his skin.

This inaction has given him far too much time to think. To think about the prisoners. About his own shifting views. Thoughts he wishes he didn't have. Thoughts that nights at the tavern have been unable to wash away. He wants simplicity: a world where the Williamites are right and the Jacobites are wrong, and he never heard a Catholic prayer murmured on that merchant ship, or thought of his mother praying the rosary.

But he can't find that world any longer. He just hopes that once they're back out at sea, they'll be thrust back into conflict, and he'll be far too immersed in whether he's going to live or die to think about what that life might look like.

Graveney doesn't even know why he's entertaining these thoughts. Leaving Ward's crew is not an option. He's far too deep in debt to step away. Without this regular income, and an officer's position to boot, he'd be curled up on a street corner somewhere in Saint Giles, stealing from the markets to survive.

Creaking davits and footsteps, and Graveney knows Ward has finally returned to the ship. Despite the hounding of his officers, he'd been adamant that they remain on the island. For what purpose, Graveney cannot quite tell. As far as he's aware, Ward hasn't found the courage to face the family in the house again. There seems to be no reason to them being here beyond the captain wallowing in his own bad decisions.

"Here we go," Hunter murmurs to Graveney, scratching at his thready white beard. "About bloody time." He clambers to his feet, leaning on the saloon wall for support, the pipe dangling from his other hand. He shuffles across the deck to meet the captain. Graveney leaps up to follow.

"Come on, Henry," Hunter says firmly, clapping the captain over the shoulder. "We've been here long enough. We've business to attend to in London, aye?"

Ward doesn't speak at once. He looks pale and drawn, with shadows under his eyes and a new slump to his shoulders. Still, his hesitation is something of a victory, Graveney supposes. Yesterday, when he and the other officers had raised the issue of leaving, Ward had lopped off the conversation and marched away without so much as a coherent response.

It had taken days for Graveney to get the full story out of him about what had happened at the house that night. Tucked away in the parlour with a bottle or two of whisky, he and the other officers had had no thought that anything was amiss until Ward had sent them out into the night to search for the cabin boy.

Ward turns to look back at the island, his eyes glassy and faraway. The ruins of the priory are washed by cloud, like a shipwreck in murky water. "I'll have an answer for you shortly," he says. Disappears into the saloon before either man can ask any more questions.

Hunter watches after him. "The man's going to stay here. I'm telling you." He shoves the pipe back into Graveney's hand. "He's going to stay here for the woman in the house. There'll be no more privateering for him. Just you watch."

The comment catches Graveney off guard. For all the captain's brooding, he'd not considered the possibility that Ward might step away from a life at sea. The thought is jarring. Doesn't quite seem to fit. Henry Ward seems like a man who does not exist outside of the confines of his ship. But Graveney knows Abigail Blake has gotten under his skin.

The notion of Ward putting an end to his privateering is an uncomfortable one. But why? Ward's leaving wouldn't mean the rest of the crew would be put out of work. Ward could just send the *Eagle* out with a newly appointed captain and collect the income due to him as the ship's owner. There's nothing about this that makes that street corner in Saint Giles any closer to a reality.

Hunter trudges back towards the saloon as the drizzle gives way to steady rain. "He's a changed man. And you ain't been yourself lately neither."

Graveney thinks to laugh it off. *What are you talking about, old man?*

He hesitates. A moment too long.

Hunter snorts. "You're still wound up over them French prisoners."

Graveney shrugs, trying to make light of the situation. "The ransom could've been made by just holding the *Fortune's* captain and master."

Hunter leans a gnarled hand up against the wall of the saloon, preventing the younger man from passing. "And? What else?"

"There's nothing else."

Hunter snorts. "Bull. You've been on about this for weeks. Something's got you, I know it." He raises thick grey eyebrows, a new look of suspicion in his eyes. "What're you hiding, John?" The words feel far too accusatory. Feel like a threat.

Graveney is relieved when the saloon door creaks open and Ward appears in the doorway. Eyes vacant as he says, "We're to sail at first light."

CHAPTER THIRTY

At first, the house seems impossibly empty. Quieter; unfilled—unfulfilled. A place so weighted by death and loss.

Abigail had chosen not to bury Oliver with Samuel. Had not claimed a place for him at Saint Aidan's, forever beside his father.

In the weeks following Oliver's death, she finds herself questioning, again and again, why she had made this decision. Perhaps she could not bear to go back there so soon, to the churchyard where she had watched her husband's coffin disappear into the earth. Perhaps it just highlighted the cruelty of being forced to bury her son less than a year after she had buried her husband.

No, it was more than that. It was the knowledge that Bamburgh had never been Oliver's home, as it was Samuel's. But it was also the dull knowledge that Samuel and Oliver had never had the kind of relationship Abigail imagined a father and son ought to have. They had never had that innate connection that Nathan and Samuel had shared, that warmth, that easy affection. In her frustration, her anger at her husband, Abigail had told herself Samuel had not tried hard enough. But she knows in truth that Oliver had not allowed it. Even as a young boy, he had never been the kind of child to build close relationships—at least with anyone other than herself. She will never know the kind of man he would have grown into.

Well, she knows. But she can tell herself otherwise.

A part of her had feared that no one would attend her son's burial.

Perhaps she had cut herself off from the village too much. Perhaps Oliver had been too challenging a child for people to wish to mourn him. Perhaps word of the accusations Abigail had flung at Mairi had filtered through the village.

But in the end, she had not buried her child alone. The tolling of the church bells had brought much of the village to Saint Mary's, and many of the same people who had attended Samuel's burial had also been there for Oliver's, including Mairi and Elias Mitchell. Abigail and Mairi had not shared a word beyond rote condolences and murmured thanks. It was far more than Abigail had expected.

In the weeks after his brother's death, Nathan is even quieter than usual, retreating to the distant world of his star maps and telescope. On more than one occasion, she catches him standing outside his brother's room, back pressed to the wall, and a look in his eyes that is at once both vacant and overflowing.

But then, unexpectedly—or perhaps not—he awakens. When they sit down to dinner—the three of them lost within the endless acres of the dining table—he tells her about comets and constellations and moons circling distant planets. She had no idea he knew about such things. Had no idea his and Samuel's love for the skies had extended into such far-reaching parts of the universe. As though encouraged by her brother's intellect, Eva's questions gain a new depth. She asks about seasons and sunrises and the world beyond the island—and how has Abigail missed her daughter turning from an infant into this bright young girl? Oliver's loss is a searing pain inside her, but it makes her even more painfully aware of how much she had been neglecting her other children.

Eva asks many more questions about Oliver's death than she did about her father's. She is nine months older, endlessly more curious. Abigail gives her the simple lie-that-has-become-the-truth she has been giving the villagers. Another fatal bout of smallpox. It's easier to tell Eva her brother died in the same manner as her father. Easier to put it into a neat box, pare it down into something her four-year-old mind will understand. The truth of Oliver's death is one she will never need to know. Abigail will make sure of it.

Lying has always come easily.

She begins to go back to the village. A church service. A visit to the apothecary, the post house. Walking Nathan to the coach that will take him up the coast to the grammar school. Abigail knows her children deserve better to than to live out their lives imprisoned in Highfield House, and there has been no sign of the thieves in the four, five, six weeks since Oliver's death. And while Abigail knows her friendship with Mairi is in pieces, Mairi's civility the day of Oliver's burial has given Abigail the strength to believe nothing will crumble if she dares to show her face in the village again.

Oliver has been gone almost two months when Donald Macauley chases Abigail out of the church after Father Dering's Sunday service. The autumn is careening toward winter, great sacks of cloud hanging low over the ruins of the priory and turning the sea to slate.

"The Baron of Milgate," Macauley says, voice low.

It's a name Abigail has barely thought of in the turbulence of the past two months. But suddenly her thoughts are back in Bamburgh, circling around thieving rings and mud-streaked alleys, and Jacobite donors with overflowing pockets. She swallows hard. Forces herself to keep her composure.

"What about him?" She dares to look at Macauley; an attempt to make light of his comment. The moment she meets his accusatory grey eyes, she regrets it.

Mrs Calloway glances in their direction, a faintly concerned look on her face. Abigail gives her a faint nod, gesturing to her to take the children back to the house. She dares to look back at Macauley. He strides towards the empty far corner of the churchyard, shadowed by the ruins of the priory. Reluctantly, Abigail follows.

"At a meeting among the rebels last night, the Baron asked what his donations were being used for," Macauley tells her. "Says he's donated over two hundred pounds to the cause this year." He pins her with hard eyes. "Our records show he's handed over far less than that amount. And on a number of occasions, he handed the money over to you."

Abigail forces herself to keep her voice level. "What are you implying?"

Macauley snorts. "You know exactly what I'm implying."

She swallows heavily. "I must say, this is all quite flimsy evidence to confront me on."

"Is it? Lord Milgate made the rest of the donations to Mrs Mitchell. And I'm far more inclined to consider you a thief than her."

Abigail tightens her hands into fists. "Why is that, exactly?"

Macauley looks caught off guard by her question. He says, "Where is the rest of the money, Mrs Blake?"

Abigail opens her mouth, the truth on her lips. But something stops her. She knows how lucky she has been that the thieves have not seen fit to come after her. She had almost begun to believe she had put the whole sorry mess behind her.

And if she speaks of them now? If she tells Macauley of the thieving ring and he goes tearing into Bamburgh to take back the Jacobite money? If she does what she promised Lizzie she would never do, and tells people of the ring's existence? She will go back to those long, fearful days of locking herself away in the house. Of fearing for Nathan whenever he is out of sight at school. Of herding Eva inside at every flicker of movement in the garden.

Even after all she has lost, there is still so much they could take from her.

"I took the money," she blurts, before she can change her mind. "I needed it. I was struggling after my husband's death. My settlement was far too small…" It's a neat, convenient story, this faux truth Henry Ward had arrived at. But she knows pity is not about to sway a man like Donald Macauley.

"I can get it back to you," she rushes, before he can get a word out. "Every penny." It's far too much money. *Every penny* will leave her almost destitute. She can manage it, she tells herself. Just. She has the settlement, and the income from the tenants in Chelsea. And, she thinks distantly, she has Henry Ward, and his safe at the Bank of England overflowing with privateering wealth.

But does she? Eight weeks since Oliver's death. Eight weeks and three days, and she has not seen a sign of Henry. Has not heard a word from him. Certainly, he has gone this long without visits before, but these are extenuating circumstances. Surely she must be in his thoughts.

Henry is keeping his distance out of respect for her, she tells herself. Perhaps out of his own guilt. He will give her the space she needs to mourn her son, and then he will return. Surely. Surely he has not disappeared forever. Surely he is not that kind of man.

Isn't he? Somewhere at the back of her mind, an unwelcome voice reminds Abigail of how little she truly knows of Henry Ward.

She finds her gaze drifting instinctively across the water. Finds it empty but for the fishing ketches and dories that usually dot the anchorage.

"Repayment," Donald Macauley says, the word yanking her away from her thoughts of Henry. "Do you really think that is all it will take?"

Fear runs through her. Because she knows that, whatever brand of justice Donald Macauley has in mind, it will not be lawful. How can it be, when he is raising funds for an illegal cause?

"Donald Macauley." Mairi comes striding towards them, eyes darting between him and Abigail. She plants her hands on her hips. "What's all this about?"

"Just addressing some pressing accusations of theft within the Jacobite movement," Macauley says pointedly.

"I see." Mairi's eyes meet Abigail's for a fleeting second. A weighted look. "Leave her be, Donald. She's done nothing wrong. Has the poor woman not been through enough?"

Macauley chuckles. "Ought to know you'd side with her, Mairi, given you were the fool who took her out visiting with you in the first place. I'm sure Elias would like to hear all about Mrs Blake's thievery. No doubt he'd have plenty to say about his wife's choice of friends."

Abigail glances at Mairi and catches the flicker of fear in her eyes she does not manage to hide.

"I can make it up to you," Abigail hears herself say. "I can give you something far more valuable than the money I took from the Jacobites."

"Oh yes? And what might that be?"

"Information. About the Jacobite leanings of a prominent Whig politician. His party would pay handsomely to make sure that information never got out."

Macauley's eyes narrow. "How do you know about that?"

"I read it in a letter. From a Scottish nobleman. A Williamite spy." She hears a sharp inhalation from Mairi.

Macauley rubs his bristled chin, considering her. "How do I know that's not a lie?"

"It's not a lie."

He gives a humourless laugh. "That information's not enough. I need the letter."

"I—" Abigail stops herself from admitting such a thing is impossible. Admitting she no longer has the letter.

Macauley seems to catch hold of her hesitation. "Can you get me that letter?" he asks. "Or was this all a load of rubbish?"

Irritation flickers inside her. "I told you, it's the truth." And then, before she can stop herself: "I'll get you that letter."

"Good," Macauley says finally. "Then you can consider your debts repaid."

Something turns over in Abigail's stomach. "I need a few days."

With each word, her heart beats faster. How can she promise such a thing? The letter is in the hands of the thieving ring. Or lying at the bottom of the sea.

No. Not at the bottom of the sea. Oliver had told her he had given it to Lizzie's mother. And Oliver never lied.

But is the letter being in the thieves' hands really any better than it lying on the ocean floor? In both cases, it is completely unreachable. But right now, all she can cling to is this look of interest in Donald Macauley's eyes. A look that gives her hope she may avoid being hunted down by the Lindisfarne Jacobites.

Macauley nods. Barks out an instruction for her to bring the letter to his farmhouse once she has it. And if nothing else, Abigail knows she has bought herself a little more time.

A little more time to do what, she is unsure. Flee to London and her mother, who still thinks Abigail is married with three children?

Mairi watches Macauley trudge out of the churchyard. She turns to face Abigail, her face unreadable.

Abigail wraps her cloak around her body, trying to slow her heart. "I don't know how to get this letter," she admits. "The thieving ring has it. Oliver gave it to them before he died. In exchange for them staying away from us."

It had worked, she thinks suddenly. She had berated Oliver for his naivety in thinking he could coerce Lizzie and her mother into staying away. But it had worked. The thieves had stayed away as he had promised her they would. Abigail feels something squeeze in her chest.

Mairi is silent for a long moment. Abigail can practically hear her turning her words over in her head, sifting through the validity of them. Finally, she says, "I can help you get the letter back."

Abigail shakes her head. "I couldn't ask that of you. It's far too dangerous. The thieving ring, they—"

"I know," says Mairi. "I know." Two older women look their way as they pass, and Mairi takes Abigail's arm, tugging her out of the churchyard. She pulls her into the shadows beneath shopfront awnings on Church Lane. "I can get into the thieving ring," she says finally.

Abigail's lips part. She doesn't speak; just lets Mairi's words fall into place. "You are involved with them," she hisses. It's not shock she is feeling. It's not shock at all. Just anger. Hot and fierce. "Were you the one who sent them after me in the first place?"

Mairi's silence is all the answer Abigail needs.

No, of course it's not shock. Because when she had first told Mairi about the thieving ring, Mairi had not asked questions. Elias and Donald Macauley had not come seeking more information about these thieves who were targeting the Jacobite cause. Had not come asking about when it had happened, or what she had seen. Of course they hadn't. Because Mairi had not spoken of the ring to anyone. Why would she? Why risk revealing her own involvement?

Mairi toys with the lacing on her shortjacket. Eyes down, she says, "I'm sorry. I never intended it to go as far as it did. Young Lizzie, she was under pressure from some of the men in the ring for not bringing in enough coin. I sent her your way after you went to see Lord Milgate. I knew they'd be especially pleased with Lizzie if she handed over money intended for the Jacobites. And I knew you'd not hurt her."

Abigail smiles wryly to herself, thinking of the way she had shoved Lizzie up against the wall of the house. Thinking of how close she had come to hurting her. "Why?" she demands. "Why in hell would you do such a thing? You and your husband are staunch Jacobites."

Mairi lets out her breath at Abigail's raised voice. "My husband is a staunch Jacobite," she says in a sharp whisper. "I've little choice but to go along with what he believes. At least outwardly."

In spite of herself, Abigail feels a fragment of her anger give way.

Mairi presses a hand up against the wall of the shop, as though to support herself against the truths she is about to admit to. "The Jacobite cause was never mine," she says. "It was always Elias's. Since the Revolution, it's all he's talked about. And after Dunkeld, it just consumed him. He came home from the war to a newborn daughter and barely even looked at her. Was far more fixated on the men who'd been lost than he was on poor Julia. He's been like that ever since. Barely a kind word for the children. Never one for me." She shakes her head, lost in her own thoughts. "He forced me into the fundraising. But why would I wish to raise money for a cause that took my husband from me?" Bitterness in her words now. "Helping the thieving ring feels like a way of taking back some small piece of what's owed to me."

For a long time, Abigail doesn't speak. She feels betrayed. She feels angry. She feels afraid. Feels the ocean of grief that has been a constant for every minute of this year surge and roll inside her. She wants to walk away. Never go near Mairi Mitchell again. But she knows she has little choice. She needs to get that letter back from the thieves—in the desperate hope they have not sold it. And the only way she will do that is with Mairi's help.

"Meet me at the Pilgrims' Way tomorrow morning," Mairi says, before Abigail can find a response. "We're going to Bamburgh. We're going to get your letter back."

CHAPTER THIRTY-ONE

Today, there is no easy chatter as Abigail and Mairi cross the Pilgrims'
Way in the wagon. Today, there is just a stilted wordlessness, filled with
all the questions that are storming around inside Abigail's head. Mairi has
not brought her baby with her today, and his absence feels notable. Feels
like they are heading into danger.

Despite the November chill, it's a hideously bright day, with sun
pouring into the wagon and making the wet sand of the Pilgrims' Way
shimmer in the light. This does not feel like a day that ought to be filled
with sunshine. There ought to be clouds and shadows and rain that keeps
prying eyes out of the streets.

"Tell me everything you know about the ring," Abigail says finally.
They have almost crossed onto the mainland, and it is the first time she
has opened her mouth since she climbed into the wagon.

Mairi looks down into clasped hands. Much of what she tells Abigail
is the same as Oliver had told her: a ring of thirty or more, active in
Bamburgh and the surrounding villages. Their thievery ranging from
simple pickpocketing to embezzlement. Many of them widows and
orphans of the Jacobite movement, seeking whatever meagre retribution
they can muster.

"The day you sought me out in the village to see how I was faring. The
day you first spoke to me about raising funds for the Jacobites." Abigail
presses her lips together at the effort of keeping her composure. Her
control comes from a need for answers, rather than any desire to be polite.

"Did you only do that in the hope I'd join the cause?"

"No," Mairi says hurriedly. "Of course not. I swear it. I only wanted to make sure you and the children were coping after Samuel's passing." There's a look of such intensity in her eyes that Abigail cannot help but believe her. However reluctantly. "When I spoke of the fundraising that day, I had no intention of involving you. The thought had not even crossed my mind. You were the one who showed an interest in the movement."

"So you thought you'd invite me along and send the thieves on my trail?"

Mairi doesn't answer. Does not need to answer.

Abigail blows out a breath. "I don't understand. If you do not want the Jacobite cause to succeed, why bring me with you to raise more money? Why not just give the ring a cut of what you yourself are taking from the donors?"

Mairi picks at something beneath her thumbnail. Avoids Abigail's eyes. "It's what I've been doing for years," she admits. "A lot of the money the ring takes helps the women and children left behind by the war. I wanted to take from the Jacobite cause, yes. But I wanted to help the people that needed it too." She begins to gnaw at her thumbnail. "I could tell Elias was becoming suspicious about the amount of money I was handing over. And I was afraid he'd find out that the records did not match what the donors were handing over—as Donald discovered with you and Lord Milgate. I thought that if I brought you along, I could still get the money to the ring for the people who needed it. And I could hand over enough from the donors that Elias and Donald would no longer question me."

Abigail does not answer immediately. Her anger is far too raw, far too sharp to cobble together anything coherent. And she knows that if she does not take a moment here to breathe, to consider, she will say something she will regret.

Perhaps she will not regret it that much.

"And here I thought you were trying to make a friend of me," she says finally. "Trying to help me get past the loss of my husband." Her words come out dripping with bitterness. She does not attempt to hold it back. "Have you any idea of the trouble you've caused me and my family?"

"I'm sorry," says Mairi. Her freckled cheeks are flushed with shame.

"I truly am. Causing you and your children trouble was the last thing in the world I meant to do." When Abigail doesn't speak, Mairi leans forward, pinning intent eyes on her. "This letter. How did you get your hands on it?"

"That's no business of yours," Abigail says tightly. "You just need to help me get it back."

Mairi nods resignedly. "Of course." She sits back on the bench, chastened.

Abigail leans against the side of the wagon, pulling her cloak tight around her. Her body rattles with the movement of the wagon. It feels as though the darkness inside her is pulsing, trying to find an escape. "Oliver said he gave the letter to Lizzie's mother. Do you know her?"

"Yes. Ailith. She lives at the far end of Church Wynd. I can get into the place without difficulty. She'll welcome me in." Mairi speaks quietly, gently, as though ashamed of all she is saying. "Ailith is one of the ring's record-keepers. She's smart. Well-educated. But she married beneath her and lost everything after her husband died at Killiecrankie. She keeps a box safe under one of the flagstones beside the hearth. Keeps the takings there until they can be divided up between the ring members. I'm sure that will be where she's keeping your letter."

"Oliver gave her the letter more than two months ago. She might well have sold it by now."

"No." Mairi shakes her head. "She's not sold it. It's far more valuable for them to keep it."

Abigail purses her lips. "She's told you about the letter before, hasn't she."

It is not a question, but Mairi nods anyway. Guilt in her eyes. "I knew of the letter. But I didn't know it came from you and Oliver until you told Donald about it yesterday." She shifts awkwardly on the bench seat. "Ailith and the others are holding tight to it to get themselves out of a difficult situation," she says. "In case the redcoats come looking." She looks squarely at Abigail. "We'll get the letter back. I promise. And we'll see to it that Donald doesn't come after you again."

It's risky, Abigail knows, trusting Mairi like this. The women in the thieving ring are friends of hers. Women whose families have become broken and disillusioned by the Jacobite cause, just as Mairi's has.

But Abigail knows she has no choice. She has promised Donald Macauley the letter, and she must find a way to deliver.

"I'll call on Ailith first," says Mairi. "Do her best to get her and Lizzie out of the house. There's a cloth window that leads from the alley into the kitchen. You'll be able to get inside through there."

Abigail nods.

Mairi looks at her pointedly. "Make sure you put everything in the house back just as you found it," she says. "I can't have Ailith getting suspicious of me. She can't know the letter's been stolen until I'm long gone. I can't have anyone from that ring coming after me. Or my children."

CHAPTER THIRTY-TWO

She wishes Oliver were here. Of course she does; she wishes it every minute of every day, with a desperation she did not know she was capable of.

But right now, she wishes it even more than usual.

Because Oliver would know what to do. Would know how to handle these people.

She closes her eyes, fighting back a swell of self-loathing. How can she be thinking such things? If Oliver were here, she ought to be keeping him as far away as possible from such things. Perhaps if she had kept a closer eye on him from the beginning, he would not have gotten involved with the thieves in the first place. Would not have given them the letter. Would not have become the kind of boy to take a knife from the water and wave it around and—

No. She is not going down that deep, dark tunnel of regret. Not now. It will do no one any good, and she needs a clear head if she is going to do as she needs to.

Abigail waits on the corner of the Wynd, crouching at the corner of the cottage opposite Ailith and Lizzie's. She can see Mairi on the doorstep, speaking to someone unseen. Mairi is smiling, laughing, waving a hand around as she speaks. Then she and Ailith step out of the cottage and head down the Wynd towards the village.

Abigail hesitates. Where is Lizzie? Is she still in the house? Was Mairi unable to convince her to leave?

She has no idea. Either way, this is her only opportunity to get the letter back. Abigail reaches into her pocket for Oliver's knife. Hates that there's a part of herself that longs to use it.

She hurries across the narrow street towards the cottage, shoes sighing through the mud. Squeezes herself down the narrow gap between Lizzie's cottage and the next. Towards the back of the house, she sees the narrow window covered in its colourless cloth.

Abigail stands motionless for several moments, listening for any sound inside the house. She hears the shout of a young boy from the other end of the street. A dog barking in the distance. Nothing from inside the house.

She takes the knife from her pocket and slices carefully along the bottom of the cloth, severing it from the nails holding it to the window frame. She pulls back a corner and dares to peek inside.

A thick gloom hangs over the cottage. A crooked table, cluttered with unwashed stew bowls and a burned-out candle, takes up most of the space. A grate holds a dwindling fire, pots and a kettle resting on the blackened stones of the hearth. The air is soured with the smell of old meat and wet wool. Ash and unwashed bodies. Abigail's gaze darts across the flagstones. Which of those hides the box safe?

Her gaze travels to a narrow doorway at the far end of the room. The bedroom, she guesses; there are no sleeping mats or washstands here in the kitchen. She holds her breath, waiting for Lizzie to appear. A cold wind whips suddenly through the alley, fluttering the loose cloth over the window.

When there is nothing but silence and stillness, Abigail hoists herself up onto the window frame. She swings her legs awkwardly over the sill, skirts tangling around her calves. Lands with a soft thud on the flagstones of the kitchen.

Fingers tight around the knife, she edges towards the grate. Kneels beside the fire, running the knife around the edges of the flagstones to find the loosened tile.

In the far corner, she feels it. Feels the blade of the knife slide beneath the stone. The smallest tile, thankfully; light enough to prise up with the knife to reveal the small ditch dug into the earth below. A wooden box sits inside the hole, fastened with nothing more than a simple latch.

Abigail leans the loose flagstone up against the wall and pulls out the box safe. Shoots a glance over her shoulder. Then she turns back and opens the box.

There's little in the safe beyond a small pouch of coins, and a spring watch she suspects is worth pennies. But there between them, lying on its side, is Henry Ward's brass box. Abigail lets out a murmur of relief she is unable to hold back. She snatches it out of the safe and opens the lid. There is the letter, neatly folded. She fastens the clasp again and buries it in her pocket.

Abigail shoves the safe back into the hole. She wrestles the flagstone towards her, easing it downwards. Cringes as it groans against the floor.

The sound is replied to by a volley of snoring, coming from what Abigail assumes is the bedroom. A man's snoring. Far too deep and loud to be Lizzie's.

The sound freezes her for a moment, then she flies into action, leaping to her feet and rushing back across the cottage. She heaves herself up through the window, landing heavily in the damp earth of the lane beside the house.

She stops for a moment, gathering her breath. *Run.* She has the letter. Has made it out without being caught. But the cloth of the window is fluttering in the breeze and the moment Ailith sees it, she will know someone has been here. She will suspect Mairi had lured her out of the house to allow thieves into the cottage.

There's a part of her that doesn't care. A part that's telling her to run, regardless. To put her own safety first. After all, Mairi had put Abigail's family in danger from the thieving ring. Why not do the same to her?

But it's this internal argument Abigail has been fighting against her entire life. This need to betray, to retaliate, to put her own selfish needs first. Mairi might be guilty of deceiving her, but her four young children are not.

Abigail fumbles with the window cloth, hurriedly yanking it downwards and hooking the torn edges over the nails on the sill. It's a sloppy, temporary solution. But perhaps it will save Ailith and Lizzie— and whoever is sleeping in that bedroom—from immediately discovering someone has been here. Perhaps it will buy her and Mairi a little time.

Abigail hurries back towards the anchorage, keeping the hood of her cloak pulled up to hide herself. She has no thought of how long Mairi will be, or where she has gone, but she can hide herself in the wagon until she shows herself.

As she is approaching the anchorage, she hears, "Mrs Blake."

She holds her breath. Keeps striding past the harbourside tavern.

"Mrs Blake!" Footsteps come thumping towards her, forcing Abigail to look up. Lizzie stops walking as she reaches her, breathless. "Aye, I thought it was you."

Abigail's heart is suddenly thundering. Had Lizzie been in the house too? Has she followed her here from the Wynd? Or has she just crossed her path in the street?

The look in the girl's eyes is not a threatening one. It's something far closer to pity. And something else too. Sadness?

"Is it true?" she asks. "What happened to Oliver?"

Abigail swallows heavily. Is it true? There's never been any truth about *what happened to Oliver.*

She wonders what Lizzie has heard, and from who. From Mairi, she supposes. Unless there are others on Lindisfarne entangled in the ring.

She gives Lizzie nothing more than a faint nod. Digs her hands into her cloak pockets—one tight around the box, the other around Oliver's knife.

"I'm sorry," says Lizzie. "I truly am." There's a depth to her voice Abigail has not heard before. A genuineness. "He was a good person."

Abigail lets out her breath. "You met because he was teaching you to pick the pockets of funeral-goers."

Lizzie's lips part. "Aye, but…" She trails off, shifting uncomfortably.

"Oliver was not a good person, Lizzie," says Abigail, hearing her voice crack. "But neither are you and I. That's why we both understood him as we did."

Lizzie hesitates for a moment. Gives a faint nod. Then, though she has just glimpsed a part of herself she would rather not acknowledge, she turns and hurries back into the winding streets of the village.

CHAPTER THIRTY-THREE

Abigail and Mairi barely speak on the way back to Lindisfarne. As they rattle out of Bamburgh, Abigail can see the tide beginning to creep towards the castle. She wills the coachman to hurry so they can get to the Pilgrims' Way before the rising water cuts Lindisfarne off from the mainland. The last thing she needs is to be stranded off the island in Mairi Mitchell's company.

Abigail grips the brass box until her knuckles whiten. Henry's box. Henry's letter. He has no idea of all the strife it has caused her. Will she ever get the chance to tell him?

"Was there any trouble?" Mairi asks finally. It feels as though she has been trying to gather the courage to ask the question since they had first climbed into the wagon.

"Nothing I couldn't handle."

Abigail toys with the lock on the front of the box. What had Oliver used to open it, she wonders? It's a question she will never have the answer to.

The moment she steps onto the island, she thinks, she will go to the Macauleys' farm. Hand over the letter. And then? If ever the thieves were going to come for her, it will be now. Now, that she has broken into Ailith's house. Stolen from the box safe. Taken back the precious letter. And been seen in the village by Lizzie.

Run away. Leave this place. The thought swings at her suddenly. Surely staying here is the height of foolishness. But she cannot bear the thought of returning to London and the grip of her mother's talons. More than that, she cannot bear the thought of disappearing without another word to Henry Ward.

She needs to see him. Needs to speak to him. Needs to tell him that sending him away that night was a mistake. And she needs to find out if *there is a place for you in my future* is still a reality. Because right now, the possibility of that future is all that is keeping her afloat.

Yes, she can leave word for Henry with his buyer, telling him of her whereabouts. But she knows there's no certainty he will return to Lindisfarne now, after she had sent him away. And she could not bear the uncertainty of never knowing if he has read her words.

She shakes Henry out of her head. Dwelling on that future—or lack thereof—right now will only cause her to make mistakes.

"Can I trust Donald Macauley?" she asks Mairi suddenly. "If I give him this letter, can I be certain he'll not come after me and my family?"

Mairi nods. "Aye. You can. He's something of a brute, but he's a man who keeps his word."

Abigail nods brusquely. It does not feel right to thank her. They sit in silence for the rest of the journey.

Abigail is on her way to the Macauleys' farm when she sees him. At the sight of him, she freezes, hand clenching around the brass box.

She has seen Noah Murray on Holy Island many times before, of course. Had heard of his wife's death, his son's disappearance. Had felt some indifferent, obligatory pity for the tragedy of him. Beyond that, she has barely paid him a second glance.

Now, the sight of the Longstone lightkeeper has her breathless. This is the father of the boy who had killed her child.

A tangle of emotions threatens to overwhelm her. She wants to fly at him, hurl abuse, hurl her fists. Blame him for everything.

She wants to tell him his son is alive.

His son is alive when hers is not.

She can tell him no such thing, of course. Could never face the questions that would come. Not least because she has no idea how to answer them. Really, she has no piece of useful knowledge to give the lightkeeper about his child; cannot even assure him the boy is still alive. If Henry Ward has had his way, there is every chance he may not be.

The man is headed in the direction of the anchorage, a brown woollen cap pulled low on his head and a large tarred greatcoat swamping his body. Dark hair hangs loose down his back, grey-flecked stubble across his cheeks.

He looks up as he crosses Abigail's path. Glances at her, as though feeling her intense gaze on him. He says nothing, and it occurs to her that he likely has no idea who she even is. Certainly, they have never exchanged a single word. Noah Murray is known to everyone on Lindisfarne, of course; the man who had built his home on the pellet of Longstone, and keeps the beacon blazing to light the dark sea. Who is she but the woman who haunts the house on the head?

She closes her eyes. Tries to breathe against the tide of fresh grief the sight of the lightkeeper has brought.

He strides past her, and before Abigail knows what she is doing, she says, "Your son. I've seen him." This has to be done, she realises. She has no real knowledge to give him, nothing that can assure him of his child's safety. But she can give him a glimmer of information. A glimmer of hope. And what she wouldn't give to have a glimmer of hope for her lost son.

Noah stops walking. Turns back to face her. His eyes are widened, lips parted. "You've seen Finn?"

"I have. But not… It's been many weeks."

"Where?"

She tightens her fingers around the box containing the letter. "He was here on the island. Sailing as a privateer's cabin boy. But he's not… He's not a part of that crew anymore."

"Why not? Where is he now? Where'd he go?" She hears the urgency, the desperation in the man's voice.

Abigail draws in a breath. She could tell him everything. Tell him all that happened that horrible night. And what will that achieve? The information will not help the lightkeeper find his son.

She knows the weight of being the parent of a lawbreaker. She does not want Noah Murray to carry that weight too.

"I don't know where he is," she says. "I'm sorry. But he is alive." At least, he was on that bleak September night.

The lightkeeper's eyes bore into her, and for a long time, he doesn't speak. Abigail feels the fierce urge to turn away, to escape the intensity of his stare. But she feels rooted in place. Finally, Noah nods. "Thank you." There's disappointment in his voice, and weight. But perhaps that fragile glimmer of hope too.

Abigail replays their conversation over and over in her head as she passes through the village. Regrets it with one step, is glad to have done it with the next.

Out ahead of her, she can see the narrow path leading to the Macauleys' farm. She slows her pace. Her encounter with the lightkeeper has made her rattled and tearful, and the last thing she wants is to face Donald Macauley in such a state. For all she tries to convince herself of her own strength, she knows Macauley would not have to try too hard to tear her down today.

As she tries to find the courage to continue on towards the farm, she hears: "Mama!"

And when she turns to sees Nathan and Eva behind her with Mrs Calloway, it takes everything in her not to sprint to their sides. She is not sure she has ever been so glad to see them. Having her children close feels suddenly so fleeting, so fragile. So precious.

They hammer towards her and she bends to gather Eva into her arms, gesturing for Nathan to come close. Doesn't bother to wipe the tears that spill without warning down her cheeks.

Mrs Calloway trots down the road to catch up with them. "Have you more errands to run, Mrs Blake?" she asks. "Shall we see you back at the house?"

Abigail gathers up the brass box she had dropped on the path in her hurry to embrace her daughter. "No," she tells the nurse. "I shall take the children home myself." She shoves the box into her pocket and clasps her fingers around Eva's. "I can finish the rest of my errands in the morning."

CHAPTER THIRTY-FOUR

Nausea has her tearing out of bed to the chamber pot and she knows she cannot deny it to herself any longer.

Abigail tells herself it's grief, it's fear, it's anger. And yes, perhaps it's all those things. But she also knows Henry Ward's child is stirring inside her. Somewhere in the back of her mind, she has been aware of this for days. Weeks, perhaps. Has not found the strength to accept it. But she knows there is little point in pretending any longer.

Her youngest child, conceived as her eldest had died.

She closes her eyes. Breathes. Presses her forehead against the cool stone of the bedroom wall.

Run away. Leave this place.

Does she have any other option? Never mind the fact that she had stolen from the thieving ring yesterday—it will only be a matter of time before the villagers come to see she is carrying a child that cannot be her husband's. She can only imagine what they will think of her then. And she refuses to bring shame to Samuel's good name.

Really, *run away* is all there is. All there can be. But how can she disappear without telling Henry about his child?

She hunches beside the bed, watching dawn light squeeze through the curtains and pick out the shapes of her bedroom. Rain is pattering against the windows, and she tries to let the calm rhythm of it soothe her.

She hovers by the chamber pot until the sickness has passed, then splashes her face at the washbin and rinses her mouth. Ties a robe around her to ward off the chill of the house and empties the chamber pot into the garderobe. She has no intention of leaving the task for Ruth, and facing any questions that might arise.

As she is making her way back to her bedchamber, in an attempt to force out another hour of sleep, a knock at the door echoes through the house. Abigail panics. Who would be here at this time? The sun has barely risen, and the rain has grown louder against the windows. Ruth has not yet arrived, and the house is cold and lifeless.

Abigail finds Mairi on the doorstep. Her cheeks are flushed, eyes wild. Rain drips off the brim of her bonnet. She steps inside without waiting to be invited.

"The letter," she says, breathless, "have you given it to Donald yet?"

"No." Abigail pushes the door closed behind her, silencing the lash of the sea. "I planned to take it to him this morning."

"You can't give it to him. Please."

"Why?"

Mairi paces back and forth across the foyer, barely looking at Abigail. Rainwater trails off the hem of her cloak, leaving a silver trail across the flagstones. "One of the Northumbrian Jacobites was arrested late last night," she says. "He was intercepted carrying messages meant for the movement in London."

Abigail swallows heavily.

"There'll be more arrests," says Mairi. "For certain. The redcoats know the movement is active up here again. If Donald and Elias are arrested and they have the letter, they'll use it to blackmail the authorities for their freedom."

Abigail frowns, not understanding. "That could save their lives."

"It will draw unwanted attention to this village," Mairi says bitterly. "It will put far too many people in danger. Perhaps even those who are not involved in the cause." She winds her hands into her tartan cloak. "If Elias is caught, he ought to be punished. It's not right for him to put others in danger for his own safety." She looks at Abigail with piercing green eyes. "You must think me a terrible person for doing this to my husband. But I've been trying to get Elias out of the movement since Dunkeld. For the good of our children. He'll not do it. Won't even listen to all I have to say." She turns away, scrubbing a hand across her face and leaving a smear of mud against one cheek. "Heaven, what you must think of me to be saying all this after all you've lost. But I—"

"Mairi." Abigail snatches her arm to stop her pacing. "I don't care what you want for your husband," she says tautly. "But I promised Donald Macauley that letter. If I don't hand it over like I promised, I'm afraid of what he will do to me. To my children." She looks desperately at Mairi. "I can't lose anyone else."

"I'll see to it that Donald doesn't come after you. I swear it."

"How?"

"I don't know," Mairi admits. "But I need you to trust me. I don't want my husband to get his hands on that letter. I don't want him to know anything about it."

I need you to trust me. Abigail almost laughs. She does not trust Mairi an inch. Nor does she have any faith in her ability to keep Donald Macauley at bay.

But it doesn't matter, she realises suddenly. None of it matters. Not anymore. Because *run away* is all there is.

"Tell Donald I could not get the letter back," Abigail says brusquely. "Or tell him I lied about its existence. Let him think I stole the money for my own purposes. It doesn't matter what he thinks of me. Or my family. I cannot stay here any longer."

Mairi frowns. Her voice softens. "Abby, you don't need to leave." Guilt in her eyes, her words. "I'll see to it that Donald and Elias—"

"I do need to leave. For many reasons." She pins Mairi with a look that tells her not to ask questions. "I just need a few days to put things in order. Can you keep Donald away from me until then?"

Mairi hesitates. After a moment, she nods. "Of course. If that's what you need." Her lips part, as though debating whether to ask more questions. But she just lurches forward, pulling Abigail into her arms. Abigail stiffens in her embrace. "Take care, Abby." Mairi's voice wavers. "And I'm sorry for everything."

Not handing the letter over to Macauley feels dangerous. Foolish. But Abigail can't deny there is something faintly steadying about having it tucked back into her nightstand where it should always have been.

Somehow, it gives her space to breathe.

Donald Macauley might come for her. The thieving ring might come for her. But she will not have to admit to Henry Ward that she cannot be trusted. And right now, this feels like the most pressing thing of all.

She sits at the desk in her husband's study. Barely any trace of Samuel in here now. The scent of his tobacco has faded, the indentations on the chair have been replaced with her own. Perhaps he is still here, if she looks hard enough. Perhaps he has faded because her thoughts are circling around another man.

No time for guilt now, or for reminiscence. Samuel is gone. Oliver is gone. She has another son or daughter on the way, and she needs to ensure her child grows up knowing their father.

Henry will not come to the house; she knows that now. Or at least, she fears it. In any case, she does not have the time to wait around for his ship to reappear; for him to fight past his regret and return to her doorstep. She cannot wait for the Jacobites, or the thieving ring, to beat him to the house. And she cannot wait for the child inside her to grow, and betray her as the woman who had taken to bed a man who is not her husband.

She will tell Henry, yes. Will write him a letter and tell him everything, raw and unfettered. And she will find out if her lost son had been speaking the truth when he had said that Henry Ward loves her.

She stares down at the blank page. She will make two copies of this letter. Will ask Henry's buyer to hold on to one copy, in case the *Eagle* comes north again to sell their cargo. The second, she will send ahead to London. Deposit it in the bank safe, in her son's name.

The plan is sound—or at least as sound as it can be. As secure a way to get word to Henry as she can manage. Not secure enough, of course. It will never be secure enough. Not unless she can look him in the eye and tell him everything face to face. But she has no time. No choice.

How does she go about a letter like this one? Straight to the point, or meandering around the issues?

She wants Henry to know all of it: of his child, of her feelings for him, of the way she wishes—needs—that future they had discussed to become a reality. The way she has no choice but to leave Lindisfarne. Not a single piece of it feels like the kind of information she ought to be conveying through a letter. *No time*, she reminds herself. *No choice.*

In the end, she decides on the same openness and honesty she has committed to each of her previous letters to him. It is so much harder given she is intending, unlike the others, for this letter to actually reach him. But once she begins to write, the words pour from her quill, filling the page with a sea of sloping letters and careless inkblots. She tells him of the thieving ring, of her true reason for stealing from the Jacobites. Tells him of the adventure his little brass box has been on. She tells him of the child she is carrying inside her.

She sets the quill back into the ink and leans back in her chair, suddenly drained. She reads over the letter as the ink dries. Soon, she thinks, she will repeat the process. Will write Henry a second letter to send on to London. But not today. Today, already, she is worn through with emotion and exhaustion. Getting the letter to the office of Henry's buyer feels like a monumental undertaking. But it must be done.

She folds and seals the page. Tucks it in her pocket and stands to fetch her cloak and bonnet.

CHAPTER THIRTY-FIVE

Ward wakes drenched in sweat, the bedsheets tangled and lying on the cabin floor. He has no recollection of what he had dreamt about—all he knows is it has left him with a sense of dread pressing down on him.

Daylight is flooding through the windows, and he reaches for the spring watch on the stand beside the bed. Almost noon. He's only slept three hours.

He sits up, scrubbing a hand across his eyes. His body feels weighted with lead, but he has no desire for more sleep—not if that sleep is going to be peppered with unidentifiable horrors.

He'd had nightmares like this as a much younger man; the same imageless, formless dreams that would cause him to wake in terror. Back then, he'd put it down to the stress of not meeting his father's rigid expectations. Now, though he has no conscious recollection of what he has been dreaming about, he's fairly certain it features Oliver Blake's glacial blue eyes staring lifeless at the ceiling of his bedchamber.

No more sleep. Since Oliver's death—since the night Abigail had cast him from her house with that look of blame in her eyes—Ward has learnt to exist on whatever scraps of sleep he can snatch—not that he has ever managed to cobble together more than a few consecutive hours when he is at sea. In any case, they will be coming up on Lindisfarne soon.

Ward goes to the washbin and splashes his face with cold water, trying to slough away that lingering anxiety. There's a restlessness in his chest he knows has little to do with his nightmares, and everything to do with the choices he is on the verge of making. He turns towards the bank of windows in the stern of the ship, trying to soak in a little sunlight. The flimsy rays that struggle into the cabin bring little warmth with them. Little light.

He pulls on a fresh shirt and rakes his fingers through the waves of his hair, tying it into a loose queue at his neck. When he has his boots and breeches on, and has managed to conjure up a little steadiness, he opens the door of the great cabin.

Instinctively, he opens his mouth to call for Finn. Stops himself at the last moment. More than two months since his cabin boy has been gone, and the ache of the loss has not yet begun to fade. He marches down to the ward-robe, seeking out Quartermaster Hunter. Does his best not to think of his cabin boy, and where he might have ended up.

Ward takes Hunter back to the great cabin. Locks the door behind them. "I'm handing command of the ship over to you," Ward says, before either of them have even managed to take a seat at the table.

Hunter nods slowly. There's no shock in his eyes.

Little wonder. Ward is well aware of how distant and distracted he has been since Oliver's death. He's made more than one bad decision at the helm—sailed headlong into dangerous weather; gone after targets far more heavily gunned than the *Eagle*. He's mildly surprised they've returned from the latest voyage in one piece. Suspects they wouldn't have if Hunter hadn't stepped in to make his captain see sense on more than one occasion.

Ward slides onto the bench at the table, nodding for Hunter to join him. "You'll need to apply for your own commissions," Ward says. "And you'll be free to choose your crew as you see fit. Take whichever of the men you wish."

Hunter scratches the white bristles on his chin. "When?"

"I'll be leaving the ship when we land in Northumberland tonight."

Hunter raises his bushy eyebrows. "These men still have four months left on their articles of agreement."

"Yes." Ward nods, feeling a tug of shame. The men will not be happy at having their agreements cut short, of course. He wishes he could make himself care a little more. But he knows now, with deep certainty, that this life is not the one he wants.

When he was a younger man, trying to scrape together a life that would please his father, he had wanted success at any cost. But he has had that success now, and he feels nothing but hollowness. His father is long in his grave, and still Ward is fighting to prove himself to some outside entity.

It had been a thrill once, this existence. But now it just makes him think of death and loss. Just makes him think of how precious and fleeting life is, and how he must find the strength to turn towards what he truly wants.

The thought of existing without the sea is a strange and hazy one. But he has full ownership of the *Eagle*, and for that, he will be paid a cut of Hunter's takings. Coupled with the money locked away in his account in London, it will be plenty to build a good life for him and Abigail. For Nathan. For Eva.

He has no idea how Abigail will react when he knocks on her door tonight. He knows there is every chance the sight of him will send her back to that dreadful night two months ago, and she will cast him from her home once again.

Even though Ward knows this is a distinct possibility, the only way he can find the strength to do this is to trust that the life he longs for will become a reality. He must make the necessary arrangements with Hunter. Must pack his belongings and prepare to leave the ship. Prepare himself to face whatever criticism he will receive from the crew when they learn he is to slice their agreements in half.

Somewhere in the back of his mind, he is toying with the alternative. Entertaining that bleak vision of what his life will look like if Abigail turns him away. He will not stay in England, that much is clear. He will take the *Eagle* to faraway colonies. Operate out of the Caribbean. And perhaps his bitterness, his despair, will reshape him. Rub shoulders with buccaneers. Blur the line between privateering and piracy.

No. That is a line he never wishes to cross. He pushes the thought away.

"What of the sale of the cargo?" Hunter asks. "Will you see to that before you leave?"

"No." He needs to do this now, before he changes his mind. "I shall leave that in your hands. Divide the takings between these men, and then you'll be free to choose your crew as you wish."

Abigail trudges through the mud of the dunes to deliver the letter. Wind whips up from the water, stinging her cheeks and turning the tip of her nose numb.

Her eyes dart as she crosses the open greenery. She is wary of Donald Macauley appearing to string her up for not handing over the Jacobite letter. Mairi had promised to keep him away from her, she reminds herself. Plus, he himself had given her a few days to produce the letter. And before those few days are up, she will be gone.

This thought, this resoluteness, keeps her moving forward, trudging over the wet grass with her skirts pulled high above her ankles.

She will deliver the letter to Henry's buyer, then return to the house and begin to pack. What else? A second letter to Henry, of course, to be left in the safe in London. But that can be written on the long journey south. She must write to the grammar school notifying them that Nathan will not be returning. Must write to Samuel's lawyer, asking him to see that the house in Chelsea is vacated. Letters of reference for Ruth and Mrs Calloway, along with their final payments. As for the possibility of leasing Highfield House, she will make a decision about that later. She doubts Samuel's lawyer will have any luck finding tenants to fill such an isolated and sea-blown wreck. She has never been able to see the allure of the place, the way Samuel and his cousin could. Perhaps, she thinks, you must have the Blakes' blood coursing through you to see the magic in Highfield House. No part of her will be sad to leave the place behind.

It all makes simple sense, this plan. All makes simple sense, as long as she doesn't think too hard on the contents of the message she is leaving for Henry. All she is telling him. Asking him. All the vulnerability she is showing him. This was a far less terrifying thing when she was determined to keep him at a distance.

Then of course, there is the issue of her mother. Abigail has no thought of how she will even begin to explain everything that has happened in the past year. Perhaps it's for the best that Susanna believes her still tucked away up in Northumberland with her husband and three children. Perhaps it's best that their lives never intersect again. Abigail shakes the thought away as soon as it arrives. It's far too cruel a thought—a thought that comes from the very part of herself she is afraid Susanna's presence will bring out into the light.

Abigail stops walking as she passes the castle. A ship is approaching the island. Three-masted barque—at the sight of it, her heart is racing. Henry's ship? Dare she hope for that? It feels as though she has willed him here.

She hurries into the village and clambers up towards the abandoned fort on the Heugh. Squints into the wall of cloud, watching the ship grow closer. And as the barque slices through the silver-grey water, she sees it—sees that regal eagle figurehead, its wooden wings frozen in flight.

Her breath is suddenly rattling against her chest in a frantic mix of relief, excitement, nerves. Because now she has a chance to tell Henry everything face to face. Now she will not have to cast this most personal letter into the depths of his buyer's office and hope it somehow makes it into Henry's hands. Now, she will be able to see the look in his eyes when she tells him everything she needs to tell him.

About the child. About her plans to leave Lindisfarne. Every true and honest detail of her entanglement with the Bamburgh thieving ring and the lies she had let him believe.

She will tell him of the life she wishes to build with him. And she will hope with every inch of her being that it is a life he wishes to be a part of. Hope he'll not look down on her for all she has been involved in. He will see past it, surely. He loves her, doesn't he? Oliver had said so.

She casts one last glance out at the ship, then turns and hurries back to the house.

Goes up to her nightstand and opens the brass box. She folds the message she had written to Henry and crams it into the box beside the Jacobite letter. Fastens the lid again and slips the box back into her drawer.

CHAPTER THIRTY-SIX

John Graveney had feared this. These were unfounded, irrational fears at first: fears that Henry Ward might choose to leave the sea behind. Fears that Ward's leaving might mean the end of his own short-lived life at sea.

Graveney had told himself that when it all came down to it, Ward wouldn't leave. He was a man who belonged on the ocean. A man who surely only felt alive when his lungs were full of salty air.

And besides, even if he did… *Even if he did*, there was no reason Graveney himself would be out of work. Hunter would become captain, and Graveney was sure he would keep him on as boatswain. He's good at his job. Reliable. Organised.

Over and over, Graveney told himself he would not become penniless. He would not die on that street corner in the London slums, or at the hands of Amos Sheffield when he could not repay his gambling debts. He would not have to resort to a life of running, of looking over his shoulder, of wondering when Sheffield might show his face. Or his pistol.

And then that conversation with Hunter the day of the Blake boy's burial. The suspicion in the quartermaster's eyes had been all too blatant.

What are you hiding, John?

In the two months since, Hunter has barely exchanged a word with him, beyond barked, necessary instructions on the smooth running of the ship. Graveney has caught the quartermaster's sideways glances; is well aware of the murmurs he's been exchanging with Ward.

Hunter's distrust of him is glaring.

Graveney does not know, for certain, what it is Hunter thinks him guilty of. French sympathies? Jacobite sympathies? He would not be wrong.

Whatever it is, it doesn't matter. All that matters is that, if Hunter takes control of the ship, he will surely not be offering Graveney a berth upon it.

Tonight, Ward has gathered the entire crew on deck. The ship is moored in the bay beyond Emmanuel Head, but in the thick cloud and darkness, Holy Island is just a vague shape in the gloom.

Henry Ward is climbing onto the poop deck. Is telling his crew their articles of agreement will be cut short tonight. Telling his crew he will he handing control of the ship over to Quartermaster Hunter.

The words echo and roll inside Graveney's head. His body is suddenly blazing, and he curls a hand around the gunwale to keep himself upright. He stares up at Ward, trying to catch his eye, but the captain has a distant look about him, as though a part of him has already left.

Voices erupt. Questions fly out of the men's mouths; questions about payment, about Hunter's plans for new articles of agreement, about whether those not chosen in the new crew will be given passage back to London. Too many questions in too many angry voices.

"Mr Hunter will arrange the sale of the cargo tomorrow morning," Ward says, without emotion. "And each man will be given the share of the payment due to him." He sounds distracted. Looks distracted, his gaze darting regularly out in the direction of the island. The house.

Hunter steps up to join Ward on the poop deck. He looks out across the heaving mass of men, his eyes hovering on Graveney for a moment too long. "I'll be offering new agreements shortly," Hunter says loudly. "The men I choose'll be given the option to continue on to the North Atlantic for another voyage with the *Eagle*."

"And what of those you don't choose?" This man's voice is laced with bitterness.

Yes, thinks Graveney. What of those you don't choose?

Distant memories swing at him of a stomach so empty it made his legs feel hollow. Of that bruising London cold, with no money for coal to keep it at bay.

Really, Graveney thinks, a life on the streets is a generous assessment of the situation. When he fails to repay what he owes, he's far more likely to face Sheffield's bullet than he is a life on the streets. He knows that, what he is really facing, when Henry Ward leaves the ship and he loses his place in this crew, is death.

That reality swings towards him, making his chest tighten. Ward steps down from the poop deck and begins to stride towards the saloon, with not even another glance at his rioting crew. Hunter opens his mouth to speak, but his words are lost over the shouting. And the crew moves towards the saloon door as one, charging after their captain.

Abigail stands at the window of the study and peers out at the ship. She can see the *Eagle's* lamps glittering through the thick bank of cloud. Why has he not come yet?

She tries to shake the unease away. Henry is the captain of his ship. No doubt he has other matters to attend to. Or perhaps he is waiting until later tonight to come to the house, so he can be sure her children are asleep. It is still several hours from midnight.

Abigail has set a lamp on the windowsill, its light beaming steadily through the study window. A beacon, making it as clear as possible to Henry that he is welcome here. She wishes there was more she could do. Prays she has the chance to tell him in person how much she regrets sending him away.

She had intended to pack up the house. She has not yet even made a start. She has managed the letters of recommendation for Ruth and Mrs Calloway. Has half-written the letter to Samuel's lawyer. But her productivity has been stolen by thoughts of Henry Ward, and all she has to tell him.

She needs him to come now, before she loses her courage.

Abigail turns away from the window. Rakes her fingers through the hair that hangs loose on her shoulders. Focus, she thinks. She has far too much to do to waste the night pining at the window. Henry will come when he comes. And he *will* come, surely. The ship would not be here otherwise.

The thought nudges her into action and she leaves the study for her bedchamber. She kneels, peeking under the bed in search of her travelling trunks. It has been more than twelve years since she has used them. Once, she had imagined the entire rest of her life would be spent up here in this wild top corner of the country.

She straightens at a sound from outside the house. The faint sigh of footsteps. Someone is here. But it's not relief that she feels. Because these footsteps are coming from the side of the house furthest from the sea. No one from the ship would be approaching from this direction.

She rushes back to the study and snuffs the lamp at the window. Curses her foolishness. With the lamp blazing so brightly, she has made herself a beacon. For Henry Ward, or for Donald Macauley, or for whoever else might wish to come here to Highfield House tonight. For whatever reason they wish to come.

She reaches into her pocket. Wraps her fingers around Oliver's knife. It has become such a part of her, she often forgets she is carrying it.

She moves through the building, dousing the rest of the lamps. Blackness falls over the house in waves. It's an almost impenetrable dark; the only hint of light travels from the coals still glowing in the parlour grate. Abigail moves instinctively through the lightlessness. Even sightless, the house feels so familiar, so knowable.

Footsteps again, much closer to the house this time. The dull murmur of voices. Abigail hurries upstairs. She may have made it clear that she is here in the house. But she will not make herself so easy to find.

Shouting. Men shoving and surging through the door of the saloon. The flash of a pistol here; a cutlass there.

Animals.

Ward supposes he cannot blame the crew for this. A few months ago, he would never have considered doing something as shameful as abandoning his own ship before the men's agreements are through. He has to admit, he's not proud of any of this. But it's what he must do. Going back to Abigail is not even a question.

He shoves away the man at his shoulder and climbs onto the table of the saloon. Slides his pistol from his pocket. He does not raise it. Does not threaten his men. But the sight of it in his hand sends a hush through the men. They stop shoving each other through the saloon door. Their shouting falls quiet.

"My decision has been made," Ward says, his voice loud, but controlled. "And I suggest you all remember that Mr Hunter is yet to choose which of you he wishes to take on. I'm sure I do not need to remind you that violence is prohibited by this ship's articles."

His warning causes a fresh murmur to ripple through the men. Ward climbs off the table and pushes his way back out onto deck. Hunter strides out behind him.

"I trust you're not going to just abandon ship with the crew in such a state," his quartermaster says tautly.

Ward lets out a short, humourless laugh. He has to admit, it's a tempting prospect. "Of course not. I've more decency than that." There are payments to arrange for the men, and ship's papers to go over with Hunter. Besides, he's barely even begun to clear the contents of his great cabin.

Ward picks up the spying glass dropped on the deck by the crewman who had abandoned his lookout post. "Get the anchor watch back in place at once," he barks to Hunter. He lifts the spying glass to his eye, trying to pull the shape of Highfield House from the darkness. He cannot see it. The landscape is black; the house has disappeared. As though it never existed. Had he seen a lamp in the windows earlier tonight? Perhaps. Or perhaps just his imagination. He has been cursedly preoccupied.

Unease tugs at him. Urges him to go straight to shore. Find her, in amongst all that blackness.

Ward looks at the house through the spying glass again. Tries to talk himself out of his unease. He is overreacting, surely. Abigail and her children are asleep in bed with the lamps doused. Nothing more sinister than that.

Nonetheless, he would feel better if he knew that for certain.

He turns at the sound of Graveney's footsteps. His boatswain is heading towards Hunter with an uneasy look in his eyes. Ward claps him on the shoulder. "I need you to take a message to the house, John. Tell Mrs Blake there's trouble on the ship and I'll be there as soon as I can."

<h1 style="text-align:center">CHAPTER THIRTY-SEVEN</h1>

Abigail pulls back the curtain of her bedroom, daring to peek out onto the dunes. She can just make out two figures moving through the darkness. A man and a woman, she thinks, draped in dark cloaks.

They are coming for her, surely. They must be members of the Bamburgh thieving ring, come to punish her for taking back the letter. Why else would anyone be here? No one comes to Emmanuel Head, other than to come to the house, at least not at this time of night.

It's not panic that overtakes her, but a strange, almost dizzying calmness. A sense of going past herself to reach this inevitability she has been waiting for since she first got entangled with the Bamburgh thieves.

Of course there is no surprise that they have shown themselves now. She knows it would not have taken Lizzie and Ailith long to realise they had been robbed. And Lizzie had seen Abigail in the village the day of the theft. Surely it had not taken her and her mother long to put the pieces together.

So there is no surprise to this. But she has not been quick enough to leave the island, Abigail sees that now. She ought to have ignored formalities such as recommendation letters and legal correspondence. Ought to have just taken her children and run, the moment she had returned from Bamburgh with the letter in her pocket.

Her need to write to Henry, telling him everything, had delayed her. And she sees now how foolish that was.

Still. There is no time for regret. No time for panic. Right now, the best thing she can do is remain calm. The thieves are outside the house, yes. But so is Henry Ward. And he will come for her. Because he loves her. Oliver had promised.

She grips the bedpost tightly, trying to order her thoughts. How will the thieves try and get into the house? Through a window? Every door is locked tight. Surely they cannot know of the passage in the walls. Even she did not know of the thing.

Unless Oliver told Lizzie about the passage. Told her of the tunnel that leads into the house from beneath Nathan's bedroom window.

Abigail rushes across the hallway and throws open the door to Oliver's room. A part of her is grateful for her urgency, because it does not allow her to feel the grief she knows would be careening into her otherwise. She has not set foot inside the room since Oliver's death. Still, his books are scattered across the desk, his clothes hanging in the wardrobe. Still, his blood is staining the floorboards. The coat belonging to the boy who had killed him is still bunched up in one corner of the mattress; the cabin boy's abandoned boots still tipped over beside the bed.

But Abigail does not think of these things. She just thinks of the double-barrel priest hole beside the fireplace, and the passage leading down, down into the walls. Easy access in and out of the house for anyone who knows how to find it.

She throws her weight against the bed, trying to slide it towards the fireplace. Trying to block the opening of the hole. It groans against the flagstones. Barely moves an inch.

Before she can try again, a volley of breaking glass comes from the ground floor and echoes up through the house. Abigail swallows her murmur of fear.

Get the children. Leave the house through the passage.

These thoughts are all she can manage.

Henry's ship is in the bay. She will get to him. She has given away the rowboat, and has never learnt to sail or swim. But somehow, she will get to him.

She flies down the hallway towards Eva's room. Can hear footsteps inside the house now. The soft click of boots on flagstones.

Abigail holds her breath. Looks down the stairs into the sea of darkness. On the edge of her vision, she sees movement; shapes at the bottom of the stairs. They catch sight of her, and suddenly the two figures are rushing up the staircase, stealing away the last of her calmness. Abigail darts away from Eva's bedroom and snatches the fire poker from Samuel's study.

She charges back into the hallway. Meets the intruders at the top of the stairs. Abigail can just make out enough in the darkness to know the woman is Ailith. Beside her is a man Abigail does not recognise. She holds the poker out in front of her. The nose of a pistol emerges from the dark, held out in the man's hand.

"Where's the letter?" he asks. His voice is deep and Scottish.

She hesitates. A click of the pistol. "Nightstand," she croaks.

The man keeps the pistol trained on her. He nods towards Ailith. "Go."

Ailith shoves her way past them. Abigail hears her throwing open the doors to first the dressing room, then her bedchamber. Hears her clattering blindly through the darkness, searching for the nightstand.

Suddenly, there are more noises downstairs. The thump of someone jumping through the broken window. Boots crunching over shattered glass. Abigail holds her breath, unable to take her eyes from the pistol levelled with her face.

A pale globe of lamplight breaks the darkness.

"Mrs Blake?" The voice rising up from the entrance hall is not Henry's. One of his crewmen? His footsteps quicken, intensify, and it causes the man with the pistol to falter.

Before the thought enters her head, Abigail is swinging the poker, knocking the pistol from the man's hands. It clatters against the floorboards. Henry's crewmate—Mr Graveney, she realises distantly— rushes up the stairs towards them. He grabs at the man, hauling him from the landing and heaving his body down the staircase. The lamp in Graveney's hand shatters, and blackness spills over the house again. Abigail hears the dull thumps of bodies falling. Drops to her knees in a desperate search for the pistol.

She feels a sharp pain as Ailith lurches into the passage and grabs a fistful of her hair; yanks her away from the weapon. Instinctively, Abigail hunches, curls in on herself, a protective arm wrapped around her middle.

Ailith stands over her and Abigail can just make out the brass box in her hands.

"Go," she manages. "Take it and go." She will not her fight for this. Will not put herself in danger for that cursed brass box. Surely, Henry will value his unborn child over his letter. Will value *her* over his letter.

Ailith meets her eyes for a second, then rushes down the staircase with the box. Abigail watches her disappear. The Jacobite letter. The letter she had written to Henry, telling him every piece of her heart.

It doesn't matter, she tells herself. Henry is here, just out in the bay. Soon, they will stand face to face and she will tell him everything.

He is here, isn't he? Why has Graveney come to the house instead? Has something happened to Henry? Has he not returned home from the Channel? Fresh panic rushes at her.

As she gets shakily to her feet, her fingers find the pistol. She tucks it into her pocket and edges downstairs.

"Mr Graveney?" Her voice disappears into the sudden stillness of the house.

"Down here."

Abigail steps slowly down the staircase. Graveney is standing at the bottom of the stairs, looking down at the limp figure of the man from the thieving ring.

Abigail swallows heavily. "Is he dead?"

Graveney nods.

"Are you hurt?" she asks.

"Nothing I'll not shake off. I had the element of surprise on my side."

"Thank you," Abigail murmurs. It does not feel like enough. She knows that, in all likelihood, this near stranger has just saved her life. But speaking it makes it too real.

Graveney looks up at her, then down at the body. "What was that about?" he asks. "Who were they? What did they want?"

"They—" She stops herself. She has no idea if Henry has told his crewmen about the Jacobite letter. All she knows is that he had told her to keep quiet about it. Keep it safe. She has failed on so many counts. "They were just petty thieves," she manages. "They must have known my children and I were alone in this house."

Graveney nods faintly.

Abigail's eyes draw downwards to the body. The man has fallen face-down, and in the pale light, she sees a thin trail of blood snaking out from the body.

She has to go. She has to go, she has to go.

The thought circles through her head without pause. She has delayed for too long, and now a man is dead.

Less than an hour back to Bamburgh on horseback, she thinks. Less than an hour before Ailith gets word to the rest of the thieving ring about what Abigail Blake has done.

But what if Ailith and the dead man were not alone? What if there are more of them out here? Abigail knows she cannot count on *less than an hour back to Bamburgh*. It is far too dark to be certain the dunes are empty.

If—when—the thieves find out one of them has been killed in her house, they will be back at her door. And there is no telling what they will do to her in retribution.

She needs Graveney's help. She cannot risk Nathan or Eva getting out of bed and seeing a dead man at the bottom of the stairs. Especially not after all they have been through these past months.

"Help me," she says huskily. "Please. I need to remove the body."

Graveney nods. "Is there somewhere we can bury—"

"No. I can't have him buried here. What if someone sees you? What if they come looking—"

"All right," Graveney says. "All right." He glances out through the broken window. "I can take him out in the longboat. Take him out to sea and dispose of the body before I get back to the ship."

Abigail nods, despite the sudden rolling in her stomach. There's something inevitable about this, she thinks dully. About her becoming the kind of woman who sees dead men tossed into the sea. She feels a pull of self-loathing. And she says, "Thank you."

Graveney rolls the body over and hauls it from the floor. Slings the figure over his shoulder. Abigail hurries into the parlour, lighting a single candle with the tinderbox on the mantel. She takes it back to the entrance hall. Its pale light illuminates the line of blood snaking across the flagstones. Abigail pulls off her shawl and tosses it onto the floor. Uses it to wipe the blood from the stone. Let there be no trace of this night left for whoever steps into these halls next. She has no thought of who that might be.

Cupping the tiny flame with her hand, she leads Graveney down the narrow passage toward the servants' entrance. Shoves on the door at the end of the corridor. It opens with a creak, cold air billowing inside.

"This will take you out onto the dunes," she says, voice low. "Do you think you can get to your longboat without anyone seeing you?"

Graveney heaves the body from his shoulder and sets it down beside the door. He steps out into the night, scanning the dunes. "It's quiet," he says. "No one out here as far as I can tell. But it's far too dark to be certain."

Abigail nods wordlessly. She sets her bloodstained shawl on top of the body. And then she asks that which she has so far been too afraid to: "Henry. Is he alive?"

"Aye. He'll be here as soon as he can."

She lets out a breath of relief she was not aware she was holding. "Take me back to the ship," she says suddenly. "My children and I need to leave this house at once. It's not safe for us here."

Graveney hesitates, eyes darting between her and the dead man on her doorstep. "I can't," he says. "I'm sorry. The men are brawling over the captain's new conditions. You don't want your children around that, aye?"

Abigail feels her hope shatter. "No," she manages. "Of course not." She swallows hard. She cannot wait for Henry. She needs to leave now.

She looks up at Graveney, meeting his eyes in the candlelight. "Will you give Henry a message?"

"Of course."

Her thoughts race. There is so much she needs to tell him. But she will not spill her heart to this man from his crew. Will just give him the bare facts.

"Tell him I need to leave at once. Tell him to come to the lodging house in Beal as soon as he is able. I shall be waiting for him there."

Graveney nods. "Of course."

"Tell him—" Abigail hesitates. *Face to face*, she thinks. But she needs him to understand the urgency of this. Needs him to understand everything that is at stake. Needs him to come to the lodging house, knowing the life that awaits him. "Tell him he is to be a father."

Something almost imperceivable passes across Graveney's eyes, but he keeps his face level. "I see." He nods. "I shall pass on your message." He looks at her squarely. "Take care, Mrs Blake."

CHAPTER THIRTY-EIGHT

Abigail rushes back upstairs to her bedchamber and pulls a pouch of money from her nightstand. Shoves it into her stays. She grabs her cloak from where she had tossed it on the end of the bed, fumbling with the hooks as she swings it around her shoulders.

Henry will find her, she tells herself. He will find them, and he will help them start again. Once they are off this island, they can begin to plan their life together.

With the candle in hand, she steps out of her bedchamber, not looking back. She strides down the hallway, keeping her eyes averted from Oliver's room. At the back of her mind is the knowledge that she is leaving her son here on Lindisfarne, alone. Guilt knifes her; not just for leaving him, but for allowing him to become what he had. Allowing him to die the way he had.

She pushes open the door to Nathan's room.

"Mama?" Nathan is already sitting up in bed when she steps into the room. How long has he been awake? How much had he heard?

She fights the urge to pull him into her arms. "I need you to get dressed, my love," she whispers. "Quickly. Can you do that for me while I fetch your sister?"

He looks up at her with wide eyes. Nods. Does not ask questions. Abigail swallows the lump in her throat. She sets the candle on the mantel.

"Good boy. I'll be back in a moment."

She hears his faint footfalls as he goes to his wardrobe, pulls open the squeaking door.

Two doors down the hallway, Eva is breathing deeply in sleep, one hand curled beneath her cheek, her dark hair fanned out on her pillow. Keeping her wrapped in her blankets, Abigail scoops her into her arms. Eva blinks sleepily, rubbing her eyes.

Abigail hurries back into Nathan's room. He has buttoned his breeches and waistcoat; is fumbling with the silk neckcloth he wears to school. "Just your coat, Nathan," she tells him. "Just get your coat and shoes. You don't need anything else."

Obediently, he tosses the neckcloth on the bed and snatches his coat from the wardrobe. Wrestles his arms into it and buttons it crookedly. Sits on the floor to pull on his shoes. On his way past the window, he grabs his telescope from its wooden stand.

He hurries to Abigail's side. Stands close, not touching.

Down the stairs; one step, the next, the next, candlelight painting long shadows over the walls.

And as they make her way towards the door, Abigail is suddenly aching for it: for this house; her prison, her protector. This house, where she had brought her children into the world, where she had fallen in love with her husband, where she had built herself into something close to a decent person.

But there is not a scrap of choice to any of this. Not a single way to stay. And it's this that keeps her walking. Keeps her leaving her house behind.

"Take hold of my skirts," she whispers to Nathan. Leads him down the passage of the servants' entrance and slips through the side door. She blows out the candle, letting the full intensity of the darkness fall over her and her children.

She does not look back at the house. Does not look out at Henry's ship, glittering in the bay. She just has to trust that he will come to the lodging house. Has to trust that this life she has laid out for him is a life he wishes to live.

"Where are we going, Mama?" Nathan asks. His voice is a murmur, but she hisses to him to be quiet, instantly regretting it.

"We need to leave," she says. "I promise I'll tell you more soon. But right now, I just need you to do as I say."

He looks up at her with a thousand questions in his eyes. Does not ask any of them. He lifts his face upwards, seeking out the glimmers of starlight between the clouds. Clutches his telescope to his chest.

The path to the village is invisible in the thick darkness, the rugged grass of the dunes far too uneven to navigate without light. Abigail hears the dull thud of hooves. Sees the glow of a roe deer's eyes. She freezes, several yards from the house, listening for any sound of humanity. Is Ailith still on the island? Are there others from the ring seeking to punish her for all she has done? She cannot even think about who might be hiding in the dunes. All she can focus on is getting off this island.

When the silence returns, Abigail keeps walking, Eva slung over her shoulder, breathing deeply with sleep again; Nathan stumbling along beside her with a fistful of her cloak. They follow the coastline in the dark; follow that line of white water that will guide their path to the Pilgrims' Way. Abigail can tell the tide is rising. They need to hurry if they are to make it off the island tonight.

Her arm aches under Eva's weight, her long legs dangling down past Abigail's hips. She is growing too big to be carried.

As Abigail tries to shift the weight of her, Eva wakes and begins to murmur—murmurs that turn to wails as she takes in the layers of night pressing down them. Abigail tries to murmur soothing words, but can find nothing. All she has inside her now is panic. Out ahead of them, the Pilgrims' Way stretches out dark and endless, the sea invisible, a constant sigh. How deep is the water? How high has the tide risen?

Hide in the village. Wait until morning.

No. She has made too many enemies for that. Father Dering, surely, would help her. But there is no certainty she will get to the vicarage without coming across Donald Macauley or Elias Mitchell, or any of the other Lindisfarne natives with a Jacobite alliance. Men who believe she has stolen from their cause. Men who will punish her before they help her. Men who will curse her family's name.

Abigail takes a breath. Grabs Nathan's hand tightly, ignoring the way his fingers stiffen and try to escape her own. She steps out onto the Pilgrims' Way, feeling her shoes sink into the damp sand. One step.

Another, another. And now here is the water, rushing up against her ankles. Soaking through her stockings, tugging at her skirts. Another step. Another.

Water at her shins now, her knees. It's a cold she has never experienced. A cold that blazes and burns and has her gasping. A murmur of shock escapes her lips. She pulls Nathan close to her, gripping hold of his coat. Pushes forward as the water tugs at her skirts, tries to pull her back onto the island.

"Just keep going," she says. Is not sure if she is speaking to Nathan or herself. "Just keep going."

Another step. Another, into and through the rising tide.

CHAPTER THIRTY-NINE

Graveney does his best not to think as he heaves the body into the water. Does not think about how easily—and how soon—it could be his body being disposed of by Amos Sheffield and his men. He does not look back at the dark circle of water where the man had disappeared. Close enough to the moment of death, he thinks, for the body to sink quickly to the bottom. For the man to just vanish from the world without a trace. Is this what will happen to him? Will Sheffield's men fling his body into the Thames when he cannot pay his debts? Will he be washed out into the ocean, with no one any the wiser? He swallows a sudden swell of sickness.

He pulls on the oars, stifling a groan. Pain is roaring through his shoulder after his tumble down the stairs. The *Eagle* is just a few yards ahead of him now, lit up in pools of lamplight. Out on Emmanuel Head, the house has vanished into the darkness. The tide is rising, he realises, and it occurs to him he had not even thought to make sure Mrs Blake and her children had a way off the island. Perhaps he ought to go back and find her.

The thought is pushed away by the cold reality of all that is going on aboard the *Eagle*. He can still hear angry voices drifting out across the water. Can tell nothing has been resolved since he had left. Hunter, it seems, has not managed to take control of his men.

Hunter, who believes him a Jacobite traitor. Hunter, who will never allow him to remain a part of this crew.

Graveney tries to tell himself this is for the best. Because each time they fire at the French; each time they steal from the Jacobites, he knows it will come with guilt. A memory of his mother. But the only conclusion he can come to is this: what kind of life is it to be penniless and starving? To live each day in fear that Amos Sheffield will hunt him down and demand payment for debts he cannot pay? What kind of life is it to die at the end of a gambling man's cutlass?

The ship is still heaving when Graveney climbs back aboard. Men are strewn about the deck, locked in heated conversations with Ward, with Hunter, with each other.

Ward looks up as Graveney approaches. Strides across the deck towards him. "Did you find her?" he demands. "Is she safe?" His eyes flicker across the water towards the darkness containing the house.

And sometimes, Graveney thinks, sometimes a man has to do what is right for himself and himself alone. Sometimes a man has to put his own needs first.

Besides, he knows Henry Ward. Henry Ward is not a man who settles down to raise children. He is a man who fights for his country. And he'll realise that, Graveney thinks. Once he's sailed out from under Abigail Blake's spell, he'll realise that the helm of the *Eagle* is where he belongs.

"The house was empty," says Graveney. "Not a soul about. Looks as though no one has been there in some time." He meets the captain's eyes in an attempt at sympathy. "I'm sorry, sir. She and her children have left."

CHAPTER FORTY

She has her answer.

When she had finally made it to the lodging house in Beal, Abigail had intended to stay awake all night. Stay alert, stay watchful of anyone who might have followed her off the island; wait for Henry. But exhaustion had pulled her down, and as she had drifted off to sleep, she had imagined being woken by Henry's knock at the door. Or perhaps, implausibly, by his breath tickling her skin as he leant over the bed, kissing her cheek and telling her she was safe.

In the end, she had been woken only by waves of nausea, to find the candle burned out and a grey dawn light slinking through the gap in the curtains.

Wrapped in blankets, with her sodden clothes drying by a restoked fire, she had gone to the window. Sat there, watching the sky lighten, exhaustion making her body ache, and the child inside her making her stomach roll. And she had looked out across the sea. Watched the *Eagle* pass. Disappear.

Henry Ward has not come for her.

Abigail sees now that she had made herself believe in a different reality. Made herself believe in all that Oliver had told her. Made herself believe that Henry Ward loved her. That he would want this life she was offering.

Had she truly imagined she might lure a man like Henry away from the sea and into some dour, city-bound domestic life?

Perhaps she is as adept at lying to herself as she is to others.

Sitting at the window, she had watched the ship disappear with a necessary sense of detachment. And, perhaps, inevitability. Because her tryst with Henry Ward has always been a little too make-believe. A little too fanciful to be reality.

With a sense of empty resignation, Abigail had stumbled back into bed beside her children. Fallen into a deep, dreamless sleep.

Late morning now—she can tell by the white light peeking through the curtains. Beside her, Eva and Nathan are sprawled across the bed in their underclothes, still breathing deeply with sleep. Abigail watches them dazedly, her mind filled with flashes of the crossing: water at her ankles, her knees, her waist. Hauling one child in each arm as she struggled through the deepest water at the heart of the Pilgrims' Way. Fearing that her decision to leave would end in all of their deaths.

But then the water had begun to grow shallower and the lights of Beal had begun to grow brighter, and the prospect of living, surviving, had begun to feel within reach.

In the early afternoon, with her skirts still slightly damp and her children still sleeping, she goes downstairs to find the innkeeper and make her arrangements. A wagon to Berwick, where they will find a coach down to London.

A piece of parchment, please. Ink pot and quill.

She writes the letter upstairs in their room while the innkeeper arranges for the wagon. Writes that long-overdue letter to her mother.

Her words are succinct. Samuel and Oliver dead from smallpox, herself carrying a child. She and her two youngest children on their way to the townhouse in Chelsea.

Her words are heavy with fresh grief, though it is not grief for her husband, who has been gone almost a year now. Not that her mother will ever know that. Nor will anyone else in London. She will return to the capital in her mourning clothes, and speak of her departed husband with emotion thickening her voice, as though he has only just left them. And the child growing inside her? Well, how could that be anything but Samuel's child? She knows Eva and Nathan are too young to question it. Knows herself an adept enough liar to let this become the truth.

And so, it will be like this:

This part of her life, she will never speak of.

The house, she will never speak of. The island, she will never speak of.

Most of all, it is Henry Ward that she will never speak of.

He has made his decision. And so she has made hers.

She will lock away the part of herself that makes dangerous, impulsive choices. Lock away the memories of this past year, and the emotions that come with it. From now on, her sole focus will be making a good life for her children. Ensuring they know nothing of the mistakes she has made, the foolish things she has done.

Rain is falling when the wagon begins to pull away from the lodging house, tapping steadily against the thin wooden roof inches above her head. Abigail sits bundled in the blankets the coachman has left on the bench seats for them, trying to ease away the last of the water's chill. Eva, still in her nightgown, is curled into her lap with her head against her mother's chest. Nathan sits close by her side, his telescope lying across his knees and a faraway look in his eyes.

As the wagon rattles down the muddy path, Abigail cannot help but look out at Lindisfarne, bathed in cloud on the other side of the Pilgrims' Way. She cannot see the house, hidden away on the far corner of the island. Is glad for it. Now that she has made her escape, she has no desire to look back.

She will never return to Northumberland—this she knows with a certainty that reaches her bones. Silence will fall over Highfield House now; the kind of silence that seems impossibly fitting. The fires she had left simmering will turn to cold ash, the food in the cupboards will become dust. Her garden will be torn at by birds and trampled by deer, and overrun by scree and wild grasses. As for all the clothes and books and pieces of lives they have left behind, the loss of them will make space for something new. Something better.

Nathan's house, she thinks distantly. It will become Nathan's house now. The manor, and all the struggles Holy Island has brought this family, will fall upon his shoulders. And for this, she pities him. Best, she thinks, that he never return either, to this tidal island; to this world of thieves and Jacobites and privateers.

Best he turn his eyes forward and build a life on more solid ground. Let every piece of this past fall away.

Book Five:

North Star Rising

NORTHUMBERLAND, ENGLAND

NOVEMBER 1725

CHAPTER ONE

His earliest memory is this: salted windows and firelight, sea at all the edges. A father who had made this rock his world. Surrendered his own freedom to save the lives of strangers.

Back then, Finn had not understood. Had run instead; sought adventure, danger, a broader life of cannon fire and privateers. Almost lost that life on far too many occasions.

But this wind-crashed island has always been here waiting for him. This place of unlikely shelter, where tides rise to his doorstep and cloud sweeps stone. Shelter, once, for his mother, his father, his short-lived childhood. And now, for the last decade, his own unlikely, growing family. They have weathered Longstone through Jacobite plots and failed Risings, births and deaths; lives saved, lost and reunited. His wife, sons, tottering daughter—some days they all still feel impossible. Even now, after all this time, Finn is still waiting for them to be a moonshine dream.

He turns up the collar of his coat and marches down the stairs at the front of the cottage to refill the firebasket. The night is deep and silver-black, a cold late-autumn wind whipping across the sea. In the brassy glow of the flames, he can see the ocean pushing up against the edges of the island. The tide is rising, drawing pieces of the Farnes below the surface.

The sound comes to him like a memory; distant, haunting. A ship's bell, tolling across the water. Finn secures the chain of the firebasket to the hook. Turns in the vague direction of the sound. Again, it comes. A metallic, musical echo.

It's rolling in from the south, out behind the cottage, where nothing but the Crumstone islet interrupts sheets of dark sea. A light there too, he realises; disappearing, reappearing, dancing back and forth behind unseen castles of rock. And suddenly, vividly, a gunpowder roar. A streak of fire brightening the sky.

Finn runs inside, taking the stairs two at a time. Snatches the spying glass from the mantel.

Eva wakes at his urgency. Slides out of bed. "What is it? What do you see?"

"Flares," he says. "Out near the Crumstone."

Eva pulls her shoes on over bare feet and grabs her cloak from the hook beside the door. Takes the lamp from the mantel as she passes. Finn hurries down the steps of the cottage and lifts the spying glass. These early-morning hours, the sea, the cloud—it changes things, makes the world hazy. Makes you see things that aren't there.

It's not the first time he has imagined a ship foundering.

There have been incidents before, of course. Near misses of herring boats. Passenger ships venturing a little too close to the reef on rainy, lightless nights. The battered dinghy that had tossed his future wife onto Longstone in the wake of Donald Macauley's death.

This feels like more than a near miss.

The ship's bell clatters through the darkness again. A scream drifts across the water. Tells him this is not the night, or the sea, or the cloud playing tricks. Tells him the ship has struck the reef, and he needs to act.

He hands Eva the spying glass. Panic in her eyes, but she does not attempt to stop him as he hurries to the jetty and unwinds the mooring ropes of the skiff. She just wraps her hand around his wrist and pulls him close for the briefest of moments. "Be safe," she says. "Come back to us."

He squeezes her fingers, thin and cold in his gloved hand. "Of course."

Finn leaps into the boat as Eva hooks the lamp to the bow. He guides the skiff carefully away from Longstone towards the light rising and plunging on the Crumstone. A second roar of gunpowder is followed by another flare, illuminating, for seconds, the peaks and troughs of the sea. It's a treacherous patch of ocean, yes, rippled with currents and hatched with reefs. But visibility is fair tonight and the sea is often far harsher than this. The fog far thicker. There are days when attempting this trip out to the Crumstone would end in certain disaster. Why a wreck tonight? A navigational error, he guesses. A compass variation. A quadrant wavering in the hand of a sailor tossed by the sea. A misreading of the stars. Perhaps they had not seen the beacon in time to correct their course.

Finn looks over his shoulder as he approaches the scarps of the Crumstone. He can see the ship now, run aground on the reef, the bulk of it emerging from the darkness. Two masts at a violent tilt, her portside languishing below the waterline. It's a packet boat, he guesses, trapped sails thudding and straining. He can tell the reef has torn one side of the ship open. He hears the screams and cries of the passengers, hears the sea thunder as it roars into cabins and crevices, the animal groan of the ship writhing against rock.

Bodies struggle over the sloping deck, straining towards the cold solidity of the Crumstone. It's a nugget of rock far smaller than Longstone. Will disappear almost entirely beneath the sea once the tide is at its highest. Finn eases his boat past the flailing hulk of the ship.

He hears shouting from the water. Looks down to see three figures thrashing towards him.

Finn reaches over the gunwale. Hauls out three young men in sailors' slops. The skiff rocks violently as they tumble inside.

"How many aboard?" Finn asks.

The responses are tangled, but he makes them out: eight passengers. Five members of crew. Passenger ship: London to Edinburgh.

"Take the lamp," he tells one of the men. "Guide my way."

Getting closer to the Crumstone is risky. He knows he is right above shards of rock that could slice the hull of the skiff from below. Men and women are scrambling up over the jagged island, trying to outrun the swell of the rising tide. A child wails in its mother's arms. Finn sees torn skin, bloodied faces, horrified eyes. Two figures—a man and a woman—lie motionless on the rock. The ship groans loudly, pummelled by the swell. It lurches, rolls, another inch of its gunwale disappearing beneath the surface.

A pull on one oar, the other, careful, muscles straining, and the skiff is close enough. Finn steadies the boat against the white water glowing at the base of the islet. The crewmen help the passengers climb aboard.

He looks down at the two motionless figures. The man, older, with a thready grey beard, has a deep gash on his head, his face awash with crimson. The woman is wearing only a thin white nightshift and dark cloak, long pale hair clinging to her face and neck. No sign of an injury— Finn guesses she has succumbed to the cold. He knows from experience how quickly the chill of the water can steal your senses. But the woman's chest is moving with slow, shallow breath. A survivor, if he gets her back to the cottage quickly enough.

A man with a thick black beard is hovering by her side. "Make room for her in the boat," he barks, stumbling back to let the sailors lift the woman into the skiff.

"She your wife?" Finn asks him as he clambers over the gunwale after her.

"No. Just someone I met on the voyage. I think she was travelling alone."

Finn takes off his greatcoat and lays it over the woman's body.

"Don't freeze to death on her account," one of the crewmen tells him bitterly. "She tried to jump from the ship before we even ran aground. Caused quite the commotion. Think she'd prefer for us to leave her out here."

Finn eyes him warily. Feels a pull of unease as he glances back at the woman. "I'll take her with us if it's all the same to you."

Too many people for the tiny skiff. He feels it sitting low in the water. One of the sailors takes an oar and together, they shove the boat away from the Crumstone. Finn looks over his shoulder. Pulls towards the light blazing on the edge of his island.

Fire, thinks Eva. Blankets. Tea and broth and warming pans. She restokes and fills, and gathers bowls and cups and spoons and cloths, mind fixed on nothing but the task at hand.

And so this is how it is: this desperate need to act, without thought of what might lie ahead. Eva has wondered. Ten years she has spent out here in the glow of the Longstone light, and at the edges, there has always been this uncertainty. This unsureness of how she would react if faced with a situation like this, with a ship foundering on their doorstep and screams echoing across the water. There has always been a fear that she might close down. Freeze up. Fail to be of use. In the past, her panic has not served her well.

But somehow, it feels as though she has always been waiting for this. Standing in the firelight and watching the sea for this moment of disaster.

She has banked up the fire and filled the kettle and pot from the rainwater barrel behind the cottage. Hung both over the flames to heat. Has gathered the blankets from her and Finn's bed, collected the covers kicked to the bottom of the boys' mattress, plucked the old shawl from the corner of Maggie's cradle. The warming pan waits beside the hearth, ready to be filled with embers and slid between the sheets of the bed.

Act, and it will stop her from thinking. From fearing.

She laces her quilted skirts and bodice on over her nightshift. Knocks the tin cups from the table in the panic she is trying not to give life to. The clatter brings Noah out of the children's bedroom, dark hair tangled on his shoulders, brown eyes hazy with sleep. He looks around the living area at the piles of blankets, the simmering pot, his mother crouched beside the table with her arms full of fallen cups.

"What's happening?" he asks, rubbing an eye with his palm.

Little point trying to shield him. Out here, they are too exposed to be shielded. Besides, he's nine now, her eldest child. Too old to believe untruths told to protect him.

"A wreck," Eva says, splattering the cups on the table. "On the Crumstone. Da has gone out to help them."

Noah's eyes widen slightly. He hurries to the window. "What kind of wreck?"

"I don't know." Eva can't tell if it's excitement or fear in his voice. A little of both, perhaps.

Noah's cousin Tom slips out of the bedroom. "A wreck?" he echoes.

Noah throws open the door, letting a blast of cold air inside. The fire dances, throwing wild shadows across the walls as the boys fly down the stairs at the front of the cottage. Somewhere distant, Eva thinks *coat, hat, shoes, gloves;* but then her son says:

"The boat, Mama. I see Da's boat."

At once it's chaos, the cottage overflowing with tearful passengers and blood-streaked crewmen, and trails of water streaking the floorboards silver. Eva helps men from sodden greatcoats, wrestles women from drenched and weighted bodices. She pours tea and serves steaming broth. Wraps shivering bodies in blankets and sponges blood from cheeks and foreheads, straps the swollen arm of a woman who holds a thrashing child upon her hip. She ushers people towards the fireplace, cramming them in between the table and chairs and fireguard hung with drying clothes. There's sobbing and murmuring, and stunned, colourless faces.

Finn carries a woman into the house; lays her on their bed in the corner of the room. Eva looks over. A motionless figure, sprawled beneath Finn's greatcoat. "Is she alive?"

"Aye. Just. We need to get her warm."

Eva hangs the kettle back on the hook and hurries towards the bed. She freezes suddenly, shock striking her beneath the ribs.

The room is shadowed. Firelit. And it's been ten years since they've stood face to face. But Eva knows without a doubt that the woman lying on the bed is her sister.

CHAPTER TWO

Eva slides the wet cloak from Harriet's shoulders, and it falls to the floor with a metallic thud. A coin pouch in the pocket, she supposes. She kicks it beneath the bed, away from prying eyes. She tugs the sodden nightdress from Harriet's body and wrangles her into one of her own dry shifts. Pulls the blankets up over her sister and shoves the warming pan into the bed.

"Some tea," Eva says loudly, panicked, not entirely sure who she is speaking to. "Bring me some tea." Her heart is hammering, her thoughts colliding. Distantly, she thinks, *there are not enough cups*. Not enough cups, not enough blankets. Not enough, not enough, not enough. The baby on the woman's lap shrieks.

On the edge of her vision, Eva sees Noah take a cup from a man by the fire. He fills it from the teapot on the table. Uses two hands to carry it over to her.

Eva slides a hand beneath her sister's head. Drizzles a little of the warm liquid down her throat. Harriet's eyelids flutter faintly. A swell of relief.

Finn had not recognised Harriet when he had brought her into the cottage, Eva is sure of it. And why would he? She and Finn had only been married weeks when Harriet had disappeared without a word ten years ago. The two of them had barely known each other.

"I'll go for help at first light," Eva hears Finn say. "I don't know if anyone on the mainland will have seen the flares." When she doesn't speak, he squeezes her shoulder. "Evie. Did you hear me?"

"It's Harriet," she says. "It's my sister."

Finn comes to stand close beside her at the bed. He is dressed in a knitted shirt and woollen cap, droplets of water shining in his beard. Eva can feel the cold radiating from him. He looks down at Harriet, and is silent for a long moment. "Did you know she was coming here?" he asks finally.

Eva shakes her head. "I've not heard a word from her since she ran away. I never imagined I'd hear from her again." Why her sister has come back is something she cannot even begin to consider right now. It's far too complicated a prospect.

She glances through the window to the dark reams of sea beyond the firebasket. "Were there any that didn't survive?"

"Aye. Several were lost on the ship, including the captain. One man passed while I was bringing them back. Bled out from a gash to the head."

Eva's stomach rolls. "Is he in the skiff?"

Finn nods. Glances over his shoulder at Noah and Tom. "It'll do him no good to be brought inside."

Eva reaches for his hand and squeezes, needing the steadying feel of him.

"They're saying…" Finn begins, then changes his mind.

"They're saying what?"

He hesitates. "One of the crewmen told me there was an incident. Involving Harriet."

Eva frowns. "What kind of incident?"

"I can't be certain. But he seemed to suggest she was trying to make her way off the ship before they were wrecked."

"Make her way off the ship?" Eva repeats. "You mean, she tried to jump into the sea?" She feels a hot pull of dread. "Do you think she was trying to… end things?"

"Try not to jump to conclusions. These people have been through a hell of an ordeal. They're likely confused about what they saw."

Eva feels eyes on her. One of the men at the hearth stumbles to his feet and makes his way towards the bed. He's tall and dark-haired, with a thick black beard and close-set grey eyes. A blanket is pulled around his shoulders and she sees the little finger on his left hand is missing at the knuckle—an old injury. He tries to peer past Eva to Harriet. "Is she alive?"

"Yes." Eva says no more. Cannot bring herself to consider why he is asking, who this man might be to her sister. She glances around the living area at the passengers and crew piled into her tiny cottage, huddled close to the fire. Noah and Tom are moving between them, refilling teacups and bowls of broth, throwing extra logs on the fire. On some sudden instinct, Eva finds herself shifting to block Tom's view of Harriet.

Finn takes the bearded man's elbow, guiding him away from the bed. "Sit," he says. "Rest. My wife will take care of her."

Eva touches her fingers to her sister's wrist, relieved to find a steady pulse. As she sits on the bed, making the mattress shift, Harriet opens her eyes. Takes Eva in. There's a look of distant bewilderment on her face, as though she is unable to determine if she is alive or dead. Or how she has ended up here.

Eva cannot make sense of it either. Was Harriet on her way to Lindisfarne? To see her family? Her son?

The son who is running around their living quarters with his cousin, completely unaware of his estranged mother's presence?

Eva fights the urge to pull Harriet into her arms. To ask questions. Demand answers. She has no thought of how any of it would be received. Has ten years washed away the bitterness that had existed between them the last time they had spoken? Eva has no idea. No idea of her own thoughts on the matter. And no idea who her sister is these days. If she is honest with herself, Harriet has always been a stranger.

But she is here, she is safe, she is alive. And right now, that is all Eva can find room for.

Harriet closes her eyes again, as though unable to even begin comprehending. Finally, eyes still closed, she says, "So, I'm alive then?"

Eva smiles faintly. "Yes, Harriet," she says. "You are."

And from the long, wavering breath that Harriet lets out, Eva cannot help but wonder if she might have been hoping for the alternative.

CHAPTER THREE

Nathan stands outside the house, squinting up at the loose boards dangling from the window casing. The oriel frame is a convoluted mess of Tudor woodwork that has spent the last century and a half rotting away in cold sea-salted air.

"See," Theodora says from beside him. "I told you it was in a state."

"Mm." She's right. The window needs fixing—but so does the back step and the rotten floorboard in the front guest room, and the loose hinge on the door of Mrs Brodie's quarters. And then there's that half-rebuilt fireplace in his mother's old dressing room he has never bothered to finish. Really, it's a rare day that there's not something wrong with this house.

Nathan has done little to the place in terms of upkeep—at least not since he'd been horsing about with his sham restoration on a search for Henry Ward's Jacobite letter. A part of him is holding his breath waiting for the house to collapse around him. And after years of to-ing and fro-ing and simultaneously loving and hating the place, he has come to the conclusion that this is not the outcome he wants. Unbidden, Highfield House has worked its way under his skin. The same way, Nathan thinks distantly, that he feels about Holy Island as a whole. Somehow, this place of stone and sea and pink-grey light has begun to feel like home. Or rather, he is reminded that it always has been this.

He shivers as wind blusters off the water, carrying the scent of drying kelp. The broken window casing shudders violently. "I'm sure there's someone in the village who can fix the thing."

Theodora leaps in with a touch too much enthusiasm. "I know someone who can help. I met a lad last week who's just arrived on the island. He's been doing odd jobs around the place for some extra coin. He fixed Mrs Emmett's roof a few days ago."

Nathan eyes her. "And how exactly did you meet this lad?"

His daughter shrugs with a nonchalance he feels certain is cultivated to annoy him. "I was just out walking. Happened to cross paths with him."

He gives her a withering look. "As a fine storyteller, you might come up with something a little more convincing."

Theodora smiles. Says nothing.

"I don't know, Thea," says Nathan. "This lad could be anyone." The thought of his pretty seventeen-year-old daughter flitting about the island with some itinerant roof-man is not sitting particularly well.

"Don't be silly. He's not *anyone*." She nods towards the window. "Besides, that thing could have someone's head off. We need to fix it."

Nathan is pleased to see their stable hand trudging over the dunes towards the house.

"You know anything about carpentry, Lewis?" Nathan calls to him, gesturing up to the window.

Lewis chuckles. "You want me to fix that? Not a chance, sir. I'm the last fellow you want with a hammer in his hand." He digs his hands into the pockets of his coat, a seriousness falling over his eyes. "You been into town this morning, Mr Blake?"

"No. Why?"

"A passenger ship was wrecked out near Longstone last night. Survivors are with your sister and her husband."

"What?" Nathan's attention is drawn away from the window. "Was anyone hurt?"

"Don't know much more than that, I'm afraid," says Lewis. "But a few of the fishermen are heading out there once the tide lifts to help take the passengers to the mainland. I'm sure one of them will take a message over to the island for you."

"Write the message, Papa," Theodora says with a shine in her eyes.

"I'll take it down to the anchorage. And I'll ask this fellow about fixing the window while I'm there."

And for far from the first time in his daughter's life, Nathan knows there's little point in protesting.

Boats come. Jostling and creaking against the Longstone jetty to ferry the survivors to the mainland. The morning is bright now, with fierce shards of sunlight straining into the cottage through the gaps in the shutters. Light falls on the aftermath of the night: on bloodied cloths and scattered cups, on bruised and sleepless faces. The sailors of the rescue boats— Trinity House seamen and a horde of local fishermen—pour into the crowded living space, helping survivors to their feet, shepherding them out of the cottage.

Eva steers the people past the bedroom door, hoping they won't wake the children. She would like, when her sons and daughter next open their eyes, for the worst of this to be over. Through the window, she can see the man in the skiff being wrapped in hessian. She watches the lifeless weight of him being passed over the gunwale into one of the rescue boats. She wraps her arms around herself, suddenly cold.

"A note from your brother, Mrs Murray." She turns at the sound of a fisherman's voice. He holds a folded page out to her. "Your niece gave it to me this morning after they heard about the wreck."

Eva takes the note, nodding her thanks. Unfolds the page and skims over it.

Finn catches her eye. "All right?"

She nods. "Just asking after us." She glances over at Harriet in the bed in the corner of the room. "I think I've a little too much to tell Nathan in writing," she says, voice low. "I'll call on him when I can."

The officer has pencil and notebook in hand now, a hundred questions on his lips. Questions for Finn, for the lost ship's crewmen, for the passengers. Time of impact? How many souls lost? Your captain among them? Cause of the wreck?

He scrawls down answers. Promises an investigation.

Eva glances at her sister. Her eyes are closed, but her breathing is shallow, eyelids fluttering. Eva can tell she is awake.

One of the fishermen steps up to the bed, nodding towards Harriet's still form. "She's the last one?"

Eva steps in front of him, blocking his way. "Yes. But she'll stay here." She cannot let her go. Not now that she has just found her again. She waits for a protest from Harriet, but it doesn't come.

Finn guides the last of the men out of the house and closes the door behind them. Shouted instructions carry in from outside, then a thick stillness falls over the cottage. The sound of voices is replaced by sea against the jetty; the rattle of the firebasket's chain. A chaotic choir of birdsong.

Eva moves around the cottage, throwing blood-splattered cloths into the washbin, collecting empty soup bowls from beside the hearth, folding blankets over the backs of chairs.

Finn reaches for her. Pulls her into him. "There's no need to do all this now."

A wave of exhaustion breaks over her and for long moments, she stands with her head pressed to his chest, inhaling the scent of sea, feeling the coarse wool of his shirt against her cheek. She had not allowed herself to consider the danger he had been in out on the Crumstone, but now the relief at his safety threatens to break over her. She tightens her arms around him, craving his nearness.

Finally, she steps away. Opens the bedroom door a crack and peeks in at the children. After being up and down throughout the night, all four are now sleeping heavily; Noah, Tom, and Archie sprawled out across the bed in a tangle of legs and blankets, Maggie on her back in one corner of her crib.

Eva pulls the door closed and looks down at Harriet. Her body is limp and weighted, and Eva guesses that this time, her sleep is genuine. Her chest is rising and falling steadily, a little of the colour returned to her cheeks.

"She seems better," says Finn.

Eva nods. "Perhaps we could take her to the bedroom? Make up a bed for the children out here by the fire? At least there she can have a little privacy."

"Aye. Of course."

When the boys are curled up in blankets by the simmering hearth, and Maggie's crib brought out to stand beside the fire, Finn scoops Harriet into his arms and carries her into the children's room. Eva watches from the doorway as he settles her onto the bed. Pulls the blankets up to her chin. Harriet stirs in her sleep but doesn't wake.

Finn steps out of the bedroom, closing the door behind him. His eyes drift to Tom. "Have you told her?"

"Not yet." Eva sinks wearily onto her bed. Her sister's wet hair has left dampness on the sheets, but it doesn't stop fatigue from tugging her down. She hopes the children are as exhausted as she is. Hopes they will sleep for a little longer yet.

Finn pulls off his boots and climbs onto the bed beside her. He wraps an arm around her, lies with his forehead pressed to hers. "All right?"

Eva meets his gaze. She sees the gold flecks in his brown eyes, threads of silver in the crags of his beard. "I ought to be asking you that. After all you did tonight."

"Aye, but are you all right with your sister being here?"

Eva cannot deny it: she feels on edge at Harriet's nearness. She is infinitely grateful that her sister is alive. But there's an old unease there; a discomfort she has not felt for years. It's just nerves, she tells herself. Nerves that come from not having seen her for so long.

But she knows there's more to it than that. A fear of what pieces of the past her sister might see fit to dredge up when she next opens her eyes. The last time Eva had seen her, Harriet had been wild with anger at her for keeping the truth of Oliver's death a secret. For marrying the man who had killed their brother. It is something they have never really discussed. A truth Eva has tucked away, buried deep. One she would be happy never to go near again. Certainly, she and Finn never speak of it; their children do not know—will never know, if Eva has her way. But with Harriet sleeping beneath her roof, the peace they have spent the last ten years cultivating suddenly feels far too precarious.

CHAPTER FOUR

When she opens her eyes, it takes Harriet a long time to remember where she is. Pale light is struggling through curtained windows, the sea hissing constant and unseen. The sound makes her feel painfully enclosed. She had hated being on the ocean, unable to escape the confines of the ship.

An easy target.

Trapped at first—and then the sea was everywhere; cold and dark and flooding into places it was never meant to be. Last night is made up of fragmented memories—the roar of the ship against rock, the shouts of the crew, the pitching of the deck, water sweeping her off her feet and stealing her breath. When she tries to grasp hold of it all, the only clear notion she comes away with is fear, and a cold so fiercely all-consuming she had ceased to be aware of it.

She is not on the ship now. Her addled brain grasps this, yes. Because that ship had succumbed to the ocean, straddled and splintered upon the reef.

Eva's cottage.

In the pale afternoon light, Harriet sees pieces of the life her sister has built: children's breeches tossed on the back of the chair in the corner, nine-pins tipped over beside the bed, a rag doll lying face down on the dresser. She hears muffled voices on the other side of the door. How many voices? Eva and Finn. Three children? Four? How do they all fit in this crumb of a cottage? How many small bodies squeeze into this bed each night? Harriet feels faint regret at taking up so much space.

The muffled voices grow steadily louder, then are hushed by their mother.

Tom, she hears. *Would you like some more bread, Tom?* The name nudges at her; an ache. She does her best to push it away. Push all of this away.

The last of her sleep is sloughed off her when Eva shoulders open the door, a wooden bowl in one hand and a water jug in the other. She gives Harriet a tentative smile. Sets the bowl on the side table and empties the jug into the washbin in the corner of the room.

Harriet takes her sister in in the daylight. Eva seems to have grown into her life here, eyes clear and blue against her tanned skin, a dark knot of hair piled messily on top of her head. She looks less coltish and willowy than last time Harriet had seen her, her body made curved and muscular by motherhood and firelight. There's a rugged strength to her that seems completely at odds with her London self—Harriet realises her sister has become an islander. Perhaps she has always been one.

"How are you feeling?" Eva asks.

"A little better." She feels cold again now she is sitting up with her arms out of the blankets; supposes it's a good thing that she's able to recognise the sensation again. She still feels drained to the core. And more than a little surprised she is still alive. Her mind goes to dark water and shouting crewmen. Arms grabbing a hold of her, tugging her back from the railings. The ship groaning, splintering.

She sits up suddenly. "My cloak. Where is it?"

"Out in the living area, drying by the fire," says Eva. "I put your coin pouch in the sideboard to keep it safe."

Harriet lets out her breath in relief. After all this, at least she will not be reduced to a penniless charity case. "Were my travel documents in there too?"

"I don't know. I'll fetch it for you."

Eva disappears for a moment and returns with the pouch in her hand. She passes it to Harriet, who opens it carefully. Her folded papers are at the top of the pouch, sodden but intact. The sight of them goes some small way to steadying her.

"There's a lot of money in there," Eva says.

Harriet eyes her. Sets the pouch on the side table. "The other survivors were all brought here?"

"Yes. No one from the mainland came until morning."

Harriet's heart quickens. "Was a man with a missing finger among them? A dark beard? Is he here?"

"He was taken to Berwick with the others," says Eva. "He was asking after you. Is he… a friend?"

Harriet looks away. "He's no one. Just an acquaintance."

"He and the other survivors will go on to Edinburgh by coach," Eva tells her. "It's where the ship was headed, was it not?"

Harriet nods. They had been due to reach Edinburgh this morning. Not that she herself was ever destined to make it to Scotland. She is fairly certain the man with the beard will not go to Edinburgh either. Likely, he will bide his time here in Northumberland until he finds her again.

Eva reaches for the door, then seems to change her mind. She turns back slowly, hesitantly. "Did something happen to you aboard the ship?" she asks carefully. "Before it foundered, I mean. The other passengers said there was a commotion."

Harriet tries to laugh away the question. "A commotion? Of course there was a commotion. The ship was sinking."

Her sister presses her lips together—an attempt, Harriet can tell, not to rise to her sharp response. Eva may have become an islander, but she has always been easy to read. "One of the crewmen says he saw…" She knots her hands together. "He thought he saw you try to throw yourself off the ship."

Harriet gives another short laugh; too forced and brassy. "Why on earth would I do that?"

Eva chews her lip. "You weren't trying to…"

"Kill myself?" Harriet finishes. "Good God, Eva, of course not. The crewman was obviously confused about what he saw in all that chaos."

Eva studies her, as though trying to find the truth behind her eyes. Finally, she says, "I'm very glad to hear that. Very glad you're safe." She hovers beside the bed, clearly waiting for more. A piece of information about what her long-lost sister was doing aboard that ship. Why she has come up here, to this part of the country she had once been so desperate to escape.

When Harriet doesn't speak, Eva takes the bowl from the side table and holds it out towards her. It's filled with a thin, watery soup, unappetising chunks of vegetables floating on the surface. "You ought to eat something," she says. "It will help you regain your strength." A clatter, then a boyish giggle from the other side of the door. Eva glances towards the sound. "You're welcome, of course, to join us outside if you wish." The offer sounds tentative, uncertain.

Harriet shakes her head. The thought of stepping out there, into all that life, feels far too overwhelming. Being face to face with her sister is hard enough. "I'd prefer to stay in here for now." She takes the bowl. Forces down a mouthful, surprised to find the soup almost edible.

Eva drags the rickety wooden chair over from the corner of the room and perches on the edge.

"You did not have to keep me here," Harriet says, cutting off her sister's questions before she can ask them. "I could have gone to Berwick with the others." She is infinitely glad, of course, not to be in the company of the man with the missing finger—although she is not entirely certain that being marooned here on Eva's island is any better. There are far too many unresolved poisons hanging in the air between them. "I'm sure it's enough of a squeeze here without a house guest."

Eva smiles slightly. "We shall manage."

Harriet swallows down another mouthful of soup. Her gaze drifts towards the door, towards the voices. *Would you like some more bread, Tom?* She swallows heavily. Feels that ache again. And she has to ask. "Your son's name is Tom?"

Eva tilts her head, taking her in. Doesn't speak for a moment. Then: "He's your son, Harriet."

Harriet closes her eyes. The answer is not a surprise, despite the sudden thumping in her chest the confirmation brings. She sets the bowl back on the side table, her stomach suddenly weighted and tight. "Why is he here?" she dares to ask. "Why is he not with his father? Is Edwin… Is he dead?" The waver in her voice surprises her.

"No," says Eva, and it brings Harriet a swell of relief. Thomas has gone ten years without his mother. She does not want him to be without his father too. "Edwin is away in Bath," Eva tells her. "He's had a string of pains and illnesses since he suffered the bullet wound during the fight with Ward's men. He brought Tom up to stay with Nathan and Thea at the house while he convalesces." She smiles slightly. "I think the adventure of staying out here held more appeal. He and Noah are the best of friends."

For a long time, Harriet doesn't speak. A thousand questions war inside her head. Questions she knows she has no right to ask. Finally, she manages, "Does he know anything about me?"

There's a brief moment of silence before Eva says, "Edwin told him you had passed. He asked that Nathan and I not speak of you to Thomas." Her voice is soft, and faintly guilty.

Harriet lets Eva's words fall into the silence. She feels the ache of them, though she knows she can expect little else. Of course Edwin had told their son she was dead. What was the alternative? To let him know his mother had seen fit to abandon him?

What was it she had told herself when she had left Thomas that night, a decade ago? That he was better off without her? That is far truer now than it ever was back then.

It feels impossibly fateful that she has ended up here, stranded on this rock with her estranged sister and son. But really, what coincidence is it? She had come to Northumberland because her family is here. As for the wreck, well, she had been anticipating disaster from the moment they had slipped out of the mouth of the Thames.

And Thomas being here? Unexpected, yes. But perhaps fate knows well she deserves this kind of punishment.

"Good," she says finally. "Then you must do as Edwin asked. It's for the best."

Eva says nothing. She takes the breeches from the back of the chair and folds them pointlessly in her lap.

"Miss Haywood," Harriet says suddenly. "That's who I am now. Miss Haywood." Their mother's unmarried name. The name she has chosen to hide behind.

Eva hesitates for a moment, uncertain. But then she nods; seems to catch the thread. Beneath this roof, Harriet is not an aunt, nor a sister. Not a mother. She is just Miss Haywood, wrecked upon the reef.

Eva swallows heavily, toying with the hem of the breeches. "Were you on your way to Lindisfarne? To see us?"

"Yes." It's not a lie. Not a lie at all. And right now, Harriet cannot find the will to give anything other than the simplest answer.

CHAPTER FIVE

Finn sits at the table in a pool of lamplight, turning through the pages of the logbook. His pencil scratches across the page.

November 8: Passenger vessel wrecked on Crumstone.

At least four lives lost on packet boat Cygnus. *Survivors taken to mainland. Trinity House investigation to follow.*

The abrupt phrases feel cold, hollow. Dehumanised pieces of the story. And so he adds: *Survivors spent the night on Longstone.* No mention of Harriet. He has no idea what the outcome of that debacle will be.

Well. He suspects. But he is willing to give Harriet the benefit of the doubt. As long as Eva comes out of this unscathed.

He leans back in his chair, looking out the window at the firebasket glowing against the darkness. The first hint of dawn is pushing at the bottom of the sky. Around him, the cottage is still and quiet; Eva and the boys all piled into the bed, Maggie snuffling softly in the crib beside the fire.

He's glad his wife and children are sleeping. All too often, their nights are broken and firelit, as he and Eva manage a juggle of lightkeeping and childrearing, and stolen, silent moments. Precious hours curled up in bed together as the beacon burns out with the dawn. Last night has broken the chaotic rhythm of their lives.

Finn stretches his arms up over his head, the muscles in his back and shoulders tired and aching. He's exhausted after last night too, and still a little on edge. Something of a wonder, he supposes, that it had taken fifteen years of him keeping the Longstone light to have had a ship founder on his doorstep. After all, it was the death of Finn's two uncles in a wreck on the Knavestone that had caused his father to build the cottage and beacon out here in the first place. To the log, he adds: *Grateful to be of use.*

Over the years, the logbooks have become far more than just a record of the weather and tides. There are entries written in Eva's neat hand; their sons' broad tangles: *Lots of seals in the water today.* Precious records: Noah's arrival; Archie's, Maggie's—born, like their mother, in the rigid safety of Highfield House. The scrawled grief of their Longstone-born daughter, arrived months too early and lost before the dawn.

Finn looks up at the soft creak of the bed. Noah's footsteps sigh over the floorboards.

"The lady in our room," he says. "Who is she?"

"Just someone your mama knows." It seems like the simplest response.

Noah slides onto the chair opposite Finn at the table; tugs the logbook towards him. "'Passenger vessel...'" He frowns in thought, a furrow appearing on the bridge of his nose. "What's that word?"

"'Wrecked.'"

"'Wrecked on Crumstone.'" Noah glances up at his father with a weighted look in his eyes. A new seriousness that makes him look like more than a child. It catches Finn by surprise.

"All right?" he asks.

Noah nods. "I'm glad all those people are gone."

"So am I."

"There was so many of them."

"Aye. Too many for this place. But they were lucky we were here."

Noah nods again slowly, still frowning over the page.

Tom rolls over in the bed, murmuring in his sleep. "Get dressed," Finn tells his son, closing the logbook. "Let's go outside. Let everyone sleep."

Noah rifles through the pile of clothes at the bottom of the bed and steps into his breeches. Finds his coat and woollen cap hung on the hook beside the door. He pulls them on, following Finn out of the cottage.

A pale grey light is settling over the archipelago, absorbing the line of smoke coiling upwards from the firebasket. Finn walks the island slowly, carefully, peering into rockpools and crevices. There will be pieces of the wreck in these waters now. Pieces of lost lives.

"What are we doing?" Noah asks.

"Just seeing what we can see."

"Pieces of the wreck?"

"Aye." Archie will be out here exploring the pools soon, like he does at every low tide. Pulling flotsam from the water, to clutter up the mantel. Finn does not want him finding anything untoward. He'd prefer for Noah not to see anything either. But then again, he'd seen plenty worse when he was his son's age.

Finn is all too aware that Noah, at nine years old, is the very same age he was when he had fled Longstone on Henry Ward's ship. When he had decided life on this island was not enough for him. He has found himself watching his son more closely these past months, trying to catch any hint of unhappiness, of discontent.

Finn reminds himself that Noah has a far different life to what he had had: he has his mother, his siblings. And, Finn hopes, better relations with his father.

None of that knowledge stops him from wondering, from worrying. It's a concern he has never shared with Eva—can't quite tell if it's because he knows how foolish and unfounded his fear is, or because it's a concern he does not want to pass on to her. A concern, he knows, that's rooted in his own regret at the way he had left Longstone without a word to his father. Left him to fret and fear, and eventually to die alone on this island. Fearing that his own son might do the same feels like the penance he has to pay.

Out on the Crumstone, the masts of the foundered ship are silhouettes against the dawn, torn sails caught by the breeze.

"It's still there," says Noah.

Finn nods. "Trinity House'll be out here soon. Examining the wreck for their investigation. Salvaging what they can."

"An investigation? To find out why it got wrecked?"

"Aye."

Noah squints. "Why *did* it get wrecked?"

"I don't know," Finn admits. *A commotion,* he thinks. But even if the crew were right about what Harriet was trying to do, that would not have caused the ship to founder. "A navigation error, I imagine."

"Maybe they got blown off course."

"Aye, maybe."

The sun has fully risen by the time they finish their circuit of the island, having found nothing more than a few stray pieces of driftwood. Finn hears voices floating out from the cottage. Fishing boats are dotting the water now. One, he realises, is drawing close to the island.

He goes out to the jetty, Noah trailing. Watches the cutter approach. He recognises the mainsail—misshapen, torn, and badly stitched. Knows the boat belongs to Martin Macauley.

It's Macauley at the tiller, two other Lindisfarne fishermen with him. The sight of them makes Finn uneasy. Macauley has been here in the past, stealing back the coal Finn had stolen from him—and then some. But that was all many years ago; these days, Finn has been doing his best to let his family's long-standing feud with the Macauleys fade.

The boat shudders as it knocks against the jetty. Finn is faintly surprised the thing is seaworthy. It feels like only a matter of time before he's pulling Martin Macauley off the Crumstone.

Macauley climbs out, leaving one of the other fishermen to secure the cutter to the moorings.

"Can I help you?" Finn asks guardedly. He slides a protective hand over Noah's shoulder.

Macauley reaches into the boat and produces a small hessian sack. "A gift from the villagers," he says stiffly.

Finn raises his eyebrows. "What?"

"For your efforts the other night."

Hesitant, Finn takes the bag with a faint nod of thanks. It's heavier than he expected—he feels the solid shape of a bottle inside. Smells a metallic trace of raw meat.

Noah wriggles a hand into the bag. "Look, Da. Apples." He holds one up with a flourish.

Finn turns to see Eva making her way down the cottage stairs, Maggie on her hip. It's the sight of Martin Macauley that has brought her out, he knows. Always, Martin Macauley is able to bring this look of unease to Eva's eyes.

Ten years ago, Martin's father had taken Eva out to sea and tried to kill her, on the belief she was spying for the government against the Jacobites. And Finn knows Eva has never forgiven herself for Donald Macauley's resulting death. Knows there has always been a part of her that fears Martin finding out the truth.

"Is there trouble?" she asks, eyes darting between the men.

"No trouble, Mrs Murray. We're just bringing over a gift from the villagers."

"A gift?" Eva asks doubtfully. "For us?"

"Aye. Father Morgan thought to put around the village for a collection as a show of thanks. Asked us to bring it over on our way out here."

"There's apples, Mama. Look." Noah waves it under Eva's nose, then holds it out for his sister to prod.

Finn wishes he didn't feel so suspicious. But trust between himself and the villagers has always felt like a fragile thing. He knows he's largely to blame—in the days before Eva, he'd stolen coal and peat from the villagers' sheds on more than one occasion. But this visit seems to suggest the villagers might willing to put the past behind them. Why is he finding it so hard to do the same? Is it because of the knowledge he carries of what truly happened to Martin's father?

"Thank you," he says finally. "That's very generous of you all. Please give everyone our thanks."

Macauley nods. He hesitates a moment, and Finn wonders if he is expecting to be invited inside. Finally, he turns to the other two men, gesturing back to the boat. "We'll leave you be then," he says gruffly.

Finn nods. Eva takes a step towards him and pulls Noah in close. Watches as the cutter slides away from the island.

Finn allows himself a faint smile. "I'm surprised he didn't choke himself trying to get those words out his mouth."

Harriet pulls the curtains back a crack. Watches through the window of the children's bedroom as the boat disappears back towards Lindisfarne. She recognises the men inside, although two have little more than a faint familiarity. Martin Macauley, though, she remembers him well. The son of the man Eva had sent to his death. He's worn and grey from his cap to his boots, hunched and rounded at the shoulders. He seems to have aged much more than a decade. So does his boat.

Through the window, Harriet sees Finn and Eva standing close to one another on the jetty. Watches them speak, eye to eye, his fingers grazing her elbow. A bonneted, pink-cheeked child is pressed between them, nightshift bunched, little stockinged legs hooked around Eva's waist. Their son is crouched at the end of the jetty, rifling through a hessian bag and exhibiting carrots like he's never seen anything so exciting. The sight of all that togetherness manages to dredge up an old jealousy Harriet had long forgotten.

Ten years ago, in a fit of rage, she had sent the authorities after the pirate ship of her father, Henry Ward, not knowing Eva's husband was aboard. Thanks to her, forty men had been sent to their deaths. Thanks to her father, Finn Murray had not been among them.

She'd followed the executions with a bleak obsession. Had felt no small amount of relief when her sister's husband had not faced the hangman. Finn's survival had felt like a reprieve from her guilt, however small. As many as forty women widowed. But her sister was not one of them.

A reprieve from her guilt, yes, but not her anger. Because Eva had knowingly married the man who had killed their brother.

But right now, Harriet is too exhausted to give any energy to that anger. Finn Murray may have taken Oliver's life. But he had saved hers.

How long this amnesty towards Finn will last, she has no idea.

Harriet can tell, by the haunted look on Eva's face as she watches the boat disappear, that there has been no resolution between her and Martin Macauley. Can tell she is still carrying the secret of how Martin's father died.

Two more boys burst from the cottage and Harriet whirls away before she catches more than a glimpse of her son. That faint, fleeting glance is enough to strike her breathless, and she stands for long moments with her back pressed to the wall, hidden from the window, trying to steady herself.

She knows she cannot stay in this room forever. This tiny island, this tiny cottage, feels stifling—far more so with Thomas here. And there is nowhere to run if the man with the missing finger shows himself. Harriet knows she needs to leave as soon as possible.

Eva has left clothes for her on the end of the bed: stays and plain linen petticoats, woollen skirts and a shortjacket the colour of rain-washed slate. Harriet goes to the washbin. Her skin is still sticky with salt, and despite the chill of the water, she scrubs until her body feels raw. She laces the bodice slowly, still heavy with fatigue, though her heart is thumping in the aftermath of Thomas. Eva's jump stays, lined only with cord, feel soft and pliable compared to the whale-boned corset Harriet is used to wearing; the storm-cloud skirts impossibly dour. She longs for her sack gowns and ribboned trims, for stomachers splashed in colour. Those purples and crimsons and fine trails of embroidery are all at the bottom of the German Ocean now. Harriet is just thankful she had her coin pouch in her cloak— with her travel documents inside—when the ship had disappeared beneath her.

She searches the dresser in the corner of the room for anything to make herself more presentable. No hairbrush, but a small wooden comb, which she runs through her tangled curls, wincing as the teeth catch on the salt-hardened snarls of her hair. She peers into the hand-mirror she finds next to the comb. Lowers it quickly. She is too pale, too weary, too colourless. Looks as though she has narrowly survived a shipwreck.

She sets the mirror back on the dresser and tugs at the shortjacket to straighten it. Then she draws in her courage and unclicks the latch of the bedroom door.

Finn and Eva are herding the children back inside as she steps out into the living area. Being in the same room as her son is an almost physical blow, and Harriet finds herself stepping backwards with the force of it.

"Oh," says Eva, her eyes widening slightly at the sight of Harriet. "I…" She gathers herself quickly. Shifts the bonneted child—a daughter, Harriet guesses—onto her other hip. "Children, this is my…" She falters. "A friend. Miss Haywood." The name—the lie—sounds awkward on her tongue. "This is Maggie and Archie," says Eva, gesturing to her daughter and younger son—five or six, perhaps—who takes one look at Harriet and disappears behind his mother. "And Noah." Eva avoids Harriet's eyes. "And this is Tom. My nephew." Harriet hears the strain in her words, the excessive, forced lightness.

"A pleasure to meet you," Harriet manages, in a voice that does not sound like her own. She tries not to let her gaze linger on Thomas. She can see herself in him, yes. Sees herself in his straw-coloured curls and sharp blue eyes. He's golden beside Eva and Finn's dark-haired flock, his coat and breeches newer and neater than Noah and Archie's, though all three boys are similarly windblown and pink-cheeked. Thomas has just an inch or two of height on Noah, though he must be more than a year older. His face is narrow and angular, Edwin's mostly, but the resemblance to her is there. Too faint, Harriet assumes—hopes—for him to see himself. She has not forgotten that unmooring feeling of standing in front of the father she had never known, and seeing herself in him for the first time. She does not want that for her son.

"Is there anything you need?" Eva asks. "Are you warm enough? Are you hungry? Thirsty? Do you—"

"I'm fine." The words come out sharper than she intended.

Archie emerges from behind Eva to inspect the bag his father has dumped on the table. Finn glances between Harriet and Eva, then looks down at the three boys. "Come on, lads," he says suddenly. "The basket needs emptying. Best we do it now before breakfast."

He herds them back out of the cottage. As the door closes behind them, Harriet lets out a breath she had not realised she was holding.

"Are you all right?" Eva asks.

Harriet nods. Seeing her son has left a quake inside her, but she does not want Eva to know that. Leaving Thomas had been her decision—the right decision. She does not want anyone to question that. Especially not her sister.

Maggie bleats and wriggles, and Eva sets her down on the worn rug in front of the hearth. She totters off towards the table on unsteady legs. "You look better today," Eva says to Harriet. "Are you feeling any stronger?"

"A little." Harriet sidesteps the baby and perches on a chair at the table, folding her hands in her lap. She wishes she had stayed locked away in the bedroom.

Eva peers into the bag on the table, rummaging through its contents. She lifts out a bottle of claret and a misshapen seedcake. Inspects a wrapped cloth package Harriet assumes is full of meat.

"A gift from the villagers," Eva tells her, tucking the meat back into the bag. "I'm not quite sure what to make of it. They've never seen fit to thank us before."

"Well," says Harriet, "I imagine you've never rescued shipwreck survivors before either."

"No. That's true. In any case, I'm grateful. I'll not turn down such an offer with so many mouths to feed." Harriet catches her faint wince. "I mean... Not that I mind. We're very happy to have him here. And Edwin made sure he was well taken care of." Her cheeks flush as she blunders over her words. "Financially, I mean."

Harriet looks down into her hands. She has no idea what to say. An apology? A thank you? She supposes both options would be more than appropriate. But she cannot find the will to speak.

Eva pulls a cannister from the sideboard and scoops its contents into a pot sitting on the hearth. She pours in water from the kettle and hangs it on the hook above the fire, she and Maggie jabbering back and forth to each other in a dialogue Harriet can barely make sense of. She feels like an intruder.

Eva looks over her shoulder. "Tell me about your life," she says, stirring the contents of the pot with one hand and herding her daughter away from the fireguard with the other. "Did you ever make it to France? Are your paintings hung in Parisian salons?"

She speaks with forced lightness, but Harriet hears the weight of the questions. She knows Eva is probing, prying, to see if there might be anything so terrible in her life that she might have no other choice but to fling herself from a ship in the middle of the German Ocean.

"They are," Harriet says. "Yes. I've a number of patrons in France. Several in England."

Maggie stares up at her with wide brown eyes, then makes a grab for a carrot poking out of the bag. She scurries back towards Eva.

"Really? How wonderful. Thank you, Maggie. Give that to me." Eva prises the carrot from her daughter's pudgy fingers. "Sorry," she says to Harriet. "Now she's walking she's into everything. I'm pleased for you. I know it was what you always wanted." She puts the carrot back on the table. "Tell me about your patrons. Are you able to make a living from your art?"

"Yes." And it brings her no small amount of pride. "Although my commissions are not always so thrilling. Usually a patron comes to a woman artist if they want a nice, polite painting of a vase of flowers to hang above the harpsichord."

Eva smiles. "A nice, polite painting of anything has never been quite your style."

Harriet traces a finger over a knot in the wood of the table. "I signed most of my landscapes with a man's name until very recently. One of my London patrons commissioned a series of pieces for a public display. I agreed to it on the condition I could use my own name." She smiles wryly. "It was a series of pieces inspired by these islands, of all things."

Eva raises her eyebrows. "Really?" She glances at Harriet, then corrals her daughter back towards the table. "You thought to paint the islands?"

"I know. I—"

"No sweetheart, you can't have that." A screech from the baby. "It's for another time."

"Perhaps we can speak later," Harriet says stiffly.

Eva gives her apologetic eyes. "I'm sorry," she says, stuffing the bag of food into the sideboard cupboard. "I truly do want to know. I'm just—"

"Raising three children and keeping a shipping light." Harriet glances down, hit with a pang of guilt. "Four children."

Eva doesn't respond at once. "Yes," she says finally. "I am. We are." She pauses. "But I do wish to hear about all these things. Very much so." Meets Harriet's eyes. "Are you happy?"

It's a complicated question, and in the tentative way Eva asks it, Harriet can tell she is aware of this.

In many ways, she has been happy. Eva is right: seeing her paintings on salon walls *is* the dream she has always wanted. She is slowly, steadily making a name for herself; pushing the boundaries of what is expected of her as a female artist, and tutoring other young women to refine their skills.

Once the fear of being out in the world alone had eased, Harriet had reinvented herself in London. Had detached herself from her old life as Edwin Whitley's wife, and yes, as Thomas's mother. A risk, she knew, to be living her unconstrained life in the city she shared with her estranged husband—the chance of being recognised was always there in the background. But she knew there was little enough crossover between Edwin's circles and her own. Knew, also, that he was unlikely to come looking for her, at least as the months turned into years. With time, the fear of being drawn back into her old existence began to fade.

Life as Miss Haywood was vivid and thrilling—a life lived in bright colours on the fringe of society. Days spent hunched over paper and inkpot, writing letters of introduction, seeking new commissions, managing patrons, setting tasks for her students. Long hours at lamplit canvases, wrangling pastels for her neat, patron-approved flowerpots. Storms of oil paint for the wild skies and islands that flowed most instinctively from heart to hand to brush.

Nights spent twined with Isabelle; talking of art, not talking of art, staring out through the uncovered window in the roof of the garret at the stars that strained through London fog.

Harriet had cared deeply for Isabelle. Cared for her far more intensely than every facet of society told her she ought to. Loved her? Perhaps, but it's an uncomfortable thought, and one Harriet rarely allows herself to go near. Because she had taken what she needed from her—shelter, a listening ear, the confidence to try and make something of herself as an artist—and then stepped out into the world alone.

When it was just the two of them together, being with Isabelle had been a solid, healing thing. Had taken Harriet away from the guilt and unhappiness that had followed her for so much of her life. But the secret of what they were to each other had begun to feel like just another weight to carry. Just another piece of herself she needed to keep from prying eyes. Harriet knew how damaging it would be if anyone discovered the true nature of their relationship. She and Isabelle would both lose patrons, students, commissions. They would be shunned as sinners—never hired again. The fear of it was a weight that Harriet could not bear. And leaving those she cared about, well that was what she did best wasn't it? In so many ways, life was easier on her own.

It has been more than five years since she has spoken to Isabelle. Since she has had more than fleeting glimpses of her among crowds—whether real or imagined, Harriet is never quite certain. She tells herself it is easier this way. Believes herself sometimes. Other times is sure it's a lie.

Eva takes a pile of wooden bowls from the top of the sideboard and fills them with porridge. Gives up waiting for Harriet to answer the question. "If you wish," she says, "I can take you to the house tomorrow. I'm sure it cannot be easy being around Tom. And I'm sure Nathan will be pleased to see you."

She does not sound sure. Rightfully so, Harriet assumes. She has no thought of what kind of reception she will get from her brother. But at least the vastness of Highfield House will give her a little space to breathe.

"Yes," she says finally. "I think that would be for the best."

CHAPTER SIX

This lad that Theodora has dug up from the depths of the island is much too preoccupied for Nathan's liking. As far as he can tell, the boy has been spending far more time chattering at Thea than he has mending the broken window casing. Nathan is beginning to wish he'd attempted to fix the damn thing himself.

Naively—or too hopefully—he'd assumed this to be a simple afternoon's work. How it has extended into a two-day ordeal, he is not quite certain. At least the sound of hammering that has finally started coming from outside the house suggests some work might actually be getting done this afternoon.

Nathan is at his desk now, trying his best to focus on the inventory in front of him. It's an exotic—and expensive—list of porcelain, silk and spices, and he'd really rather not be distracted by thoughts of Thea's roof-man.

Nathan had been pleasantly surprised at how quickly he had managed to rebuild his professional life once he had made the decision to stay here in Northumberland. Had fast recognised the gap in the market—and the number of gentry from Auld Reekie to Newcastle eager to part with their money for a glimpse of the Far East. In little more than a year, he'd managed to rebuild the thriving Northumbrian merchant business his father had once had—and rebuild a little respect for his family name while he was at it. The villagers had been far more welcoming once they had realised he was not spying for the government—these days, it's easy chatter and friendly greetings he gets when he walks the streets of Lindisfarne, instead of turned backs and looks of suspicion.

Nathan loves the challenge of his work, loves the scents and colours of the goods he deals in. The regular excuse to travel to Edinburgh to meet ships and retailers, and snatch a reminder of his old, chaotic city life. Usually, he returns to Holy Island exhausted, exhilarated, and glad to be home.

He realises the hammering has stopped. He looks out the window, straining to see down the side of the house to the broken casing. Hears the dull murmur of voices. A bubble of laughter from Theodora and the boy.

There is a definite ease to their interaction. This boy is no stranger to Thea—of that Nathan is certain. He does not believe for a second that she had just crossed paths with him on her way to the village.

The realisation is uncomfortable. Headstrong and self-assured as she is, Theodora has never been one to lie to him. Challenge him, frustrate him to no end, yes. But never lie.

Why is she feeling the need to do so now?

Probably, Nathan thinks dully, because she had anticipated him acting like a possessive madman at the first hint of some young lad snaring her affection.

He shoves open the window of his study and pokes his head out into the cold air. "I thought I was paying you to fix my window," he calls.

Thea and the boy whirl around, starting at the sight of him glaring down on them from above.

Theodora's cheeks blaze. "Papa," she hisses. "Don't be rude. I was just telling him there are extra tools in the cart shed if he needs them."

Nathan would like to believe that. Does not believe that.

He is not looking forward to the day when Theodora marries and leaves him to start her own life. He wants her to be happy, of course. Wants that more than anything. But he cannot bear to think how empty this house will feel then. Or how much he will miss her when she is no longer sitting across the table from him at breakfast time, chattering away about the story she had stayed up all night writing. For so many years, it has just been the two of them, tucked away in the cradle of Highfield House. What will he do when she is no longer there to call out to when the sky clears and the stars light the darkness, or he sees auroras glowing at the window?

Thea is still months from her eighteenth birthday; up until now she has shown little interest in any lad she has crossed paths with—at least to the best of his knowledge. Nathan had told himself he still had a year or two at least before she settled down with a family of her own. But given the way she is creeping around the place with this boy, he is beginning to wonder if he may have misjudged the situation.

The boy glances at the broken casing, then back up to Nathan's study window. He looks distinctly uncomfortable. "Thank you, Miss Blake," he garbles at Thea. "I'm sure I'll manage to find the tools on my own." He bobs his head at Nathan. "Window should be finished this afternoon, sir. Tomorrow morning at the latest." He hurries away, disappearing around the side of the house.

Nathan watches him vanish. When he looks back down at Theodora, her hands are planted on her hips and her flushed expression suggests she is wild with either anger or embarrassment. Probably both.

"Did you really have to do that?" she demands. "I was only telling him about the tools. Honestly."

"I think that boy's done quite enough work around here," Nathan says tautly. "It's time I sent him on his way and found someone to do the job properly."

"No!" she cries. "Papa, you can't! I swear, he did nothing wrong." She stares up at him, pinning her blue eyes to his. "Do you not trust me?"

"It's that lad I don't trust."

She doesn't look away. "That's not what I asked you."

Her brassiness makes Nathan curl his hands around the windowsill in frustration. Somehow, she always manages to back him into a corner. He'd hoped he might have learnt to deal with her better after seventeen years of being her father, but he seems to be getting worse at it. Or maybe she is getting better.

"Of course I trust you," he says.

"Good. Then you'll forget this nonsense about letting him go. The job's half-finished, after all."

"That's exactly my problem. The job's half-finished. He's a little too preoccupied for my liking."

Theodora turns, catching sight of a small single-masted boat gliding towards the embankment. "Oh thank heavens," she says dramatically, tossing her cloak for full effect, "Auntie Eva is here to talk some sense into you." She frowns. Looks up at Nathan. "Who's that with her?"

Nathan looks out to watch the boat approach, and suddenly the boy at the broken window is the furthest thing from his mind. He swallows, unsure exactly what to make of this creeping sense of unease. "That's your Aunt Harriet."

CHAPTER SEVEN

Nathan has no idea how to greet her. No idea what it is he is feeling towards her, this long-lost half-sister of his, who had disappeared from all their lives—her own son included. Anger? Relief? Gratitude at finding her alive?

He realises Theodora has disappeared inside the house. It's unlike her, Nathan thinks distantly. She is usually more than welcoming of any guests.

"Harriet," he manages, as his sisters climb the embankment towards the house. "It's good to see you." He has no idea if he's speaking the truth.

Harriet nods. There's a distant, dazed look about her. The bewilderment of being back here, perhaps? It seems like something more. Harriet has always worn an invisible weight around her, but it seems to have intensified in the time she has been away. Her blue eyes feel harder, somehow. Colder. She is wearing dark-grey skirts inches too short for her, and the ill-fitting clothes only add to the discordance of her being here.

Eva puts a hand to Harriet's shoulder. "I assume you've a bed for her here, Nathan." She gives him a look that acknowledges his questions. A look that promises to answer them.

"Of course, yes. You're always welcome here." The response comes out sounding forced. He goes back to the house, Eva and Harriet following. Rings the bell in the entrance hall for the housekeeper. When Mrs Brodie appears, he says, "Please find a room upstairs for my sister."

A faint look of surprise crosses the housekeeper's face. She must remember Harriet, surely. But she asks nothing. Just says, "Of course, sir. I've a guest room already made up." She turns to Harriet. "This way, madam."

Nathan flashes his sister a strained smile. "Make yourself comfortable upstairs, Harriet. We shall talk soon. If you wish." He watches after her and Mrs Brodie as they disappear up the staircase. Whirls around to face Eva, eyebrows raised in question.

"She was on the ship that was wrecked," she tells him, voice low. "Finn pulled her from the water half frozen to death."

Nathan lets out a breath. "Did she come looking for Tom?"

Eva shakes her head. "She had no idea he was here."

"And does she know now?" Nathan asks. "Does he?"

"Harriet knows who he is. Tom doesn't know who she is."

"You mustn't tell him," says Nathan. "Edwin—"

"I know. I'll not say a word."

"Was she coming up here to see us?" he asks finally.

"That's what she says." There's a thinness to Eva's words.

"You don't believe her?"

She doesn't answer at once. Glances up the staircase. "I want to believe it," she says. "But I can't help thinking she's hiding things from us. One of the ship's crewmen said she tried to throw herself off the ship before it struck the Crumstone. Harriet denies it, but I have no thought of whether she's telling the truth."

Harriet stands in the doorway of the room the housekeeper had led her into, letting her brother and sister's voices float up the staircase. For the love of God, do they really think she cannot hear them?

"Do you really think she would do something so dreadful?" Nathan is asking. "I hope her life isn't so terrible…"

Anger flickers inside her. Is that really what Nathan and Eva think her life has become? Do they really imagine she might have failed so spectacularly out on her own that she had no choice but to end things in the black water off Northumberland, of all cursed places?

"I don't know what to believe," Eva says again. "Honestly, I have no idea who she really is these days. I'm not sure I ever have."

"Nor I. I don't think she has ever really wanted us to know."

Harriet feels a pull of bitterness. In a way, Nathan is right. There have always been parts of her she has not wanted her siblings to see. Things that are far too dangerous to ever speak of. Her feelings for Isabelle, yes, but more than that too. Those knots of darkness she has always felt present within her—coils of selfishness and deceit and self-loathing. Things she could barely put into words, even if she wanted to. Things she knows Nathan and Eva would never understand.

Nonetheless, a part of her wants to be open with her siblings, if for no other reason than to stop their painful dithering. She wants to tell them what happened on that ship, tell them why she is really here. Wants to tell them of the beacons of light that shine in her life, beneath those knots of dark. But right now, the weight of it all feels far too great. A physical thing that has melded with the bone-deep exhaustion the wreck has left within her. She feels like a part of herself is still trapped under the waves.

Harriet closes the bedroom door, silencing her siblings' voices. She had hoped for a little trust from Eva and Nathan. But she supposes she does not deserve it. After all, isn't it honesty that leads to trust? She's never been brilliant at honesty.

Nathan and Eva have always been close. Harriet can tell their bond has only solidified over the past decade, out here in the isolation of the islands. Has she ever been anything but the outsider?

She perches on the edge of the narrow bed. This room the housekeeper has led her to is her sister's old bedroom. Harriet is glad of it. She had feared she might be shunted into the room she had once shared with Edwin, or worse, the room that had been her son's nursery.

Eva's old bedchamber is sparsely decorated, with more empty space than anything else. An old chest of drawers takes up the corner beside the washstand; the chipped gold-rimmed mirror atop the mantel the only hint of opulence. Harriet catches the faint musty smell of time and neglect that had hung in so many of these rooms the last time she was here. She imagines Nathan has few overnight visitors. Why would anyone come out to this island by choice?

She goes to the window, drawing the curtains to block the view of the Farne Islands. She can certainly do without the sight of that damn place flooding into her dreams.

She has never felt as though she belongs here, in this house of the Blakes. She feels an intruder into someone else's story. She's wrong of course, because this house is her story: it's her meeting her real father, and abandoning her son, and watching her painted moonscapes swallowed by flames. It's her lies and her betrayal of her family and all the worst parts of herself.

Harriet hates who she is inside this house.

CHAPTER EIGHT

Theodora has not slept. She has been sitting up in bed for hours, half-formed sentences scrawled in the notebook in her lap. She still feels wide awake.

Her father says it's her choice of writing topics that cause her broken sleeps. She supposes he has a point: she has been losing herself in worlds of selkies and bogles and bluecaps for as long as she can remember.

And then there's the Lady in the Dunes. A making of Theodora's own imagination.

The Lady in the Dunes has been floating around her mind for years. A character that had emerged to her half-formed, then taken shape over time, populating several of her stories. The lost and wraithlike Lady in the Dunes—not quite alive and not quite dead. Sometimes wandering the dark island alone, looking for something unknown. Sometimes standing at the water's edge, watching for a ship, waiting to be saved.

The folk tales ingrained in this part of the country have always intrigued her. Have always given a sense of magic to the place. The Lady in the Dunes feels like Theodora's own folk tale. A story grown from her own little piece of the world—the lonely dunes surrounding this lonely house on this lonely, windblown island.

A lonely house, yes, but she has always loved it, fiercely and possessively. In all likelihood, it will be hers one day, and she cannot abide the idea of having to hand it over to a husband. She loves its cobbled-together walls of stone and brick, the ivy that tickles the salt-streaked panes, loves the way the years have worked their way into everything, like the rotting old window casing she'd sent B up here to prod around at. She loves that every time she opens a door, she finds another dark corner she does not remember exploring. She loves how full of secrets Highfield House has always felt.

When her father had invited her to choose a room to make her own, she had had no hesitations about choosing this one. This room Papa had tried to keep her out of as a child; this room with the priest hole within the wall. She knows, of course, that things have happened here in this room. Knows it from the look of hesitation on Papa's face when she had told him which room she wanted. Knows it from the priest hole, and the passage going down, down into the house, blocked up at its end now to keep intruders out. And she knows it because every part of this house has its own memories and stories, as though it has been here alone on Emmanuel Head for as long as the stars have burned.

Theodora knows there are pieces of the past she has not been told. She is all right with that. Just fills the gaps with imagination and story.

But tonight, her writing is just a distraction.

Theodora remembers her Aunt Harriet. She remembers her well. How could she not?

She had been seven years old when she had stepped into the parlour and seen Harriet with a pillow in hand, holding it over her husband's face as he lay on the settle with a bullet wound in his side.

Even at such a young age, Theodora had recognised what Harriet had been about to do. When she was younger, she had made excuses for what she'd seen; tried to convince herself that perhaps her aunt was simply tidying the bedclothes, or picking up a pillow that had fallen. But deep inside, she has always known the truth.

When Harriet had disappeared, it had loosened a knot that had begun to form in Theodora's stomach. She is well aware that her catching her aunt in the act had likely played a part in her decision to leave. Her decision to abandon her son.

Theodora has never told anyone this. Not a single piece of it. But every time she looks at her cousin Tom, she cannot help but feel guilty. If she had not barged into the parlour unannounced, would Harriet never have left him?

Perhaps. Or perhaps she would have succeeded in smothering her husband to death.

Despite everything she had seen that day, Theodora has always been fascinated by her aunt.

She remembers asking her father questions when Harriet had first disappeared. Where she had gone. Why. When she was coming back. Even as a child, it had not taken her long to realise Papa did not have the answers.

As the years turned over, Harriet became a piece of the past they rarely discussed. After all, what was there to say? No one had any knowledge of her, nothing to add to the conversation. She had been slipped into that same dark corner of family stories as Oliver, the other whispered name.

The secrecy—or rather, the lack of knowledge—had only made Harriet come alive even more vividly in Theodora's mind. She was fascinated by these flimsy pieces of her aunt's story: an artist, a woman who had fled the life she had been handed, the pirate's daughter who had vanished without a word.

Now that Harriet is here in the house, there are so many things Theodora wants to ask her. Needs to ask her. Does not know if she will ever find the courage.

She'd had to summon a sizeable helping of bravery just to venture down to the dining room for supper tonight. Had been spared the unease by Harriet staying in her bedchamber, claiming she was too tired to eat. Theodora had been grateful for the comfortable familiarity of eating just with her father. Grateful for the chance to ask questions. Harriet had been on the Crumstone wreck, Papa had told her. But he seemed to know little of why his sister was here. Just like all those years ago, Theodora had come away from her questioning with few answers.

Now, as she sits up in bed with scrawls of disjointed writing on the page in front of her, she hears the door across the hallway creak open. Sees a globe of candlelight dance through the darkness. She hears the footsteps, somehow avoiding the squeaking floorboards like she herself never manages to do.

She slips out of bed and is through the door before she can change her mind. The light is coming from the study, and for a moment, she wonders if the footsteps might just belong to her father. No. Papa is one to go clomping down the hallway regardless of the hour; these footfalls had been too light and soundless to belong to him.

She creeps down the hallway and pushes open the study door.

At the groan of the hinges, Harriet turns, looks up from where she is rifling through the desk drawer. "Theodora," she says.

Theodora is faintly surprised Harriet has recognised her so quickly. But then she supposes, *Who else would I be?*

She holds up her candle. Even with deep shadows on her cheeks, her aunt is painfully beautiful, with coils of dark gold hair spilling over her shoulders and intense blue eyes. There's something wraithlike about her, standing here pooled in candlelight, in nothing but a nightgown and shawl. Theodora thinks, *The Lady in the Dunes.*

She wonders if some intuitive part of her had pieced together the story of the Lady in the Dunes from the fragmented, weighted memories she had of her aunt. Theodora's folk tale—her way of making sense of the world. Making sense of all that had happened during those turbulent months when her family had first returned to Holy Island. Making sense of what she'd seen when she had peeked into the parlour that day.

Her Aunt Harriet has long been a mysterious, displaced figure on the fringes of Theodora's memory. Little wonder she has worked her way into her stories.

"Are you looking for something?" Theodora asks.

Harriet looks faintly guilty. "A notebook," she says. "And a pencil. Most of my belongings were lost in the wreck."

Theodora sets down her candle and pulls open the bottom drawer, where Papa keeps his spare ledgers. She has pilfered a few of them herself over the years, when struck by inspiration. She hands an empty notebook to Harriet, along with a pencil taken from the cup on Papa's desk.

"Thank you."

Theodora nods. Hesitates. "Do you make a living from your art?" she asks curiously. "Without a husband?"

"Yes. Or at least, I did."

"Why not anymore?"

Harriet shakes her head. "I don't know when I'll be back in London. That's all."

"But you do plan on going back?"

"I hope so, yes."

Theodora can tell there is plenty her aunt is not sharing. "I want to write," she blurts. "Or rather, I do write. But I want to publish my work. I want people other than my family and friends to read it."

The small smile on Harriet's face is suddenly genuine. "I remember your writing. I'm glad you're still doing it."

"Do you paint under your own name? Or do you use a man's name?"

"Both, depending on the client."

"I want to use my own name," Theodora says. "Do you think I could?"

Harriet smiles faintly. "That depends on how wild and inappropriate your stories are."

Theodora returns her smile, feeling her cheeks colour slightly. She tugs her shawl around her shoulders, suddenly awkward. Is about to leave, when Harriet says:

"Do you write about the island?"

Theodora thinks of the Lady in the Dunes wandering through streams and rises in the vast rolling centre of Lindisfarne. Standing on the shore, waiting forever for a ship that never comes. "Of course," she says. "How could I do otherwise?"

"It's like that, isn't it. The way it works its way inside you." Harriet sounds faintly bitter, as though this is inspiration she has not sought. Memories she does not want.

Theodora feels uncertain. Like an intruder in her own house. "Is there anything else you need?" she asks stiffly.

"No. Just the notebook. Thank you."

Theodora is glad of it. Glad for the excuse to hurry back to her bedchamber, close her own notebook and keep the Lady in the Dunes at a distance tonight.

Theodora remembers; Harriet knows this without a doubt. Remembers seeing her in the parlour that day. Remembers what she had tried to do.

She listens as her niece's footsteps disappear back down the passage. Waits for silence to fall over the house again.

Harriet clutches the notebook to her chest and carries it back to the guestroom. She is exhausted, wishes she could sleep. But her thoughts are charging far too rapidly for that. Thoughts of the man with the dark beard and the little finger hacked off at the knuckle. The memory of water closing in around her. And now, the aching reminder of what she allowed Theodora to see, all those years ago.

At least now she has a pencil and paper—an outlet for the storm inside her head.

She pulls the guestroom door closed and curls back beneath the covers, opening the notebook and letting the pencil glide across the page. Above her head, the thick beams of the house moan. A log shifts and turns black in the grate.

Though the curtains are closed, Harriet finds her eyes darting constantly towards the window. The man with the missing finger prowls in her mind's eye. She has only vague ideas about who he might be, but she is certain that whatever he wants with her, it is nothing good. What if he goes back to Longstone searching for her? What if, somehow, he finds her here in Highfield House?

Things have not worked out the way she planned when she had first decided to return to Northumberland. And the last thing she wants to do is to put her family in danger.

Tonight, she has too little strength to do anything but stay here with Nathan and Theodora. But in the morning, she will go to the lodging house across the water in Beal. Put some distance between herself and her family. She knows it's risky. But far less so than staying here.

CHAPTER NINE

Nathan is not surprised that Harriet is leaving. That's what she does, isn't it? Runs and hides and leaves questions and worry in her wake? At least this time she has told them where she is going. He tries not to be offended that she is choosing to stay in the Beal lodging house rather than in the family home.

He wants to be pleased his sister is here. Wants to be pleased to see her. She has been in his thoughts so much over the past ten years. He has worried for her, missed her, agonised over his own role in her fleeing. What might he have done, have said, differently, to keep her from leaving? Would such a thing even have been possible?

But when Eva had appeared yesterday with Harriet in tow, and Nathan had looked his youngest sister in the eye, all he could think of was the way she had abandoned her child. Abandoned her husband in the midst of a long, slow recovery from a bullet wound. Left them all with so many unanswered questions, so much uncertainty. Being pleased to see her feels like something of a challenge.

His anger at Harriet is not helped by the reappearance of The Boy. Unsurprisingly, the window is still not fixed.

Nathan had known from the beginning that the boy had come here with ulterior motives. But now he's starting to doubt whether he has any carpentry skills at all. Or whether his sole ambition in life is gambolling about the place with Theodora.

Nathan is out on the doorstep with Thea, reciting obligatory pleasantries to Harriet—*are you quite sure you'll not stay?*—when the boy and his futile toolbox appear over the dunes. It's a heavy, grey day, with an icy wind spitting sand up off the embankment and doing nothing to improve Nathan's mood.

Harriet climbs into the wagon Lewis has waiting. Nathan watches as it rattles away down the coast path.

"Good morning, Mr Blake," says the boy, swiping a swathe of dark hair from his eyes. He gives Thea a rakish grin. "Miss Blake."

Theodora turns away from watching the wagon. "Good morning." Her smile doesn't quite reach her eyes. She has seemed uneasy with Harriet around. Had denied any issue when Nathan had asked her about it, but he is not convinced. He wonders if his sister had said or done something to put Theodora on edge.

In spite of his irritation at the boy, he is glad to see at least a semblance of a smile back on his daughter's face.

Theodora grabs at her shawl before the wind snatches it off her shoulders. "I've asked Mrs Brodie to make some tea," she says suddenly. "Would you like a cup before you start work this morning? It's dreadfully cold." Before Nathan can react, she has opened the front door and is ushering the boy inside.

Nathan stifles the urge to follow them. Mrs Brodie is in the house, he reminds himself. It's not as though they will be left to their own dubious devices. And yes, he wants to trust Theodora. Desperately wants to trust her. As hard as she is making it right now.

He lets himself inside and hangs his coat on the hook beside the door. Hears murmured voices coming from the downstairs hallway.

"This is a bad idea," he hears the boy say. "Your da doesn't trust me. We ought to have just told him all of it from the beginning."

Nathan abandons his plan to return to his study. Sidles across the entrance hall, trying to remain silent.

"No," Theodora hisses. "It's better this way. Trust me. Papa will come around. Just finish fixing the window." She pauses. "You do know how to, don't you?"

"Of course I do. But—"

"Good," she says. "That will put you on the right side of Papa. And then we can tell him everything."

In an instant, all the calm Nathan has been trying to cultivate is washed away. "Tell me what?" he demands, marching into the hallway.

Theodora whirls around. "Oh," she says. "Papa…"

The boy blusters towards the door. "I'm sorry," he says. "This was a mistake. I should—"

She snatches his wrist. "Please just tell him. It will be all right, I promise."

Nathan's eyes dart between the two of them. "Tell me what? What in heaven's name is going on here, Theodora?"

Thea looks pleadingly at the boy. He scrubs a hand across his face, then draws in a breath, as though trying to find his courage.

"I'm Bobby Mitchell," he says. "Back when I was a child, you and my mother, Julia, were… Well, I don't really know what you were. But I hope you've not forgotten her. Because she really needs your help."

CHAPTER TEN

Forgotten her? Nathan almost laughs. In ten years, he's not come remotely close to forgetting Julia Mitchell. Has come to the conclusion that such a thing will never be possible.

He feels suddenly unsteady. Feels as though the ground is shifting beneath him. Julia has never left his thoughts, but it has been almost a decade since he has spoken of her.

"What do you mean she needs my help? What's happened? Where is she? Why—" He presses a hand to the wall in an attempt to stop the barrage of questions falling out his mouth.

"She's in Bamburgh," says Bobby.

Nathan swallows heavily. Whenever he thinks of Julia, he always imagines her in Scotland or London—somewhere far further from here than Bamburgh, just across the water. A necessary act of self-preservation. The knowledge that she might be so close—might have always been so close?—is dizzying.

"She's got caught up with some bad people," Bobby tells him. "Thieves."

Nathan's stomach rolls. He thinks of the way Julia had packed up her beloved curiosity shop on Church Lane and left Holy Island. Had put distance between herself and him after things had fallen apart between them. "She's been thieving to survive?"

Bobby rubs the dark stubble on his jaw. Glances at Theodora. She nods at him to continue. "It's more complicated than that," he says. "There's a thieving ring been operating out of Bamburgh for years. Part of the anti-Jacobite movement. Ma got caught up with them a couple of years ago."

A thousand thoughts rush at him. Guilt and regret, mostly, at having let Julia walk out of his life—and into this one. "Why doesn't she leave?" he asks Bobby. "Money?"

Bobby shakes his head. "Once you're involved with the ring, it's hard to step away. I suppose they're afraid of turncoats going to the authorities. I've tried to convince Ma to leave. But she says it's too dangerous. Says she has nowhere else to go." He digs his hands into his pockets, broad shoulders rounding. "I'm sorry to come to you like this, Mr Blake. I don't know what there was between you and my ma. All I remember is that she used to speak well of you. But she needs help and there's no one else I can ask. My Uncle Angus is in London and Ma's other brothers died in the Rising. I even went looking for my grandfather, hoping he might help. I couldn't find him. I suspect he's dead."

Nathan nods slowly. "How can I help her?"

"She needs somewhere safe to stay."

"For how long?"

"Honestly, I don't know," Bobby admits. "She just needs to get out of Bamburgh. Get somewhere the thieves can't find her if they decide to punish her for leaving."

Nathan leans up against the wall. Hears Mrs Brodie clattering around with the teacups in the kitchen. "Why not tell me all this straight away?" he asks. "Why all this rubbish about fixing the window?"

"I—"

"That was my doing," Theodora cuts in. "Please don't be angry with Bobby, Papa. I overheard him in the village asking for directions to the house. He told me why he was coming here, and what he planned to ask you. I said it would be best if you warmed to him a little first. I know things ended badly between you and Bobby's mother, and—"

"How do you know that?" Theodora had been a child when Julia had last been on the island. How does she have any idea that there were *things* between the two of them to have ended badly in the first place?

Theodora waves a dismissive hand. "Auntie Eva told me all about it."

"Of course she did."

"*Anyway*," Theodora says pointedly, "I wasn't sure how you would react to what Bobby's asking. I thought you'd be more likely to agree to it if you got to know him a little first. And if he helped you with the window." Her cheeks colour. "I didn't know you were going to accuse him of trying to court me."

Nathan rubs his eyes. He's not in the least surprised by this elaborate plot of Theodora's. She has always had a flare for the dramatic. But she is wrong about one thing: none of this was necessary. It does not matter what had passed between him and Julia. How can he do anything but help her?

"Bring her back here," he says. "She can stay as long as she needs."

A look of surprise flickers over Bobby's face. "Thank you," he gushes. "Thank you so much."

Nathan nods, steeling himself against the torrent of emotion that rises in his chest. "You have the means to get out to Bamburgh and back? Before the tide cuts off the island?"

"Aye, we'll manage."

Nathan doesn't like *we'll manage*. "Lewis will be back from Beal with the wagon shortly," he says. "Have him take you over." But no, he doesn't like that either. He had left Julia to her own devices before. Has no intention of doing that now. Getting her away from the thieving ring suddenly feels like the most pressing thing he has ever had to do. He marches back into the entrance hall and takes his coat from the hook. Looks over his shoulder at Bobby. "And I shall come with you."

The lodging house in Beal is tiny; just three or four rooms upstairs and a cramped public house on the ground floor—lopsided chairs and tables jostling one another for space, and a Hanoverian flag hanging above a fireplace in desperate need of sweeping.

Harriet chooses the dormitory on the top storey. She much prefers her own space—hates cramming into shared beds with strangers—but she figures having other people around will protect her somewhat if the bearded man somehow manages to find her.

But when she pushes open the door to the communal lodging space, she finds the room empty. Two large beds, wide enough to hold four people each, are untouched, dust speckling the surface of the water in the jug beside the washbin. Harriet is reminded of what an outpost this place is. Reminded she is not in London anymore.

She sets her miserable luggage—a cloth bag containing just a clean shift and underskirts borrowed from Eva, and the notebook and pencil Theodora had stolen on her behalf—down beside the bed and perches on the edge. Runs her fingers over her bodice, feeling the swell of the purse tucked inside her stays. She coughs loudly, just to make a little noise.

She pulls the notebook from the bag and opens to a fresh page. Sketches the outlines of the image beyond the window: shimmering mudflats tying Lindisfarne to the mainland. Once, years ago, she had almost drowned out there in that patch of empty sea. What an odd thing it is to look at it waterless; to stare at the ocean floor at the place the sea had once consumed her. After the wreck, it feels like painful symmetry.

Her pencil glides and scratches, forming pools and pebbles and gulls; the gentle slope of the island on the other side of the water. She has no desire to commit this image to memory, but the simple act of putting pencil to paper has always been able to calm her. Bring order to her most chaotic thoughts. Lindisfarne has found its way into her artwork on far more than one occasion—most recently at Lord and Lady Allbridge's public exhibition. The pieces had churned their way out of her faster than anything else she had ever painted: rising water at the Pilgrims' Way; storm-tossed dunes; a castle siege. Each drawn just as instinctively and necessarily as these mudflats. A sign, Harriet knows, of how deeply Holy Island has worked its way inside her.

Notebook still in hand, she stands, peering through the glass to take in as much of the land around the lodging house as possible. She realises it has become more than the act of an artist observing her surroundings. Has become the act of prey seeking to hide from her hunter. Perhaps that's what it has always been. She sees no one, just mudflats and green. Is not sure if that stillness, that emptiness, makes her relieved, or as unsettled as this empty room does.

How long will it be before he finds her?

She appreciates the irony. She had come up here to Northumberland in the hope of finding a safe haven. Has brought the danger with her.

Now she has nowhere to go, but at least she is out of her family's way. They are safe from her and the trouble she always manages to drag along behind her. Her sister. Her brother. Nieces, nephews.

Her son.

The bearded man may come for her, but her family will not be caught up in any of her mess. And at least, she thinks; at least that is something.

"I'm sorry for all that horsing about with the window," says Bobby. He and Nathan are sitting opposite one another in the wagon as it jolts through muddy farmland towards Bamburgh. "And I'm sorry if you thought I was being too forward with your daughter."

Nathan gives him a short smile. "I know Thea well enough to be certain most of that was her doing." He looks out the window as they rattle past rolling farmland and overgrown grass, trees bent crooked with decades of sea-wind. Focusing on their surroundings goes some small way to settling the chaos inside him. Light rain is sheening the windows, making the images blurred and hazy.

Nathan's heart is thundering at the thought of seeing Julia again. At the thought of what he might say to her; how he is to act around her; what he will feel in her presence. The last time they had stood face to face, they had spoken in bitter half-sentences, and he had let her disappear from his life.

No. The last time they had stood face to face, they had spoken in bitter half-sentences, confessed their love for one another, and then he had let her disappear from his life.

He knows that, in the wake of all the lies and distrust he and Julia had entangled themselves in, letting her go was the only way forward. But at the thought of facing her again, all that clarity is crumbling.

"Has Julia been in Bamburgh this whole time?" he asks. "Since the two of you left Lindisfarne?"

"No." Bobby looks down. "We went up to Scotland first. Were in Edinburgh for a few years."

"Why return to England?"

He hesitates. Picks at a loose thread on the cuff on his grey coat. "Things changed."

"What things?"

Bobby shrugs, avoiding Nathan's eyes. "Work. Life. Just… things…"

Nathan feels a faint needling of suspicion. "Why have you come to me now? You said she's been caught up in the ring for the past two years."

"I've been away working in North Sunderland," Bobby says. "Ma wanted me to leave Bamburgh. She wanted me to get out while I still could, before I got caught up in the ring too. But when I came back to see her last week, I realised that was the wrong thing to do. Things have gotten worse. I should never have left her. And now I just want to help her get out."

"Why have things got worse? What's happened? Why are you so determined to get her out now all of a sudden?"

Bobby hesitates. "The thieves in the ring, they've got her keeping their records. Book-keeping, like. You know, as she did in her shop."

Nathan nods faintly.

"She keeps a box safe in her tenement with some of the takings in it."

"Things that people in the ring steal?"

"Aye. It's all pooled together, like. Ma keeps records of what's come in, and from who. It all gets distributed between the ring members. The leaders like to make out as if it's all a fair game. But do you think they share it out even?" He snorts. "I hate that they make Ma keep all the takings under her roof. It's not safe. Anyone could come for it. Especially now."

"Why?" Nathan pushes. "What do you mean, especially now?"

Bobby shakes his head. Shrugs again, folding his arms across his chest. "It's like I said, things change. That's all. Nothing more." He turns to look out the window; an attempt to end the conversation.

Nathan grits his teeth. "Bobby," he says, trying to rein in his frustration, "what are you not telling me?"

"Nothing." After a moment, he sighs resignedly. Turns away from the window to face Nathan's expectant look. "Fine," he says. "Things are worse now because he's left her. Or rather, he's disappeared. And now she's on her own."

Nathan's chest tightens. "Who's disappeared?"

"Calum," Bobby says finally. "Ma's husband."

CHAPTER ELEVEN

Nathan feels a violent, falling sensation in his stomach. "Julia has a husband?"

"Aye. They met in Scotland. Not so long after we left Lindisfarne." Bobby is deliberate in not meeting his eyes.

For a long time, Nathan says nothing. He feels utterly foolish, sitting here agonising over the last conversation he and Julia had had. Agonising over what he might say to her now. What she might say to him. Because of course she has a husband. Ten years have passed since they have seen each other, and Julia is vibrant, intelligent, striking. Of course another man has claimed her.

Nathan feels cold and hollow. "Interesting that you did not share any of this with me before I agreed to help you."

Bobby nods, absorbing his anger. But then he dares to say, "Does it make a difference?"

Nathan lets out his breath. He pounds on the wall of the coach, urging Lewis to draw the horses to a halt. He leaps out before they come to a complete stop. Bobby climbs out behind him.

"Of course it makes a difference," Nathan says tightly. He paces through the mud on the side of the road. "I cannot bring another man's wife to stay in my house."

"Ma said Calum disappeared a few weeks ago," Bobby tells him. "She said something passed between them, but she wouldn't tell me what.

Whatever it was, it made him angry enough to leave."

Nathan eyes him. "Leave. For good?"

"I don't know," Bobby admits. He folds his hands behind his head. "Ma hasn't heard from him. She doesn't know if he's coming back. But that's the thing. She's on her own now. Keeping that damn box safe under her roof. And that makes her a target."

Nathan stops pacing. He leans back against the coach, lifting his face to the sky. The rain is cold against his cheeks. Anger bubbles inside him at this man, this faceless stranger, who had married Julia and left her to her own devices, at the mercy of a band of thieves.

"Mr Blake," Bobby says, yanking him from his thoughts. "I'm sorry I didn't tell you about Calum before. But I'm desperate for your help." He digs his hands into the pockets of his coat, shoulders rounding. "I can't leave Ma alone in the tenement. She refuses to let me stay with her because she doesn't want me caught up in the ring. And if she tries to leave without having anywhere safe to go, I'm afraid the thieves will catch her. Punish her."

Emotion in Bobby's voice. Fear for his mother.

Nathan rubs a hand across his eyes. *Of course it makes a difference*, he had said. No. That was wrong. Because this has always been about helping Julia. Getting her to safety. For a moment, he had tried to make it something else. But it is far too late for that. Right now, Julia is in trouble—and what choice does he have but to help her?

He pulls open the door of the wagon and climbs back onto the bench. "Get in," he tells Bobby. "We need to hurry if we're to make it back before the tide."

When she hears the stairs leading up to her tenement creak, Julia's first reaction is fear.

No, not fear. She doesn't allow herself to call it that. Alertness.

Her body feels taut and breathless, her heart overbeating, fearing thieves. She tries to guess by the intensity of the creaks who might be on the other side of the door.

Calum, perhaps, is the most likely candidate. Or the least likely. Julia has no thought of whether she will ever see her husband again. Nor is she sure if the thought of Calum returning home ought to make her more or less afraid. Alert. When he'd blustered out of here three weeks ago, she had never seen him so angry.

There's a soft tap at the door. "Ma?"

At the sound of Bobby's voice, relief makes her shoulders sag. She throws open the door and pulls her son into her arms. He's far too transient a figure in her life these days, as he traipses around the nearby villages doing itinerant farm work. Still, it's better than him staying here, waiting for the thieving ring to entrap him as it has her. It was why she had insisted on him leaving in the first place.

He glances around the tenement, taking in the bed in the corner with its blankets heaped at the bottom, the half-drunk teacup and empty plate on the table, the underclothes drying on the pulley above the fireplace. Rain has soaked through the cloth window, leaving a pool of water on the floorboards.

"Has Calum come back?" Bobby asks, voice low.

Julia shakes her head. "I've not heard a word from him."

Her son has a slightly frantic look in his eyes. He stands close, towering over her. "Are you safe?" he asks. "Has there been any trouble?"

"Of course I'm safe." It feels like a lie. She is unharmed, yes, but Julia knows there is no guarantee things will stay that way. The box safe of takings beneath the bed has always made her feel like a target. She knows the thieves tucked in away in every corner of this town are not above stealing from their own ring. And if any of them discover she is here on her own, she is sure it will make them even more likely to do so.

Julia has kept to herself since Calum's disappearance; has told no one but those closest to her about his leaving—half out of a need for safety, and half out of a need to avoid the shame. But she is certain that news of her husband's disappearance will have filtered through the ring by now. After all, it's been three weeks since anyone has seen him.

But she does not want her son to worry for her. She suspects, however, that she is far too late in wishing that. Bobby had been frantic when he had returned from North Sunderland last week to find Calum gone and her alone. She hates that that worry is there. She ought to be the one fretting after him, not the other way around.

Bobby glances over his shoulder towards the door. "Pack your things, Ma."

Julia sighs. "I can't leave, Bobby. I've told you that before. I can't just walk away from the ring. The last time someone was caught trying to leave, the ringleaders put a bullet in his chest."

"Calum left," Bobby says—as if she needs reminding.

"And I've no idea where he is. No idea if he's dead or alive. There's every chance he's been caught too." And if her husband is dead, well, she cannot even think about that. Dead because he had left on account of his anger at her. "Do you not think I would leave if I could?" Irritation rises in her voice. "I can't try to run with nowhere to go."

"You do have somewhere to go, Ma. We're going to Lindisfarne. To Highfield House."

Julia's stomach dives. She has not heard that name spoken in a decade. But it has always been on the edge of her thoughts, a memory that refuses to fade.

She cannot make sense of what Bobby is saying. Are they to hide out in the house? Squirrel themselves away in the attic like her brothers did during the Rising? Surely he cannot think this is the way forward. "What are you talking about? Is the house empty?" Julia realises her heart is racing.

"The house isn't empty." Bobby looks down. "But I went to Mr Blake. I—"

"Please tell me you're lying." Julia inhales sharply, a flush of dread heating her face.

"It's all right, Ma. He wants to help you."

She turns away, scrubbing her hands across her eyes. A wellspring of embarrassment bubbles up inside her. The thought of Nathan knowing anything of where she has ended up… "No," she says. "Absolutely not. I couldn't."

"Yes you can, Ma. You have to."

"There is no way, Bobby. Absolutely no way. Not after…" Julia fades out. Shakes her head. "There is no way." Leaving Nathan Blake was the hardest thing she has ever had to do. The hardest—but also the simplest. In the wake of all that had happened, it had been far too clear there was no way forward for them.

"Wait here," Bobby says.

"Where are you—"

He disappears out of the tenement, his footsteps pounding down the staircase. Julia curls a hand around the top of a chair. Her entire body is blazing, heart knocking hard against her ribs. She can't quite untangle the storm of mixed feelings she has towards her son right now.

The stairs creak again beneath the rhythmic thud of footsteps. The door scrapes open against the floorboards. Nathan Blake steps into her tenement.

Julia stumbles backwards, her spine pressing hard against the wall. She wants to turn away. Hide herself. Hide from the shame. But she feels physically unable. Nathan is both the last and only person she wants to see.

He stands close to the door, hands folded in front of him, and she can tell he too is feeling the supreme awkwardness of this. He says, "Please come to the house, Julia."

He meets her eyes for a long second, and she feels almost painfully exposed beneath his gaze. Nathan is well dressed, polished, in a light-grey justacorps, deepened slightly at the shoulders with rain. The dark waves of his hair are unpowdered, and tied back neatly with a length of black ribbon. He looks as though he has found success, satisfaction. Happiness? The look in his blue eyes is too complicated for her to know the answer to that. At the sight of him, she is just as skittish as she was a decade ago. Everything and nothing has changed.

She cannot bear to be a burden to him. Not again. Not anymore. "No. Thank you. I could never ask that of you." She hates how cold and formal she sounds. Wishes very desperately that her underskirts were not hanging from the ceiling.

"You're not asking it of me," says Nathan. "I'm asking it of you." He clears his throat. "Bobby told me about the thieving ring. And I want to help you get out." She hears the thinness in his voice; the strain of being around her. Some distant, unbidden part of her is relieved she still has an effect on him. It's the most useless of thoughts, and she shoves it away quickly.

"There's a wagon waiting at the top of the street," Nathan continues. "It will take us less than a minute to reach it." He shifts slightly, the floorboards creaking beneath his weight. "No one need have any idea where you are. How would they know? And Highfield House is secure. The tunnel entrance has been filled in. Even if anyone sees you leave Bamburgh, you'll be safe there." He swallows visibly. "Far safer than you will be here, at least."

Julia looks down. How many times had she crept into Highfield House through that passage, sneaking food and water to her brothers in the attic? But in spite of all this blazing humiliation, she can't deny the appeal of secure walls around her.

"He's right, Ma," Bobby puts in. "You'll be far safer at the house than here on your own."

"There's room enough there for you and Bobby," Nathan says. "And there's room enough for you and I to..." He clears his throat again. "Well. You never need even see me if you don't wish it."

Julia dares a glance at him. Is that what he believes she wants? For the two of them to avoid one another? Certainly, it must be what he wants. How could he wish for anything else?

And what is it that makes her nod in agreement? Is it the desperate desire not to wake in the night from fear? The hope of getting away from the ring before Bobby is entangled too? Or just the pull of Nathan Blake?

She cannot dwell on her reasons.

"Good," Nathan says. He rubs a hand across the back of his neck. "Pack what you need. I shall be waiting by the coach when you're ready."

CHAPTER TWELVE

Julia yanks her underclothes from the pulley and shoves them into her duffel bag. Knocks her comb from the side table in an overflow of nervous energy. "How much does he know?" she asks Bobby, grabbing the comb and shoving it into her bag. "Did you tell him about… Does he know that I…"

"He knows about Calum, Ma. If that's what you're asking." Bobby takes her elbow in an attempt to calm her. "It's all right."

Julia feels the heat in her cheeks intensify. She is not sure what's worse: Nathan knowing she had married another man, or Nathan knowing her husband had seen fit to leave her.

She kneels and pulls the box safe out from beneath the bed. Fishes out the key from inside her bodice and unlocks the lid. The safe is half full of petty takings: coin pouches and pocket watches, hat pins and brooches. Loose pages of notes she keeps in case her books are ever stolen or damaged: records of who had procured what, from where, and when.

Keeping records for the ring was never something she had wanted to do. But she had found out quickly that what she wanted was of little concern to anyone. She had the book-keeping knowledge, the experience. She was valuable to these thieves, many of whom could barely read or count. And, as she had found out some months after arriving here, her own mother had had connections to this ring in the years before her death. Somehow, that made Julia trustworthy among these people. For better or for worse.

She begins to rifle through the safe. The last of her own money is hidden away in here too. A few coins, and pieces of jewellery that had once lined the shelves of her curiosity shop. She has never told Calum about them. Perhaps a part of her had foreseen something like this. Foreseen the moment when her husband realised she was never meant to be a wife. Without them, she is penniless.

There's a loud knock at the door as Julia is reaching deeper into the box, hunting for the pouch containing her own treasures. Bobby opens the door a crack.

"Who are you?" barks the woman on the other side. "Where's Julia?"

Julia recognises the voice of Lizzie Barrett, the older woman who lives in the tenement below her. "It's all right, Bobby," she says. "Let her in."

Bobby hesitates for a moment, then steps back, letting Lizzie inside. Her neighbour is draped in an oversized striped neckerchief and patched brown skirt, a moth-eaten shawl knotted around her shoulders. Grey-streaked hair hangs loose down her back, partially obscuring the large round birthmark on her cheek. She gestures to Bobby with a flick of her head. "Who's this?"

"No one," Julia says quickly. "It doesn't matter." She trusts Lizzie, yes. The older woman has always been kind to her. Had guided her through the maze of the ring, having been caught in the enterprise for most of her life. She had met Bobby, here at the tenement, in the days before Julia had sent him off to North Sunderland. But despite her trust for Lizzie, Julia is glad her neighbour has not recognised her son. She needs to keep him as disconnected from the ring as possible.

"He here about Calum?" Lizzie asks, eyes drawn downward to the open safe on the floor beside the bed.

"No." Julia stands, shifting to hide the half-packed bag sitting on the mattress. Perhaps when it comes down to it, her trust for Lizzie is not as solid as she believed it to be. "What do you want?" she asks the older woman. "Why are you here?"

Lizzie looks at her dubiously. "Came to see how you were faring," she says. "And to tell you there was word of Calum up north."

Julia's heart jolts. "What?"

"Mr Cameron says he saw him in Edinburgh. Says Calum was being real slippery about what he was doing up there. But he mentioned he was planning to head south again soon."

"I see." Julia sinks onto the bed. So her husband is alive. And there's certainly relief there, though it's rooted mostly in her own guilt. Can she really leave now, with the knowledge that Calum is as close as Edinburgh? That he is planning to head south? What would he do if he returned and found the tenement empty? What if he went looking for her and somehow found her beneath Nathan Blake's roof?

Lizzie looks past Julia to the bag on the bed. "You leaving?"

"Aye," says Bobby, before Julia can speak. "She is." He looks at his mother pointedly.

Lizzie hesitates, gnawing on a grimy thumbnail. She glances again at Bobby, then turns back to Julia. "Have you somewhere safe to go? You know O'Donnell and the others don't like people just walking away."

"I'm well aware. It's all right. I've somewhere to go. And a wagon waiting outside." Somewhere safe? She hopes so, for Nathan's sake more than anyone's. The last thing she wants is to bring more trouble to his life.

"All right," Lizzie says finally. "It's a good idea, I'd say. Keep yourself hidden until that rogue husband of yours decides to show himself again."

Julia nods. "I'm sure I can count on you to keep quiet about my leaving?"

"Of course." Lizzie nods down at the safe. "What are you planning to do with that? Not take it with you, I hope."

"Of course not. Do you think I'd be so foolish?"

Lizzie gives her a crooked smile. "I'd hope not." Before Julia can react, she swoops down and slams the lid. Heaves up the box and tucks it under her arm. "I'll keep an eye on it. Make sure no one untoward gets their hands to it." She holds her palm out flat towards Julia. "You got the key?"

Julia hesitates, eying the box. She needs her coins, those pieces of jewellery. Without them, she has nothing. Dare she tell Lizzie she has her own money in there? Does the trust between the two women extend far enough for Lizzie to believe her? Or will Lizzie try and gain a little favour by turning Julia over to the ringleaders for pilfering from the safe? She doesn't know. But it's a risk she cannot take. She takes the key from the table and presses it into Lizzie's palm. Feels something sink in her stomach.

Lizzie steps forward and tosses her free arm around Julia. Gives her a quick squeeze. "Take care then." And Julia watches sickly as she carries the box out the door and disappears into the darkness of the hallway.

Bobby strides down the street towards the coach, a faded blue duffel bag tucked beneath his arm.

"Where's your mother?" Nathan asks. "Has she changed her mind about coming?"

Bobby opens the coach door and tosses the bag inside. "Nah. She's just fetching Minerva."

"Minerva?" Nathan swallows. "Her daughter?" he asks stiffly.

Bobby's lips quirk. "Her cat."

"Oh. Yes. Of course." He had forgotten about Julia's cat. Cannot quite determine if this is a better or worse outcome than her having mothered Calum's daughter. "It's still alive then."

"Aye." Bobby smirks. "Still alive." He glances over his shoulder, then nods towards the coach. "Best we get in rather than waiting for her out here. Less suspicious."

"Is it really that bad?" Nathan asks, voice low. "Is there really a chance someone will try to stop her from leaving? Surely she must have cause to leave the village from time to time."

"Aye. But her husband disappearing like he did will have set the ringleaders on alert. They'll be expecting Ma to leave. And they'll not want that. Not given everything she knows about the ring—who's leading it, what they do, where to find them…"

"I see."

Nathan hears footsteps behind him as he is climbing into the carriage. Turns to see Julia striding down the street in a dark green cloak and black woollen bonnet, a bulbous ginger cat beneath her arm. The bulk of her fiery hair has been shoved beneath her hat, a few stray curls escaping out the sides. She accepts Bobby's hand and climbs into the coach. Tucks her grey woollen skirts around her legs. When, Nathan wonders, had she stopped dressing in yellows and blues and pinks that clashed so brilliantly with her flaming hair? It feels like she has become accustomed to hiding herself. Doing her best to disappear into the background.

Sitting opposite her, he feels painfully breathless. Briefly considers climbing into the box seat beside Lewis for the journey back to Holy Island. The height of cowardice, he knows. But cowardice feels preferable to this.

The cat inspects him with shrewd gold eyes, then turns away in disinterest. Nathan raps on the carriage wall and it begins to rattle over the cobbles, away from the colourless corridor at the back of Church Wynd.

As they turn into the main street, he hears a sharp inhalation from Julia. She presses herself hard against the wall of the wagon, hiding herself from the window.

"Who is it, Ma?" Bobby asks, glancing out into the street.

Julia tugs him back, out of sight. "Just someone from the ring. I don't want him to see me leaving." Her voice is low, and Nathan hears the shame in it. Can tell she does not want him to hear her.

"I don't think we've been followed," Bobby says finally, as the road opens out onto rain-drenched grassland, leaving the village behind.

Julia sinks back against the wall of the carriage. She pulls the cat to her chest and closes her eyes for a moment.

The sight of her here, so close that he could touch her, has stolen Nathan's ability to speak. Has reminded him of how things could have been.

No, perhaps *could have been* is wrong. Because really, is there any other way things could have gone but the way they did? *Ought to have been*—this is closer. *Wishes they had been.*

Julia does not say a word to him either. As the carriage trundles along the coast road, she is acutely focused on Bobby, asking him question after question, about his work and his lodgings and the stain on his coat—Nathan can tell she is deliberately avoiding so much as glancing in his direction.

He has thought often about how things might have been different if he had gone after Julia ten years ago. If he had convinced her not to leave Lindisfarne. Asked her to stay with him. Each time he considers it, he reaches the conclusion that doing so was an impossibility. But right now, he cannot seem to remember the reasons for letting her go.

Yes, a lack of trust. Their inability to be truthful with each other. Her brothers hiding in his attic. Government spies at Highfield House. A dead man in her cellar and blood on her hands.

In the dim light of the past, all those secrets seem meaningless. But he knows he cannot be that foolish. Cannot let himself forget.

He shakes the thoughts away. All of this *is* meaningless. Or at least pointless. Because Julia has a husband.

He dares to glance at her. Her expression is almost impossibly weighted: guilt, shame, regret—he sees it all. Finds himself wishing he could take it away. But even if he knew the right words to say, he feels physically incapable of opening his mouth.

"Thank you," she says to him.

And it's all he can manage to nod.

CHAPTER THIRTEEN

When the wagon jolts off the sand onto Holy Island, Julia feels an unexpected swell of joy.

It had been with no small amount of reluctance that she had left the island; had spent so many years swearing that this would be home forever. But in the midst of the Rising, staying had not been an option. Her brother Hugh had killed Joseph Holland, the government spy, and the two of them had disposed of his body in the ocean beyond the Farnes.

Julia feared that, if she stayed, she would be found out. Surely someone had seen Holland walking into her shop the day of his death. Surely people would begin to ask questions. And surely, if anyone looked too closely at her curiosity shop, they would see the faint rusty bloodstains she had been unable to properly scrub away.

And then, of course, there was Nathan. Even if it weren't for Joseph Holland's death, their parting had made staying on Lindisfarne an impossible thing.

But here on the island, she is buoyed by a sudden lightness. The sky has begun to clear, and the pink late-afternoon light is making the mudflats glitter. She leans forward, straining to glimpse the village through the carriage window; to catch that achingly familiar silhouette of castle and spire and the ancient stone of the priory.

Holy Island washes aside the stress of the thieving ring, and Calum's disappearance, and of this excruciatingly wordless carriage ride with

Nathan. Those stresses, those struggles, she knows will come flooding back in soon, but right now, she allows herself to enjoy being here. Being home. She swallows down a swell of emotion. Hugs Minerva to her chest.

By the time the wagon is rattling over the rugged path carved through the grassland, all that lightness is gone. Highfield House towers from the dunes, inky and solid against the sky. It reminds her of all the duplicity of the past; reminds her of what has always stood between her and Nathan. She thinks of the way she had crept up to the house in the depths of the night, stealing in through the passage in the walls to feed her brothers. Thinks of Harriet's husband casting her from the house moments after she had learnt of her brother Michael's death. Thinks of a night spent out on the dunes with Nathan, their eyes turned to the glitter of the sky, to help soften her grief.

Spending even a single night here suddenly feels impossible.

The carriage draws up in front of the house and a young woman steps out to meet them. Theodora, Julia assumes. She's grown lithe and elegant, dressed in neat sky-blue skirts and an embroidered stomacher, long blonde hair pinned back from her face. She has a far more open and welcoming expression than her father.

Bobby leaps out of the wagon first, offering Julia his hand. She climbs out hesitantly.

"Oh!" Theodora rushes forward to scratch Minerva's ears. "You brought your cat. How wonderful." She looks up at Julia. "Bobby and I are so glad you're here."

Nathan climbs out after them. His eyes dart between his daughter and the cat, then he looks hurriedly downwards. "I'm sorry, but I'd best get back upstairs," he says. "I've a lot of work to do." He vanishes into the house, not waiting for a response.

Theodora watches after him for a moment, then turns back to Julia. "You'll have to excuse Papa," she says. "He doesn't have too many house guests these days. It seems his manners have fallen by the wayside." There's an airy, joking tone to her voice, the bright smile not leaving her face. But Julia can sense the uncertainty, the concern, beneath her words.

Theodora leads her up the staircase to a small guestroom at the end of the hallway, with a window overlooking the ocean. The washbin has been filled and a fire is simmering in the grate. She has clearly been expected.

Theodora holds out her arms for the cat. "Can I take her downstairs? Find a treat for her in the kitchen?"

Julia smiles faintly. "I don't think your father will like her roaming the house. He's not fond of cats."

Theodora waves a dismissive hand. "He's not. But we should definitely not let that stop us." She scoops Minerva from Julia's arms. Nuzzles the cat's pink nose with her own. "Let's go to the kitchen," she tells Minerva in a sing-song voice. "Let's see what we can find for you, shall we?"

Julia thanks Theodora and sets her bag on the chair in the corner of the room. She will not unpack it. Will not make herself at home. Because being here can only be the most fleeting of solutions. All those reasons why she had to leave Lindisfarne ten years ago feel just as pressing and present as they have always been. Besides, there is every chance Calum will be back in Bamburgh soon. And then she will return to her old life as the ring's record keeper. Will do her best to temper her husband's anger.

She peers out the window. The embankment is blissfully empty; just grey sheets of water rolling steadily towards the shore. The discomfort and shame of being here in Nathan's life is almost overwhelming. But for the first time in months, the fear—alertness—she feels in the thieving ring's orbit is gone.

Unbidden, Julia finds herself wondering whereabouts in the house Nathan is. She remembers his study had been up here on the second floor. Is he just a few doors down the hallway, locked away with his ledgers?

Once, she had allowed herself to imagine becoming the mistress of this house. How distant and dreamlike those thoughts feel now.

A knock at the door and Bobby pokes his head inside. "Are you settled?" he asks.

Julia smiles wryly. "I'm not sure 'settled' is the right word."

"Don't worry about your money," says Bobby. "It will be all right. We'll find a way to get to it."

Julia says nothing. How exactly it will be all right, she cannot even begin to imagine. If Calum fails to return, and if she fails to get her money out of the safe, she will be completely penniless. But she has no intention of entangling Bobby in this any more than he already is.

He steps into the room, closing the door behind him. "I'm really glad you're here, Ma. I hated the thought of you alone in that place."

Julia pulls him into her arms and kisses his bristly cheek. His coat is still damp and fragrant from the rain. "I wish you didn't worry for me so. You know I can take care of myself. I always have."

Bobby nods noncommittally. "There's supper waiting for us downstairs."

Julia hesitates. Her stomach is groaning with hunger, but the thought of sitting across the table from Nathan is unbearable. She shakes her head. "I don't think—"

"Thea says her da will take his supper up in his study," Bobby cuts in. "You and I can eat with her downstairs. And then I'll leave you to get a good night's rest."

"You're not staying here?"

"Nah. I'm going back to my lodgings. I don't think Mr Blake is too fond of me. He thought I was trying to get up Thea's skirts."

Julia rubs her eyes. "And were you?"

Bobby chuckles. "Course not. We both just wanted to convince him to come and get you."

She manages a faint smile. "Good. Because that's a complication I really don't need." She draws in her breath and smooths her skirts. "All right," she says finally. "I suppose I could use a little supper."

As she follows Bobby down the hallway, past rows of closed doors, Julia realises she is holding her breath. But for all the stress and unease that being here brings, she is grateful for a night within the security of these walls, where the Bamburgh thieving ring cannot find her.

"So you put two cards down," says Tom, "and then you add them up, and then you turn over three—no, four more and add them up…"

"No, that's not right," Noah tells him. "You put three cards down, then choose one to get rid of, then you turn over three more and add them up." He deals the cards around the table. "I think that's right…"

Finn has no idea what game they're supposed to playing. Is fairly certain Tom and Noah have no idea either. He chuckles. Counts the eight cards in his hand and puts one back into the pile. "Where'd you learn this game?"

"My papa taught me," says Tom, casting his two—or three—cards down on the table.

Noah says, "I learnt it from Thea. But she might have made it up."

Finn catches Eva's eye across the table and smiles.

Most of the time, he is able to see that his fears of Noah leaving are founded on nothing but his own uncertainties and guilt. After all, this cottage is a far different place to what it had been when he had run away. Back then, in the wake of his mother's death, it had been a place of arguments and anger—all, no doubt because he and his da were so damn similar.

These days, it's far closer to the place he remembers when his mother was alive: a place of bedtime stories and warm, civilised conversation. He wishes he could remember more of the tales his ma had told him when he was a boy, curled up in that bed where his sons sleep now. Wishes he remembered more than snatches of her lilting Gaelic.

Oidhche mhath.

Tha goal agam ort.

Archie kneels up on his chair and spreads his cards out on the table for everyone to see, the sleeves of his nightshirt hanging down over his hands. "What does seven plus five equal?"

"You can count that yourself," says Eva.

She's come to parenthood much more naturally than him, Finn thinks, with her innate warmth and caring, fiercely maternal before she ever had a child. He still feels like he's stumbling through the whole thing. Still, they've been blessed enough to see two of their children through the deadly first five years. And while the loss of their first daughter is a thorn he knows will never leave them, it has made him fiercely grateful for the three they have. Fiercely grateful their lost child had not claimed her mother's life too. Finn knows far too many who have not been so lucky.

"Auntie Eva," Tom says suddenly, "did you and my mother play cards? When you were girls, I mean?"

Something flickers across Eva's eyes. It's not the first time Tom has asked about his mother, and Finn can tell how uncomfortable Eva is with the questions. Far more so now, he assumes, that Harriet has returned to their lives.

"Sometimes," she says. Finn can hear the forced lightness in her voice. "She was very good at Piquet. Always used to beat me." She clears her throat. "Your turn, Archie. Which cards are you going to put down?" She leans over, helping him sift through his hand. "You have to put two cards down and then choose another one… or, um… Noah, explain the rules again for your brother."

Tom is still leaning forward, as though hoping for another snippet of information. Edwin might have asked Nathan and Eva not to mention Harriet, but he had clearly failed to account for his son's curiosity about his mother.

"Da," Noah says suddenly, "it's stopped raining. We should light the basket. There might be ships out there." There's a new seriousness in his eyes—has been there since the wreck.

He's at the door before Finn even has his boots on, Eva calling after him to remember his coat. Tom follows them down the stairs. Noah is already rattling the barrow over the rocks towards the coal shed.

The darkness has fallen thick and hard, a hint of the long winter stretched out before them. The light from inside the cottage spills out across black rain-slicked rocks, lighting the path from the coal shed to the beacon. The bedsheets on the washing line beside the shed seem to glow in the darkness, catching the breeze and billowing like sailcloth.

One of the slate tiles has slipped from the roof, Finn notices. It's lying in shards at his feet. He picks the pieces up and flings them into the sea.

He leaves the boys to lower and stoke the basket. Picks his way out across the rocks to a stray nine-pin Noah and Tom have forgotten to collect. Thanks to the boys' nine-pins escapades, one ball has already been condemned to the ocean. A second is sitting at the bottom of the rockpool, waiting for some brave soul to jump in and collect it. Finn has lost count of how many times he's suggested nine-pins might not be such a good outdoor game.

The stray pin is lying on a flat stretch of rock not far from the jetty. Right where Finn had found his father's body, a decade and a half ago, when he had returned to Longstone after seventeen years of running in the wake of Oliver Blake's death. He'd abandoned his father for Henry Ward's ship, without a word. Left him to die alone on the island.

Sometimes—often—he walks past that unassuming rock without a thought to that most shameful piece of his past. Other times, like now, he inexplicably gets caught in the memory.

A burst of light as the beacon flares to life. Finn watches as Tom and Noah heave on the chain, sending the light into the sky.

"I can't see any ships," Noah reports, trudging out to the end of the jetty and panning his gaze across the ocean. "I'm glad no one came out here when the light wasn't lit."

And perhaps his concerns about his son leaving Longstone are unfounded—yes, more often than not, Finn can see this. But he's no more certain that he wants Noah to spend his life on the rim of this island, with his eyes turned out to the sea.

Nathan has heard the footsteps, the voices. Knows Theodora spent the evening at the dining table with Julia and Bobby. A scene from an alternative life.

He knows it's the height of rudeness to have tucked himself away in his study with his soup on a tray on his desk. Also knows Theodora is going to hound him for it in the morning. But he cannot bring himself to leave the safety of this room.

His heart is a steady drumbeat against his ribs, the numbers on the ledger in front of him an incoherent mess. He has long given up on trying to get any real work done. With Julia in the house, it feels like a complete impossibility. He feels constantly breathless, overwhelmed by her nearness.

Julia has always been able to bypass his fear of human contact, get closer to him than almost anyone, at least since his late wife Sarah. But he cannot think of that. She is only here for her safety. Nothing more. It cannot be anything more.

He attempts a mouthful of soup, turned cold now from having sat untouched for so long. He pushes the bowl away. What is he to do? Stay locked away in here until Julia is sleeping? Spend the night in his desk chair? If he was going to squirrel himself away like this, he might have had the presence of mind to do it in his bedchamber.

And what tomorrow? He knows he will have to face her at some point.

But right now, he cannot think further than the next moment ahead. And that moment is most certainly going to involve him locking himself away with a bowl of cold soup and doing his best not to think of Julia.

There's a soft knock at the door and Theodora pokes her head into the room. "You've been working in here for an awfully long time."

Nathan forces a smile. "Up to my neck in accounts, I'm afraid."

"I see." He can tell she is not even close to believing him.

He squeezes the bridge of his nose, trying to ward off a headache. "I'm sorry, I should not have left it to you to see to it that our guests were taken care of."

"They're fine." Theodora drags the chair from the corner of the room and sets it in front of his desk. Perches on the edge. "Everything is fine."

Nathan sits his quill back in its pot. Leans back in his desk chair. "So," he says, "did you break the window casing on purpose just to get Bobby here?"

Thea gives a short laugh. "Do you really think I would do such a thing?"

Nathan smiles. "Honestly, I would not put it past you."

"I didn't break the window casing. I just brought it to your attention. It was broken for days before you noticed it."

"I see. And there's nothing between you and Bobby then?"

She laughs airily. "Of course not." She twines a loose strand of hair around her finger. "Bobby didn't really fix Mrs Emmett's roof though. I just made that part up. Made a more convincing story."

Nathan closes his ledger, shaking his head with a chuckle. "How did I end up with you, Theodora?"

"Through a brilliant stroke of luck." She bends to catch his eye, her smile fading. "Are you all right, Papa?"

He nods. Hates that she worries for him. That protective instinct he has towards her—he knows it goes both ways. "I'm all right," he assures her. "I'm sorry for behaving like such a coward tonight. I promise I'll do better tomorrow."

Theodora doesn't return his smile. "Was it the wrong thing to do?" she asks. "Having Bobby bring his ma here? I never meant to hurt you."

Nathan reaches across the desk and gives her wrist a quick squeeze. "It was the right thing to do, Thea. Julia wasn't safe in Bamburgh."

Theodora opens her mouth to speak again, then seems to change her mind. She nods towards the telescope set up by the window. "Is it clear enough to see anything?"

Nathan slides around on his chair. He looks out through the window then presses his eye to the lens of the telescope, guides the shaft up through the cloud bank until it catches the faint glitter of Polaris and its snaking constellation.

He shifts his chair away, nodding for Thea to look through the eyepiece.

"The North Star is just visible," he says.

Theodora smiles as she lowers her eye to lens. "The star of guidance. How fitting." A reminder—not that he needed one—that his daughter is well aware of the internal chaos Julia's arrival has caused in him.

And though the night sky has long had the ability to calm his thoughts and make his troubles fade, tonight the star of guidance is offering little in the way of answers.

Theodora leaves and the house falls quiet. Nathan gets to his feet, deciding now is the opportune time to escape to his bedroom. A flash of movement in the dark outside the window catches his eye. He looks down; sees her.

Julia has her dark cloak wrapped around her body, her coppery curls loose and tangled on her shoulders. He watches her walk across the embankment in shadow. Watches her sit on the edge of the beach.

He knows how much she had loved this island. Knows how much it had pained her to leave. He has wished, many times over the years, that he had been the one to leave—though he knows Julia could not stay here while questions about Joseph Holland's death were swirling.

He watches her for several long moments, the small figure of her almost lost against the darkness. Catches a glimpse of that life that could have been. And he hopes that being back here has brought her a little peace.

CHAPTER FOURTEEN

Getting her money from the box safe in Lizzie's tenement involves, as a first step, leaving the safety of this bedroom. Facing the risk of seeing Nathan. Right now, that feels far more terrifying that anything the thieving ring might dish up.

Julia glances out the window. The tide is high; if she is to make it to Bamburgh this morning, she will need a boat to do so. She had seen a small sloop beached on the curve of the embankment when she had arrived at the house yesterday. Suspects it belongs to one of the workers—the coachman, perhaps? She has a hard time imagining it might be Nathan's. For a man who lives on the edge of the sea, he is painfully awkward on the water. Perhaps she can convince the coachman to sail her across to the mainland—or let her take his boat, in any case.

She pulls on her cloak and bonnet and opens the bedroom door a crack. The house is quiet, but she can hear Theodora chattering away to Minerva downstairs. Hears a muffled cough come from a few doors down. Nathan's study.

Julia hovers outside it for a moment, debating whether to knock. To wish him good morning. To thank him for the tea and toast he had had Mrs Brodie bring to her door. It would be the decent thing to do, after all.

But then she thinks of how quickly he had leapt from the carriage yesterday and bolted up to the safety of his study. And she makes her way down the staircase, without looking back.

She steps out of the house into a damp white morning. After the rain of yesterday, the dunes are still wet and fragrant, weak threads of sunlight straining through the clouds. Julia eyes the embankment. The sloop is gone.

She curses under her breath. Weighs her options. Wait here for either the boat to return or the tide to fall, or head for the village and its sea of familiar faces. She had had a number of friends on the island before she had left. Yes, she had been looked down upon by much of the village for mothering a child out of wedlock. But there were also people she had been close to: Alice Emmett, who ran the dame school; Molly Granville, whose father had fished with Julia's. The Macauleys, too, had always shown her kindness, on account of her father's staunch Jacobite beliefs. Will she be welcomed back to the village? Or treated with suspicion for the way she had so hurriedly disappeared?

Julia has no idea—all she knows is that she needs to get her money from the safe as quickly as possible. If she doesn't hurry, there's every chance her belongings will be divided up amongst the ring members when the takings are next dispersed.

She gathers her skirts in her fists and strides down the narrow path that cuts across the middle of the island. Wind careens across the ridges of the dunes, whipping her skirts around her legs. She is almost grateful for her urgency; for the excuse not to stop and walk the too-familiar lanes of the village. Grateful not to pass the cottage she had grown up in, no doubt filled with another family now. Grateful for an excuse to avoid her curiosity shop. An excuse not to peek inside, see what remains of her old life. What remains of Joseph Holland's blood, tainting the cellar stairs.

Did anyone ever suspect she was involved in his disappearance? She knows most of the islanders are Jacobites. And there were rumours circling about Holland spying for the government in the months before his death. There are many people on the island who would have made likely suspects if anyone ever went digging into his disappearance. But none of that makes this any easier to carry.

She reaches the anchorage. The village is far busier than she had hoped, with handcarts rattling over the cobbles and the streets alive with chatter. Market day, she realises; though most of the herring boats seem to have already left on the high tide. Instinctively, unconsciously, she has pulled the hood of her cloak up over her bonnet, hiding as much of her face as possible. Once upon a time, she had known everyone on this island. And while she suspects that, after ten years, that is no longer the case, she is sure there are still far too many familiar faces here for what she is about to do.

She hides herself behind one of the fishing huts that stands crookedly on the sand. There are still a handful of fishermen milling about the pier— men who had sailed with her brothers and father, no doubt. A woman walks past with a basket pressed to her hip. Julia lowers her eyes to hide her face. Does not want to recognise, or be recognised.

The fishermen climb into a dinghy roped to the jetty, and row out to a larger boat moored in the middle of the anchorage. She waits impatiently for them to climb aboard. Waits for them to rope the dinghy to the stern of the boat. For them to disappear around the point.

When the anchorage is quiet, she hurries out onto the pier. Unties the mooring rope of the first small sloop she comes across. She leaps into it and begins to row before her common sense can catch up with her.

She keeps her eyes pinned on the jetty, making sure she has not been followed. Perhaps she ought to have done this the right way: waited patiently at the anchorage until she found someone willing to ferry her over to the mainland. Somehow, that feels even riskier than stealing the boat—she has no thought of how the villagers will react when they see her, and she needs to get her belongings from Lizzie's tenement as quickly as she can. Besides, there's something mildly ironic about abiding by the law on her way to break into someone's house.

One day soon, Julia tells herself, she will leave all this thievery and law-breaking behind.

When she is clear of the anchorage, she unfurls the mainsail and lets the wind carry her over the storm-cloud sea. It has been years since she has sailed; years since she has even been on the water, but the feel of the rope sliding through her hands, the boat rising and falling beneath her, turning at her command, is steadying, somehow. A part of herself she had forgotten. It reminds her, suddenly, of all she had been, done, achieved, in those distant years of her old life. Before she had given up and made herself a wife.

Julia has no thought of whether, after that had passed between them, Calum still considers her his wife, his responsibility. Really, she will not blame him if he doesn't. Calum MacNeill is a proud man, a man of God. He had seen it as his duty to care for her, and for several years, he had done a good job of it. Theirs had never been a marriage full of passion, but nor had it always been unhappy. In the early years as Calum's wife, Julia had felt respected, protected. Had experienced a security she had never known before.

That pleasant, agreeable partnership is in the past now, she is certain. But she has no thought of whether her marriage is too. She doubts it. Calum is not the kind of man to abandon his wife. He would not want that stain on his character. Or perhaps she has it wrong. Perhaps *she* is the stain on his character. Perhaps putting as much distance as possible between the two of them is all Calum can think of to do. His actions would certainly suggest as much. Leaving the ring, even in the middle of the night, as he had done, had been impossibly risky. An all-too-glaring reminder of how furious he had been at her.

After she had left Holy Island, had closed up her curiosity shop and sent her brother Hugh off to die on the battlefields of Lancashire, Julia had taken Bobby north. Over the border to seek work in Edinburgh. Had hoped the Scottish roots of both her parents might anchor her somehow. Moor her after all she had lost, all she had given up—willingly or otherwise.

She had found kitchen work at a manor house on the outskirts of the city, scrubbing dishes and wiping tables, with Bobby assisting in the stables.

And then there was Calum MacNeill, who had come to the house to install new locks on the doors and windows. He and Julia had got to talking when she had brought him bread and cheese for noonshine, and they had found an easy and unexpected connection. When he had finished the job and moved on, Calum had taken Julia and Bobby with him.

In the wake of Nathan Blake and the hollow that leaving him had carved inside her, Julia had had no intention of marrying. But after running her own shop for four years, being a wealthy couple's employee was a bitter pill to swallow. Julia knew that, without the security of a husband, her life would be an endless drudge of counting pennies and scrubbing pans. She'd had far too much of struggling. Of counting pennies. Of craving security.

She had no illusions that she was anything more to Calum than a necessity. He was well past thirty, with no children to pass his locksmith business or his small West Port cottage onto. For Julia, the security being a wife brought was a fair enough exchange for being Calum's necessity. Their marriage was a business-like affair, a thing of handshakes and platonic conversations, but she had always done far better at business than love.

Her new husband was passionately anti-Jacobite. They had married and set up their home in Scotland in the aftermath of the Rising. The cause had split Calum's family down the middle—like Julia, he had lost brothers on the battlefields, had lost friends and family members on account of his pro-government beliefs. He and Julia had bonded over their shared losses, their shared anger at the Jacobite cause. And she had done her best to put the past behind her.

But Calum had been unable to let go of his anger. When he had discovered the Jacobite links of one of his wealthy clients, he had used his position as locksmith to break into the man's private offices and steal a raft of sensitive political documents. And though Calum had once fought passionately as a militiaman for King George's cause, he'd veered too far from the law for the authorities to turn a blind eye.

Two years ago, with redcoats on their tail, Calum and Julia had had no choice but to flee their home. He knew people, Calum had told her, as they had crossed the border back into England. People in Bamburgh who could offer them protection. A place to hide. For the second time in her life, Julia found herself fleeing, with all her belongings crammed hurriedly into trunks.

"Protection in exchange for what?" she asked. In her experience, nothing was ever given for free.

"In exchange for nothing," Calum told her. "Just consider it an act of decency."

She'd believed him at first; had chosen to believe him. Chosen to believe there was nothing untoward about his sudden habit of returning home late at night, or his insubstantial answers to her questions. A mistress, she assumed, and couldn't find the will to care.

Julia had done her best to make their tenement—far smaller than their cottage in West Port—liveable and pleasant, keeping the floor swept and the table laid, and coal simmering in the grate. Had made an effort to befriend Lizzie, who lived in the tenement below. She would make the most of this, she told herself. Would not overthink what Calum might have involved himself in. Would not let herself consider how close she was to Holy Island, and the life she had left behind.

An afternoon spent in Lizzie's tenement had changed everything. Over refilled whisky glasses, Julia had found herself opening up, saying too much. Loose words of Lindisfarne, of her curiosity shop, of her lost and faraway brothers. Michael, Angus, Hugh.

"You're Mairi's daughter," said Lizzie. "Aye, she used to talk about you and your brothers a lot. Used to bring you along with her when you were tiny." She leant across the table and topped up Julia's glass. "She was one of us, you know."

Julia barely remembered her mother. She was seven when Mairi died, and her memories of her had become frayed and faded. "One of us?" she repeated. "What do you mean?"

"Part of the ring," Lizzie said, too easily. She raised her dark eyebrows. "Or has your husband not told you what he's doing here?"

Lizzie laid it all out for her then: a band of thieves formed in the final years of last century, following the Glorious Revolution. Founded by men and women resentful of the Jacobite cause. Still today, rigidly anti-Jacobite. Their hands in everything from pickpocketing to embezzlement.

And though she remembered little of who her mother was, Julia knew exactly who her father had been: a cold, resentful man, made that way by the failures of the Jacobite cause and the bloodshed of Dunkeld. It made perfect sense that Mairi might have involved herself in such a thing. An outlet for her anger, her frustration, her pain.

It also made perfect sense that it was among people like this that Calum had chosen to hide. Anger at her husband swelled inside her. How long had he imagined he might be able to keep all this a secret?

The next day, Julia sent Bobby away. Told him to make his way south; look for work in North Sunderland or Newcastle. She had always wanted him to have a better life than she had had. Had fought for it with every fibre of her being. She would not let all that hard work be undone by letting him get caught up in the thieving ring.

Julia knows she is entirely to blame for the collapse of her marriage; for her husband's anger and subsequent disappearance. But in reality, there were fractures from the beginning, wrought by her pain at leaving her old life; the impossibility of forgetting Nathan. Fissures widened by her inability to give Calum a child. A bitter irony, she knows, that she had fallen pregnant with Bobby after barely so much as looking at his father, and yet she and her husband had spent years failing to conceive. After a while, they had just stopped trying.

Julia leans on the tiller, watching the shadow of the mainland sharpen. Tries to focus on the task ahead.

This stay at Highfield House can only be the most temporary reprieve. But going back to the tenement without her husband cannot be an option. Bobby is right—it's not safe. She has made it out without being caught, and now Calum has left—possibly forever—the threads tying her to the thieving ring have been frayed. She has a faint glimpse of an escape. A life on the right side of the law. And she must turn that faint chance into something more. If she can just get her money from the safe in Lizzie's tenement, perhaps she can make for the anonymity of London. Perhaps even find her brother. It has been years since she has seen Angus. Her missing him is a deep ache inside her.

And if Calum sees fit to return? If he has not been captured and killed by the ring for fleeing? If, somehow, he manages to track her down on the way to London? Well, she can tell him she had no choice but to leave. Will tell him his disappearance had put her in far too much danger, alone in the tenement with the box safe beneath her roof. She will concoct a story—not so far from the truth—of men pounding on the door and waving pistols beneath her nose. Even in his anger for her, even in his rage for the lies she had told, she knows he will never be able to argue.

If she is to go, to take this chance, it must be soon. Because Calum will not be able to argue if he catches her fleeing to London.

But she does not dare imagine what he will do if he catches her on Lindisfarne, beneath the roof of the man she has not for a minute stopped loving.

CHAPTER FIFTEEN

"And so," Theodora pauses for breath as she and Eva stride over the dunes towards the house, "Aunt Harriet is gone, but Bobby's ma is there, and her cat, and quite honestly, I don't think Papa knows what to make of the whole thing."

"Goodness," says Eva, "I really am missing all the excitement."

"You are."

Eva smiles. "After the few days we've had, I'm rather glad to hear it." Though she doesn't want to admit it, a part of her is relieved that Harriet has left the house. She had made this reluctant journey over to Lindisfarne to see her; had detoured to the market as a form of procrastination rather than any real need to buy anything. She can't help but be grateful for the reprieve. Around her sister, she has felt almost painfully on edge.

She wishes she and Harriet could put the past behind them. Though they've never been close, they'd once had a far warmer, more caring sisterhood than the stilted thing they'd stumbled through when Harriet had washed up on Longstone.

But moving forward has not felt possible. Not with Harriet so full of secrets. Eva is aware of the hypocrisy; knows things with her sister would not have fallen apart so spectacularly if she had not tried to keep the truth of Finn and Oliver a secret.

But for all of this, she cannot shake her worry. She wants to believe Harriet is telling the truth about not trying to take her own life. Wants to think the men who saw her trying to jump from the ship were mistaken. But if she allows herself to believe that, is she pushing the worst of realities aside?

She is relieved that Harriet being on the ship does not seem to have found its way into common knowledge—especially with Tom here. Eva knows all too well how much this town loves to gossip. At the market this morning, the villagers had been full of questions for her, seeking to fill in the gaps in the stories that have no doubt been spreading in the five days since the wreck. How many survivors? How many dead? Had any boats come from the mainland, or had Finn gone out to the wreck alone? No mention of Harriet. They'd been full of praise too—kind words that Eva had been unsure how to reply to. She and Finn have been gossiped about for so long that anything else feels unnatural. Sidelong glances feel far simpler to deal with than *do take some of these sweetmeats for the children, Mrs Murray,* and *I hope you enjoyed the seedcake I sent over.*

A part of her wonders why. Why is she finding it so difficult to accept the village's thanks?

Another part of her knows exactly why. Knows that, if the village knew the truth about the deaths of Oliver and Donald Macauley, there would be no heartfelt thanks. No sweetmeats. No seedcake.

Eva tightens the shawl keeping Maggie strapped to her back and calls to the boys, who are lingering by the rockpools. Three sets of footsteps hammer past her.

"How's your father?" Eva asks Theodora, trying to pull her thoughts back from the channel of guilt they so often manage to veer down. Nathan has never spoken to her openly about Julia, but Eva knows their broken relations had cut him deeply. After Julia had left, Nathan had been withdrawn and painfully quiet. Fixated on his work. It had taken Eva months to chisel out even a fraction of the story. And now, for Julia to be at Highfield House—while she is married to another man? Eva hopes Nathan knows what he's getting himself into.

Thea's smile fades. "I think it's harder on him than he'll admit to me. But I know he wouldn't think of doing anything but helping her."

Eva nods. She knows Theodora is right. "I hope he doesn't mind us calling on him. It sounds like he has more than enough to manage at the moment."

"Oh, don't worry about that." Theodora grabs her skirts in her fist as she rounds a mud puddle in the middle of the path. "He loves when you call on him. Besides, it's good for him. Stops him from turning into a grumpy old man before his time."

Eva laughs.

"Thea!" Tom calls suddenly, waving to them from rocky edge of the headland. "Is this where the Lady in the Dunes appears?"

"No," says Noah, "it's over here by the stream. Isn't that right?"

Theodora grins. "Actually, you'll usually see her right over there on the embankment, waiting for a ship that never comes." Her voice grows more theatrical. "Or sometimes you'll just see her wandering lost on the dunes. Just before it gets dark."

Eva elbows her. "That's enough. Last time you told them this story, Archie didn't sleep for a week."

Theodora smiles to herself. "Sorry." She doesn't sound sorry.

"I saw her once," Noah announces, bellowing at them from the edge of the stream. "Right over there on the beach. Waiting for a ship to come."

"You did not," Tom barks back.

"Yes I did. How would you know?"

"I saw her too," Archie volunteers.

Noah gives his cousin a broad grin. "See? Told you."

Theodora's private smile widens. She tries and fails to look away before Eva catches it.

The boys reach the house first and ram the knocker into the door, the sound thundering out across the dunes. Mrs Brodie opens the door and the children barrel inside. Eva hears herself rattle out some well-worn line about taking off their muddy boots before they go into the parlour.

When she and Theodora reach the house, Nathan is making his way downstairs, brought out of his study, no doubt, by the apocalyptic roar of the doorknocker. Thea ushers the boys down the hallway to search for the cat as Eva swings Maggie around to her front and unties the shawl. Sets her daughter down to totter off after the boys.

"Sorry for the chaos," she tells Nathan, kicking the pile of boots out of the middle of the doorway. "I hear you had quite a day yesterday. Is Julia here?"

"No." Nathan has a slightly bewildered look about him. "She's not. She's… I don't know where she is. I told her I'd give her her distance."

Eva tries to meet his eyes. "Please be careful, Nathan," she says gently. "I don't want you to be hurt by her again. I know last time was—"

"If you're here to see Harriet, you're too late," he says, blundering past her comment. "She left for the Beal lodging house yesterday morning."

"I know. Thea told me. I thought to come and see you anyway. See how you were faring with… well. Everything."

"I'm fine," Nathan says. "Why would I not be?"

Eva sighs inwardly. She can needle him for a more honest answer later. "We ought to go and see Harriet," she says. "I'm worried for her."

"Mm." He sounds as hesitant as she feels.

Eva hears a burst of Tom's laughter floating out from the parlour. Lowers her voice. "He was asking about her again last night."

"What did you say?"

"I just answered his question. Told him Harriet and I used to play cards when we were girls. Didn't make me feel any less awful about it, carrying on the lie that his mother is dead, when she was right under his nose just a day ago."

"I know." Nathan's glance flickers towards the parlour. "He's asked me about her before too. I hardly knew what to tell him. But you know this is what Edwin wants."

"I really don't think this is the situation Edwin anticipated, do you?" Eva sighs. Looks up at her brother. "Will you come to Beal with me? Make sure Harriet is safe? I'm worried it will only be a matter of time before she disappears again."

Nathan hesitates. "Do you really think she cares to see us? She made it perfectly clear she doesn't want to be in my company." Poorly hidden anger in his voice. "She could hardly leave the house quick enough."

"Let me go." Theodora appears in the entrance hall. Glances between them. "I can ask Aunt Harriet how she's faring. Make sure she's all right."

Eva feels a tug of guilt.

"What's this about, Thea?" Nathan asks. "You've been on edge since Harriet arrived. And now you want to call on her?"

Theodora hesitates, mulling over her response. "The Lady in the Dunes," she says finally. "Aunt Harriet is the Lady in the Dunes."

Eva raises her eyebrows, but Nathan just says, "I see."

Thea twines a stray strand of hair around her finger. "I'm curious about her is all. I'd like to get to know her a little better. To… help my writing."

Nathan shrugs. "Far be it from me to stifle your creativity."

"Good." A satisfied smile appears on Theodora's face. "I'll call on her this afternoon. Once the tide's gone down. Save you both the journey." And she disappears into the parlour before either of them can argue.

Nathan shakes his head as he watches after her. "I've learnt to ask as few questions as possible."

Eva snorts. "Especially if it gives you an excuse not to call on Harriet." The knot of guilt in her chest tightens. "You and I really are completely pathetic, aren't we."

Nathan returns her wry smile. "Incredibly so."

Julia moors the boat in the shadow of Bamburgh Castle, splashing through the shallow water onto the beach. She is grateful for the rain that has begun to fall—hopefully it will keep people off the streets. Prevent anyone from seeing her.

Her eyes dart as she walks into the village, seeking to avoid any familiar faces from the thieving ring. The end of her shawl unravels as she walks and she knots it at her throat in irritation. Her feet squelch in waterlogged shoes. Her body is blazing, palms stinging after relearning the feel of the sloop's ropes against her skin.

This cramped and cobbled village has always been familiar to her, just a few miles from Lindisfarne. She knows now there has been thievery woven into the fabric of the place for her entire life. Since the early days of the Rising, Bamburgh has been known as a Jacobite town—it makes sense, she supposes, that those with a hatred for the cause might have planted themselves here, to try and tear things down from the inside.

These days, when she walks these streets, she does not think of childhood adventures of sailing over here with her brothers, or of bringing Bobby here as a boy so he could admire the great sprawl of the castle. Does not even think of the miserable cottage her father had set himself up in after he had fled Lindisfarne, unable to shoulder the shame of his bastard grandson and unmarried daughter. These days, all she thinks of is alertness; of watching, waiting—for capture or collapse.

Julia lets herself into the tenement house, praying she has not been seen. Instead of going upstairs to her and Calum's quarters, she takes the downstairs passage toward Lizzie's lodgings. The hallway is dark and damp; smells of earth and woodsmoke and soured meat. Julia sees no one, but hears the clatter of pans coming from a tenement at the end of the passage. She presses an ear against the door of Lizzie's lodgings. Hears the faint clop of footsteps. She kneels on the flagstones and peeks beneath the door. A swell of patched grey skirts moves across the room.

Julia debates whether to knock. Decides against it. If she is to get her belongings out of the safe, there is every chance she will have to take them without Lizzie's knowledge. She does not want her to know she is here.

She slips out the door at the end of the hallway. A dark mop of hair is poking out from behind the wash house at the back of the building. Julia's stomach plunges.

"Bobby!" she hisses, tramping through the mud towards him.

His eyes widen and he tugs her down to crouch behind the wall beside her. "Why are you here, Ma?"

"Why are *you* here?" His words from last night rattle through her head: *Don't worry about your money. It will be all right. We'll find a way to get to it.* Dread roils inside her. She nods towards Lizzie's window. "You're trying to break in?"

She regrets not reminding Lizzie who Bobby was when she had seen him yesterday. If she catches him out here—and believes him a stranger— there is no telling what she will do. What in hell was he thinking, charging off like this to play the hero?

Bobby looks indignant. "I'm trying to get your money back. Lizzie's in there now, but if she leaves I can be in and out in a second."

"You are not breaking into her house," Julia snaps.

"Why not? How else do you plan to get your money?"

Julia grits her teeth. "It's my problem, Bobby. I will take care of it."

"How?"

Rain soaks through her shawl and runs down the back of her neck. "I don't know yet."

"If you won't let me break in, why don't we just go and ask her for your money back? Show her the book-keeping records. I thought she was your friend. Don't you think she'll believe you when you tell her the money's yours?"

"I don't know," Julia admits. "I can't take that risk. Lizzie won't want to be held responsible for anything that goes missing on her watch. I don't think she'll just let me take something from the safe."

"This is madness," Bobby says. "Stay here. I'm going to go and speak to her." He gets to his feet and strides towards the door.

Julia lurches after him, grabbing his arm. "Don't. If she—"

The back door of the tenement house flies open, knocking Bobby backwards. Lizzie blusters out, greying hair blowing around her cheeks, a pistol in her hand.

Julia darts in front of him. "It's all right, Lizzie. He's my son. You remember Bobby, aye?"

Lizzie narrows her eyes, looks at them warily. Doesn't lower the pistol. "What you both doing out here?"

"I was looking for Ma," Bobby says quickly. "She weren't upstairs and someone told me she might be out in the wash house."

Lizzie glances into the empty wash house, the pistol wavering. Julia reaches out and touches the nose of it, pushing it gently downwards. "Will you put that thing away, Lizzie? Please?"

Lizzie tucks the pistol into her apron, but pins suspicious eyes on Julia. "What are you doing back here? You know it's not safe."

"I know," she says quickly. "I left in a hurry yesterday. Forgot some things. I saw Bobby out here when I was going on my way." She clenches her hand around her son's wrist. "We'll be off now. Please don't tell anyone you saw us."

Lizzie eyes them, considering. "Go on then," she says finally. Glares at Bobby. "Watch yourself, lad. Stop prowling around beneath people's windows. You're lucky I didn't blow your damn eyes out."

CHAPTER SIXTEEN

The lodging house has been getting steadily busier as the morning has stretched into afternoon. Three more women have appeared toting travelling trunks and saddle bags; Harriet has spent the last few hours planted on the side of the bed closest to the door, a silent marking of her territory. The only thing she hates more than sharing travelling beds with strangers is being stuck in the middle of travelling beds with strangers— and she figures she would like to be as close as possible to an escape route if the man with the missing finger decides to show himself.

Two of the women, both older than Harriet, with matching clouds of grey hair, are chatting loudly to one another about the food in some Newcastle tavern—Harriet cannot tell if they are friends, or if they'd simply met here at the lodging house. The third woman, miraculously, is sleeping through the whole exchange. Harriet keeps her eyes down. Tries to focus on her sketching. Unbidden, it's the man with the missing finger that has appeared on the page today. She had had no intention of committing his image to memory. She is no portrait artist; that had been Isabelle's domain. And in a way, she hates that he has taken over her notebook, with his hellish black beard and close-set eyes. But there is something faintly calming about drawing her pursuer; identifying him, shaping him like this. Somehow, it gives her back a scrap of the power he has taken from her.

The older woman—Peggy, she has gathered from the dialogue being hurled across the room—pulls on her boots. "I'm starved," she announces. Looks to the other woman. "Food?"

"Aye, I'm famished."

"What about you, Leonardo?"

Harriet smirks. "No thank you. I'll stay here." Really, her stomach is groaning. There's little more she would like to do right now than go downstairs and eat. But it still feels too risky. Far too few days have passed for her to be certain she has not been followed here.

"You sure?" Peggy tugs the notebook out from under Harriet's pencil. Looks down at the sketch of the bearded man. "Who's this, then? A lover?"

"No" she says. "Nothing like that."

"The man you wish was your lover?" She holds the book up, displaying the page to the other woman.

Harriet says, "It's the man who's trying to kill me."

Peggy lowers the page. "Bloody hell." Tosses the book back on the bed. "That why you don't want to come downstairs?"

Well, thinks Harriet, there are a lot of reasons. Beginning with the fact that this woman is painfully irritating. But nodding feels like the simplest answer. The quickest way to get these people out of here.

"Well then." Peggy grabs her hand and tugs her off the bed. "You'd best come with me and Martha. You need to eat. And safety in numbers and all that."

Harriet begins to protest, but it doesn't stop Peggy from sweeping her down the staircase into the public house.

It's busier downstairs than Harriet had expected; she's faintly relieved to see three other tables of guests. Rain is tapping steadily against the misty windows, a puddle of water beginning to seep beneath the door. A sorry-looking fire is spitting in the grate, most of the travellers still wrapped in coats and hats. Harriet wishes she had thought to bring her cloak.

"Here." Peggy guides Harriet and Martha towards a table in the back corner of the room. "We'll be hidden here. With a good view of the door. Easy access to the stairs in case we need to make a quick exit."

Harriet smiles faintly. "Thank you." There's something steadying about following Peggy's brusque orders. Since she had set out into the world on her own, it's a rare day that she allows herself to be directed, even when it comes to something as simple as where to sit or what to eat. There's something strangely blissful about relinquishing control.

She sits opposite Martha while Peggy disappears to the bar to order their food. Harriet feels Martha inspecting her, taking her in with shrewd blue eyes. Can practically feel her considering whether sitting here with a woman someone is trying to kill is an inordinately bad decision.

"I don't know for certain he's trying to kill me," Harriet blurts. She feels her cheeks redden, as Martha's thin grey eyebrows rise. "I'm sorry. I assumed you were wondering…"

"I wasn't, actually," Martha says. "I was thinking about the wreck."

Harriet swallows. "The wreck?"

"I heard there was a shipwreck out near here a few days ago. Some people were talking about it on the coach. I heard the lightkeeper pulled the survivors off the reef. Him and his wife kept them all at their cottage until the rescue boats came."

"Is that so?" Harriet can't quite make sense of why Martha's words are needling her so much. She knows all too well that Finn and Eva had saved her life—and the lives of many others. Doesn't stop her from being irritated by it.

More than that, she doesn't like the knowledge that people were talking about the wreck on Martha's coach. It feels too dangerous. How far has the news spread? Does anyone know she is here?

Peggy returns to the table with three tankards, dumping them unceremoniously on the table. Harriet brings one to her lips, gulping down a mouthful of lukewarm ale. It manages to take a scrap of the tension from her shoulders.

"Who is he?" Peggy asks, sliding onto the chair beside her. "And what did you do to make him want to kill you?"

Martha gives Peggy a smirk that tells Harriet she does not believe her story.

"I didn't do anything," Harriet says anyway. "And I don't know who he is. He's just… after me." The words feel pathetic. Weak. She hates that she has been reduced to this.

She wants to say more. After days of secrecy under Eva and Nathan's roofs, there is something almost liberating about sharing even these tiny pieces of the story. Peggy and Martha may well judge her, doubt her, but tomorrow morning they will be gone, and what they think of her will be of no consequence.

She wants to tell them of the way the bearded man had first appeared on the closing night of Lord Allbridge's exhibit, when she had displayed her paintings of Lindisfarne. Wants to tell them of the way he had followed her out of the Allbridges' manor house and right up to her carriage. She had approached him then, assuming him just an overenthusiastic admirer of her work. Had begun to grow suspicious when he had walked away from her without a word. All the way back to her rented rooms that night, she had been unable to shake the feeling she was being followed.

After that, he had appeared to her on several more occasions—on her way to a student's house; while returning from a dressmaker; in the middle of Leadenhall Market. And then that terrifying night when she had woken to hear someone prising open the ground-floor window of her lodgings. Just as the lock had sprung open, she'd heard a man's voice calling out to the intruder; heard a pistol shot splintering the sky.

Three days later, she had climbed aboard the *Cygnus* to escape London, only to find the bearded man had followed her aboard.

She tells Peggy and Martha none of this. Knows it is too dangerous. These women are strangers. Harriet has no idea if she can trust them.

Peggy takes a long gulp of her ale. "Why don't you just take care of him?"

"You mean, kill him?"

She nods.

"I couldn't do that."

"Why not? Sounds as though he deserves it."

Harriet lets out a long breath. Allows herself, for a moment, to imagine she is capable of such a thing. Would it feel liberating? Or would it be a weight she would never be free of? She thinks of all the men who had been sent to the gallows because of her. No part of that has ever felt liberating.

And yet, the bearded man has forced her from her unconstrained London life; the life she had crafted from nothing. To have had it stolen from her like this, without a scrap of explanation, feels like a cause for retribution.

Three bowls of stew land on the table in front of them. Though the meat is gristly and dark, Harriet swallows it down quickly. The idea of killing the bearded man seems to have only increased her appetite. She is not sure what, exactly, that says about her, but she is fairly certain that whatever it is, she is aware of it already.

The door creaks open and Harriet whirls towards the sound, heart jolting. It is not the bearded man.

Theodora shakes the rain from her hood and glances around the tavern, a faintly bewildered look on her face. She heads towards the counter, changing course when she catches sight of Harriet at the table in the corner. Theodora glances between Martha and Peggy, then looks back at her aunt. "May we speak a moment?"

Harriet nods hesitantly, surprised to see her. She doesn't like it. The last thing she wants is to put Nathan's daughter in danger. She slides off her chair, ushering Thea away from the table. She's been sent here by her father, no doubt. Probably to find out why her troublesome aunt had tried to fling herself off a ship.

"You didn't need to leave the house," Theodora blurts, before Harriet can speak.

She frowns, taken aback by Thea's outburst. "It's all right. It's best this way."

Theodora hesitates. Looks at Harriet, then glances away. Harriet can tell she is unnerved by her. After a moment, Theodora says, "Did you leave because of me?"

"Why would I leave because of you?" The moment Harriet asks the question, she knows the answer. And a for a horrible, fleeting moment, she is back in the parlour at Highfield House, holding a pillow to her husband's face, feeling a million dark, conflicting thoughts batter through her head. Has she ever been at a lower point in her life than that day she had thought to kill her own husband? She cannot think of many.

Theodora toys with the edge of her damp cloak. "I've never told anyone what I saw that day. And I never will. I swear it."

Harriet is grateful. Manages a shameful thanks. Briefly, she considers giving her an explanation—*a terrible point in my life; I never intended to really do it*—but she knows there are no words that will make what Theodora saw any less dreadful. Does not even know if those words are true.

"Does your father know you're here?" she asks instead.

"Yes. But he doesn't know why I wished to speak to you. I just made something up about one of my stories. Well, no, I didn't make it up, but I said that I…" She shakes her head slightly, flustered under Harriet's questioning. Her cheeks flush and she swallows heavily. "Are you safe?" she asks. "Are you well?" And this, Harriet knows, is why Nathan has agreed to his daughter being here in this miserable tavern; this is Theodora's task. To determine if her aunt is safe and well and not the kind of person to throw herself into the ocean.

The corner of Harriet's lips turn up. "Did you father tell you to ask you that? Or was it Eva?"

Theodora gives a tiny smile. "Both."

Harriet puts a hand to Thea's shoulder, ushering her towards the door. "How did you get here?"

"I walked."

"Then you'd best be on your way. Unless you fancy swimming back." It's the worst of excuses. Even through the foggy, rain-streaked windows of the lodging house, Harriet can tell the tide has completely drained away. But she does not want Theodora here for a moment longer than she needs to be. She cannot take that risk.

Thea doesn't argue. Allows Harriet to walk her to the door. There's a new lightness to her, Harriet notes, now she has learnt she was not to blame for her aunt absconding from the house. This family, Harriet notes, has always been painfully good at shouldering blame.

Thea pauses in the doorway. "You're certain you'll not come back to the house?"

"I'm certain," says Harriet. "I'm better off here. Truly. But thank you."

"What was that about?" Peggy demands, when Harriet gets back to the table. "If you got a house to stay at, what you doing in this place?"

Harriet raises her eyebrows.

"I got the hearing of a wolf," Peggy grins. "Serves me well from time to time."

"I can't stay at the house," Harriet says shortly. "Not when I've got someone after me." She swallows down a mouthful of stew. It's beginning to grow cold. She feels a tug of guilt at putting the other women in the dormitory in the same danger. "Perhaps I ought to ask for a private room.

Just in case he—"

"If that bastard shows his face in our room tonight, I'll take him down before you even know what's happened," Peggy announces. "Got a pistol between my treasures."

Harriet covers a faint laugh. What would it be like, she finds herself wondering, to be the kind of woman who carried a pistol in her underclothes? The thought brings her an unexpected surge of power. She'd like to see the look on the bearded man's face if she pulled a pistol out from inside her stays.

Martha snorts. "Lucky you." She cocks her head toward the innkeeper. "The bastard made me turn mine in at the door."

Peggy grins. "Should have kept it somewhere he wouldn't go looking."

CHAPTER SEVENTEEN

Julia sits shivering in the boat she had stolen, blowing on her hands in an attempt to keep warm. The sloop rocks on the silver water out beyond the Lindisfarne anchorage. The sun is leaving golden pools on the horizon, the last of the light refusing to drain away. The air smells bitingly cold. The first snow of the season will be here soon, she thinks. A time for making wishes.

"You don't have to be here," she tells Bobby, for at least the fourth time. "Why don't I take you back to your lodgings? Once it's dark I'll just tie the boat up where I found it and be on my way."

"No. I'll see you back to the house. Just in case we've been followed."

The insistence in his voice is beginning to annoy her—his worry for her starting to become less endearing and more patronising.

"You shouldn't have come to Bamburgh today," he says. "If you hadn't, I'd have got your money from Lizzie's safe already."

Julia snorts. "If I hadn't come to Bamburgh today, Lizzie would have put a bullet between your eyes."

Bobby doesn't speak. Just folds his arms across his chest, a deep frown creasing the bridge of his nose. With this pinched expression on his face, he looks infuriatingly like his father. "I've a little money of my own we can use," he says finally. "Won't get us as far as London, but it'll get us clear of Northumberland. Out the way of the thieving ring. If we used that, you wouldn't need your money from the safe."

"No." Julia's response is instinctive. Fleeing with nothing but Bobby's pennies is bound to lead to trouble. Besides, the money her son has earned is supposed to be for him to build his own life. One free of the thieving ring, and the Jacobite cause, and all the other things his mother has dragged him into over the past eighteen years.

"But Ma, I—"

"I said no." Julia shifts awkwardly on the bench, tugging her cloak tighter around her. "I've money in the safe. Enough to start afresh if Calum decides not to come back. I just need to get to it."

"And how do you plan to do that?"

She tries to swallow her irritation. "Sunday morning Lizzie will be out of the tenement at church," she says tightly. "She never misses a service. I can go back for the money then. Alone." It's a flimsy plan, but far more solid than anything else she's come up with since finding herself at Highfield House.

Bobby doesn't respond. Just huffs again and turns to look out over the ink-black water. Julia can tell he's annoyed with her. Good. She's annoyed with him too.

She stares out across the leathery sea, watching the black interruptions of seals out past Saint Cuthbert's Island. "It's dark enough," she says finally. "Let's take the boat back."

Refusing Bobby's offer to take the oars, she guides the sloop carefully towards the mouth of the anchorage, peering over her shoulder into the darkness. She sees the street lamps pooling their light on the cobbles; lanterns flickering in windows. But the wharf is dark. She pulls the boat back to the jetty. Snares it to the mooring post and rushes up the beach.

Head down, hood up, she begins to walk, turning right towards the castle and the coast path. The dark is thickening and she would rather keep to the lamplit streets than attempt a lightless trudge along the edge of the island. But she does not want to risk anyone seeing her, on her way back from returning a stolen boat.

Bobby jogs to keep up with her. "I'll see you back to the house," he says again.

Julia doesn't bother to argue.

They walk in silence for a long time, picking their way through the disappearing light, watching as the dunes roll into blackness. A few faint stars peek out from between the clouds, a sliced moon trying to light their way. Julia stumbles over the uneven ground, sloshes through an unseen stream. Hears the distant knock of deer hooves, the rhythmic burble of owls. She is almost relieved when the lights of Highfield House finally lift the darkness.

She leaves Bobby at the edge of the path leading up to the house. "Wait here," she tells him. "I'll fetch you a lamp to find your way back." She knocks tentatively on the front door. Hears a rapid volley of footsteps, then the door flies open. At the sight of Nathan, Julia's heart skips. She had been expecting the housekeeper.

He is without a jacket or cravat, his shirtsleeves rolled to his elbows and the top button of his simple blue waistcoat undone. Coils of dark hair have come loose from his queue and tickle the top of his shoulders. "I thought you had left." He swallows. "And forgotten your cat."

Julia can't help but smile. "No, I… I had some errands to run, is all." It's the flimsiest of excuses, she knows. What kind of questionable errands would have her creeping about the place in the darkness?

For long moments, neither of them speak. Julia inches backwards, out of the puddle of light cast by the lamp hanging above the door. Tries to hide her mud-caked skirts in the shadows. Her feet are frozen inside her wet shoes.

The aroma of roasting meat drifts in from the kitchen, making her stomach groan loudly. She cringes, feeling colour rush to her cheeks.

"I apologise if I made you feel unwelcome," Nathan says. "If you felt the need to stay out of the house tonight."

A sudden urge comes up on her to pull him close. Press her head to his shoulder and inhale the rosewater scent of him she has conjured up in her mind so many times in the last ten years. She pushes the thought away. "You've nothing in the world to apologise for," she says, a faint waver in her voice. "I'm very grateful for all of this." She clears her throat. Takes another step away from him. "Could you spare a lantern for Bobby to take back to the village?"

"Of course." Nathan takes the lamp from the hook in the entrance hall. Steps outside and passes it to Bobby. "You know there's a bed for you here if you need it," he tells him.

"Thank you, Mr Blake. But I'm quite all right in my lodgings." Bobby takes the lamp. Murmurs a strained goodbye to Julia. She watches after him as the light disappears into the dunes. Tries to let her annoyance at him dissipate. She knows, after all, that he just wants what's best for her. Just as she does for him.

She can tell Nathan is still behind her. His presence feels weighted, magnetic. She draws in her courage and turns to face him.

He holds her gaze for a long second. "Are you safe?"

"Yes," she says, too quickly. "Of course."

He hesitates for a moment, as though debating whether to push the issue. Whether to seek a more honest response. Finally, he nods. Clasps his hands in front of him. Unclasps them again. "Very well. If there's anything you need…"

Julia nods. "Thank you."

He flashes her a short smile that doesn't quite reach his eyes. Turns to leave.

"Nathan," she says suddenly.

He looks back to face her. "Yes?"

"Was there ever any suspicion? About… the way Joseph Holland died?"

He doesn't look surprised at the question. "There was talk," he admits. "After Holland disappeared, everyone came to assume he was a government spy. But no one ever suspected you or your brother were involved in his death. At least not to the best of my knowledge."

"Even though I left the island so quickly after his disappearance?"

"I think…" He shakes his head. "Rather, I *know* people came to suspect there was something between you and me that… well. That fell apart." He looks down, away from her eyes. "I did not deny it. I allowed people to believe that was the sole reason behind you leaving." There's a rigidity to his voice, a formality. The words come out devoid of emotion—betrayed only by the rapid rise and fall of his chest.

Julia's throat tightens. "And my shop?" she asks. "The blood on the stairs?"

"There's an apothecary there now."

Minerva stalks into the entrance hall on silent paws. Circles Julia's legs. "Have you been inside?"

"Once or twice. There's blood on the stairs if you know to look. I suspect you and I are the only ones who know to look."

She dares a small smile. "I'm glad of it." Catches herself quickly. "Not that it matters, of course." She scoops Minerva from the floor. Holds her against the place her heart is thumping. "It's hardly as though staying on the island has ever been an option."

CHAPTER EIGHTEEN

"I want him to come here tonight," Harriet says suddenly.

The dormitory is dark, the bar downstairs quiet. Soft snoring is coming from the two women in the opposite bed, intermittent rain tapping against the windows. Harriet has been lying awake, staring into the blackness for hours. Can tell by Peggy's breathing that she's awake too.

"I want him to come here tonight so you can take care of him."

Peggy shifts to face her, making the mattress sag. In the faint light shining beneath the door from the lamp in the hallway, Harriet can just make out her storm cloud of hair. Her wild, determined eyes. "Why don't you take care of him the next time you see him?"

Harriet sighs, rolling onto her back. It's not like she hasn't thought about killing the man with the beard. She's thought about it a lot, although it's always been some vague, intangible concept, rather than anything solid to be acted upon. She'd never have the strength to do something so dangerous. So final. Strength—is that even the right word to use when it comes to killing someone? Anonymously sending men to the gallows is far more her style. "I couldn't," she says.

"Why not?"

Harriet is silent for a moment. Why not? Because she does not want to take a life. But hasn't he taken hers? He's forced her to flee London, leaving behind her commissions, her friends, her students and sponsors. Though she has spent a decade working and fighting and struggling to make her dreams a reality, in so many ways, she still feels weak. Still feels, sometimes, that she is caught in the same current of life she had been as Edwin's wife. Tossed and towed by rips she never meant to get caught in. Yes, she had found the courage to break free from her marriage. But she had let society tell her to leave Isabelle. Had let the man with the beard force her from her home.

"I don't have a weapon," she says.

"Ought to get yourself one."

"Where from, exactly? We're miles from any gunsmith." Harriet can hardly believe she is even having this conversation.

Peggy tosses the blankets off them and slides out of bed. "Come with me. We're going to find a way to get rid of this bastard."

Harriet doesn't move. But something stops her pulling the covers back over her body.

Peggy tugs her boots on over bare feet. "Come on," she hisses.

Harriet finds herself obeying. She pulls on her shoes and shawl and follows Peggy into the dark hallway. "Where are we going, exactly?"

"Innkeeper took everyone's weapons at the door," Peggy whispers as they tiptoe down the creaking stairs. "He must be keeping them somewhere."

"And you don't think they'll be locked up?"

"Probably. Maybe we can break in."

This feels like a terrible idea. "Break in to where?"

Peggy shrugs. Doesn't answer.

They reach the dark tavern. The remains of the fire are glowing in the grate, and the room still holds a thick warmth, along with a heady smell of old stew and ale. A mouse scuttles across the flagstones at the sound of their footsteps. Disappears into the kitchen.

Peggy runs her hand along the top of the mantel until her fingers land on the tinderbox. She lights the candlestick sitting beside it. Pans it around behind the bar.

The pale light falls over rows of barrels and bottles, and a trough filled with dirty tankards. A wooden locker is tucked in against the wall. "There," Peggy says. She hurries towards it. "I bet this is where he's keeping the weapons." She rattles the lid. Hands the candle to Harriet. "Hold this. The damn thing's locked."

Of course it is, Harriet wants to say. She glances edgily towards the staircase.

She stands over Peggy while the older woman crouches by the chest and jams the prong of a fork into the lock. Wiggles it around. Harriet can tell she has no idea what she's doing.

Peggy gets to her feet with a grunt. Tosses the fork back onto the bar. "I don't think that's going to work."

"Let's go back upstairs," Harriet whispers, gripping her shawl tighter around her body. "We're going to get caught down here. And the last thing I need is for the innkeeper to throw me into the street. Besides, you don't even know that the weapons are in there."

"Let's try the innkeeper's room," Peggy says, as though Harriet has not even spoken. "You can be sure he'll be keeping a weapon under his pillow. Just in case. Who knows what kind of mad things come through this door?"

Harriet smiles wryly to herself. She's fairly certain she's with one of those mad things right now. Is also fairly certain she's becoming one herself.

A loud creak sounds at the top of the staircase. Instinctively, Harriet crouches, hiding herself behind the bar. She looks wide-eyed at Peggy.

Another creak, followed by the soft thud of footfalls.

"Someone down there?" The innkeeper's voice. Harriet's heart speeds. She can't be thrown out of here. She can't. She already feels as though she has nowhere in the world to go. What was she thinking following this madwoman down here on a misguided search for weapons? Even if they had swung open that storage chest and found it full of pistols, Harriet knows she would never have had the courage to pull the trigger.

Peggy blows out the candle. Gestures with her head towards the door in the corner, leading to what Harriet assumes is the kitchen. The creaking of the stairs grows louder. Closer. Harriet darts into the kitchen behind Peggy.

The room is hung in shadow, the glowing coals in the fireplace picking out a long wooden table, shelves stacked with jars and barrels, a side of meat dangling grimly from a hook on the ceiling. A flicker of light from the innkeeper's candle pans across the doorway.

Harriet drops to her knees beneath the table, tugging Peggy down to do the same. As the older woman crouches, she knocks a knife sitting on the edge of the table. Sends it clattering to the floor.

Harriet sucks in a breath. Hears the innkeeper's footsteps coming towards the kitchen. This is it, she thinks, she's going to be caught down here on this most foolish of missions, with this most foolish of women, all because of her foolish need to let someone else take the reins of her life for a moment. When has that ever led her anywhere but into that suffocating undertow she has spent so long trying to thrash her way out of?

"Pardon me, sir," Peggy blunders, sickly sweet, getting to her feet as the innkeeper steps into the kitchen. "Thought I left my purse down here when I came for supper tonight."

The innkeeper grabs a hold of her arm, tossing her back into the bar. "Left your purse in my kitchen, did you? Have to try harder than that."

Peggy wavers. Beneath the table, Harriet curls her hands around her knees. Holds her breath.

"All right," Peggy says finally. "Was after a drink to put me sleep. Get bad nightmares you see. A dram of whisky usually does the trick."

"Get out of here." Harriet hears the innkeeper's voice moving towards the staircase. Hears the loud groan of the steps as two pairs of footsteps disappear into the darkness.

Harriet waits huddled under the kitchen table for what she guesses to be close to an hour. Long enough, she hopes, for the innkeeper to have fallen back to sleep. Peggy too, if she's lucky. If the older woman is still awake when she gets back to the dormitory, Harriet knows she'll not manage to hold back the harsh words on the edge of her lips. Especially not given how many mice have been tickling the hem of her nightshift, and how deeply the chill of the kitchen has seeped into her bones.

She creeps upstairs on silent feet. Pushes open the door of the dormitory and slides into bed.

The mattress shifts. "Sorry," says Peggy. "Don't suppose that was the wisest of ideas."

Harriet doesn't speak. She tugs the blankets up to her chin. Shivers. Her feet feel like they've forgotten what it's like to be warm.

Peggy wriggles around again and Harriet is about to bark out an order for her to go the hell to sleep, when she feels something cold and hard nudging her shoulder. A pistol, she realises. "Here," says Peggy. "Take this."

Harriet rolls over to face her. "Where did you get it?"

"It's mine. I want you to have it."

Harriet hesitates. Finds the other woman's eyes in the darkness. "I couldn't."

"Yes you could. You need it more than I do. I don't have some lunatic chasing me."

I couldn't. The thought comes to her again; comes from the part of her that is still afraid, still doubting. Even after all this time. Even after all she has achieved. She allows herself to reach out and touch the cold metal. Feels the weight of it in her palm. Real power, she thinks. Not the imagined kind that comes from sketching the man so his likeness stares up at her every time she opens her damn notebook.

She lies in silence for a long time. "In the morning," she says finally, "will you teach me how to shoot it?"

CHAPTER NINETEEN

Finn curls his hands around the top rung of the wooden ladder and looks out across the roof of the cottage. He'd woken to find several more tiles lying in pieces on the rocks beside the front door. Sees now that others are close to following.

He uses his hands to prise off a slipped tile that seems to be hanging by a thread.

"How bad is it?" he hears Eva call from below. He looks down to see her tying her bonnet beneath her chin.

"Worse than I'd hoped. Better than it could be."

She smiles. "At least that's something. Fixable?"

"Aye. If I can get my hands on enough slate. Could take a while to get the tiles out here. I'll ask around the farm when I go over there next week. See if anyone can help." He climbs down the ladder. "You're going to see Harriet?"

Eva nods, pulling in a breath. "Yes. Before I change my mind. I've set the boys to their schoolwork. Maggie is sleeping." She looks up at the roof again. "Is there anything I can do to help?"

Finn smiles. Nudges her towards the jetty. "Go and see your sister. The roof will still be here when you get back." He chuckles. Kisses her lips. "I hope."

He watches as the skiff pulls away from the island. Tosses the cracked tile into the sea. He hopes the worst of the autumn rain holds off until he has what he needs to fix the roof. With all these gaps in the slate, they're likely to wake one morning and find a lagoon in their living area. Still, this house has stood more than fifty years. He's sure it will stand another fifty yet.

As the thought comes to him, he glances up through the window at his sons, dark heads bent over their texts, quills in hand. This house may stand for another fifty years, but is this really the life he wants for his children? Thanks to Eva, both boys are on their way to being well educated; he has no doubt Maggie will be too. Finn wonders what his parents would think if they knew their grandchildren were studying arithmetic and Latin at that table, where they themselves had counted pennies and re-tarred their boots. Heaven knows these children could have far more from their life than to be marooned out here on Longstone forever. Could have that broader life Finn had once longed for for himself.

For not the first time since he had taken up the role of lightkeeper fifteen years ago, the thought of leaving Longstone flickers at the back of his mind. It's chased away by the thought that always follows it: that he cannot leave this patch of sea dark. The wreck of the *Cygnus* has only solidified how much he and his family are needed out here. In the face of all the recognition and thanks he and Eva are finally getting, are they really to turn away and leave the Farne Islands lightless?

They won't, of course. He won't. And at the back of his mind, Finn knows the reason is not the children, or the wrecked ship. It's because his being here is what his father would have wanted. Really, that's what this has always been about. He had left Longstone and abandoned his father to die alone; and in the midst of that broader life he had once sought so desperately, he had killed Oliver Blake. And for all of that, Finn knows he needs to pay a penance.

He takes the ladder to the shed and leans it up against the wall beside a mountain of peat. Yanks hard on the door, which has become warped with time and moisture. It squeals loudly against the stone floor as it closes.

As he returns to the house, he sees a small sloop sailing steadily towards the island. He makes his way out to the jetty.

Finn has not thought about the man at the tiller for many years. No, that's not right. For many years, he has done his best not to think about the man at the tiller. And yet somehow, he has never been far from the front of his thoughts. Finn knows Henry Ward has made far too big an impact on his life—for better or worse—for things to ever be otherwise.

He lifts a hand to shade his eyes from the pale sun bouncing off the water. Watches Ward approach. He feels an old, instinctive unease. But perhaps that unease does not need to be here. After all, after his pirate ship had been captured, Ward had told the authorities that Finn was his prisoner. Had saved him from the hangman's noose.

Ward secures the sloop to the jetty without speaking, then climbs out with one large stride. Though he must be past sixty, he still stands rigid, upright, arctic blue eyes spearing Finn from beneath the brim of his black tricorn hat. His sharp jaw is clean shaven, a long coil of white hair hanging down his back. He gives a brusque nod of greeting; a weighted gesture. Finn feels a thousand unspoken words pass between them. After a moment, Ward says, "It's good to see you, lad."

Finn is not sure he can say the same. How does he greet this man who has made such a deep impact on his life? Over the three decades he has known Henry Ward, Finn has revered him, been awed by him, felt protected by him in his father's absence. Feared him, hated him, been simultaneously overcome by anger and gratitude towards him. He has never had a chance to thank him for his freedom—indeed, he had expected Ward to die on the gallows after the *Eagle* had been captured.

Since he had learnt, some years ago, of Ward's unexpected survival, Finn has toyed with the idea of hunting him down to give him his thanks for sparing his life. Has always discarded the idea as soon as it arrives. Because how can he thank Ward for the reprieve when his former captain had been the one to force him aboard his ship in the first place? Thanks to Henry Ward, Finn had come painfully close to leaving Eva a widow with their son growing inside her.

Ward's glance drifts past him, and Finn turns to follow his gaze. Three small faces are lined up at the window, their schoolwork apparently forgotten.

"You've made quite a life for yourself out here," says Ward.

"Aye. I have." Finn decides not to tell Ward one of the boys at the window is his grandson. He shifts instinctively, to block Ward's view of the children. "Have you been in Northumberland all this time?" he asks, trying to divert the conversation away from his own life.

"No." Ward turns up the collar of his coat as wind barrels off the sea. "I've only just returned. I have pressing business up here."

The response feels deliberately vague, and Finn cannot deny a hint of curiosity at what Henry Ward's life might look like now. At exactly how he might have escaped the gallows. He supposes that, for a man with connections high up in the government, and the damning information he had had about the Whig party, wrangling his freedom had not been so difficult. But that curiosity is not powerful enough for him to want Ward here, encroaching into this life Finn was sure he would once be denied. "Why are you here?" he asks.

Ward doesn't look surprised at his bluntness. And perhaps he is in no mood for conversation either. Because there's a look of intensity in his eyes that Finn had not caught before.

"I heard news of the wreck of the *Cygnus*," says Ward. "And I need to find my daughter."

CHAPTER TWENTY

Eva knocks tentatively on the door of the dormitory. "Harriet?"

There's a knot in her stomach as the door clicks open. Harriet does not look surprised to see her. Perhaps just surprised it had taken her so long to appear. Eva has spent almost a week trying to work up the courage to face her sister. She wants the truth about what happened on that ship. But she also fears that truth. Is afraid of what Harriet might have tried to do. And why.

Only once in the last ten years has Eva tried to find her sister. She had written to Edwin and several of Harriet's acquaintances in London, asking if anyone had had word from her. Edwin's response had come back clipped and empty; it was more than Eva managed to get back from any of Harriet's friends. She was not sure if they knew nothing, or if they were keeping quiet at Harriet's request. Either way, it was clear enough that she did not want to be found.

Eva wonders if she had given up too easily. If she had let her anger at Harriet get the better of her. Perhaps she ought to have pushed aside that bitterness and kept looking until she knew her sister was safe. Happy.

She steps inside the dormitory, pulling the door closed behind her. The room is large, filled with two hastily made beds. She and Harriet are the only people inside. "You have this place to yourself?"

Harriet sits back on one of the beds and picks her notebook and pencil up off the side table. "Only because there are so few travellers in these parts." She sketches as she speaks, not looking at Eva. "There were three other women in here last night. They all moved on this morning."

Eva smiles faintly. "I'm glad you didn't see fit to join them."

"Are you?"

"Of course I am. We've barely had a chance to speak since you came back."

Harriet doesn't look up from her notebook. "I thought we'd had plenty of conversation."

Eva stays hovering in the doorway. Swallows down her irritation. "It's a beautiful day." She tries to keep her voice light. "Shall we take a walk?" It feels safer, somehow, to be out in the open than locked in here with Harriet, and the years of resentment that have been simmering between them.

"It's freezing," Harriet says, without looking up.

"Put your cloak on then."

"I'd rather stay here."

Eva presses her lips together, stifling a sigh of annoyance. She unbuttons her cloak and hangs it on the hook beside the door. Comes to sit beside Harriet on the edge of the bed. Eva peers over at her notebook. Recognises the sketched shades of Lindisfarne, the view through the lodging house window.

"It's beautiful," she says.

Harriet closes the book and sets it on the side table. Turns to face her sister expectantly.

"How are you?" Eva asks.

"I'm fine."

"Really?"

Harriet sighs. "Yes, Eva. Really. Do you wish it to be otherwise?"

"Of course not," she says tautly. "I'm just worried for you, is all."

"Why?"

Eva knows the question is designed to irritate her, and she forces herself not to rise to it. "Because I don't know what happened on the *Cygnus*," she says evenly. "If you would just tell us what—"

"What's there to tell? The ship ran aground on the reef. The crew were young and inexperienced. I can promise you, the investigation will show nothing different."

Eva hesitates. Toys with a loose thread on her shortjacket. "And you didn't…"

"Try to drown myself? Of course not." Harriet gets abruptly to her feet. She begins to pace in front of the bed, anger clouding her eyes. "I had my coin pouch with me. With my travel documents in it. You were the one who took them out of my cloak to keep them safe. If I was trying to end things, why would I bother taking my damn travel documents with me?" She shakes her head incredulously. "I can't believe you would even think such a thing." Her voice begins to rise. "Is that really what you imagine my life has become?"

"What else was I supposed to think?" Eva demands. "The crewmen said they saw you trying to jump from the ship. One of them said he pulled you back—"

Harriet lets out a cry of frustration. She scrubs a hand across her face. When she looks back at Eva, her eyes are hot and glimmering with emotion. "What else did they tell you? Did they tell you about the man who was after me? Who's been after me since London?" Her voice wavers slightly. "The man I got on the ship to try and escape, only to find he'd followed me aboard?"

Eva feels suddenly hot, then cold. "The man at our cottage?" she asks sickly. "The man with the beard? He followed you up here from London?"

"Yes."

"Who is he?"

Harriet goes to stand at the window. She wraps an arm around her middle. Gnaws at a thumbnail. For a long time, she doesn't speak, and Eva suspects she is about to shut down again. But then, in a half-voice: "I don't know. I don't know what he wants with me. I first saw him at an exhibition one of my patrons was holding. After that, he started following me around the city. When he tried to break into my lodgings one night, I knew I had to leave. I thought I could hide away in Northumberland for a while. Let him lose track of me and go back to London when it was safe. I didn't realise he had followed me onto the ship until we were out at sea and it was too late to get off."

Eva lets out a breath. "Have you been to the authorities?"

"Of course I have. They didn't do a thing. I had no proof for them of who he was or what he'd done. Do you have any idea how quickly men like that will disregard a woman without a husband?"

Tentatively, Eva moves to stand behind her sister at the window. "Why did you not tell us all this before?"

No response.

"Did you… do something you were afraid to tell us about?" Eva ventures. "The money in your pouch…"

Harriet whirls around. "What?"

Eva swallows heavily. She shakes her head. Regrets her words. "Never mind. I—"

"You think I stole the money in my pouch? You think that's why this man is after me?" Harriet's eyes are blazing. "I earned every penny of that money," she hisses. "I wrote letter after letter of introduction and I tutored half the young women in London and I stayed up painting every night until my damn eyes gave out. I worked so damn hard for all of it." She shakes her head. "*This* is why I didn't want to tell you anything, Eva. Because of the suspicion. The distrust."

"I'm sorry," Eva says. "And I'm sorry for assuming…" She hates that her sister had thought to keep all this a secret. Hates that she can expect nothing else.

Outside the door, footsteps thump down the hall. When they disappear into the room next door, Eva says quietly, "You tried to get off the ship to escape the man who was after you? Is that why the crewmen saw you trying to jump?"

Harriet leans back against the window and nods faintly. "We were due to land in Edinburgh the morning after the wreck. I knew that once the ship docked, he would come after me, just like he had in London. I knew I'd have no chance of losing him, not when there were so few of us aboard the ship." Her eyes turn downward, fixing on a knot in the floorboards. "When I came out onto the deck that night, I saw how close we were to the Farne Islands. I thought getting off the ship with a buoy was my best chance of escaping." Her voice rattles. "I didn't realise we were not supposed to be that close to the islands. I didn't realise we were off course. Or that the ship was about to be wrecked."

Eva feels an ache in her chest. She can hardly bear to think of how desperate and frightened Harriet must have been to have considered such a thing. "The waters near the Farnes are so dangerous, Harriet. You're so lucky to be alive." She swallows hard. "Or did you choose those waters because you did not wish to be?"

"I chose those waters because I knew you were there!" Harriet's voice wavers and it catches Eva by surprise. She cannot remember the last time she saw her sister cry. "I thought I could make it to the islands with the buoy," she says. "Maybe make it to Longstone." She swipes angrily at a tear as it slides down her cheek. "I could see the firebasket." She turns away. "In any case…" Coughs down her tears. "I'd rather die by the sea than at the hands of a man."

For a long time, Eva doesn't speak. She wants to believe all this. As horrifying as it is to hear this man has been following her sister, it's a better outcome than Harriet wanting to end her own life. She dares to take a step towards her. "What can we do to help you?"

"Nothing."

"Harriet—"

"There's been no sign of him since the wreck," she cuts in. "I don't think he knows I'm here." She gives a murmur of humourless laughter. Wipes her eyes with the back of her hand. "Seems like my plan of throwing myself into the water worked. In a roundabout way."

For a moment, Eva doesn't speak. "What will you do? Stay here in Northumberland?"

"I don't know what I will do," Harriet admits. "But no, I'll not stay here. This isn't where I belong. Coming here was a mistake."

Eva tries not the let the hurt show on her face. Is Harriet completely oblivious to the sting of her words? Or does she just not care?

She tries to let her anger slide. After all, she can hardly begin to imagine the fear Harriet must have gone through—not just on the ship, but in the days and weeks beforehand. And then to wake up at their cottage to find herself in her son's presence…

Eva knows seeing Thomas had cut Harriet deeply. Also knows she will never admit it. She thinks of all the questions Tom has asked her and Nathan. Thinks of that look in his eyes as he sought scraps of information about his mother. Thinks of everything she has kept from him. Half-truths that had hurt to tell.

She sinks onto the edge of the bed. "I've been thinking about Tom," she says stiffly. "And I wondered if you might… care to spend a little more time with him. If you wish, I can—"

"No," Harriet says quickly. "No."

"Are you sure? It's not too late. He—"

"Not too late?" Harriet repeats, laughing incredulously. "He thinks his mother is dead. I am not going to upturn that for him. I am not going to put him through the same kind of upheaval I went through when I learnt who my father was."

"Do you not think he might wish to know you?"

"The mother who abandoned him?" Harriet says bitterly. "No, Eva, I don't think he might wish to know me. Do you?" She shakes her head. "He is better off without me. He always has been."

"Do you really believe that? Or is that just what you tell yourself to excuse your leaving him?" Eva's own bitter words surprise her. Words she has been holding in for longer than she has been aware of them.

"Why are you even asking me this?" Harriet hisses. "I thought you were under strict instructions from Edwin never to even speak my name around my son."

"Well," Eva says shortly, "I don't imagine this was quite the situation Edwin had in mind when he made that request. I can only imagine how I would feel if I were face to face with my own son and couldn't speak openly to him."

"I'm not you, Eva. And I don't want Thomas in my life."

"And what about what he might want?" Eva feels her anger pulsing beneath the surface. The response feels so cold, so unfeeling. Inhuman. "It's all about you, isn't it, Harriet. It's always all about you. No thought to anyone else, even your own son." She gets to her feet. "You were sleeping in my children's bedroom, and you did not even think to ask me a single thing about them. Not even their names. You were at our cottage for two days and you didn't ask any of us a single thing about our lives. I would have thought that after ten years, even you might have had a little curiosity about someone other than yourself."

"I almost died," Harriet hisses. "I was hardly thinking clearly."

"No," Eva says. "You're never thinking clearly. You're never thinking about anyone but yourself. How could you just leave without a word to any of us?" She hears old, unresolved anger bubbling up in her voice. "How could you cause us to worry like that? On top of everything else we were going through back then?" She had not intended to take this abrupt dive into the past. Had come here only to ask about Harriet's safety. At least that was what she had told herself.

But none of this is in the past, she realises. It has not been washed away by time, or by all Harriet has just told her. It is all right here between them, as if it had happened yesterday.

"Could you not even have managed a single letter?" Eva pushes. "Anything to let us know you were safe? Offer any word of explanation…"

"An explanation for what?" Harriet shoots. "For why I left?" She laughs coldly. "Believe me, Eva, you of all people do not want an explanation for that."

"What is that supposed to mean?"

"I would have thought you were glad I left," Harriet says, avoiding the question. "Given what I knew about Finn and Oliver." And here is Harriet's own unresolved anger, Eva realises. Rage at her sister for marrying the man who killed their brother. For trying to keep it a secret.

"I'm sorry," she says, swallowing hard. "I ought to have told you about… all that."

Harriet smiles wryly. "You cannot even say it, can you."

Eva looks down, avoiding Harriet's eyes. Feels a knot tighten in her stomach.

"Do you and your husband ever speak of it?" Harriet presses, coming to stand close. "Do your children know? Will you ever tell them?"

Eva pushes past her suddenly, striding across the room to put space between them. "I told you I was sorry." Her voice rattles. "I never should have kept it a secret from you."

Harriet snorts. "You're only sorry I found out about it. You would have kept it a secret forever if you could have. Anything to keep from disrupting your perfect life."

"A perfect life?" Eva repeats. "Is that what you think I have? You've always been the first to tell me just how pathetic our little cottage is. The first to list all the reasons why I would never be happy there." She shakes her head. "Is that what this is about, Harriet? You're angry at me because

I'm happy and you're not?"

Harriet stumbles backwards as though the accusation is a physical blow. She gathers herself quickly. "Please," she snorts, "I would choose my life over yours a million times over."

In a way, Eva is glad for this outpouring of anger. It feels like a release of something held far too tightly for far too long. Not just the past ten years, but for Harriet's entire life. Her sister has always been this: selfish, angry, lost in her own world. Abigail had always made excuses for her. Why? Because she was the youngest? Because she wasn't Samuel's daughter? Because she was so precious, born in the wake of Oliver's death?

Harriet, with her impossible beauty, and her prodigious talent. Too young, too flighty, too lost in her own world. Always one excuse after another.

Harriet turns to face her, blue eyes icy. "I would have liked to reconcile with you and Nathan," she says bitterly. "But the first thing you did was blather on to one another about how much you distrusted me."

"The first thing we did was save your life," Eva snaps.

"Yes. You and your husband are heroes." Harriet turns to give her a thin smile. "I wonder what everyone would think if they knew the truth about Oliver's death. Or Donald Macauley's."

And it comes from nowhere: an old fear, one that had been buried deep. The same fear Eva had felt towards her eldest brother. Innate and unplaceable. She has no idea why Harriet's words have sparked it, or how her sister has been able to dredge it up from so deep within her.

She only sees now that what she ought to have recognised from the beginning: that this could only end here, with anger and bitterness and not a hint of resolution.

Eva snatches her cloak from the hook and throws it over her shoulders. And she leaves the dormitory without looking back.

Harriet stands leaning up against the wall for a long time after Eva leaves, her body hot with anger.

You're angry at me because I'm happy and you're not?

The accusation feels impossibly brutal.

Somewhere inside, Harriet knows this is what this has always been about. Eva was supposed to be the dreary, rigid sister, the one who lived a tiresome life in the confines of all that was expected of her. She was supposed to watch from the corner while her sister made a name for herself painting the skies.

Eva was not supposed to be the one who defied convention and married for love and had the villagers fall at her feet for saving her lost and broken sister from a shipwreck. She was not supposed to represent everything Harriet knows she will never have. Can never have.

Worst of all, is that, in spite of all this, in spite of all her failures and imperfections, Harriet *had* found something close to happiness. Had found pride in the life she had built for herself, had found joy in seeing her dreams of being an artist come to life. Happiness—or at least some watered-down form of it.

But all that has been stolen from her by this nameless black-bearded man, and she has no understanding of why. Now she has nothing but the bleakest unhappiness and a pistol in her pocket, with nothing close to the courage to use it.

She watches through the window as Eva's boat shifts steadily towards the horizon. Lets the curtain fall.

She paces back and forth across the dormitory, rage simmering inside her.

Harriet hates that she had not fought back against the marriage Nathan had laid out for her, as her sister had. Hates that she had blindly married Edwin, had allowed herself to be walled into a life in which she had felt no choice but to abandon her child. She hates that she is incapable of loving a husband as Eva does. And she hates that she had not had the courage to keep Isabelle in her life.

She knows these were all choices she could have made. But none of them had felt even remotely possible. She hates that dour, colourless Eva was the one brave enough to build a life that has made her happy. Most of all, Harriet hates that she cannot manage any more self-loathing, so the only place she can lump all this hatred is on her sister. Heroic, lightkeeping Eva, who has Donald Macauley's blood on her hands.

Harriet knows it will do no good to wish this part of her did not exist.

That bitterness, that angry jealousy simmering inside her, sometimes hidden, sometimes pushed aside, is always there. She cannot remember a time she was without it.

Right now, all she wants is retribution. Wants her sister to hurt, as she herself is hurting. *You're angry at me because I'm happy and you're not?*

Harriet reaches for her notebook. Tears a page from the back and stares down at the blank paper, her pencil hovering inches from the page. Rage pulses, hot and guilty.

This is justice, isn't it? Eva and Finn have both taken lives. Both evaded punishment for their crimes. Instead, they have been rewarded with these accolades. Yes, she thinks. Justice.

Harriet writes the letter, doing her best not to think; not to feel.

CHAPTER TWENTY-ONE

Harriet marches down the stairs. Do not think; do not feel. She strides through the public house and hands the letter to the innkeeper.

Don't think; don't feel.

"I need this delivered. And I need a coach out of this place."

The innkeeper takes the letter. "Tuppence to deliver this," he tells her. "Next coach out of here is in two days. London via Newcastle."

"Two days?" Harriet says tautly. "Are you certain? There's nothing before then?"

He chuckles. "Fairly certain, aye. You'll just have to make do with our fine hospitality for a little longer yet."

She grits her teeth. She had hoped to be out of this damn place by tomorrow morning at the latest. Leave all this mess behind her. At least, she thinks, the coach is going in the right direction. Back to London, and not dragging her up into the heathen wilds of Scotland.

Is it dangerous to go back to London? Perhaps. But the last she had heard from the bearded man, he had been carted up to Berwick. If he has gone north, best that she goes south.

The innkeeper nods down at the letter. "You want this delivered or not?"

Harriet huffs at his impatience. "I suppose I'll have to wait two days for that to be sent as well?"

The innkeeper gives her an insincere smile. "Lucky for you, it'll make it over to Lindisfarne tomorrow morning."

Lucky for you.

Really, she thinks, it would be lucky for her if she was far from this place by the time the letter reaches its destination. Should she wait until she leaves to send the thing?

No. Do it now. Before she loses her nerve.

She digs into her coin pouch and hands the innkeeper the money.

As she is turning to go back upstairs, Harriet hears someone call her name. An unfamiliar voice. No, it's not unfamiliar. It's a voice that's deeply known to her—just unexpected. She knows before she turns around that it's her father.

Ward is standing beside a chair in the corner of the tavern, his coat and hat tossed across the table. Has he been down here waiting for her to show herself? How in hell does he know she is here? She has not seen or heard from him in ten years.

His being here does not make sense. Does not feel real.

At the sight of Henry Ward, Harriet's thoughts are back on that cold and clear night when she had sent the authorities after his pirate ship. They are back in Wapping, as she stands at Execution Dock with her eyes on the hangman's noose, waiting to watch her father die. The sight of his face brings all that guilt surging to the fore.

And it's all she can do to rush back to the safety of her room.

From his precarious perch on the roof of the cottage, Finn sees the misshapen sail heading straight for Longstone. Feels that old unease at the sight of Martin Macauley. He climbs down the ladder and looks out towards the water. Today, Martin is alone. And there's a look in his eyes that suggests this visit is about far more than a bag of apples and seedcake from the villagers.

Finn looks over at the boys. The three of them are teetering around the edges of the rockpools, inspecting the lobster pots. "Inside, lads," he says. "Quickly now."

Macauley's cutter thuds against the jetty. He climbs from the boat. Stands inches from Finn. "I need to speak with your wife."

"She's not here," Finn lies. "You can speak with me."

Macauley shoves a crumpled piece of paper into his hand.

"What is this?"

"A letter," says Macauley. "That I found most interesting." He narrows his eyes on Finn. "If you can't read it, I've come to know the contents quite well. I can recite them for you if you like."

"That's not necessary." Finn opens the page. Looks down at lines of small, coiled pencil strokes; the neatness of the handwriting betraying the brutality of the words. A letter to Martin Macauley. Outlining the circumstances of his father's death. Brusque and matter-of-fact words: *German Ocean* and *blow to the head* and *Eva Blake.*

Who had Macauley asked to read him the letter, he wonders? Who else knows about this? He screws up the page. "These are all lies."

"For what purpose?"

Finn hears Maggie squalling inside the cottage. He prays Eva doesn't see Macauley. Prays she stays occupied with their daughter. When she had returned from seeing Harriet yesterday, Eva had been wound up and on edge, wild with rage, and yet convinced her sister wasn't safe. The last thing she needs is to hear all this. He knows how much she has feared the truth of Donald Macauley's death coming out.

"If this were true," Finn says to Macauley, "why would whoever wrote this wait ten years to tell you? Your father was lost at sea. They found his boat."

"Aye. Floating out near Longstone."

"And why would you think Eva had anything to do with that? She was living at Highfield when your father disappeared."

Macauley stares him down. "Eva was on Longstone the night my father disappeared. I saw you bringing her home the next morning."

Finn folds his arms. "What, the day you tried to kill me with your hunting musket?"

Macauley snorts. "If I wanted to kill you, you'd be dead."

Finn shoves the letter into his pocket. "Look," he says finally. "I know there's always been bad blood between your family and mine. But that's between you and me. Leave Eva out of this."

Macauley chuckles. "And just forget everything that's in that letter?"

Finn hesitates. "What do you want?" he asks finally. The question is an admission of sorts; yes, he realises that. At least, as much of an admission as Macauley is ever going to get from him. But he needs to know where this is going to lead.

Macauley takes a step back, eyes narrowing. What's that look on his face? Indecision? He's come here on a whim, Finn realises. Come here in a burst of anger—likely the moment he heard the contents of that letter. Has not considered at all what he plans to do with this information. He steps into his boat, looks back at Finn. "Just tell her I know."

CHAPTER TWENTY-TWO

Eva dreams about her dead brother. Oliver is faceless, wordless—but she knows it's him from the fear that consumes her. She dreams of Oliver and she dreams of Harriet, and she dreams of Donald Macauley. Dreams that this time it's her plunging downwards into dark water, never to resurface.

She sits up in bed with a racing heart, and the relief of being awake is sloughed away quickly by the harshness of reality.

Just tell her I know.

There's a pale dawn light reaching through the gap in the curtains. Finn is sleeping lightly beside her, his skin fragrant with woodsmoke. She guesses he has just come to bed. Eva reaches out to lift the curtains; sees the last glow of the firebasket simmering in the grate. Tendrils of pale blue mist are coiling off the sea, hiding the rest of the world.

Just tell her I know.

Martin Macauley's words have been circling through her head since Finn had—all too reluctantly—relayed their conversation last night. She wonders if he would have told her any of it if she had not caught sight of Macauley leaving the island.

She shuffles across the bed, curling up against Finn's warm body. She wants to wake him; is craving his company. She won't of course—sleep is far too precious a thing, especially these days. He'll wake soon enough when the boys come barreling out here with bright eyes; will do his best to squeeze in a few more hours' sleep in the children's bedroom. Keeping the light had been manageable with one child, challenging with two. Life is utter chaos with three.

And how could she want anything but this chaos? How can she regret what happened to Donald Macauley when his death had led her to Longstone? If he had not forced her into his boat that day; if he had not rowed her out into the ocean and raised his musket on her—and if she had not swung that oar and knocked him into the sea—she would never have found her way to this island. She would not have her husband. Would not have her children. She would have lived a stilted, loveless life as Matthew Walton's wife.

Donald Macauley's life for her sons' and daughter's. Donald Macauley's life for her happiness. How can she have regrets?

And yet, the guilt is searing. Always has been. She has struggled for ten years to force it to the back of her thoughts. Has searched for some sense of absolution each night she has set the firebasket burning. Each night she has foregone sleep to keep the Farne Islands illuminated.

"He has no proof of anything," Finn had told her last night. "As far as he knows, this is nothing more than gossip."

There's a part of her that wants to speak openly to Martin Macauley. Tell him everything; answer his every question. She wants to rid herself of this weight of guilt, and let whatever is to come of it come. But perhaps Finn is right; perhaps right now Macauley has his doubts, his own uncertainties—if not of her guilt, then at least of what to do with this new knowledge. If she stands face to face with him and tells him how she knocked his father into the sea—and thought to hide the truth for a decade—there is no telling what he might do.

Finn rolls over and wraps an arm around her in his sleep, and she runs her finger over the coarse skin on his knuckles. Chaos, she thinks, but this is the ordered, beautiful chaos they have built together. A life of lobster pots and made-up card games, clothes that smell of woodsmoke and sea. A life that has held the deepest grief and the most profound and dizzying happiness. Right now, it feels completely precarious. And sitting here, doing nothing, waiting for Macauley to act feels foolish.

Feels as though she has built a life on foundations of sand and now she is standing back, watching, waiting for the tide to rise.

Sometimes, Nathan is able to forget everything that had happened between Eva and Donald Macauley.

When he thinks back to those stormy months during the Jacobite Rising, it's his own weighted memories that come to the fore: the ball in Edwin's side and his long, incomplete recovery; the inevitable choice to let Julia walk away; the heat of the pistol in his hand as he had cast John Graveney's body onto the dunes. There is little room for Donald Macauley amongst all that chaotic memory. Yes, Nathan can still conjure up rage at the man if he allows himself to. After all, he had tried to kill his sister. But Macauley has been long forgotten, by most of Lindisfarne. And in the end, her desperate night on Longstone had led Eva to happiness.

In the end—no. There is no end. Not yet at least.

Nathan looks across the tea table at his sister. She is perched on the edge of the settle, turning a cup edgily around in her palms. Her eyes are underlined with shadows of sleeplessness.

"Have you any idea who told Macauley?" Nathan asks. "Or why?"

Eva shakes her head stiffly. She glances down at her two youngest children, who are petting Julia's cat beside the fire. Minerva lies stretched out on the hearth, patient as the children prod at her ears. "I can't imagine why anyone would see fit to tell him after so long." Her response does not feel entirely honest. Feels like a lie to cover a truth she does not wish to disturb. And yes, Nathan understands. Because this he knows: two women have returned to Lindisfarne now, when talk of Donald Macauley's death has resurfaced. Two women who both know the truth of how the man died.

He can think of no possible reason why either Harriet or Julia would do this to Eva. But he cannot ignore the coincidence. Which is worse, he wonders? For him to have brought Julia back into their lives and for her to have told Martin Macauley about his father's death? Or for Harriet to have done this to her own sister?

He does not speak of it out loud. Can tell this is a conversation Eva cannot bring herself to have. But he knows he needs to speak with Julia. A proper conversation, not a few stumbled sentences in the doorway. He needs to find out if there is any possibility she might have been the one to go to Martin Macauley. He cannot imagine what she would stand to gain from doing so. But Nathan knows Julia's life has complications in it now that he cannot even begin to comprehend. Perhaps it always has.

That evening, he finds some hidden reserve of courage and knocks on the guestroom door. He hates that Julia feels the need to lock herself away in her room like this. Not that he can blame her. He's hardly been a picture of hospitality. Nonetheless, he's relieved that she is here tonight, instead of out running whatever questionable errands saw her and Bobby blundering over the dunes in the dark the night before last.

Surprise on her face when she pulls open the door and sees him.

"Will you join me for supper?" he asks, blurting the words out before he can change his mind. His heart quickens at her nearness. Though she is still in her grey woollen skirts, she is wearing a neckerchief splashed with pinks and blues and yellows today, her fiery hair spilling loose down her back. She makes Nathan think of blazes, and sunlight, and sea-thrift and orchids exploding across the dunes.

Her lips part. "Are you sure that's what you want?"

"Yes," he says. "It is."

She swallows. "I… All right. If you're certain." The cat stalks out of her bedroom and disappears down the staircase. "Shall I tidy myself? Pin my hair, or…"

Nathan manages a faint smile. "There's no need for that. I'd just like your company." The words spill out thoughtlessly. This is not supposed to be about enjoying her company. It's supposed to be about determining if she was the one to go to Martin Macauley.

Julia follows him downstairs into the dining room. Candles are lit in the centre of the long table, bread plates and wine glasses already filled. Julia takes in the two place settings. "Theodora won't be eating with us?"

"No. I've asked her to take her supper upstairs. She's more than happy to be up in her room writing."

"I see."

Is she suspicious of this? Nathan knows he could have spoken to Julia about Martin Macauley anywhere: a quick aside in the hallway, or outside the house, in bright, searing daylight. Instead, he had chosen this private, candlelit table, just so he might catch a glimpse of that life he had let pass him by.

He pulls out a chair for Julia, then slips into the seat at the head of the table. Tries to order his thoughts. "I'm sorry for being so distant these past few days," he begins. "I'm not usually quite so rude."

"I know you're not." Julia shakes her head. "There's nothing to be sorry for. This is hardly the easiest situation. Our children have a lot to answer for." She lifts her wine glass and takes a shallow sip.

Nathan smiles. He appreciates her bluntness. "They do. But I'm glad you're here. Glad you're safe."

Julia turns as Mrs Brodie enters, carrying two plates filled with roast meat and potatoes. She sets them down on the table then disappears, pulling the door closed behind her. For several moments, they eat without speaking, forks clinking against the plates and steam curling silver in the candlelight.

"I imagine you have questions," Julia says finally.

Nathan puts down his fork. "Only if you wish to answer them."

"What do you wish to know?"

Tread carefully, he thinks. He cannot ask her the things he wants to ask her. Because really, the things he wants to ask her have nothing to do with Martin Macauley and his father's death. No. He wants to ask Julia if she has been happy, and if she regretted leaving Holy Island. Whether she has thought of him at all in the last ten years. *Tread carefully.*

"The thieving ring," he says instead. "How much do you know about it?"

Julia turns her wine glass around by the stem. "It's been in place since last century. It began with women stealing from Jacobite fundraisers because they lost their husbands to the rebellion in '89. My mother was one of them," she says. "Not that I knew that at first."

Nathan raises his eyebrows. "Your mother?"

She nods. "I was surprised at first. I never imagined her as a thief. But it makes perfect sense that she'd want to rebel against the Jacobites after what the cause did to my father. It didn't make her a widow, but it may as well have, for all the care Elias showed her after he returned from Dunkeld."

"How did you get involved with them?" Nathan asks.

Julia lowers her eyes. "Calum is passionately against the Jacobite cause.

He was a militiaman during the Rising. But he went too far. Stole from one of his clients when he found out he had Jacobite connections. We had to leave our home in Edinburgh and go to Bamburgh to seek the ring's protection."

Nathan catches the faint colouring of her cheeks. She takes a hurried mouthful of wine.

"Is that why you married him?" he asks carefully. "Because you wanted to rebel against the Jacobite cause too? For taking your brothers?"

"Rebel against the Jacobite cause? Do you not think I had enough of that madness during the Rising?" She shakes her head. Looks down for a moment, then back up to meet his eyes. "I married Calum because I was too proud to scrub dishes for the rest of my life. If I didn't want to do that, marriage was my only option."

Nathan feels an apology on the edge of his lips. Perhaps marriage was her only option, but it ought to have been to him. All too easy to say that now, he knows. It had not felt possible to look past their differences ten years ago, when Joseph Holland's blood had stained the steps to Julia's cellar.

He knows they would not have had a good life together. How many times had they looked one another in the eye and lied? They would have been forever questioning. Forever doubting. Distrusting. He knows that. But seeing her here, her green eyes shining in the candlelight, and her curls falling loose over her shoulders with the casualness of a woman at home, those reasons feel far too flimsy.

He dares to ask, "Do you love him?"

Julia looks down. She slices her meat, but doesn't eat.

"I'm sorry," Nathan says. "That was too forward of me. I—"

"I care for him," she says. "But no, I don't love him."

Nathan wishes her answer didn't bring him quite so much satisfaction. A strange thing, he thinks, that Julia might be so open and honest with him now. Where would they be if they had managed a little more of that ten years ago?

"He's not…" She fades out, then tries again. "He's not a bad man. He's always treated Bobby and me well."

"He left you alone with the thieving ring." The words fall out before Nathan can stop them.

"Yes," Julia says. Doesn't look at him. "He did. Not that I can blame him."

"What happened?" Nathan asks. "What did you do to make him leave?"

She runs a finger around the rim of her wine glass. "I lied to him. When we first met. I told him I'd been married to Bobby's father. Widowed. I knew Calum wouldn't have me as his wife if he knew I'd had a child outside of wedlock. It would have offended him. Disgusted him." She sighs. "The lie was good enough when we were up in Scotland. But down here… Too many people knew my father. Knew why he'd cut his ties with me. I've never seen Calum as angry as he was when he found out the truth. He went on and on about all the shame I've brought him and his family name."

Nathan doesn't speak. Doesn't trust himself to say the right thing. He dares to ask the question that has been circling through his head most violently since Julia had stepped inside his house: "Do you think he will come back?"

"My neighbour's friend saw him in Edinburgh," she tells him. "Calum was talking about heading south. There's a chance he's on his way back to Bamburgh."

"I see." The words come out sounding too thin. Before he can speak again, Julia says:

"You've made a good life for yourself here, I can tell."

It's a blatant attempt to divert the conversation away from her husband, and Nathan is all too willing to oblige. "I have," he admits. "Business is good, and I think I've finally regained the trust of the villagers." He chuckles. "I don't think our family name is spoken with quite so much disdain as it once was."

Julia smiles. "You must be a very hard-working man."

He laughs. "Indeed."

"Theodora seems to love it here too."

"She does. She's very inspired by the place. She loves the folk tales from this part of the world. Has she told you her story about the lady in the dunes yet?"

"Not yet. I shall have to ask her." Julia shifts in her chair so she is facing him squarely. "Didn't I tell you, this is where your home is? Some part of you has always been Northumbrian."

"You may be right. There is something about the place that I can't help but love." Nathan smiles. "You'll be pleased to know I'm even learning to sail. I thought it was long overdue." He chuckles at the look of open surprise on Julia's face.

"I never thought I'd see the day," she grins.

"Lewis is teaching me," he tells her. "The man has the patience of a saint. I've nearly run us aground on more than one occasion and he still insists on taking me out for more lessons."

Julia brings a forkful of potato to her mouth, her eyes not leaving Nathan's. "Well," she says, "you are quite full of surprises. The next thing I know, I'll come home to find you with Minerva on your lap." She swallows heavily. Looks down. "Come *back*, rather. I didn't mean…"

Nathan just smiles, all too willing to overlook her misstep. "Let's not get carried away. I'm certain that cat can see right into my soul."

Julia laughs. "Oh she can," she says. "And she can read your every thought."

Nathan chuckles. "And what does Calum think of the cat?"

"He loves her."

"Of course he does."

Julia gives him a crooked smile. Peers at him over the top of her wine glass. "It's good to see you," she says finally.

"It's good to see you too." Nathan feels something shift in his chest. This feels easy. Too easy. And far too dangerous.

Somewhere in the back of his mind, he acknowledges that finding out who had written to Martin Macauley was just an excuse to put aside his unease and his guilt and the shadow of Calum, and sit down with Julia and hear about her life. Nathan has known this from the beginning.

And if he acknowledges this, he must also acknowledge the other, more brutal truth. That Harriet was the one who had told Macauley what had happened to his father. A brutal truth, yes. But not a difficult one to believe. Harriet has always had it in her to do something of this magnitude.

Nathan does not understand why she had done it. But when has he ever understood anything about his youngest sister?

Right now, he does not want to think about Harriet. Not now, when he is sitting face to face with Julia, with this lightness in the air and this warmth in his chest.

She takes another mouthful of meat, her free hand resting on the table beside her bread plate. Her fingers are inches from his.

It would be easy, he thinks. Easy to place his hand over hers. Feel her fingers twined with his own. Perhaps, easier than it has ever been for him. This desperate need to be close to her, after so many years, it washes aside his fear of physical closeness. Outweighs it. The need to feel his skin against hers is almost overwhelming.

The crunch of footfalls sounds outside the window. Julia sucks in a breath and pushes her chair back abruptly, making it squeal against the flagstones. She hurries to the glass and peeks through the gap in the curtains.

Her panicked reaction catches Nathan by surprise. He comes to stand beside her; looks out onto the dark roll of the dunes. "It was just a roe deer," he says. "They often come close to the house."

Julia looks unconvinced. Nathan thinks of the way she had sat so rigid in the coach out of Bamburgh. Thinks of the way she had pressed herself against the carriage wall, desperate not to be seen.

She rushes out of the dining room towards the front door. Opens it a crack and peeks out, a bluster of cold air billowing inside.

Nathan takes a lamp from the hallway and follows her out of the house. "No one from the ring has come for you," he says. "No one knows you're here."

"You don't know that." There's a hard look in her eyes now. A fierce alertness.

In spite of himself, his heart is quickening. It has been a long time since he has been alert to people creeping around Highfield House. He's taken back, suddenly, to a time when this house had felt anything but safe. Anything but home. A time he does not want to return to.

He pans the lamp over the embankment, then steps out onto the dunes and circles the dark bulk of the house, Julia at his shoulder. The flimsy light of his lantern is swallowed by the empty island. But he sees no movement, no sign of any figure.

"Roe deer," he says again.

Julia glances at him, eyes hard in the lamplight. "Or thieves. I heard footsteps. It did not sound like a deer."

Nathan decides not to press the issue. He puts a soft hand to her shoulder, leading her back into the house. Feels his fingertips pulsing at the touch. "Well," he says, "if there are people from the ring out here, you're far safer inside." He pulls the door closed, turns the key. Hangs the lamp back on its hook, its beam passing over the painted eyes of an ancestor staring down from the wall. Julia wraps her arms around herself, her hair blown wild by the wind.

Nathan wishes he could take away some of her anxiety. Wishes he could take them back to that easy warmth of the dining room. He can't, of course. Because that easy warmth was never meant to last. Pretending otherwise will do neither of them any good. "What do you intend to do?" he asks instead. "Will you go back to Calum if he returns to Bamburgh?"

"Yes," she says after a long silence. "I have to. He's my husband."

Nathan tries not to let his anger show on his face. Anger at Calum for leaving her. For marrying her in the first place. Anger at himself for letting her go. "And if he doesn't return? What will you do then? How long do you intend to wait?"

Really, he does not want to speak about what is next for her, because he knows that what is next will be her leaving his house, his life—no doubt, forever. He wants to keep talking about Thea's folktales and Julia's cat and his shore-hugging sailing lessons. But he also wants her to see a way out. Wants her to see a life in which she does not panic at every sound in the night.

"I need to go back to Bamburgh," she says. "I've some money of my own in a box safe. If Calum doesn't return soon, I can use it to get to London." She picks at her thumbnail. "The safe has ended up in the home of one of the other thieves. I need to get to it without her knowing about it."

"Is that what you and Bobby were doing when you were out the other night?"

Julia's cheeks flush in the lamplight. "It's what we were trying to do. Bobby went off like a half-cocked madman trying to break into Lizzie's tenement right beneath her nose. He's lucky she didn't take his damn head off." She leans up against the banister. "Lizzie will be out of the house at church on Sunday morning. I'll have a much better chance of getting to the box safe then. Especially if I leave my cavalier of a son behind."

Nathan wants to argue. Wants to tell Julia she has no cause to be breaking into the homes of thieves. Wants to tell her he will give her whatever she needs. But he knows he is far too late for that. And so he does the only thing he can do from here. Says, "I will come with you."

CHAPTER TWENTY-THREE

It's late—those dream-blurred hours between midnight and dawn. Long hours at this time of year; days are short and nights endless.

The light of the firebasket reaches in through the unshuttered window, casting long shadows over the cottage. Eva is sitting at the table with a pile of the children's clothes in front of her, head bent over her sewing. Finn sits opposite her, twining the frayed edges of the lobster pot ropes. He has barely got more than one-word answers out of her all night. The hiss of the lamp on the table between them punctuates their wordlessness.

Finally, Eva looks up. "I'm not going to sleep tonight," she says. "I'll stay up and watch the light. You get some rest."

Finn reaches across the table, takes her hand. "I don't need to sleep yet. And you ought to try."

It's rare for the two of them to be alone, awake, in the quiet like this. He's missed it. But he knows it's Eva's fears that are keeping her from sleeping.

Since Martin Macauley had paid them a visit two days ago, she has only left Longstone to take Thomas back to Highfield House—to endless pleas and protesting from both Tom and Noah—convinced she is unable to keep him safe here on Longstone. As for their own children, she has hardly let them out of her sight. Has spent far too long standing at the window, waiting for Macauley to reappear and enact his retribution.

She has phases of this, Finn has come to know. This intense awareness—sleeplessness, alertness, periods of violent concern. Those surreal, dazed weeks when they'd first become parents. The murmured prayers and fuming pots when an influenza outbreak had torn across the county. And yes, those long-ago nights with Henry Ward's ship on the horizon. Just as he had been unable to take away his wife's fears then, Finn knows he can do little to stop her agonising over Martin Macauley now. Not that that will stop him from trying.

He tightens his grip on her fingers. "He's not going to act on this, Evie."

She raises her eyebrows. "Not going to act? How can you say that?"

In truth, Eva has not been the only one preoccupied by Macauley since he'd appeared on Longstone yesterday. Finn's thoughts have been circling around and around the issue. How can they do anything but?

And this is the conclusion he has reached. "If Martin does a thing to harm you, people are going to start asking what his father did to you." He releases Eva's hand and she goes back to her sewing, the needle darting furiously in and out of the cloth. "Everyone knows you weren't spying for the government during the Rising. If word gets out that Donald tried to kill you, think how badly that'll reflect on him and his son. Besides, surely Martin must have some doubt over this letter. It's been years. How does he know for sure it's telling the truth?"

"It is telling the truth," Eva says stiffly.

"Macauley doesn't know that. And he doesn't need to. Let him have his suspicions. They can't hurt us."

Eva sighs, tying off her sewing and yanking violently at the thread. "I wish I had your faith in the matter."

"Then let me have faith in the matter for the both of us."

She manages a pale smile. Reaches for the next piece of clothing.

Finn wonders if she's going to speak of it. Or if she's going to pretend she doesn't know it was her own sister who has done this to her. Finn is under no illusions. And neither is Eva—he is sure of it. There are only a handful of people who know the truth of how Donald Macauley died. And for this letter to have appeared the day after Eva had fought so bitterly with Harriet?

Finn had been reluctant to show her the letter in the first place. Would likely have thrown it in the fire and never spoken of it if Eva had not seen Macauley leaving the island. He had hoped that seeing those words—in her sister's handwriting—would make the truth undeniable. But Eva is continuing to deny.

He wishes she would confront the reality of who her sister is. Wishes she would stop trying to make their relationship into anything other than the poisonous knot it has always been. Harriet has been taking up space in Eva's thoughts for the past ten years. Probably for her entire life.

Finn says, "I assume you've not spoken to Harriet lately."

Eva looks at him for a long second. She knows the conversation he is trying to guide her towards, he has no doubt. "No," she says shortly. "You know I've not left the island since I took Tom back to the house."

"And do you mean to—"

"I want to speak to Martin Macauley," she says suddenly. "I want to tell him the truth."

Finn's stomach tightens. "Why? Why on earth would you want to do that?"

She stands up and begins to pace. "I can't bear the guilt. And I can't bear the uncertainty of waiting to see what he intends to do to me. To us."

"So instead you'll just hand yourself over to him? Tell him everything and let whatever is to come of it come?" It's the worst of ideas—he hates every piece of it. He and Eva have had to fight so hard for this peaceful, uninterrupted life. The letter Harriet had written to Macauley has knocked that peaceful life off its axis; Eva confessing to everything will shatter it completely.

He gets up from the table. Takes her shoulders gently. "You have nothing to feel guilty for," he says. "Donald Macauley was trying to kill you. All you were doing was trying to save your own life."

She looks at him squarely, and Finn can tell she is thinking of Oliver. Thinking of the utter frailty of these words—because was that not exactly what he had been trying to do the night he had killed Eva's brother? Trying to save his own life? That has not saved him from years of guilt and regret. He knows it will not save Eva either.

He wraps his arms around her. Presses his nose into her hair. Feels the faint tremor of her body.

"Do you truly believe he is not going to act on this?" she asks, her voice muffled against his chest.

"Yes," says Finn. "I do." And he believes this with conviction. "Digging into the truth of what happened will reflect far worse on Martin's father than it will on you. He's not going to want to pry. He's not going to want the truth of this to become public knowledge." He steps back slightly. Looks her in the eye. "Please, Evie," he says, "just leave him be. Let him have his doubts. Confronting him on this won't achieve a thing."

Eva slides out of his arms and goes back to her sewing, not speaking.

"Eva," he pushes. "Please tell me you'll not go to Macauley."

She nods faintly. "I'll not go to Macauley." But her words are far from convincing.

CHAPTER TWENTY-FOUR

Nathan cannot quite determine which particular detour in his life has led to him sitting in this coach beside Julia, rattling his way towards the Bamburgh thieving ring. He was under the mistaken impression that he'd left all this cavalier madness behind years ago.

"We ought to have sailed over," Julia says, peering out the window at the grey pall of the ocean. "It would have brought me great joy to see you at the tiller of Lewis's sloop." She's had an intense seriousness about her all morning, but now a faint glimmer appears in her eye.

"That would not have allowed for a quick getaway," Nathan says with a smile. "Believe me."

Lewis draws the carriage to a halt at the edge of the village. Nathan climbs out, offering Julia his hand. "Wait for us here," he tells his coachman. "We'll not be long. I hope."

Julia is already striding into the snarls of the village. Nathan jogs after her.

"You don't have to be here," she says, looking back over her shoulder at him. "I'd hate for this to reflect badly on you. I know you've worked hard to build a good name for your family again."

"I'm already here, Julia," he says. "There's no need to have this conversation again." He puts a thoughtless hand to the small of her back. "Let's just get your money and leave as quickly as possible."

She nods. Keeps hurrying towards Church Wynd with her head down and her hood pulled high. There's a heaviness to the air this morning; the sky is vivid white and smells of rain. Despite the chill in the air, Nathan is hot and breathless by the time they reach Julia's tenement building.

Her glance shifts upwards to take in the second-storey windows. "Wait here," she says tautly. "I need to go upstairs for a moment."

"Why? I thought you wanted to get in and out of Lizzie's lodgings as quickly as possible."

"I do. But…"

Something sinks inside him. "But you need to see if Calum has returned."

She nods faintly, not looking at him.

Nathan swallows hard. Bites back angry words intended for her husband. "Of course. I shall wait for you across the street." He forces himself to keep his voice even. "And if you don't come back, I'll…"

"I will come back," Julia promises. Her fingers brush his gloved hand, so softly he is not certain he didn't imagine it. "Even if Calum is there, I will come back to tell you. I'll not leave without saying goodbye."

Nathan nods. He turns away, unable to watch as she opens the front door and makes her way up to her tenement. He hates every part of it: this squalid, teetering building, this town overrun with thieves, Julia's bastard of a husband who had seen fit to leave her alone in the midst of all this.

He thinks of the unease in her eyes as they had searched around the house last night for what Nathan was certain was just a deer. He thinks of her fear they had been followed the day he had first brought her to the house. And he thinks of following her upstairs to make sure she is not in danger.

He cannot do it, of course. Because there's a chance her husband might have finally decided to show himself. And if Calum is upstairs in their tenement, then Nathan crashing through the door on some ill-advised rescue mission is the last thing Julia needs.

He begins to pace the street, shoes sucking through the mud, arms folded across his chest. He's making himself a suspicious character, he supposes, but he has too much nervous energy to stay still and hide like he probably ought to be doing.

He is dreading Julia coming down here to tell him Calum has returned—and yet isn't that what's best for her? For her husband to have returned? For her to no longer be alone?

It doesn't feel like what is best.

Nathan reminds himself that her staying at Highfield House was never an option. Cannot be an option. As much as he had loved her company last night, he knows that having her at the house is no good for either of them. It can lead nowhere but to that same cold devastation he had felt when she had disappeared from his life a decade ago.

Julia reappears at the doorway of the tenement house and waves him over.

"Has Calum returned?" he dares to ask.

"No." She avoids his eyes. Whispers, "What time is it?"

Nathan checks his pocket watch. Forces himself to keep his expression neutral. "Almost nine."

"All right. Lizzie ought to be at church by now. We need to hurry." She leads him around the side of the building and squints through the gap in a cloth window on the ground floor beside the wash house. "I don't see anyone inside," she reports.

She reaches into her pocket and produces a small fishing knife. How long has she been carrying that for? It reminds Nathan of the blade Oliver used to carry around—the blade that had been pressed to his own skin on far too many occasions. The sight of Julia using it to carefully cut the window open makes something tighten in his chest. He hates that this is where she has ended up. And he hates that he has had no choice but to follow her here.

She pushes aside the cloth and hoists herself up on the windowsill. Gathers her skirts in her fist and wriggles through the narrow space.

Nathan closes his eyes for a moment. Julia is right—the last thing he wants to do is make a bad name for himself and his family again. But there is also no way he can leave her to do this alone. He heaves himself up onto the sill and clambers inside.

Lizzie's tenement is small and dark, with a wooden table in the centre of the room and a straw sleeping pallet pushed up against one wall. The bricks above the fireplace are blackened, the faint glow of the coals suggesting Lizzie has just left—or plans to return soon.

Julia goes straight to the flagstones beside the hearth. Begins to trace the shapes of them with her knife. "Lizzie said her ma used to keep the takings under the stones of the hearth when she was a child," she explains. "I thought maybe she might do the same. Makes a good hiding place, I suppose." She moves from one stone to the next, tracing, prying. Nathan hovers over her, eyes darting edgily towards the door.

Julia groans in frustration and gets to her feet. "None of them are loose." She turns in a slow circle. "Where else could she be keeping it?"

She lifts the blankets of Lizzie's sleeping pallet, peeks behind the cannisters on the shelves. When she lifts a pile of what look to be discarded underskirts, she lets out soft cry of elation. Dumps the wooden box safe on the table and rattles the lid. "Locked," she says matter-of-factly. She turns the box over and digs the blade of her knife beneath the lid, sliding it over to the edge of the table. "I need you to help me," she tells Nathan. "Push down on the lid with all your strength. Lever it open. I'll hold the box steady."

There's a fierce determination to her now. It's a side of her Nathan has never seen—but not, he imagines, a new side. He joins her at the table.

He does not want to break into a safe belonging to a ring of thieves, any more than he had wanted to break into Lizzie's tenement. But he cannot help but feel responsible for this, at least in part. He had let Julia go. And this is the life she had found in exchange.

He pushes down hard on the handle of the knife and the lid pops open with a loud splintering sound. Instead of the metallic rattle of coins he was expecting, there's a dull thud as a small cloth bag drops to the floor. Julia kneels to inspect it. Curses under her breath.

"Look at this." She holds the bag up under his nose. It's filled to the brim with oats. "Damn Lizzie."

"Is it the wrong box?" Nathan asks.

"No. This is definitely the one I gave her. She's taken everything out of it. Moved all the money."

"Stolen it?"

Julia begins to pace, eyes darting. "She wouldn't have risked that. She's been caught in this ring for most of her life. She'd know better than to steal the takings. She'd know what the repercussions would be."

"Maybe she's escaped?"

Julia glances around the room, tapping her chin in thought. "I don't think so. Her belongings are still here. Her clothes. Her comb. Her food. And she left the fire lit." She looks back at the empty box. "Maybe she was using this as a decoy. You know, in case anyone came to steal it. They'd take this safe instead of the one with the actual valuables in it." She shoves the box back beneath the pile of underskirts. "We have to keep looking."

Nathan wants to tell her to stop. Stop tearing Lizzie's home apart. Stop digging herself deeper and deeper into the mess of this ring.

You're out, he wants to tell her. *You got out. Don't force your way back in.*

Instead, he finds himself rifling through the wood pile and peering beneath the sleeping pallet. Lifting the lids from pots and pans.

"Julia," he says. "Look."

She comes to stand beside him and peers down into the soup pot at a second smaller wooden box. She grabs it. Dumps it on the table and hacks at the lock again.

She pulls at the lid as it breaks open, exhaling in relief as she pulls out a pearl necklace.

"Your things?" Nathan asks.

She nods.

And why does he feel such a pull of disappointment?

At the click and scrape of the front door of the tenement building, they both turn towards the sound. Julia drops the necklace back into the box and shoves the lid back on.

"Come on," she hisses, snatching his wrist without warning and sending a rush of energy searing up his arm. "We need to leave."

CHAPTER TWENTY-FIVE

Julia darts towards the door of Lizzie's tenement, tugging Nathan out behind her. They turn down the lightless tunnel of the hallway as the footsteps grow louder. Julia slows to a walk so as not to attract attention, and climbs steadily up the stairs to her tenement. Nathan follows close behind, unable to help a glance over his shoulder. He hears footsteps from down below. Sees nothing but the shadows of the stairwell.

Julia unlocks the door of her lodgings and sets the safe on the table. She sinks back against the door, staring down at the box with its broken lid. "Hell," she hisses, "what am I going to do? Lizzie's going to see the torn window and she's going to realise the safe is gone."

"She'll not know it was you who took it."

Julia exhales sharply. "Except that she saw Bobby prowling around her window the other day looking suspicious as all hell."

Nathan takes a step towards her. Stifles the urge to pull her close. Before he can speak, the stairs creak loudly. Julia whirls away from him, looking towards the sound. Fear in her eyes—and yes, Nathan feels it too. He knows she is expecting her husband. He also knows that Calum finding her here with another man will be far worse for her than him finding her with a box safe stolen from inside Lizzie's soup pot.

"Mrs MacNeill? Are you in there?"

The fear in Julia's eyes intensifies. "It's O'Donnell," she hisses. "One of the ringleaders."

And it's blind impulse that makes Nathan snatch the safe from the table. Blind impulse that makes him dart into the empty bed-closet and yank the door closed behind him.

He hears Julia's footsteps tap across the tenement. Hears the click of the front door. "Mr O'Donnell," she says. "Mr Briggs. Can I help you?" Her voice sounds thin, taut. Sounds like someone else.

"We're looking for your husband," says one of the men. "He wasn't at church again today. As I suspect you well know."

The men are inside the tenement now, Nathan can tell. He presses a hand to his mouth to silence his breathing. Clutches the safe to his chest.

"I don't know where he is," Julia admits. "I've not seen him in more than three weeks."

Nathan understands the danger this admission has just put her in. Now, the ringleaders know she is without the protection of her husband—just another reason, he thinks, why she needs to get out of this place and never return.

"I see. And you've not heard word from him?"

"No," she says stiffly. "I haven't."

There's a moment of silence, and Nathan can almost sense the men sifting through Julia's words, trying to determine the truth beneath. The floorboards creak as footsteps come towards the bed-closet. Nathan holds his breath.

Finally, one of the men says, "You'll be sure to let us know if you hear from him." His words are spoken simply enough, but Nathan can hear the threat beneath.

"Of course," says Julia.

"And we shall see you at the end of the week for the allocation."

"Yes. You shall."

Footsteps clop towards the door, and as he hears the latch click closed, Nathan lets out his breath.

Julia throws the door of the bed-closet open. She lurches for him, then seems to remember herself and pulls away at the last moment. Her eyes glisten with unshed tears. "Thank you," she says. "I'm so sorry to have dragged you into this mess."

A coil of coppery hair falls across her eye and Nathan stifles the urge to touch it. "Get your things from the safe," he says gently. "Lewis is waiting for us in the square."

Julia shakes her head. "It's not that simple. Now the ringleaders know Calum is gone, they'll be watching me. Waiting to see if I try to leave too. Besides…" She glances at the box still clutched to Nathan's chest. "What am I to do with that? I can't just leave it here. If Lizzie finds it in my tenement—"

"So take it with you," Nathan says.

Julia's eyes widen. "Do you have any idea of how much trouble that would cause?"

"You said yourself, they are already going to suspect you of stealing it," he says, voice low. "And you can't keep it here."

Julia lifts the edge of the cloth window and peers down into the street. "The ringleaders will be keeping a lookout for me. Even if I wanted to, there's no way I could get the safe back to the wagon without them seeing."

"They're not keeping a lookout for me," Nathan says. Before he can change his mind, he unbuttons his coat and slides it off his shoulders. Slings it over his arm to hide the box from view. "I'll go to the carriage. Wait a while before you follow. Let the ringleaders think you're just going for a walk in the square, or to the market, perhaps." He is on his way to the door before Julia can protest. "Lewis and I will be waiting."

CHAPTER TWENTY-SIX

When Julia finally makes it to the carriage, the panicked look in her eyes has not abated. She accepts Nathan's hand and tucks herself hurriedly onto the bench seat, pressing her back against the wall of the coach to keep herself hidden.

Nathan raps loudly on the wall, urging Lewis to leave.

Julia sets the basket she has brought with her on the floor beside her feet. A few loose potatoes and carrots are rolling around in the bottom of it—Nathan is not sure if she had actually made a detour to the market, or if this is just part of her ruse to keep the ringleaders away.

For a long time, her gaze lingers on the safe sitting on the bench between them. "I ought to get rid of it," she says finally. "Throw it in the ocean or something."

Nathan doesn't respond. He can think of far more useful things to do with a safe full of jewellery and coin—fund a life away from Calum MacNeill, to begin with. But he feels fairly certain his suggestion will not be welcome.

Julia produces a bag of coins from the safe and carefully counts out a sum. She shoves the coins into her own purse, along with the pearl necklace. "All I wanted was what belongs to me," she says distantly. "I never intended to become a thief."

But Nathan is only half listening. His attention is snared suddenly by a small brass box sitting at the bottom of the safe.

The memory comes from nowhere, flying at him with ferocity. He has seen this box before. Has held it in his hands. It's an instinctive piece of knowledge, a memory so deeply ingrained it had kept itself hidden for the past thirty years.

I've a new game, said his brother. *It's called Plundering.*

Oliver sending him to their mother's nightstand to fetch this box. Nathan handing it over for his brother to hide in the priest hole.

And this tiny, tarnished brass box, it contains the Jacobite letter Henry Ward had once been so determined to lay his hands on. Nathan is suddenly certain.

He reaches down and grabs the box. Exhales. All these years, all that searching, and this piece of knowledge has been hiding within him all along. That precious letter that had once caused him so much trouble— he had held it in his hands as a young boy.

Oliver had had Nathan steal this box for him from their mother's nightstand. What had he done with it then? How has it ended up here in the possession of the Bamburgh thieving ring? Nathan can only guess at answers, of course. But he feels as though he has returned to the beginning of a vast, far-reaching circle.

The box is far smaller than he had imagined it to be when he had been searching the house for it. Its lock is broken and the lid swings open easily. Nathan pulls out the folded page inside. It is faded and soft with years.

He reads the words slowly, carefully.

We ought to meet urgently, Henry…

A morsel of information to whet your appetite: Lord Haver, prominent Whig party politician, is harbouring Jacobite tendencies…

Meaningless now—Lord Haver has been in his grave for several years, after slinking away from politics and disappearing into obscurity. But how valuable this must have been all those years ago, when the rebellions and Risings were finding their feet. Nathan is not surprised Henry Ward and his crewmen had been so determined to get their hands to the damn thing.

"What's that?" Julia asks, setting down her coin pouch. "I've not seen that brass box before. It must have been among the takings Lizzie was guarding."

"It's Henry Ward's letter."

Julia frowns. "The one you were looking for when you first returned to Lindisfarne?"

He nods.

She leans over, peering down at the faded page. "Why is it here?"

"I've no idea."

It feels implausible that he might be holding such a thing in his hands. But also, in a strange kind of way, it feels as though he has been led here. Feels as though he was supposed to find this. Find Julia again.

No. No, no, no. Julia is another man's wife. He cannot look past that. He had had his chance with Julia, and he had not taken it.

She points. "What's that?" There is a second folded page in the brass box, Nathan realises. It has been hurriedly stuffed into the bottom.

He takes it out carefully. Turns it over in his hands. Henry Ward's name is written on the front in his mother's handwriting, the ink faded with years. The seal is unbroken. Ward had never read this letter.

Nathan snaps open the seal. The sight of his mother's words scrawled across the page makes something ache in his chest.

Dear Henry,

I hardly have a thought of where to begin. There is so much I need to tell you. I wish we could speak of these things face to face, but I fear that will never be. I must leave Lindisfarne, for reasons I will explain, and I do not know when, if ever, you intend to return to the island.

And so, where to begin? My heart is pounding as I write, at imagining your response to everything I am to tell you. I have not been entirely truthful with you—and I suppose this is as fine a place to begin as any. As you know, I have been stealing funds from the Jacobite cause, and I allowed you to believe I was doing so out of financial necessity. This was an easier story to speak than the truth: that I was coerced into such actions by a thieving ring entangled in the Jacobite movement. The thought of telling you this made me feel unbearably foolish—far less shameful to be a penniless widow than to admit I was naïve enough to fall into a thieving ring's trap.

The tale is too tangled to tell you everything here—I will simply say that your letter full of Jacobite secrets and its little brass box have been of great interest to the Bamburgh thieving ring, thanks in no small part to the actions of my late son. This is just one reason why I must leave Lindisfarne for the relative safety of London.

And as I am speaking of my dear late son, I must tell you how much I regret sending you from the house the night of Oliver's death. I know I let you believe I held you responsible for all that happened. But I know who my son was, and I know placing blame will do no good. The past cannot be changed. I only hope you can forgive me for sending you away.

The night Oliver died, you told me there was a place for me in your future. I pray you still feel this way, after everything that has happened, and everything I have told you here. For what I must next tell you is this: you are to be a father, Henry. I hold my breath as I write this, in anticipation of your reaction. I hope that, with this knowledge, this is a future you still wish to be a part of.

I understand the gravity of all I am asking you. To have a life outside of your ship. To raise another man's children alongside your own. And if this is not a future you wish to be a part of, I will understand. But as this letter is my attempt to unburden myself of all my secrets, I want you to know that I love you.

If you feel as I do, you will find me in London, at the address penned below. I hope and pray we will see each other again.

Ever yours,

Abigail

Nathan releases a slow breath as he stares down at the page. He feels the weight of it, the complete upturning of everything he thought he knew about those years.

For a decade, he has not questioned his belief that Abigail had fled Lindisfarne to keep Ward from finding out about his daughter. Had been certain his mother had hauled him and Eva through the rising water of the Pilgrims' Way so she might keep her secrets intact. But Nathan sees now that he has cobbled together the pieces to make an image that does not reflect reality. And in his clumsy reconstruction of the past, he has let Harriet believe she was a shameful secret. The mistake that had caused them to flee.

Other truths here too, just as powerful. *Coerced by the thieving ring... Just one reason why I must leave Lindisfarne...*

Nathan has made an uncomfortable peace with the knowledge that his mother had been thieving from the Jacobite cause. Henry Ward had told him as much, back when they had been searching for the letter. But here, in her own words, her own handwriting, is the proof that she had not been stealing for her own purposes. Here is the proof that, just like Julia and Mairi Mitchell, his own mother had been entangled in this cursed thieving ring. *Just one reason why I must leave Lindisfarne…*

He feels an odd sense of things unravelling.

Julia peers over at him. "What is it, Nathan? What have you found?"

He clears his throat. "I'll have Lewis take you back to the house," he says. "Have Mrs Brodie prepare you something to eat if you wish."

She frowns. "Where are you going?"

"I'm going to the lodging house in Beal." He tucks the box into the pocket of his coat. "I need to find Harriet."

CHAPTER TWENTY-SEVEN

Harriet knows she has stayed here in Northumberland far too long. Has been far too destructive. With the benefit of hindsight—or whatever it can be called when she is still stuck right in the middle of all this—she sees what an inordinately stupid idea it was to have come up here in the first place. How could she have imagined it would end any other way than with her counting down the minutes until the coach comes to take her away?

She is sitting in the corner of the public house with a bowl of lukewarm porridge in front of her, the pistol Peggy had given her heavy in her pocket. Head lowered, doing her best to hide herself. This morning she is the only person in the public house besides the innkeeper, who keeps shooting bemused glances at her from behind the counter.

She hates being down here in the wilds of the tavern where anyone could find her; she had fought her hunger for as long as she could. But she knows she needs to eat something before she gets on the coach in a few hours' time.

Yesterday, she'd only had half a bowl of stew, forced down in a single breath before she'd hurried back up to the safety of the dormitory. Now her father has reappeared, she has two people to try and keep her distance from.

She can't determine who she is more afraid of seeing: Henry Ward, or the bearded man. It does not feel coincidental that they are both here. Harriet has come to learn that nothing about her father is coincidental.

She has no thought of how Ward even knew she was in Northumberland. The last time they had spoken, her father had told her he did not want her in his life. Had believed that was what Abigail had wanted. In return, Harriet had reported his pirate ship to the militia. Almost sent her own father to the gallows.

She forces down a mouthful of porridge, her stomach churning and tight.

With her eyes down, she sees movement on the edge of her vision. Sees a dark-coated man approaching her table. She holds her breath as she looks up, but it is not the man with the missing finger, or her father.

Nathan takes off his black felt hat as he cuts a deliberate line towards the table. He must know, surely, that she had been the one to tell Martin Macauley that Eva had killed his father. But his expression gives nothing away. "I'm glad I found you, Harriet," he says. "There's something I need to show you."

For a long time, they sit opposite each other, not speaking, the brass box on the table between them. Harriet stares down at the letter in her hand, her heart knocking hard.

She had spent the first nineteen years of her life believing she was Samuel Blake's daughter. Has spent the last ten years believing a lie about what her mother had felt for Henry Ward. Believing herself a shameful mistake. The consequence of a bad decision.

She has no thought of how this letter came to be among a thieving ring in Bamburgh. Nor does she have any thought of why, if her mother had loved her father, she had grown up believing she was Samuel's child. They are questions Harriet knows she will never have the answers to. Abigail has been in her grave for fifteen years.

Harriet keeps staring down at the page. She does not want to look at her brother, for fear he will see the emotion in her eyes. She can feel him watching her as he sits silently on the chair opposite.

Harriet feels a deep, aching sense of loss for what might have been. But something more than that too—something far more steadying. Something far closer to peace. Somehow, in spite of all the lies, and all the mistakes, this new knowledge comes close to being enough.

Finally, she lowers the page, pushing her bowl of porridge away with the back of her hand. Still, she cannot look at Nathan.

"Are you all right?" he asks.

She nods, not trusting herself to speak.

There is so much she wants to ask her brother. So much she needs to know. What, if anything, does he remember about Ward coming to the house? How had Abigail had behaved around him? Had their mother truly loved her father?

Harriet desperately hopes this is the case. She wants to believe everything Abigail had tried to tell Ward in this letter—and yes, she realises, she does believe it. As unmooring as it is, she lets herself accept this new truth.

And it changes things. Though Abigail has long passed, and her father is a figure she can never have back in her life after everything that has happened, this knowledge, it makes her see herself in a new light. She is not the result of a night her mother had regretted. She was not a secret Abigail had never wanted Ward to know about. The truth of that is right here in faded, thirty-year-old ink: *You are to be a father, Henry* and *I want you to know that I love you.*

Harriet wants to speak openly to her brother about all of this. Wants to release the weight of it by speaking it aloud. But she cannot bring herself to open her mouth. She does not know how to do this—to be open. The thought of that vulnerability is terrifying.

Nathan clears his throat, and Harriet is afraid he is going to speak of these things—ask questions that have answers she does not know how to put into words. But he says, "I don't suppose you have any thought of how to find your father? I'm sure this is a letter he would like to read."

Harriet shakes her head. "I don't know how to find him. We've not spoken in ten years." It's not a lie. And though she knows there's every chance Ward might come looking for her again, this letter does not change the fact that she and her father cannot be in one another's lives. This letter, it rewrites many things, but it does not undo the fact that she had tried to send Henry Ward to the hangman.

Nathan nods. Nudges the box towards her. "You ought to keep it," he says. "And if you ever do see him again…"

"I won't," she says. "But thank you."

Nathan is at the door of the lodging house before he changes his mind. He cannot do it, he realises. He cannot leave Harriet to her own devices, however much he might wish to. Especially now, after all she has just learnt.

He turns back and returns to the table. Harriet is still sitting with the letter in her hands, staring down at their mother's words. There's emotion in her eyes, but at the sight of him, she steels herself quickly.

"Eva told me about the man pursuing you on the ship," Nathan says. "Has there been any sign of him?"

Harriet shakes her head stiffly. "There's no need to involve yourself in my problems. I can take care of myself."

Nathan sits back down in the chair opposite her. "I'm your brother, Harriet. And whether you believe it or not, I care about you. I want you to be safe."

She sighs. Folds Abigail's letter carefully and slips it back inside the box. "I've not seen him," she says finally. "I don't think he knows I'm here. And I'll be leaving on the coach in a few hours."

"Where will you go?"

She traces a finger over the tarnished brass lid of the box, not looking at him. "I'm not sure yet. Back to London, I hope. If it's safe."

"Why didn't you tell us the truth about why you came up here?" Nathan asks. "Why keep all this to yourself?"

Harriet is silent for a long time, and Nathan doubts he will get an answer. But then she says, "Because I did not want to involve you and Eva in all this mess. When I left London, I had no idea I was going to be followed up here."

"Do you have any thought of why this man is after you?"

She shakes her head. "I don't know who he is. Or what he wants with me. But I didn't want any of you in trouble on my account."

"If that's how you feel, why did you tell Martin Macauley how his father died?" Nathan keeps his voice level.

Harriet is silent for a long time. He can tell she is unsurprised by his accusation. "It's just what I do," she says. "I ruin people's lives. I sent the authorities after my father's ship ten years ago to punish him for not wanting me in his life. His crewmen were sent to the gallows. Finn was almost one of them. And I told Martin Macauley about his father because I wanted to punish Eva for having all the things I will never have."

"What things?" Nathan pushes. "A husband? A family? You had those things, Harriet. You chose to leave them behind."

She shakes her head. "I couldn't expect you to understand."

Nathan waits for her to continue. When she doesn't, he says, "Eva is terrified of what Macauley is going to do to her and her family. She brought Thomas back to the house because she's so afraid of Macauley coming to Longstone to punish her."

Harriet looks down. Swallows visibly but doesn't speak.

Nathan leans back in his chair. There's anger there at her, of course. Wild anger, if he thinks too hard on it. The truth of Donald Macauley's death is one they had managed—rightly or wrongly—to keep buried for a decade. But there's no part of him that is surprised at what Harriet has done. He has long known she has it in her to do something like this; to upturn her sister's life on account of her own pettiness.

But he is not going to let that anger out. Not here, not now that Harriet has finally been open and honest with him. And not now, after learning the truth of what her father had meant to their mother. That knowledge has left him questioning everything he thought he knew about the past. He can only imagine how unbalanced Harriet must feel.

"Are you certain you want to leave?" he asks. "Will you not come back to the house like you first planned to do?"

She smiles faintly. "After all I've done? I don't think so."

"It's your home, Harriet. You're always welcome there, regardless of anything else."

"No," she says. "It's not. And I'm not. But thank you." There's a genuineness in her voice that Nathan rarely hears. "I'll be leaving on the coach in two hours. It's for the best. I think we both know that."

When will we see you again? Nathan wants to ask. But he feels he knows the answer. Knows that, had Harriet not found herself in trouble, she would never have come up here in the first place. Would have been content never to see her family again.

What would their life have looked like if Henry Ward had received that letter? Would they have stayed here in Lindisfarne? Would there still be such a gaping divide between Harriet and the rest of the family?

Nathan knows there's little point dwelling on what might have been. He stands. Looks down at his sister. Can tell from the expression in her eyes that she intends this to be a final goodbye. What will she go back to when she leaves this place, he wonders? He hopes there is someone for her to return to, in whatever shape her life takes now. He swallows down a swell of emotion. Swallows down all the useless phrases like *if you change your mind,* and *you know where to find us.* "Take care," he says instead. And, "I hope you find what you are looking for."

CHAPTER TWENTY-EIGHT

When she hears the front door of Highfield House click open and closed, Julia feels a fluttering in her stomach. She knows it's foolish to let Nathan's return conjure up these feelings. But it does not seem to be something she can control.

She feels a storm of emotions: gratitude at his helping her, guilt over allowing him to become so entangled in the thieving ring, and at the danger she had put him in. And yes, unbidden, the lingering warmth of their supper together last night. There's no future to this, of course—can be no future. But just for now, she will allow herself to enjoy his company.

His footsteps clop towards the parlour. Julia is perched on the edge of the settle, her money on the table in front of her, along with a scrawled page of sums. Calculations of how far these elaborate riches will get her. The total is nothing grand, but nor is it the most dire of prospects.

"I'm glad to see you in here," Nathan says, stepping into the parlour and closing the door behind him. "Glad you're no longer feeling the need to hide yourself away."

Julia returns his smile. "I could say the same for you."

He nods down at the piles of coins she has stacked neatly on the tea table. "Where did you put the safe?"

"Theodora took it. Said she had a good place to hide it."

Nathan smiles wryly. "Inside the priest hole, I imagine."

"I'm sorry, I didn't mean to involve her. She saw the safe when I came inside. I couldn't think of a lie quick enough." She regrets the words the moment they are out—knows in Nathan's eyes she has never been short of a lie.

But he just gives her a faint smile. "It's all right. She would have wrangled the truth out of me sooner or later. I'm sure it will inspire her next story. What will you do with it?" he asks. "Do you really intend to throw it in the ocean?"

"It's the safest thing to do," Julia says. "Dispose of it all, where the thieving ring cannot find it."

Nathan nods. He reaches into his pocket and passes her a folded note. "Here. Mrs Brodie gave me this to give to you. From Bobby, perhaps?"

Julia looks down at her name on the page in her son's messy scrawl. She opens the note. Feels her stomach fall.

"Is everything all right?"

"Yes, of course," she says stiffly. She tucks the note into her pocket. "Did you find Harriet?"

"I did."

"And?"

Nathan sinks into the armchair opposite the settle. Lets out a long breath, his shoulders sagging. "And she's just as difficult as she's ever been. Although I do hope that letter of Mother's might change things for her somewhat. That may be wishful thinking." His eyes drift back to the coins. "Where will you go?" he asks. "Now you have your money?"

Julia can't look at him. She thinks of Bobby's note:

I've just seen Calum in Bamburgh. I told him you'd been staying with an old friend in Berwick and that you need him to collect you. He's gone up there now—should give you time to get back before he does.

And yes, she will tell Nathan the truth of this. Will tell him her husband has returned, and that she must return too. Must face Calum, and hope his anger at her has settled enough to allow them a civil marriage. She cannot imagine that will be so easy, especially when he realises Bobby has led him off to Berwick on some completely fictitious mission.

She knows Calum's return is not a truth that Nathan will want to hear. But she will not let herself lie to him any longer. After all he has done for her, she will give him the honesty she ought to have given him years ago.

But not quite yet. As soon as this conversation is over, she must go upstairs and pack her things, and leave Highfield House for the last time. And so just for now, she will let herself imagine that other life. The one where she takes her hard-fought-for money and builds a life of her own again. Perhaps, in this other life, she also allows herself to take the contents of the stolen safe and reopen her curiosity shop. In this other life, there is no guilt at doing so; no fear of the thieves coming after their takings.

It's not a possibility, of course. Taking the safe is far too dangerous; far too grating against the morals she is trying so hard to cling to. And her scribbled sums tell her that if she were to take her own money and run, she would have the life of a scullery maid over the life of a businesswoman. That is even less appealing than trying to salvage something from the ruins of her marriage.

But to Nathan, she says, "Perhaps I'll follow Bobby down to North Sunderland. See if I can find work there too. Or perhaps go down to London to find my brother."

"Would it not make you sad to leave Northumberland? I know you love it so." No mention of Calum. And so this is the game they are playing: the game where nothing is impossible. The game where they let themselves imagine these prospects are real.

"Yes," Julia says, "it would make me sad to leave." *Perhaps I shall find a way to stay.* The words are on the tip of her tongue—because this is the game they are playing, after all. But she knows from experience that allowing herself to imagine that future will only bring her to her knees. She had given herself permission to believe in it once before, and it had taken every ounce of her strength to pull herself from the despair that had engulfed her when the life she had imagined had not come to pass. She will not put herself through that again. Will not put Nathan through it either.

She scoops the coins from the table and tucks them back into her purse. Says, "But that's the way things have to be."

The afternoon is turning, a raft of blue-grey clouds beginning to gather at the bottom of the sky. It's the kind of weather she would paint; angry colours hurled across the canvas. Make a thing of beauty from all this natural anger.

Today, it doesn't feel beautiful. It just feels foreboding.

Harriet is the only person out here, waiting for the coach by this thin ribbon of road. She finds it hard to believe the carriage won't just rattle right on by her. Up the hill out of the village and disappear. She glances over her shoulder. Sees only rolling grassland and the gnarled black fingers of trees. She shivers, pulling her cloak tighter around her body.

Finally, the coach approaches, four dappled horses trotting steadily down the narrow road, mud spraying from the carriage wheels. Harriet wills it on quicker. She cannot wait to leave this place behind. Her thoughts are charging—full of Thomas and Eva and Martin Macauley. The brass box containing her mother's letter to her father. Every piece of being here feels like a mistake, and yet somehow, she cannot quite find a way to regret it. If she had not come back to Northumberland, she would never have learnt the truth of what her father meant to her mother. She would never have learnt what might once have been.

The coachman tugs on the reins, drawing the horses to a halt. He leaps from the box seat. Looks down at the small cloth bag sitting at Harriet's feet.

"That all the luggage you got with you, ma'am?"

"Yes. Thank you."

He nods. Opens the door of the coach.

He is there as though he has been waiting. As though, somehow, he knew she would be here on this lonely road, with clouds sucking away the light, having fractured all her relationships beyond salvageability.

The man with the missing finger is sitting right by the door, and his grey eyes meet hers squarely. Some distant part of her sees that perhaps he has not been waiting for her at all; had just sought this coach back to London—this coach that has come from Edinburgh, from Berwick, where the survivors of the wreck were taken. But right now, that logic means nothing—not to her, and not to him; this she knows by the sudden look of recognition in his eyes, the upturning of his lips beneath the dark storm of his beard. A look that recognises that, in spite of all the bad luck that has befallen him, things are finally going right.

Harriet does not think. She just runs. Grabs her skirts in her fists and tears down the road, away from the coach, back towards the village.

She hears the coachman call after her. Doesn't look back. Is the bearded man following? Footsteps thunder in her ears—just hers? Or his as well? Surely he must be chasing her. He had trailed her across the capital, and all the way up the country. Had tried to break into her bedchamber. He is not going to let this opportunity slide.

Another shout from the coachman. And then the steady clop of hooves as the carriage pulls away from the village.

Harriet crouches in the narrow gap between two cottages, gulping down her breath. Her lungs are burning, straining against her tightly laced stays.

Where does she go from here? The tide is low—she could make it across to Holy Island. But out on the open sands of the Pilgrims' Way, there is nowhere to hide.

The public house, she supposes, is her best chance. Likely the first place he will look, but there will be other people around—the innkeeper at the very least. Perhaps from there she can get word to her brother. Beg for the help she was too proud to ask for just a few hours ago.

She hurries across the narrow street, eyes darting. Sees movement on the edge of her vision. She tears away, past the jetty, footsteps thudding in her wake. Feels a presence bearing down on her. A hand reaches out, grabbing her arm from behind.

Harriet whirls around. Comes face to face with her father. At the sight of the blatant panic in her eyes, Ward releases his grip on her arm. Harriet cannot make sense of why he is here. He feels like a vision she has conjured up in her guilt-ridden imagination. Instinctively, she breaks into a run again. Past the lodging house, past the jetty, out towards the Pilgrims' Way.

Ward calls her name. Charges after her.

"Goddamn it, Harriet," he barks. "Stop running." And somehow, the intensity of the command makes her obey. She hunches over, gulping down her breath. Finally dares to look up at her father.

"There's a man after me. I—"

"I know," says Henry Ward. "This way. I've a boat." And it's all she can do to follow.

CHAPTER TWENTY-NINE

Harriet sits alone below deck on her father's small sailboat, feeling the vessel career across the water. She has no idea where they are or where they are going. No idea if she ought to feel safer here on Ward's boat, than being pursued by the man with the missing finger.

The space below deck is cramped and airless, with benches tucked around a narrow, rough-hewn table, and a sleeping pallet rolled up in one corner. It smells of the sea, of whisky and potted meat. Of her father.

After what seems an eternity, Harriet hears a metallic groan and clatter, and the rattle of what she assumes to be the anchor chain. The hatch groans open, letting in a shaft of pale daylight. The ladder creaks and Ward appears from above. He takes off his coat and tosses it over a storage chest in the corner. Slides onto the bench on the opposite side of the table to Harriet.

"Where are we?" she asks.

"Just outside Beadle Bay. I've seen no sign that we've been followed."

Under her father's gaze, Harriet feels jittery and on edge. Her heart is still thumping after being chased across the village, her shift clinging to sticky skin. "Is this your boat?" she asks. Right now, all the other questions she needs to ask feel far too weighted.

Ward nods. "Not quite as big as the *Eagle*." Smiles. "But it does what I need it to do."

She looks at him for a long second. His face is weathered and worn, and though his eyes are still fiercely blue, there's a weariness to them. A deep exhaustion.

"How did you know where I was?" she asks. "How did you know I was in trouble? Have you been following me?"

He sighs heavily. Rubs a scar on his knuckles. "The man that's after you," he begins, "he's pursuing you because of me. He is the brother of one of my former crewmen who was executed ten years ago."

"What?" Her voice comes out strangled.

"When Mr Lawler learnt I had been spared the hangman when his brother died, he hunted me down. Demanded some form of compensation. I paid him handsomely with what wealth I had that wasn't seized by the crown on my arrest. Several years later, he found me again. Demanded more. More than I was able—or willing—to give."

For long moments, Harriet doesn't speak. The sea clops rhythmically against the hull of the boat. "Why is he after me?" she dares to ask. Could he possibly know she had been the one to send the authorities after Ward's ship? How could he know? Her knuckles whiten as she grips the edge of the bench seat.

"Lawler knows you're my daughter," Ward says. "He imagines, I presume, that he can get to me through you."

"By kidnapping me?" Harriet swallows hard. "Or killing me?"

Ward is silent for a moment. "I'm not certain."

She thinks of Lawler prising open the window of her bedchamber in London. Thinks of him trailing her across the city. Onto the *Cygnus*. Thinks of the thinly veiled threats he had whispered as he passed her in those narrow, creaking corridors of the ship.

We're not far from Edinburgh now.

See you when we land.

All this had been because of whose child she is?

"I'm not certain how he came to know I'm your father," Ward says, before she can ask. "Lawler knew I'd spent much time on Lindisfarne. Perhaps he made the connection when he saw your paintings of the island. And there's a certain family resemblance…"

"My paintings of the island? How do you even know about those?"

Ward is silent for a moment. There's an uncertainty in his eyes now.

The same vulnerability she had seen from him the day they had first met. A vulnerability so far removed from the unyielding façade he presents to the outside world. "I admit I've been following your work in London," he says. "I read about the commissions of a painter using your mother's unmarried name. I suspected it might be you." He smiles faintly. "You're a fine artist. Very fine. You have my mother's talent."

Harriet feels her chest tighten. "Really?" The word comes out strained.

"Yes. She was a landscape artist like yourself. Wished to push the boundaries of what was expected of her as a female painter."

Inexplicably, Harriet feels tears gathering behind her eyes. Cannot make sense of why, after all she has just learnt, it is this piece of information that has struck her the hardest.

The faint smile disappears from her father's face. "I saw you presenting your work at the Allbridge exhibit," he says. "And I'm afraid Lawler followed me there. I assume that's how he came to know of you."

Harriet knots her fingers. "He came to my lodgings one night," she says. "Tried to break in. It was you who stopped him, wasn't it." Some part of her has known this all along, she realises. Some part of her had recognised her father's voice when he had called out to Lawler to scare him away from her window. It had felt like a truth too difficult to acknowledge.

Ward nods. "I fired a warning shot before he got through your window, but he got away before I could catch him. When I realised he had left on the *Cygnus*, I came up here as quickly as I could. I heard of the wreck when I landed in Edinburgh. I went to Berwick, then to Longstone searching for you. Finn told me you were staying in Beal." He shifts on the bench, leaning forward to meet her eyes. "I'm sorry," he says. "I truly am. The last thing in the world I wished to happen was for you to be put in danger because of me."

Harriet looks down, unable to hold his intense gaze. As frightening as it is to know Lawler is after her to punish Ward, there's something steadying about sharing the strain of this. Of having the support of her father. And perhaps it's this that frightens her more than anything. She is not used to feeling supported. No—she is not used to allowing herself to be supported. Not anymore.

"Why did you follow my work?" she asks. "The last time we spoke, you said you wanted nothing to do with me. Because you thought that was what my mother wanted." Instinctively, her fingers slide into her pocket. Graze the lid of the brass box.

Ward glances down. What is that look on his face? Regret? "I suppose narrowly escaping death changed my outlook somewhat." He keeps rubbing at his knuckles. "I read about the work you had been commissioned to do. When I heard your sponsors were opening their salon to the public, I admit I found it difficult to stay away."

Harriet swallows heavily. "You did not approach me at the Allbridges'."

"No." He manages a wry smile. "Too much of a coward, I suppose. It felt like the wrong thing to do, given I was the one who told you we ought to stay out of one another's lives." He sighs, leaning back against the bulkhead. "I did try to find the will to approach you that night, once or twice… or several times. I suspect that told Lawler all he needed to know."

Harriet feels a deep, hollow discomfort in her stomach. When she had first met her father, she had longed for a connection with him. Had longed to mean something to him. And if she is honest with herself, that desire has never really left her. If he has been following her and her work, he likely knows she has left her husband and son. What must he think of her? She supposes it doesn't matter. Because even after all her father has told her; even after Abigail's letter, how can she have a life with him in it when she had tried to send him to his death? This is what she does: destroys people's lives. Chips away at the foundations of every relationship she has until they crumble and shatter at her feet.

"How did you escape the gallows?" The words come out husky. "Was it because of the information you had about the Jacobite cause? The information in the letter you were trying to find at Nathan's house?"

He nods. "I gave up Lord Haver's name in exchange for my freedom."

Harriet closes her eyes, feeling tears well in her throat. They spill down her cheeks with little warning. She brushes them away hurriedly. "The night your ship was captured," she blurts. "It was all my doing. I sent the authorities after you. I told them there was a pirate vessel leaving the bay." As the words fall into the silence, she feels the ugliness of them, their petty brutality. She hates that she is the kind of person to have done such a thing. Hates that she is *this*.

She dares to look at her father, an apology blazing in her eyes. Does not speak that apology. Doing so feels far too flimsy, far too trite.

Ward leans back on the bench, studying her for a long time with an expression that is impossible to read. After a moment, he says, "Why?"

Fresh tears gather in her throat and she swallows past the pain of them. "I was hurt because you chose to leave. Because you did not want me in your life."

Ward pins his gaze on her, not speaking until she looks up and meets his eyes. "It was never a matter of not wanting you in my life, Harriet. I was only doing what your mother would have wanted."

She closes her eyes. Tightens her fist around the box in her pocket. A part of her is desperate to give it to him. Let him read Abigail's words, thirty years too late.

A bigger part of her is too afraid. Because Abigail's letter will be permission for Henry Ward to seek a life with their daughter in it. It's permission for him to be her father. And the thought of that is far too terrifying. Having her father in her life is just another relationship for her to shatter and destroy.

"I'm sorry," she says. "I was young and foolish and angry. Not that I'm any less foolish now."

Ward gives a short chuckle. Shakes his head. "You sound like the daughter of a man who's made his own lifetime of mistakes."

Harriet looks up at him in surprise. "You're not... Should you not be feeling a little more... furious?"

"What point would there be in that?"

She lets out an incredulous breath. "What *point* would there be?"

Ward takes a tarnished spying glass from the table and turns it around in his hands. "I'm an old man. I don't want to spend what years I have left holding a grudge against my only child."

Fresh tears spill, faster than she can blink them away. This unexpected reprieve is far too difficult to navigate. She wants his anger. Wants that old belief that Abigail had never wanted her to know her father. Those things were easier than this.

No. She doesn't want those things back. She wants the truth of Abigail's letter. *I want you to know I love you.* She wants her father to know that truth too. Wants the courage to tell him.

She swipes at her tears. Draws in a breath in an attempt to steady herself. "What do I do now? How do I rid myself of Mr Lawler?" Perhaps she cannot open up completely; cannot tell her father everything she ought to tell him. But Abigail's letter gives her the strength to ask him this. To seek his advice. His help. "I don't have information to blackmail anyone with. I don't have a safe home to return to. And I've ruined things with my family so badly I can never go back to them." She looks to her father with desperate eyes. "How do I escape this?"

Ward stands. "It's not your plight to escape, Harriet. It's mine."

"It's my fault Lawler lost his brother." And somehow, because of this, it feels only right that he has come after her.

Ward doesn't respond. Just looks down at her, taking her in. What would it have been like, Harriet finds herself wondering, to have grown up with Henry Ward as a father? What would her life have looked like if he had read Abigail's letter thirty years ago, when she had first written it?

"I'll see to it that he doesn't come near you again." There's a resoluteness to his voice. A determinedness.

"How?"

Ward goes to the storage chest and clicks open the lid. Produces a pistol and a handful of shot. "I'm going back to Beal," he says, pulling on his coat. He slides the weapon into his pocket. "I ought to have gone after Lawler earlier. But I wanted to get you to safety."

Harriet swallows hard. "What makes you think you can stop him now if you couldn't in London?"

"This is a far emptier part of the country. A far easier place to… do what is needed. I've no desire to find myself back on the gallows again."

Harriet's stomach turns over. Her father could die for this—could die because of events she herself had set in motion. He needs to see her mother's letter. She cannot let him die without knowing the truth of it. The urge to give it to him, to show him what had been in Abigail's heart is almost overwhelming. But so is the fear of where this could lead.

Ward steps onto the ladder and shoves open the hatch, leaving Harriet down below, fingers curled around the brass box in her pocket.

CHAPTER THIRTY

"Evie." She feels Finn's hand on her shoulder, tugging her out of a dream. Shadows and crashes and water rolling down the walls of their home. "Evie." He shakes her gently and she thrashes, panicked, against him. "It's all right."

She opens her eyes, disoriented and breathless. Muted grey daylight is streaming in through the window. She had closed her eyes for a moment after putting Maggie down in her crib. Had not intended to fall asleep.

She sits up hurriedly, making her head spin. "Where are the children? I was—"

Finn takes her shoulder to steady her. "They're fine," he says. "The lads are outside. Maggie's right here."

Eva turns to look at him. He has their daughter in the crook of his arm, she realises. The sight of Maggie pressed to her father's chest is faintly steadying. But she needs the boys here too.

"They can't be outside." She slides out of bed. "It's not safe."

Finn catches her hand, tugging her back gently. "Eva. Come on. It's all right. They know to keep away from the edges of the island."

"Macauley," she manages. "What if he…"

"Macauley is not going to come for our children," says Finn.

"How do you know that?" Eva goes to the washbin and splashes her face, trying to let the cold water sear away her nightmare. "I didn't mean to fall asleep."

Finn sets Maggie on the floor. Stays sitting on the edge of the bed. "I'm glad you did. You were awake most of the night."

Eva uses the cloth beside the washbin to dry her face. She still feels painfully unsteady. Exhausted to the core. Not just from lack of sleep, but from a lack of peace. From the constant pulse of guilt that has been inside her for a decade. It has grown from a murmur to a roar since Martin Macauley learnt the truth about his father's death.

She needs this to end. She knows she will never be rid of the shame that comes from having killed a man. But she can rid herself of the guilt of keeping secrets.

She tugs on her shoes and strides towards the door, snatching her cloak from the hook on the wall.

Finn scoops Maggie up again and follows Eva out the door. "Where are you going?"

"I need to speak to him." She can see Noah and Archie on their knees at the edge of the rockpool. The clouds at the bottom of the horizon are beginning to thicken, darken. A pulsing surrounds her—in the air or in her chest, she cannot tell.

Finn hurries after her. Lurches for her wrist. "Stop," he says, voice low. "Think about what you're doing."

She keeps walking. Finn marches over to the rockpool and hands Maggie to Noah. Catches back up to Eva as she steps onto the jetty.

"Since the wreck, we're finally being treated like decent people," he hisses. "We're finally being treated with some respect. Why in hell are you trying to undo that by bringing up the past?"

"Because there's never been any decency about this, Finn!" she cries. "There's been nothing decent about keeping the truth of Donald Macauley's death a secret for ten years. Martin should never have found out through some anonymous letter. He ought to have found out from me."

Finn blows out a breath. "Anonymous letter? So that's what we're doing? We're not even going to acknowledge the fact that that letter came from your own sister?"

Eva turns away. Can't look at him. "You don't know that."

"Yes I do. So do you."

Eva is silent. Perhaps he's right. Perhaps there's a part of her that does know the letter was Harriet's doing. But acknowledging that is far too brutal. She would rather the letter have come from someone nameless, faceless. "It doesn't matter where it came from," she says tautly. "I need to speak with Macauley. I need to explain myself. I cannot keep it all inside anymore."

"And do you think that's something he's going to want to hear? That his father tried to kill you?" Finn takes her hand and tugs her close. His grip on her is firm, possessive. "Let him have his doubts," he says. "Haven't we had enough trouble? Why would you go looking for more of it?"

"I'm not *looking* for trouble. The trouble is already here. Martin already knows."

The island feels suddenly stifling. Oppressive and constrictive. And for the first time, with her husband's hand snared around her own, she lets herself imagine it: that other life she could have chosen. That ordered, respectful life she was supposed to have had. The life Nathan had laid out for her.

An easier life.

The thought comes to her like a physical blow and she curses herself for even thinking it.

She looks across the island at her children. How could she even for a second have allowed herself to envisage a life they are not a part of?

But the thought is there in the front of her mind now, pulsing and violent. She cannot push it away.

She had not chosen that easier life. She had chosen this one: this challenging, sea-drenched, firelit life. A life of love—intense, consuming love—but a life of guilt and struggling too. Because in this life she has chosen, she had killed Donald Macauley, and tried to keep it a secret. And now she must face the consequences of that decision.

As she reels towards the skiff, Finn grabs her arm, tugging her back. "Please, Eva. Don't." He wraps his hands around her shoulders, looks at her squarely. "I know how you feel. You know I do. I know how it feels to carry the weight of the life you took. But do you really think confronting Macauley is going to make it any easier?"

"You have your absolution," Eva says bitterly. "Oliver's death is not a secret anymore."

She sees something flicker and harden behind Finn's eyes. It has been a long time since they have spoken of her brother. Years since they have spoken his name.

"Absolution?" Finn repeats. "Is that what you think I have?"

There's an incredulous tone to his voice and it makes Eva's anger rise. "You have far more absolution than I've ever had. Nathan and Harriet both know how Oliver died. You don't need to keep it a secret any longer." She forces herself to keep her voice to an angry hiss. "I need to tell the truth about Macauley's death too. I can't carry it any more. You of all people ought to understand that."

"Eva. Please." His grip on her wrist tightens. "I have never forbidden you from doing anything as your husband. But I am begging you not to do this."

She yanks her arm back and Finn lets his hand fall. "I have to," she says. "I'm sorry. But I have to. I don't have a choice."

CHAPTER THIRTY-ONE

This is the second time Nathan has had to restart the letter to his distributor. It's been a chaos of clumsy wording and spilled ink; he's been far too tangled in thoughts of Julia and Harriet and his mother's involvement in the thieving ring. When the knock at the door comes, he is relieved at the distraction.

Julia steps inside the study, her gaze drawn to the telescope set up at the window. She smiles faintly. "I'm glad you're still using it."

Nathan returns her smile. "It's a fine piece."

She hovers in front of his desk for a long moment, hands clasped in front of her. "Calum is on his way back to Bamburgh," she says.

The words feel like a physical blow. "I see. And are you…"

"I have to go back," she says. "Yes."

He waits, hoping for more. Nothing comes. "Are you certain?" he dares to ask. "You could—"

"I'm certain," Julia says tightly. "Calum is my husband. I cannot just walk away from my marriage. That's not the kind of person I want to be."

"Of course. I'm sorry, I did not mean to suggest…" He fades out, lowers his eyes, not entirely certain of what it is he is trying to say. For several moments, neither of them speak. The window rattles with a loud gust of wind.

Nathan turns his quill around in his fingers. "I know it's no place of mine to ask, but when he returns… will you be safe? Given how angry he was with you when he left?"

Julia stares at her feet, colour rising to her cheeks. "He's never hurt me. And I don't believe he would."

"Even now he knows the truth about Bobby's father?"

"Yes. I trust him. I do. He's not a violent man."

Nathan nods. He's glad of this, of course. He must be glad of it. But there is something galling about Julia's blind trust for her husband when she had never managed such trust for him. He stands. Folds his hands behind his back and clears his throat. "Shall I ask Lewis to take you over?"

"No. It's all right. I can make my own way." Her voice is clipped. Deliberately so, Nathan can tell. Already, she is putting distance between them. Necessary distance, he reminds himself. It's what they ought to have been doing all along.

"Do you have your cat?" he asks.

A faint smile flickers on Julia's lips. "I shall make sure I don't leave her behind. I'd not do that to you."

Nathan tries and fails to return her smile. He takes a step closer to her. Drinks in the sight of her: her gold-flecked eyes, her freckled cheeks, her chaos of coppery curls. He's sure it will be the last time he ever sees her. And the words fall out before he can stop them: "Is this really what you want?"

Julia's lips part. "What I want has nothing to do with anything." He hears the ache in her words. Or perhaps that ache just belongs to him.

And suddenly the words spill out, angry and unbidden. Nathan hears his own voice say, "You can't go back to him."

Julia blinks, eyebrows shooting skyward. "I beg your pardon?"

Words keep tumbling out before he can rein them in. "How can you turn around and walk straight back into the thieving ring?" His voice rises. "How can you go strolling back to the man who left you alone in the midst of all that?"

Julia blows out a breath. "I'm *strolling back* to that man because I'm his wife."

"He abandoned you, Julia."

"No, he didn't. He's on his way home. And I need to be there when he returns." Her green eyes flash. "Besides, what choice do I have?"

"You have a choice," Nathan pushes. "You have all that money in the box safe."

She gives an incredulous laugh. "I am not using stolen money to leave my husband." Shakes her head. "Do you really think I want to be that kind of woman? Don't you think I've had enough of being looked down upon in my life?"

"So you'd rather stay with the man who left you alone with the thieving ring?"

She wraps her arms around her body. Begins to pace as she gnaws on a thumbnail. "You talk like the alternative is so easy, Nathan. I've been out on my own without a husband before, and I never knew if I was going to be able to keep a roof over my head. Never knew if I was going to be able to feed my son. I will not go back to that life again."

"So use the money in the safe."

"I am not using stolen money," she repeats through gritted teeth.

Her stubbornness is infuriating. "Why do you care so much about breaking the law?" he snaps. "It's not like it's ever bothered you before." He regrets the words the moment they are out.

Julia's eyes flash, and for several moments she stands wordless behind his desk, jaw clenched. When she finally speaks, her words are clipped and controlled. "I was dreading leaving you," she says tautly. "I was dreading saying goodbye. I'm grateful to you for making it so easy."

CHAPTER THIRTY-TWO

Julia knocks on Theodora's bedroom door. No answer. She clenches her hands into fists. Anger is coursing through her, and all she wants to do is get the hell out of this house. What was she thinking, coming here in the first place? How was it ever destined to end in anything other than carnage?

Carnage, she supposes, is better than the deep, aching emptiness she anticipated feeling when she left Nathan for the last time. Right now, she never wants to look at him again.

She hovers impatiently outside Theodora's door, Minerva mewling and squirming like a terror beneath her arm. She needs to get inside; get the safe out of the priest hole.

She needs to get out of this house.

Which is worse, she wonders: letting herself into Theodora's bedchamber uninvited? Or leaving the safe under her and Nathan's roof?

She is saved from the decision when Theodora appears on the staircase. At the sight of Julia waiting outside her door, she hurries down the hallway. "Is everything all right?" she asks.

"Yes," Julia says tightly. "I just need to collect the safe from the priest hole."

Theodora glances at Minerva, then catches sight of the duffel bag slung over Julia's shoulder. "Are you leaving?"

"Yes."

Julia is glad Theodora doesn't push the issue. She follows her into the room. Watches as she pushes on the panel of the fireplace, the priest hole swivelling opening beneath her hand. She bends to collect the safe and hands it to Julia.

"Are you sure you want to leave?" Theodora asks. "Is it safe? You're always—"

"I'm sure. Thank you." Julia hugs the box to her chest. With Minerva under her other arm and her duffel bag lolling on her shoulder, the safe feels too heavy, too unwieldy. She can't wait to rid herself of the damn thing. Can't wait to hurl it into the ocean and let every piece of this be forgotten.

She forces a smile. "Thank you for your hospitality, Thea. You've been more than kind."

Theodora says nothing, just gives a short nod, and Julia can tell she has not bought her forced brightness. She can't make herself care. She just needs to get away from this place, away from the memories. Away from Nathan, before he knocks the ground out from beneath her again.

She doesn't look back as she charges from the house. Doesn't dare to look up at the study window to see if Nathan is watching. She just tramps over the dunes, mind on nothing but escaping.

The tide is rising, but there's still only a thin sheen of water covering the Pilgrims' Way. Too shallow for a boat. Too deep for shoes. She charges into it anyway, tightening her grip on Minerva. What are wet shoes and cold feet if it means she gets far away from Nathan and this cursed island? *Why do you care so much about breaking the law? It's not like it's ever bothered you before.*

She'll wave down a wagon when she gets to the mainland, or walk to Bamburgh if she must. Hopes she makes it back before those potato sack clouds above her head spill open.

Hopes she makes it back before Calum returns from Berwick.

The water is only at her knees in the middle of the steppingstones, but she cannot bear to look at the safe for a minute longer. With a loud cry of frustration, she hurls it into the ocean. The broken lid swings open as it flies through the air, coins and jewellery splattering down into the shallow sea. The half-empty box lands with a weighted splash. It tilts and hovers on the surface for a moment, then disappears into the water.

Eva has not been this close to Martin Macauley's farm since before she had killed his father. Ever since, she has always given the place a wide berth; has taken detours around the village to make the chance of seeing him as remote as possible.

But somehow, standing here outside his gate like this has always felt inevitable. Some part of her has never doubted that one day Martin would come to know the truth of his father's death. Heaven knows there have been times over the past years when the guilt has been so strong she has teetered on the verge of coming here and telling him everything.

She thinks of Finn. Thinks of the anger, the pleading in his eyes when he had tried to stop her from leaving their island.

The emotion of their argument is gathered in her throat, knotting her belly. There's a deep regret in her for going against what he had asked of her. And yes, she knows the danger of what she is about to do.

But she also knows this is the only way forward. She cannot spend any more of her life carrying this weight. She has no thought of what Macauley will do with this information, this confirmation. All she knows is that she has no choice but to confess.

She lets herself through the gate. Trudges through a trough of ankle-deep mud past a gnarled, bare apple tree. Knocks on the door of the farmhouse.

Macauley appears from around the side of the house, carrying a shovel. A worn knitted cap is pulled down to his grey eyebrows, his dark coat patched and riddled with holes. The look he gives Eva is blazing. "Wasn't expecting to see you here."

Her heart thunders against her ribs. "May we speak?"

Macauley steps past her, tossing down the shovel and shouldering the door of the farmhouse. It opens with a shudder and groan. He stands at the doorway, gesturing for her to enter the single room of the cottage. He pulls the door closed behind her. Turns the key in the lock and slides it into his pocket.

The place is just as worn and threadbare as Macauley's boat and jacket, with an icy draft sifting between the beams of the roof, and an earthen floor beginning to turn to mud. One window is boarded up and the door of the sideboard is dangling off its hinges. It makes the cottage on Longstone feel like a palace. Have the Macauleys always been so hard-pressed? Or has Martin fallen to hard times after the death of his father? It's a question Eva cannot bear to follow too far.

He drops into a seat at the table. "Why are you here, Mrs Murray?"

At the look of blatant animosity in Macauley's eyes, panic squeezes her lungs. She thinks of her children; suddenly craves the safety of Longstone. But it is too late for regret.

She hovers by the table for a moment, then sits opposite Macauley. Dares to look him in the eye. "I came to tell you I'm sorry."

A cold smile appears in the corner of his mouth. "That's not why you're here."

Eva lets out a breath. He is right, of course. At least on some level. And the least she can offer him is the truth. She says, "I've come to find out what you are going to do to me."

Macauley leans back in his chair, studying her wordlessly for several long moments. Wind makes the cloth window drum. Sends a frigid draught snaking through the cottage. A tree branch taps steadily against the window frame.

"What do you think I ought to do?" he asks. "A life for a life? Is that a fair trade?"

Eva squeezes her hands together in her lap, fear pulsing inside her. Finn was right—she should never have come. But she *has* come, and now she must see this through. Wherever it takes her. This is what she wanted, she reminds herself. For her guilt to be laid out in the open. For her confession to ease the constriction of it.

"If you wish to kill me, I cannot stop you," she says. "But you do not want that on your conscience. Believe me." She hears her voice waver.

Macauley is silent for a long time. He keeps his eyes down, picking at the splintered edge of the table. When he speaks again, a little of the venom is gone from his voice. "What did he do to you? Why were you out at sea with him? I don't suppose you were there by choice."

"He believed I was spying for the government against the Jacobites. He forced me into his boat and rowed us out to sea. Once we were far enough from shore, he raised his musket and tried to kill me."

"And you defended yourself."

"Yes."

Macauley gives a short, humourless laugh. "He always was a stupid old bastard." He folds his wiry arms across his chest. "The innkeeper in Beal said you were staying at the lodging house the night of Da's death. How d'you get him to lie for you?"

Eva swallows hard. The truth, she knows, could lead to more trouble. But the truth is why she has come here. "The Beal innkeeper is staunchly anti-Jacobite," she says huskily. "We promised the government spies use of Highfield House in exchange for him accounting for me at his lodgings."

Macauley snorts. "Always knew your family were in Geordie's pocket."

"No," Eva says quickly. "No. It's never been like that." She feels a rush of regret. How hard has Nathan worked to regain the villagers' trust? To rebuild their family's good name? "We were never spying for the king. My brother only ever agreed to it to help me. He's never been involved in the government cause. I swear it." She feels as though she is back in that dinghy with Donald Macauley, pleading with him to accept the truth of her family's innocence.

Donald's son eyes her. Does he believe her? It's impossible to tell.

"I'm so sorry," she says. "Truly. I'm so sorry for all of it. And I'm sorry for keeping it a secret. I know it was the wrong thing to do." And they are out now, the words she has imagined speaking for the last ten years. Her absolution? It does not feel like it. Speaking of what happened just makes the past feel so much more present. Her guilt has not eased. It has just become more precarious.

Martin doesn't respond. Doesn't look at her. Just keeps picking at the splinters on the edge of the table. The tree branch knocks and knocks and knocks.

And what now? Does she turn and walk out the door, and hold her breath, praying he does not produce a pistol and shoot her from behind? Is Martin Macauley that kind of man?

Martin Macauley is the son of the man who had tried to kill her on account of rumours.

Martin Macauley had put a bullet in Finn's calf on account of a little stolen coal.

So, yes, she realises sickly. Martin Macauley is the kind of man to produce a pistol and shoot her in the back as she walks out of his cottage.

But she is here now, and the thing is done. And now she has to leave.

She gets to her feet, dizzy with the racing of her heart. She looks down at him for one last moment, waiting for him to speak. When she gets only silence, she turns. Walks towards the door of the farmhouse. Waits, with held breath, for him to unlock the door.

She hears no movement. No click of a pistol. But her pulse is roaring in her ears, drowning out all other sound.

He will always know, now. And perhaps he will tell others. Perhaps he already has. And this will be her punishment, she thinks. Every time she sees Martin Macauley, she will think of what she did to his father. And she will wonder who else might know of her direst of mistakes. But if this is the weight she must carry, she can manage it. Because the burden of her guilt has been lightened, if only a fraction, by this confession. She will take a fraction. She will take whatever she can get.

"Why are you leaving?" Macauley says suddenly. "You've not got the answer you came for."

Eva swallows. Turns to face him. "What?"

"You came here to find out what I was planning to do to you. And I've not told you."

She squeezes her hands into fists, trying to stop them from shaking. Presses her spine against the door and dares to look into Macauley's eyes. "What are you planning to do to me?"

He looks at her for a long second, and she sees more in him now than she did before. That blatant animosity has become hatred; has become his father's anger. And Eva sees that, just as her guilt has been festering for the last ten years, so too has Martin Macauley's anger at the unanswered questions about his father's death. And now, after so much uncertainty, he finally has a place to put that rage.

His colourless lips part, but he doesn't speak. Just stares her down—a look of blazing anticipation. Then he stands, comes towards her with slow, measured steps. He leans over her, accosting her with the stink of sweat and animals and unwashed skin. Slides the key into the lock and shoves the door open. Cold, damp air punches into the cottage. Eva looks up at Macauley, but he says nothing, leaving her with no choice but to start walking.

She steps from the farmhouse into icy, rain-heavy air. Wonders if perhaps her direst of mistakes was not Donald Macauley's death, but this moment, right here, right now.

CHAPTER THIRTY-THREE

Nathan has a lot of regrets when it comes to Julia. But he is not sure any quite match up to this.

Now she has left, the house feels almost unbearably quiet—perhaps just made that way by the deafening rattle of his thoughts. He hates that he had said such terrible things. Hates that she had left on such terrible terms.

Most of all, he hates the inevitability of it all. Julia was always going to leave. Was always going to go back to Calum. And Nathan was always going to behave like a complete arse about the whole thing, because he couldn't manage anything different.

Clouds are drowning out the last of the sun, the lamp on his desk doing little to lift the long shadows that have fallen across his study.

Theodora and Tom are out turning wild on Saint Cuthbert's Island, and Nathan can hear no sign of Mrs Brodie. He had sent Lewis home to the village not long ago, so he might be saved from travelling once this downpour inevitably hits.

Nathan has stayed planted at his desk in the two hours since Julia left, finally finishing the bungled letter to his distributor and making arrangements for his next trip to Scotland. Throwing himself into his work had seemed like the best way through this. A desperate attempt to distract himself from his own stupidity.

Go after her. It's a thought he's been trying to push away all afternoon. A thought that refuses to be silenced.

Go after her. Go after her. Go. After. Her.

It's almost overwhelming. There can be no future for them, of course. But he feels certain this is the last time Julia will ever be a part of his life. And he cannot bear for his last words to her to be so bitter and hurtful. For all the turmoil Julia has brought him, his feelings for her are undeniably precious. Undeniably rare.

He looks out the window, grateful for the gunmetal tide locking him onto the island. Good. He needs this—this emphatic reminder from the natural world that going after her can achieve nothing.

But his eyes are drawn to the sloop outside the window.

He pushes the thought away as soon as it arrives. The daylight is beginning to fade, and the wind is whipping the sea into choppy grey peaks. He is still far from a confident sailor. Trying to sail over to Bamburgh would be madness.

Of course it would. It would be madness for far too many reasons— his sailing abilities being the very least of them.

But he cannot stop thinking. Thinking about the regret of the last ten years, and the aching bitterness of their parting argument. The constant replaying of conversations, trying to determine if he might have done something, said something, different, to keep Julia from leaving. And there is nothing to lose. Not a thing. He lost Julia years ago.

He is out of the house and marching towards the boat before his good sense can catch him.

CHAPTER THIRTY-FOUR

This wind has whipped four more tiles off the roof, doing nothing to help Finn's terrible mood. By the time he makes it over to the farm next week to ask about the tiles, there'll be little of the damn thing left. This house has begun to feel far too flimsy, far too susceptible to the elements—and to the storm he can see gathering on the horizon. Has begun to feel like far from the beacon of solidity it has been for so much of his life.

He can't quite make sense of what he's feeling when he looks out from atop the ladder and sees Eva draw the skiff up towards the jetty. Violent relief at her safety, yes, but there's far more anger and bitterness than he has ever felt towards her before. An old anger—the kind Henry Ward had spent two years trying to scrub out of him. He hates that it has returned; hates even more than it was Eva who had sparked it.

Finn had spent most of the hour she had been gone debating whether to go after her. Calculating the risks of piling the children into the longboat and following her to Macauley's; of leaving Noah here to guard his siblings with the weather turning and roof tiles shattering. Eva had made her decision, he had decided finally. And now they have to face whatever is to come.

Since she has been gone, Finn has turned into all the parts of his own father he swore he would never be—short-tempered with his children, barking at their waterlogged boots, their stream of questions, their dropped cups of milk. He was almost relieved when Noah had corralled his brother and sister into the bedroom to get away from him. At least this way he couldn't make things worse.

He climbs from the ladder and waits for Eva on the edge of the jetty. The sea is grey and heaving, spitting up over the edges of the island.

"Did you speak to him?" he asks tautly.

"Yes." She winds the mooring ropes. Doesn't look at him.

"And? What did he do? What did he say?"

He offers her his hand to help her out of the boat. She doesn't take it—whether out of spite or anger, or just a deep distractedness, he can't quite tell. She looks flushed and windblown, her blue eyes full of an emotion he can't quite read. Finally, she dares to look up at him. "I don't know what he's going to do," she admits. "I told him the truth and he gave me little in response." He hears the fear in her words.

Finn had truly believed that Macauley would not act on the information Harriet had given him. Why would he want the truth of what his father had done to become public knowledge? But now, with this fear in Eva's voice, he cannot help but wonder if perhaps he was wrong. If perhaps Martin Macauley is far more vindictive than he had imagined. If perhaps he does not care what the village thinks of his father, as long as he has his retribution.

Finn turns away. He can't look at Eva in case he says, does, something he regrets. The thing is done. She has made her choice. And now all they can do is wait to see if Macauley retaliates.

How hard had he and Eva fought to find peace and security? How many times had they nearly lost each other? How hard have they worked to build this uninterrupted life for themselves and their children? Now all that security is at risk again. Now, they are condemned to going back to those nights of watching the horizon, keeping the beacon burning, and waiting to see who might appear on their island. Easy targets. It feels like this is what they have always been.

His anger, Finn realises then, it's not directed at Eva. Not entirely, at least. Yes, they had had their peace. And it had been upturned.

By her own sister.

Finn sucks in a breath, trying to remain calm. He cannot remember the last time he found it such a struggle. They need Harriet out of their lives. Right now, it's the only thing he can see with clarity. Right now, he feels like he would do anything to make that happen.

"You and the children need to get off the island," he tells Eva stiffly. "There's a storm on the way and I don't know how secure the roof is. I don't want any of you here tonight. It's not safe."

When she looks up at him, he sees the unease behind her eyes. But she keeps her voice level. Expressionless. "What about you?"

"I've things I need to do."

"What things?"

He shakes his head stiffly. "It doesn't matter." This is not a conversation he can have with her now. He doesn't trust himself to keep his anger in check.

Eva is silent for a moment, as though debating whether to press the issue. She keeps her distance from him, arms wrapped tightly around her body. "There'll be no chance of keeping the beacon lit when this rain comes," she says finally.

"No."

She unfurls her arms. Takes a tentative step towards him. "Will you come to the house when you're done with… whatever it is you need to do?"

Finn hesitates. He had intended to come back here to Longstone. Lock himself away and try to let his anger dissipate. But he knows that's a foolish thing to do, now that Martin Macauley has become such an unknown threat. He needs to be wherever his family is—and they'll be far safer in the solidity of Highfield House than on this crumbling sea-swept island.

He nods stiffly. "Aye. I'll see you at the house. But you need to go now. Before the weather gets any worse."

He stands on the jetty and watches them leave. Eva doesn't look at him as she pulls the boat away from the island and it leaves a dull ache in his chest. He hates her leaving with things so strained and bitter between them. Still, it's best this way. Safest.

Finn waits until the skiff has disappeared into the wall of cloud. He climbs into the longboat. Heads for the mainland to find Eva's sister.

Hours have passed and Ward has not returned. The last of the light is draining from the day, and up here on the deck of her father's boat, Harriet can smell the rain in the air. Gulls soar over the water in perfect formation, stark white against the darkening sky.

She grips the gunwale. Squints into the fading light out across the village of Beal. She sees globes of lamplight behind the windows of the lodging house, and in a couple of cottages further up the hill. No other signs of life.

Her father had moored his boat here at the jetty, across the water from Lindisfarne, and stalked off into the village with his pistol in his pocket. If he has found Lawler—or if Lawler has found him—she has seen or heard no sign of it. The fearful anticipation has made every muscle in her body taut. Her stomach is a constant roll, her skin hot and sticky beneath her shift.

She reaches into her pocket. Feels the weight of Peggy's pistol. And beside it, the brass box, smoothed with time.

Harriet has to admit she is grateful for this second chance she has been given, to see Ward again, especially in the new light of her mother's letter. But having him in her life can only be a fleeting thing. Abigail's letter does not change the fact that she destroys every relationship she ever has. It's far easier, far safer, to keep her father on the fringes of her life. Let him remain this half-mythical figure she thinks of sometimes and tries more often to forget.

She wishes she was a stronger person. Once, she had been so proud of the life she had built, out in the world on her own. That unhemmed-in life that had once felt so unobtainable. But now that life doesn't feel like something to be proud of. Now, all she can think about is all the trouble she has caused. All the terrible things she has done. That poisonous streak inside her that wants to hurt and punish others on account of her own failings.

There can be no rebuilding from here—yes, she understands that. She has damaged things with Eva far too completely for them to ever be rebuilt. There can be no rebuilding, but perhaps there can be some attempt at making things right.

To do that, she needs to get back to Lindisfarne. Right now, the tide is high, locking her out. What an irony, she thinks, that she is standing here on the deck of a boat, looking longingly across the water at an island she cannot reach.

She will find someone to take her over. There will be someone at the tavern she can ask. Someone who owns one of these sorry-looking dinghies knocking against their moorings beside her father's vessel.

She gathers her skirts and climbs onto the jetty. And she follows the curve of the road up towards the lodging house.

In the fading light, something glints on the edge of her vision. She sees a gold pocket watch protruding from the wet sand. Thoughtlessly, she pulls it from the water. Shoves it into her pocket.

Her fingers graze the brass box and she stops walking suddenly.

She cannot take this with her as she goes back to Holy Island, trying to undo what she knows can hardly be undone. She cannot take it with her into a life she does not want her father in. She cannot take this box away, without him knowing what is inside.

She climbs back onto the boat. Steps back down the ladder, hearing it creak beneath her weight.

She takes the box from her pocket and sets it in the centre of the table. Her father will return, she tells herself. And he will see Abigail's letter, and he will read it, and he will know the truth of *I love you* and *you are to be a father, Henry*. And he, like his daughter, will think of faded things that once could have been, and now never will.

CHAPTER THIRTY-FIVE

Harriet hears the boards of the deck creak above her head as she is making her way back to the ladder. Her father has returned, she thinks. Her gaze goes to the brass box on the table. She feels a sudden, instinctive need to hide it. She wants him to read Abigail's letter, yes. But she does not want to be here when he does. Cannot face the vulnerability of what it may lead to.

Before she can reach the table, the hatch groans open. A man appears, swallowing the last of the daylight. He's tall, stocky, his face half-hidden behind a thick black beard. His hand curls around the top rung of the ladder, little finger missing at the knuckle. Harriet hears a frightened murmur come from deep in her throat. She stumbles backwards, clattering against the bulkhead. Lawler lowers himself down the ladder in one swift movement.

"Where is my father?" she asks, hearing her voice rattle.

"I was hoping you might tell me that. It would save us both a lot of trouble."

She tries to read beneath his words. See behind his grim grey eyes. Is he playing with her? Has he already found Henry Ward? Has he already delivered his own retribution for his brother's death upon the gallows?

Harriet's heart thunders against her ribs, fear blurring the edges of the room. But this man will not kill her. That is not what this is about. Lawler wants her because she is Ward's daughter—a far more precious commodity alive. But as she tries to cling to this thought, she realises its blatant untruth. Perhaps Lawler wants to kill her to punish Ward. Her life for his dead brother's.

Perhaps Lawler wants to kill her because he knows she was the one who had sent the authorities after Ward's ship. No. Because the only way he would know that would be if Ward had told him. And somehow, whether foolishly or not, she trusts that her father would not do that to her. Trusts, somehow, that he will do all he can to protect her.

But she has no idea if her father is still alive.

Perhaps Lawler has already found him.

He takes a step towards her, rounding the blockade of the table. Instinctively, Harriet tries to back away, stumbles against the storage chest. She grapples at the bulkhead, hand knocking against a solid weight in her pocket.

She remembers. Peggy's pistol. She fumbles for it, feels it cold and heavy in her palm. Brings it out in a shaking fist. Prays Lawler will retreat at the sight of the weapon.

There's a faint quirk beneath his beard—perhaps he is laughing at her. Perhaps he knows she cannot do this. Perhaps he can see the utter incompatibility of this woman and this pistol.

She pulls the trigger. Sends a wild shot flying into the ladder, the jolt of the pistol coursing through her body. Lawler ducks. Curses. Pitches towards her. Harriet drops the empty weapon. Instinctively, her hand closes around the spying glass sitting atop the storage chest. She swings wildly. The metal shaft cracks against the side of Lawler's head, broken glass spraying out across the cabin. His torso thuds against the table before he crumples to the floor at her feet.

Dizziness swings over her as she bends to collect the pistol. She scrambles up the ladder, stepping, repeatedly, on her skirt hems. Thudding to her knees against the deck. She bolts the hatch closed. Lurches to the gunwale and empties her stomach into the sea.

She hunches for a moment, shaking, sweat prickling her forehead. Is he dead? Surely not. Surely she did not strike him hard enough. She cannot bear the thought of him being dead. For all he has done to her, she does not want the weight of his death. Does not want to carry him wherever she goes.

Silence from down below. A deafening, sickening silence, but it gives Harriet a moment to breathe.

She is thinking of her sister. Thinking of the weight of death Eva has been carrying for ten years. And Harriet thinks of the letter she herself had written, bringing that weighted truth out into the light.

She gets to her feet, skirts tangling around her legs. She needs to leave this place. Needs to leave before Lawler wakes and forces his way out of the hatch.

But before she runs, before she disappears, she needs to go back to Lindisfarne one last time. Needs to try and make things right.

Harriet stumbles off the ship and down the jetty. Dark water laps against the hulls of the boats tied to the moorings, the sea whipped into peaks by the swirling wind. Somewhere distant, thunder rumbles low. The lights of Lindisfarne village glow behind the cloud.

Harriet puts her head down and strides towards the lodging house, trying to will away the weakness in her legs. She will find someone in the tavern, she hopes, willing to take her onto the island. She glances over the shoulder at her father's boat. Thinks of Lawler's motionless body lying at the foot of the ladder. He will wake soon, surely. Will force his way out of the hatch. Will find her like he has managed to find her so many times before.

Panic rising, Harriet breaks into a run. And as she rounds the bend towards the tavern, she collides with her sister's husband. She has never been more grateful to see him. "A boat," she garbles. "You have a boat?"

Finn blinks in surprise. "Of course." His eyes narrow. "Why?"

"I need to get across to the island. Quickly."

"Why?" he asks again.

Harriet tugs at his arm, pulling him back towards the water. "There's someone after me." Breathless. "Can you help me get away?"

For a second, Finn doesn't speak, and Harriet can practically see his thoughts racing. His eyes reflect his contempt for her, his complete distrust. Finally, the faintest of nods. He strides towards the water. Helps her into the longboat and shoves it out onto the sea.

Eva drags the skiff up onto the embankment beyond Highfield House, Noah tugging on the gunwale beside her and Archie climbing carefully over the beach with his sister in his arms. The last of the light is disappearing behind the horizon, any hint of starlight lost behind thick banks of cloud. Eva smells the rain, feels the air pulsing cold against her cheeks. Wind slaps at the dunes, bending the grass into rigid angles. The gale had blown up on their way over and her arms are tense and aching from the strain of the journey. She casts a quick glance over the water, hoping to see Finn's longboat. He'd not have sent them over here without him if he'd known the wind was going to strike up like this, Eva knows. She has no thought of where he has gone. But she knows he cannot be far away. For all his anger at her, all that tightly coiled rage she had sensed in him when she had returned from Macauley's farm, she knows he would never leave them.

She takes Maggie from her brother and ushers the children towards the house. Noah pounds the door knocker. A flurry of footsteps, then Theodora pulls the door open.

"My goodness, that wind," she says, as another violent burst careens into the entrance hall, making the lamps flicker. "Did you sail over here in this?"

"Wind picked up as we were on our way over," says Eva, handing the baby to Theodora and bending to help Archie unbutton his coat. "We need to stay here tonight. It's not safe out on Longstone."

At the sound of their voices, Thomas thunders down the stairs.

"Where's Da?" Archie asks, for the third time.

Eva hangs the coats. Can't bring herself to look him in the eye as she rattles out the same empty response. *He'll be here soon. He has things he needs to do.*

"Did you fight with Da?" Noah asks.

"A little. But everything is all right." She knows her words sound anything but believable. She is convinced she can see the doubt in Archie's eyes. Is certain she can see it in Noah's. But neither of them protest.

Theodora leads them into the parlour, where a fire is roaring in the grate. Thea sets Maggie down on the rug and goes to the window. Peeks through the curtains. She's on edge too, Eva can tell. Can sense the unease pouring off her. She joins Thea at the window. Slides an arm over her shoulder. "Are you all right?"

Theodora wraps her arms around her slender body. "I don't know where Papa is. When Tom and I got back from Saint Cuthbert's, he wasn't here. It's so unlike him not to leave me a note. And the boat was gone."

Eva feels a swell of unease at the thought of Nathan at the helm of that rickety sloop. She knows he's been turned upside down by Julia's presence—also knows he would never admit to it. Still, her brother is rarely one to act rashly. Eva can tell the platitudes she churns out to Theodora—*the weather is turning, he's likely decided to wait out the storm*; and, most foolishly, *try not to worry*—are doing little to convince her of her father's safety. And she feels the unease inside her simmering, threatening to tear itself free.

"Were you going to the house?" Finn asks Harriet, pulling on the oars and guiding the longboat away from the Beal jetty. The sea is blue-black, churning. Seesawing the boat and spitting salt into his eyes.

Harriet glances over her shoulder. She's trembling hard—Finn can't tell if it's from cold or fear. Her chest is heaving with rapid breath.

"No," she says. "Just to the village."

"Good."

She eyes him. "Why is that good?"

"Because Eva is at the house and you've done enough to her." He pulls through the swell. Tries to rein in his anger. Letting it out here, with the sea and sky rolling and someone on their tail, will do neither of them any good.

"Is that why you came to the tavern?" Harriet asks. She is without a bonnet or cap, and the wind is whipping her pale hair wildly across her face. "To berate me for what I did to Eva? To tell me to stay away from her? To tell me you don't want me in your lives?"

Finn doesn't answer. Suspects he doesn't need to. Harriet seems to be under no illusions as to what he had been doing at the lodging house. "Eva knows you were the one who gave that letter to Macauley," he says finally. "But she doesn't want to admit it. She doesn't want to accept that her sister would do such a godawful thing."

Harriet looks down. "Eva knows who I am." Her voice is thin.

"Is that supposed to be an excuse?"

"No. Just an observation."

Finn doesn't speak at once. She's impossible to read. Has been for as long as he has known her. He has no thought of who Harriet really is. He wonders if anyone does.

He guides the boat past the Pilgrims' Way. From out here, he can see the lamplight of the village. Cannot see Highfield House. Eva and the children will have made it there safely, he tells himself. She's a competent, confident sailor. Noah is becoming one too. They've both managed far worse conditions than this. Nonetheless, he can't shake the regret at not taking his family over to Lindisfarne himself. He'd not expected the gale to blow up this ferociously. He hates that he had let his anger get the better of him.

His frustration at himself sparks his rage at Harriet. "Why in hell would you do something like this to your own sister?" he demands.

She looks at him squarely. She's entirely Henry Ward, Finn thinks. Age has made her look even more like her father. She's got his hardness too; that dark streak that teeters into cruelty.

"I know it was wrong," she says. "I know it was a terrible thing to do. And I know there is no point trying to explain any of it to you." She looks away. "You're far too besotted with my sister to ever see from anything other than her point of view."

Finn snorts. "I'm sorry you resent us for that."

Harriet wraps her arms around herself. "Just take me to the village," she says. "Please." She looks past him, eyes fixed to the faint glow of light coming from the town. Thunder rumbles dully.

Finn rows in silence for several minutes, relieved when the swell tosses the longboat into the mouth of the anchorage. "Was that Ward's boat by the jetty in Beal?" he asks finally.

Harriet nods.

"He found you then?"

No reply.

"Where is he?"

"He went looking for the man who came after me. I don't know where he is now. I don't know what's happened to him."

In her voice, Finn hears her fears for her father's safety. The glimpse of genuineness surprises him. "You think he's been hurt?"

Harriet looks down. "Or worse. He went after Mr Lawler. But Lawler found me on his ship."

"Lawler was the man from the wreck? The man with the beard who asked after you?"

"Do you really want to know?" she asks tautly. "Don't you want to wash your hands of me?"

Finn ignores the question. "Is Lawler likely to follow you onto the island?"

A short laugh. "Why do you care? You came to the lodging house to get rid of me, didn't you?"

She's right. He had come out here to demand that Harriet keep her distance from Eva and their family. And he will not let himself be drawn in by the constant chaos of her.

He eases the longboat up towards the Lindisfarne jetty. Harriet grabs at the mooring post and stumbles out, skirts held above her knees. She looks back at Finn for the briefest of moments. "Thank you." And she is off towards the beach without looking back.

Finn hesitates for a moment. He needs to get to the house. Needs to get to his family. The need to see Eva is suddenly overwhelming. Ought he take the longboat around the coast to Emmanuel Head? Or try and cross the dunes on foot?

He pulls on the oars. He knows the coast of this island better than the tangle of inland paths. He'll stay close to land, avoid the worst of the wild weather. With luck, he'll be at the house before the clouds break open.

Another vessel out here, he realises, as he traces the coast out of the anchorage. A small cutter perhaps, barely bigger than his longboat. The sail backs, and the cutter's lamp flashes and flares. Finn lurches across the longboat for his own lantern. He holds it up, out towards the cutter.

A figure is waving him down. Calling his name.

He draws the longboat closer, shoulders burning as he drives the oars through a wall of water. Henry Ward looks down over the gunwale at him, panic in his eyes.

"I took Harriet into Lindisfarne," Finn tells him. "Lawler came after her."

Ward nods. "I know. I found him on my boat. She struck him with my spying glass and locked him below. Where was she going?"

"I don't know. She didn't tell me. Into the village somewhere."

Ward nods brusquely. "All right. Thank you." He hesitates for a moment, gesturing out to the dark water around the Farnes. "What are you doing here, lad? Why are you not on Longstone?"

Finn says, "I can't light the beacon in this weather." But as he speaks, he sees the untruth of it. Rough seas tonight, yes. Thunder and thickening darkness. But so far, the rain has stayed away. The firebasket could still be lit.

"Are you certain?" Ward raises his eyebrows—it's a critical look that Finn has seen all too many times. A look that makes him feel like a child again, hunched at the table in Ward's great cabin, weathering the captain's scolding. "You're needed out there," he says—and those simple words strike a physical blow. Finn hates that, after all these years, his former captain can still affect him so deeply. Why—how—does he still hold such power?

You're needed out there.

He closes his eyes, feeling the longboat careen on the water.

Go to the house. Eva is waiting. His children are waiting.

And he had left Henry Ward behind years ago.

But: *you're needed out there.* Yes, he sees the truth of it.

Lighting the beacon, lighting that treacherous patch of sea—this is the responsibility he has agreed to carry on his shoulders. A responsibility that feels like his dues. *You have your absolution,* Eva had said. And perhaps in some ways, he does. The truth of Oliver's death has long been known, at least by Nathan and Harriet, and Finn has come out of it with his marriage—and his life—intact. But the guilt, both over Oliver's death, and the way he had abandoned his father, is still a sharp, pulsing thing inside him. The blazing beacon has always gone some way to easing that. Some way to fading the image of his father's lifeless body on Longstone; dulling the memory of Oliver's blank eyes and the trail of blood snaking out from the back of his head.

The wreck of the *Cygnus* has only served to remind him of just how crucial it is that he is out there. Of how selfish it would be to turn this boat to the left instead of the right and return to Highfield House. He wants Eva; wants to tell her he is sorry for sending her to the house without him tonight. Wants to tell her they will carry the weight of Donald Macauley together. But: *you're needed out there.* If Henry Ward says it, it must be true. As long as this rain keeps from falling, that beacon needs to light the sky.

CHAPTER THIRTY-SIX

Nathan's legs are a little unsteady as he walks into Bamburgh, wind whipping the hem of his coat and pulling his hair loose from its queue. He's still in some kind of disbelief that he has made it here in one piece. At the back of his mind, behind all the madness, he regrets not leaving a note for Thea. She will worry for him, he knows, especially when she sees the boat gone.

But tonight he feels foolishly reckless. Incapable of rational thought. And that recklessness, it keeps pushing him forward, through the streets towards the narrow end of Church Wynd. Up the stairs to Julia's tenement.

He stops outside the door. Raises his fist to knock.

Christ Almighty, what is he doing? Julia is another man's wife. How could he have lost sight of that, even for a moment? More than that, there is every chance her husband is here right now, beneath this roof, ready to answer this knock at the door.

Nathan turns to leave, the floorboards creaking loudly beneath his weight.

"Who's there?" Julia calls sharply. She bursts through the door with a knife held out in front of her. Her shortjacket is half unlaced, her hair falling loose and wild over her shoulders.

"It's all right. It's just me."

She lets out her breath. Lowers the knife. "I'm sorry. I'm on edge. The safe, and Calum, and I—" She shakes her head. "Why are you here?" Suspicion in her voice? Anger?

Nathan looks down. "I shouldn't be. It was a mistake. But I…" Her husband is not here, he thinks distantly. She would not be standing on the doorstep speaking to him like this if her husband was here. He tries to silence the thought. It can lead him nowhere good. "I came to apologise," he manages, "for those terrible things I said to you. I did not mean a word of it. I just… I did not know how to let you go." His words fall heavily into the silence and he forces himself to hold her gaze. "I should never have said what I did. And I had no right to get angry at your leaving." His voice is husky. "I had no right to feel anything at all. I had my chance to make you my wife long ago and I didn't take it."

Julia reaches for his wrist. Curls her fingers around it, sending a pulse of energy through his body. She looks at him for a long second. "Do you wish you had?" she asks, voice trapped in her throat. "Made me your wife, I mean."

Nathan swallows. "Of course I do."

Julia doesn't speak. Just stares at him with her lips slightly parted. Her fingers move almost imperceptibly against his wrist. The movement feels enormous, consuming. She tugs him gently into the tenement. Closes the door behind them and sets the knife down on the table.

The feel of her has become almost a part of him now, Nathan realises. He cannot quite tell where her fingers end and his wrist begins. And it's not her who's tugging him forward. He's pulling her towards him. Seeking her nearness. Craving it. He is suddenly breathless for her.

He kisses her without thought. He's had ten years of thinking about Julia and it has led him nowhere but in empty, painful circles. And this, he knows, is by far the most thoughtless thing he could be doing. Her lips part beneath his, inviting him deeper.

He finds the curves of her, his hands remembering, relearning, what it is to feel a woman beneath his touch. He feels her chest straining against her stays, her body seeking his. Wind pounds against the cloth window, makes the beams above their head groan.

"Are you all right?" she asks on an exhalation. "Is it too much?"

Yes, it is too much, but it is also nowhere near enough. And now he has Julia close, he needs every inch of her. But: "Is this what you want?" He can hardly bear to think of him, Calum MacNeill, who might walk through this door at any moment. The thought of what that would mean for Julia is enough to make him loosen his grip on her. Enough to make him step away.

She pulls him close again, fist tightening around the hem of his justacorps. "Yes," she says. "This is what I want." She slides his jacket from his shoulders. Pulls at the buttons on his waistcoat. Nathan's fingers slide though her hair, then trail downwards to the lacing on her bodice. He feels breathless, vivid, almost painfully alive.

And he says, "I love you."

Julia pulls away from him slightly, just enough for him to see the faintest of smiles flicker on her face. "I love you too."

And suddenly her lips are crushed against his, last thoughts, last hesitations gone from his mind. She is consuming him, intoxicating him, tugging him down onto the bed with her, as laces come loose and linen falls with a sigh against the floor. Her hands skim over the blazing skin on his back, untouched for so many years by anyone other than himself. It has been so long since he has felt a woman beneath him like this; not since Sarah, whose memory is beginning to fade.

"I'm not…" he says, unsure of what it is he is trying to say. "I don't…"

Julia silences him with a kiss. And she is everywhere, all at once, shifting and writhing beneath him, her breath hot and short and fast against his ear. Tomorrow, she will go back to being someone else's wife. And though he is certain he has no hope of ever making it so, Nathan knows that this, right now, must somehow be enough.

CHAPTER THIRTY-SEVEN

Harriet is relying on hazy memories to find her way to Martin Macauley's farm. She stumbles around the rim of the village, past Saint Cuthbert's and the ghost of the priory, streets dimmed as the lamplight is snatched by the wind. She heads blindly towards the farmland that feeds into the dunes. Tries one property after another until she finds the place she is looking for.

In the pale light glowing behind the cloth window, she can tell Macauley's farmhouse is in tatters: the grass overgrown, the roof tilted, a second window covered with boards. She shivers hard, wind slicing through the layers of her clothing.

And though her hands are still trembling from her attack on Lawler, she fumbles with the pistol and slides in a fresh ball.

She trudges through the mire at the front of the cottage and pounds on the door, unsure if it will be heard over the rattling of the window frame, or the steady thudding of a tree branch against the side of the house.

Lamplight filters under the large gap beneath the door. It opens a crack, letting out the stench of tallow and damp. Martin Macauley's bristly grey head pokes through.

"Who are you?"

She swallows hard. "My name is Harriet Whitley." Using her husband's name feels bitter on her tongue; it has been years since she has done so. But she suspects that, with hearing Edwin's name, Macauley will remember her. And yes, she sees that look of recognition fall across his face. Not just recognition: anger too. Bitterness.

He spears her with hard eyes. "You're Eva Murray's sister."

She nods. "May I come in?"

Macauley chuckles. "I'm honoured the two of you thought to visit me today."

Harriet feels a pull of dread. "Eva was here?"

He doesn't speak.

"What did you… talk about?"

Macauley snorts. "I don't imagine you need me to answer that."

No. Because the question she really wants to ask is, *What did you do to her?* "Did you harm her?" she blurts.

Macauley tilts his head, considering her. "Is that why you're here? Because you think I harmed your sister?"

Harriet feels the weight of the pistol against her thigh. She would do it, she thinks distantly. Every piece of this is her own doing, yes. But if Macauley tells her he has hurt Eva, she would pull that pistol from her pocket and fire. It could not worsen the guilt she already feels.

"I didn't touch her," says Macauley. "I'm not that kind of man."

Harriet swallows down her murmur of doubt. "May I come in?" she asks again.

Macauley hesitates, then pulls the door open, gesturing for her to enter.

He does not offer her a chair at the table. Just stands facing her with his arms folded across his chest, waiting expectantly for her to speak. Unbidden, Harriet finds her gaze drifting around the shadowed interior of the cottage. Searching for lies, she realises. Searching for anything that might suggest Macauley has laid a finger on her sister.

The house is a near ruin, with its boarded window and muddy floor and the sideboard door dangling on broken hinges. Roof beams hang low, as though threatening to swallow this miserable excuse for a house. It bodes well for her, Harriet thinks. This place sings of desperation.

She reaches into her coin pouch. Pulls out the gold pocket watch she had found in the water and sets it on the table. "Take this," she says. "Sell it and use the money to start again. Find a landowner who'll rent you someplace decent."

Macauley looks down at the watch glinting in the lamplight. "I don't know what you're trying to get out of me, lass, but it'll take a lot more than some little trinket."

Harriet narrows her eyes. "It's pure gold."

He snorts. "Do you really imagine me so desperate?"

She hesitates a moment. Her hand slides into her pocket, fingers gliding over the pistol. She pulls her bulging coin pouch from her pocket and sets in on the table. Macauley peers inside, his eyes widening slightly at the contents.

I wrote letter after letter of introduction and I tutored half the young women in London and I stayed up painting every night until my damn eyes gave out. I worked so damn hard for all of it.

Harriet pushes aside the ache. She takes her travel documents out of the purse and nudges it forward. "Is this a more suitable sum?"

Macauley eyes her. "In exchange for what?"

"In exchange for you leaving Lindisfarne tonight. Leaving my sister and her family be."

For several moments, he doesn't speak. Just glances between Harriet and the pouch she had placed on the table. "Your sister killed my father," he says finally.

Harriet stares him down. "Your father tried to kill my sister. Eva was just defending herself."

Macauley stares back at the pouch, then shakes his head. "This place is my life. I'm not leaving it."

"This place is on the verge of collapse," Harriet hisses, waving a wild hand at the boarded window. "When was the last time you made a damn penny from this farm?"

Macauley doesn't answer.

"There's enough money in there to start again," Harriet tells him. "Somewhere far better than this." He folds his arms across his chest, making her release a breath of frustration. "This cursed island. Why are you all so tied to this damn place? Can you not see that things could be so much better for you elsewhere?" She reaches down to grab the purse.

"Wait."

Harriet straightens.

"How do I know this isn't a trap?"

"What kind of trap?"

"How in hell should I know?"

She sighs. Lowers her eyes. "I was the one who wrote the letter telling you about Eva and your father," she admits.

"Why would you do that?"

"Because I was angry," she says tautly. "Angry and bitter and jealous. And now I'm just trying to undo a mistake." She nudges the pouch towards Macauley. Without it, she has nothing. Without it, she is that penniless charity case she has always feared being. Without it, her only chance of survival is to rely on the family she has shunned. Pray they will let her back beneath their roof. "There is no trap," she says. "Just take the money."

For long seconds, neither of them speak. Macauley stares down at the coin pouch on the table. The cloth window drums loudly. The fire simmers weakly in the grate. Harriet shivers. Edges towards it.

Finally, Macauley takes the pouch. Shoves it into his pocket.

Harriet nods faintly. "You must leave tonight," she says.

"I can't leave tonight. There's a storm about to hit."

"Then you'd best not delay." He could strike her down; Harriet is all too aware of that. Could strike her and take the money and leave her unconscious out on the island somewhere. He could. And yet, he doesn't. Instead, he shuffles around the cottage, shoving shirts and breeches and underclothes into a bag. He takes a tarred greatcoat from the hook beside the door and pulls it on.

"I've animals," he tells her. "A horse. Sheep. I need to take them over to the next farm. Can't just leave them here."

She nods. "Do what you need to do. As long as you leave once you're done."

Macauley eyes her for one last moment, then turns and marches out of his cottage, leaving Harriet standing alone beside the dying fire.

She waits in the cottage for some time, sitting at Martin Macauley's kitchen table, listening to the tree branch thudding against the window frame. Listening to thunder rolling out across the ocean. She feels an unbalancing lightness at both the loss of her money, and the loss of a fraction of her guilt. She has nothing now. No way of getting back to London. No way of continuing her glittering, unhemmed-in life.

She stands from the table and walks from the cottage. The door groans and sticks as she tries to pull it closed behind her. She lifts the lamp, trying to pick shapes from the inky darkness. Where to now? The wind is swirling and she feels flecks of ice in the gale.

She feels painfully adrift. Untethered. The thought of letting herself blow wild at the mercy of the wind is almost appealing. Where else does she have to go? What else can she do?

She stumbles away from the farm, out towards the dark heart of the island. She is walking towards Highfield House, she realises. Because where else is there to go?

CHAPTER THIRTY-EIGHT

Lamps are glowing in the downstairs windows of the house, the upper storey almost lightless. Harriet stands outside it for a long time, her cloak pulled tight around her trembling body. Wind whips her hair around her face, obscuring her view of those bleak stone walls.

Some fragile part of her, the part of self-preservation, urges her to take the final few steps towards the house. Knock at the door. Step inside and escape the coming storm.

But it feels, suddenly, as though something almost physical is preventing her from doing so.

Eva is in this house. Thomas is in this house; this house where his mother had abandoned him.

This house is not yours. The knowing comes from deep inside her. Not your house. Not welcome here.

Harriet understands the alternatives. The cold. The wind. The untethered wild. But none of that has the power to overrule the knowing that she cannot step through that front door.

Finn ought to be here. He promised he would be here.

Eva is at the window of her childhood bedroom, peering out over the dark sea. How many times, before they had married, had thoughts of Finn brought her to this window, as she sought the reassuring glimmer of the

Longstone light?

Tonight, there is no glitter in the blackness. Nothing to assure her of Finn's safety. She can see little through the window, but can hear the sea throwing itself against the embankment. Hears wind rattling the time-worn edges of the house. Beams groan loudly above her head.

She tries to push aside the knot of worry in her stomach. Finn had promised he would come to the house. And he will come. Whatever else had passed between them today, he will come.

Soft footsteps in the passage and she turns to see Noah in the doorway.

"Can you see Da?" he asks, coming to stand beside her at the window. Eva slides an arm over his shoulder, pulling him close.

"Not yet, my love. But he'll be here." Lightning jags, illuminating, for seconds, the empty troughs of the sea.

"The weather's bad. There's going to be a storm."

"I know. But it's not here yet. And Da is a good sailor."

"Shall I stay here and watch for him?"

And this is what she and Finn have raised their son to be: a watcher of the sea; a protector, like his father and grandfather before him. But it's not a weight she wants him to shoulder—not yet, at least.

"Let's go back to the parlour," she says. "See what Tom and Thea are doing. Da will come."

Noah hesitates, then nods finally. Lets Eva walk him back downstairs.

He hurries off to the parlour as she peeks in on Archie and Maggie, asleep in one of the old servants' rooms. When she returns to the parlour, she finds Noah, Tom, and Thea on their knees around the tea table, a pack of cards spread out in front of them.

Noah looks up at her. "Will you play, Mama?"

"In a moment." She can't help going to the window. Can't help lifting the curtain; peeking out onto the dunes.

She sees a flash of movement. Pulls the curtain back further. Squints. Just her imagination? No, there it is again: a shadow moving through the darkness. Person, not animal—she can tell no more than this.

Noah scrambles to his feet. "Who's outside?" he pushes. "Is it Da?" Tom trails him to the window, cards abandoned.

"I don't know." Finn would most likely have sailed straight to Emmanuel Head. Unlikely to have come across the dunes. Unless he had thought it safer to moor in the village.

Noah and Tom chase her into the entrance hall. "Stay here," Eva tells them, snatching her cloak from the hook.

Her son looks up at her wide-eyed. "You can't go out there by yourself. It's so dark. And windy."

She feels a swell of love for him. Presses her hands to his cheeks, his shoulders. "Stay here," she says firmly, meeting his eyes. "I'll be back in a moment. I'm only going out to see who's there."

Theodora steps from the parlour, calling the boys back. "Go on," says Eva. "Finish your game. I'll not be long."

She steps out of the house and pulls the door closed before her son can protest.

Harriet hears her sister's voice bouncing across the dunes. Sees the light from Eva's lamp struggling and flickering against the wind. She hurries away from it. She cannot bear to face her sister after all she has done to her.

The ground rolls and lurches beneath her feet as she stumbles further from the house. Eva is still following her, lamplight moving through the darkness like a will-o'the wisp. Harriet crouches behind the rise of the earth. Wills her sister back towards the house.

The light of Eva's lamp disappears suddenly, snatched by the wind. With the stars and moon lost behind the cloud bank, the only light is the distant glow behind the curtains of Highfield House. Harriet is far from the manor now; a hundred yards at least. She cannot tell how near to her Eva is. Wind swirls, whipping the hood of her cloak off her head. The cold seeps through to her bones.

"Finn?" Eva calls again. "Are you there?" She is closer than Harriet expected. She sees the shape of her emerge from the dark. "Harriet. What are you doing out here?"

Harriet turns away. "Go back inside. Leave me be."

"Don't be foolish. I'm not leaving you out here. What are you doing?"

And what other response is there but the truth? There is no lie she can conjure up that will satisfactorily explain her being here, crouched behind the dunes, hiding from her sister. Although perhaps the truth will not do that either.

"I thought to come to the house," she admits finally. "But I know it's not my place."

"What do you mean? Of course it's your place."

"No. It's not."

Eva steps close. Wind whips dark hair across her cheeks—Harriet sees now that she has come marching out here without her bonnet or gloves. In a sudden spear of lightning, Harriet can see the tangle of emotions on her sister's face. She wonders if Eva is going to tear her apart for telling Macauley about his father, out here in the dunes, with the weather turning wild around them. Instead, she takes Harriet's arm firmly and begins to stride back towards the house.

Harriet feels her muscles tighten as the manor grows closer. Is not sure she can bring herself to go inside. But what choice does she have with Eva latched to her like this, refusing to let go?

The front door comes into view and Harriet finds a fresh surge of determination. She pulls free of her sister's grip and stumbles away.

"Harriet—" Eva whirls around, but her attention is snatched by Theodora bursting from the house.

"Are they with you?" Thea demands.

"Who?"

"Noah and Tom. I can't find them. Their coats are gone."

Harriet hides herself around the corner of the house. Does not want Theodora to see her. Does not want another voice urging her through that front door.

"I'm so sorry." Theodora's tears spill. "Noah wanted to come out and find you. Help you. I told him to stay inside. But then I heard Maggie crying and I went to her, and when I got back, I couldn't find the boys…"

Eva squeezes Theodora's shoulder. "It's not your fault." She takes the lamp from her, tries to shield it from the wind. Hands her the lantern that had blown out. "Go back inside. Stay with Archie and Maggie. I'll find the boys." Harriet hears the poorly hidden panic in her sister's voice. And she realises that yes, somewhere deep, she is feeling it too. A flicker of maternal instinct she has not managed to bury. This place is far too dark, far too wild, far too sea-hemmed for children to be running around unseen.

For her child to be running around unseen.

The wind catches the front door and slams it shut. Eva strides back down the path, lifting the lamp and spearing light into Harriet's eyes. "Are you coming?" she asks, steel in her voice.

And Harriet finds herself saying, "Yes."

CHAPTER THIRTY-NINE

"They'll be all right," Eva is saying. "They'll be all right." Over and over. "They're sensible boys. They'll not do anything foolish."

Is she trying to placate herself or her sister? Harriet cannot tell. She doesn't tell Eva that if the boys were as sensible as she believes, they would not have come charging out here like this with wind tearing across the dunes and the sky about to open. Knows she has no right to do so.

Eva calls their names, wind carrying her voice away. "They cannot have gone far," she says. "They won't have gone far. They won't." She lifts the lamp, panning it around the dunes. The light flickers. Catches the rugged scarps on the edge of the headland.

"We should check the water," Harriet says stiffly. "The rocks. In case they…" Fear lurches inside her. Stops her from finishing the sentence.

"They wouldn't have…" Eva says, but she is hurrying towards the violent lash of the sea. *Noah*, she calls. *Tom*. Harriet feels a sudden, violent urge to call for her son. Stops herself. Thomas had ceased to be her child a long time ago.

Eva stops walking suddenly and lifts the lamp out over the water. "No," she says suddenly. "No."

Harriet feels her stomach dive. But Eva is not looking down at the base of the headland anymore. Her eyes are fixed on the horizon, and the faint glow of light coming from the Farne Islands.

"He promised he would come to the house," she says. "Why is he—" She shakes herself suddenly. "Our boat," she says. "Is the boat still there?" She hurries over the embankment, lamp swaying in her fist. Lets out a breath of relief when she sees her skiff still sitting high on the beach. Waves are hurtling over the sides. "I was afraid the boys tried to get out to Longstone," she said. "Finn was supposed to come to the house. But he… we…" She scrubs a hand over her eyes. Crouches suddenly, as though cowed by the weight of her emotion. Her exhaustion. "We fought." She looks up at Harriet for the briefest moment. "We fought over my going to see Martin Macauley."

Harriet looks away. "I'm sorry." She knows there's no need for elaboration. Knows it will achieve nothing.

Eva is silent for a moment, hunching on the ground with her head bowed. She stands suddenly, lifting the lamp and panning it over the dunes again. "We need to find the boys." She pushes past the rattle in her voice. "They must be out on the dunes somewhere." She calls their names again. Follows the curve of the island past unseen rockpools and streams. "Noah is too protective of me when his father's not around," she says, almost to herself. "He's always been like that. The wreck seems to have made it worse. I don't want him to shoulder such responsibility. Not yet, at least. I'm not sure I ever want that for him."

Harriet doesn't respond. She knows this is not a conversation she is meant to be a part of. Knows this is just Eva's way of making sense of the thoughts, fears, inside her head. She and her sister could not have ended up living more different lives. And yet, for all that, here they both are, stumbling through the darkness, carrying their guilt and their fears, searching for their lost sons.

"Mama." Two small shapes burst from the darkness towards the lamp and Noah throws himself at Eva. She wraps her arms around him, sets down the lamp, pulls Thomas close too.

Harriet hangs back. Just watches, listens as Eva is the one to scold the boys for leaving the house, to tell them how relieved she is they are safe. For a moment, Thomas looks past Eva to catch Harriet's eye. She feels a jolt inside her.

"Mama," says Noah, "the firebasket. You said Da was coming to the house."

"Yes," she says. "I did…" Eva has one arm around each of the boys' shoulders, her voice thin, uncertain. "I…" And then she lifts the lamp from the ground again and shines it out over the sea. There's a boat on the water, not far from shore; Harriet sees its lamp diving, disappearing and reappearing beneath the slope of the swell. The boat is small; seems flimsy, misshapen, almost. It pitches across the water, out in the direction of the Farne Islands. And the sight of that flimsy boat with its misshapen sail, it makes a look of dread pass across Eva's face.

"I need you to take the boys back to the house," she tells Harriet.

Noah looks up at her, eyes wide. "Where are you going, Mama?"

"I need to go back to Longstone. I need to find Da."

Harriet keeps her voice low. "Eva. Are you sure that's a good idea?"

"I've no choice," she hisses.

"Why not? What's happening? Whose boat is that?" Harriet knows she does not deserve the answers to these questions, and Eva does not give them to her. When she looks back at Harriet, there's a look of fierce determination in her eyes.

"Please," she says. "Just take the boys back to the house. Make sure they're safe. Tell Thea I'll be back as soon as I can."

Harriet's stomach knots at the thought of being alone with the boys, but she knows she can do nothing but agree.

"Get yourself warm too," Eva tells her. "You're shivering." When Harriet doesn't respond, Eva takes her elbow. "Promise me you'll not stay out here. Go inside and get warm." She looks at her pointedly. "You belong there just as much as the rest of us do."

And Harriet says, "Of course."

She walks with one hand to each of the boys' shoulders in an attempt to keep them from running again; from following Eva; from attempting more heroics. She tries not to focus on the feel of Thomas's lithe body beneath her fingers. Tries to focus on her footsteps, and the intensity of the cold seeping inside her. Because she cannot focus on this.

She stops at the top of the path leading up to the house. Lets her hands fall. They are both staring up at her, she realises. Wide-eyed. Bewildered. Neither of them seem to recognise her from the two days she had spent at Eva's cottage. "Go," she tells them. "Inside."

"Aren't you coming in?" Thomas asks her.

She swallows. "No. I can't."

"Why not?"

She closes the space between them without even being aware of it. Her hands find his shoulders again, tracing the shape of him. Her icy fingers feel the smooth skin of his cheeks, the soft curl of his hair. Thomas stands motionless, lips parted, eyes meeting hers. It's dizzying and dreamlike, and the moment she catches what she is doing, Harriet steps away.

The sky opens, spilling fat drops of rain across the island.

"Inside," she says. "Go and get warm. Quickly."

Thomas hesitates for the briefest of moments, then turns and chases Noah into the house. Does he look back at her? She would like to imagine so, but it's dark, and she is already backing away towards the embankment, and she's starting to feel those same hazy edges to the world as when she had been shipwrecked. But yes, she wants to believe her son looks back at her. Acknowledges her. And perhaps, on some innate level—recognises her.

The door of Highfield House thumps shut, swallowing the blaze of light pouring from the entrance hall. And where does she go from here?

She should not be out here. Should not be doing this. Eva knows that. She knows this weather, this ocean, the maze of rocks and reefs surrounding her home.

But her fear of what Martin Macauley might do to her family pushes aside every other concern. It's a fear she has had for ten years—a fear that has intensified a hundredfold these past few days. At the sight of Macauley sailing out towards Longstone, she knows she has no other option but to be out here, taking on the wind, the sea, the rain.

What reason would Macauley have for being out here in weather like this, other than to seek his retribution? To reach Longstone, when there is no risk of anyone else being out near the Farnes tonight. No herring fishermen in this weather. No passenger ships passing. Just Finn alone in their fragile house, fighting against the rain to keep the firebasket alive.

Eva leans on the tiller, trying to quarter the waves. Her arms are burning, eyes stinging. She doesn't care. All she can think about is getting to Longstone. Getting to Finn. Warning him about Macauley. Because it's not just her fear that has sent her out here; it's her profound love for her husband. A desperate need to tell him how sorry she is for going against his wishes, and for the hurtful words she had spoken. For letting herself imagine, even for a second, that he might have put Oliver's death behind him.

The knot in her stomach tightens as the lights of Highfield House vanish behind sheeting rain. The sea rolls into castles around her, threatening to consume the skiff. And for a moment, she is back in Donald Macauley's dinghy, alone on the ocean, with his body disappearing into the water beneath her.

She shakes herself out of the memory. She is not the same woman she had been that night, more than a decade ago. She is not helpless at the helm of a boat; she is not lost in this new land; she is capable of far more than she had ever imagined herself to be that day. The night she had killed Donald Macauley, she had made it to Longstone. Had made it to Finn. And she will do the same tonight.

The skiff dives forward into a wall of water, sucking the light from the lamp. Water soaks through her cloak, settles in the bottom of the boat.

Eva keeps her eyes on the firebasket. Tries to let the sight of it steady her, pull her thoughts from the terrified spiral they have begun to career down. The flames of the beacon waver wildly, dimming against the rain.

Eva realises she has lost sight of the boat with the misshapen sail. Has Macauley's lamp blown out too? Is he here on this ocean with her? She cannot even bring herself to consider the alternative. Her arms burn as she throws her weight against the tiller. She feels the sea overpowering her, tossing the boat away from her island. She heaves and lurches, driving the skiff away from the Knavestone.

The rain grows heavier, sucking the last threads of light from the beacon. She is close now. She squints through the rain to catch a glimpse of lamplight inside the cottage. Sees just a faint flicker of light—she can tell Finn has closed the shutters to prevent the windows from breaking. To prevent the sea from finding its way inside their home.

Wind tears through her, tosses the skiff forward. And at once, she is too close, the rugged shards of Longstone coming up on her with far too much speed.

Eva reaches desperately for the oars, trying to steer the boat away from the teeth of the rocks. She is too far from the jetty, waves throwing themselves against the edges of the island.

She shouts for Finn. Cannot even hear herself over the roar of the sea. The skiff lurches and dives. And then she is flying, falling, as the sea grabs her boat from beneath and flings her into the waves.

She will die for this, Eva thinks suddenly. Cold water tightens her lungs as she thrashes and kicks and grabs at her cloak, trying to tear herself free from its tangled weight. Flashes of lamplight and air for a second as she breaks through the surface, but they are sucked away before she can grasp them. The skiff growls as it is thrown against the edge of the island, the mast splintering. And as she kicks hard, trying to keep her head above water, she sees Finn running from the dark firebasket over the rocks towards the sound. Sees him pitch towards the water.

She will die, she thinks. And maybe so will he. For her fear and her love and her most foolish of choices, perhaps the both of them will die.

CHAPTER FORTY

Finn has one hand gripping hers, the other reaching for the rocky shards protruding from the sea.

This is their island; surely it won't let them die. He has a hand on her, now she is stolen away, now he reaches her again. The sea tosses them against rock and pain sears the side of his body. Tears at his hands as he tries to pull himself from the water. Another swell of the sea and the edge of the island slips through his fingers. He digs his hand into the laces of Eva's bodice; tethers himself to her. He kicks, resurfaces; sees dark and dark and dark, unbroken only by the faint flicker of light glowing between the shutters.

He kicks towards the island again and this time the wave lifts him; allows him to feel solid rock beneath his feet. He lurches forward, pulling Eva from the water with the next violent surge of sea. The wave crashes over them and Finn braces himself against the rock, covering her body with his.

He scrambles to his knees. Leans over her. Her eyes are closed. Not breathing. The panic is dizzying, blinding. He sucks down a breath before it consumes him.

They are here, he realises, on this cursed plane of rock where he had once found his father's body, colourless, lifeless, succumbing to the sea. He rolls Eva onto her side, his frozen fingers fumbling as he tries to loosen the laces of her stays. "Evie," he says. "Evie." Maybe if he keeps calling to her, he can bring her back. Stop this from being real. He leans over her, thumping his hand hard between her shoulder blades. Again. Again. Calling to her.

And suddenly she is coughing, gasping, emptying the sea from her lungs. The cry of relief comes from deep inside him.

He wraps his arms around her, legs around her. Holds her as another waves crashes over them. Keeps saying her name. *Evie, Evie, Evie.* His voice disappears into the roar of the sea. Rain pelts down on them from low-hanging clouds.

He hears Eva speak close to his ear; words that sound like *Martin Macauley.*

"What?"

She tries to sit up. "Martin Macauley. He's coming here."

Finn brushes her tangled hair from her face. "No. I saw his boat passing by the islands just now. Heading towards the mainland. Don't know what he was doing out in weather like this." He presses a hand to her cheek. "Is that why you came out here? Because you thought Macauley was coming?"

Eva pulls herself into sitting. Wraps her arms around his neck. "I was so afraid of what he might do to you." She pulls back to look him in the eye. "Why are you here? You promised you'd come to the house."

He nods. "I know. I'm sorry." It is not enough. It is not close to being enough. Had he lost Eva to the sea, it would never have been enough.

He closes his eyes for a moment, feeling a too-familiar chill beginning to pull him down. Feels water pelting him from above, rain and sea. And he hears Eva's voice:

"We need to get inside."

Her words spark him into action and he stumbles to his feet, helping her stand. He wraps an arm around her waist. Guides her slowly, carefully, over the rocks. Crouch low, he thinks, to avoid being swept off his feet by the waves tossing themselves at the island. Wind sweeps across the sea, snatching more tiles from the roof. The lightless firebasket sways wildly.

In the light and the warmth of the cottage, the pain hits, blazing down his side where his body had slammed into the rocks. His hands are stinging, palms flecked with blood. Torn patches on the sleeves of his shirt, washed crimson. He stumbles towards the fireplace and throws two more logs into the grate. He lowers Eva onto a chair at the table, reaches for the lacing on her shortjacket. He shivers hard, his fingers seizing.

She lifts his hand away from her laces. "I can manage, Finn," she says gently. "You need to get out of your wet clothes too. Quickly."

When the fire is roaring in the grate, their wet clothes in a pile on the floor, Eva goes into the children's bedroom in her dry nightshift. Returns with her arms full of blankets. She piles them onto their bed and tugs Finn down onto the mattress beside her. *Shipwreck survivors*, he thinks.

He intertwines his legs with hers, holds her close, feeling her heart beat. Water plinks steadily into the pot he has placed on the floor to catch the drips from the hole in the roof. Another stream drizzles down the wall near the children's room, pooling on the top of the sideboard.

Finn doesn't speak. There is so much he needs to say. He hardly knows where to begin. So he just lies in the silence, feeling her body bring warmth back to his own.

Finally, Eva says, "Why did you come out here?"

"I felt like I had to." Right now, it feels like the simplest answer. He does not want to speak of Henry Ward. Ward has come between them on far too many occasions. And there's also a part of him that doesn't want to admit he had let himself be led out here by his former captain. He's far too ashamed of it. He ought to have stopped taking orders from Henry Ward when he was an eleven-year-old child. And here he is, still bending to Ward's will thirty years later. "I had to light the beacon," he says. "If anyone else came out here tonight, they'd be wrecked without it." There's a hollowness to his words. Finn can sense Eva sifting through them, turning them over in her head. She shuffles back on the mattress, running her finger gently over the gashes in his palm. "How much of you being out here is because you want to save lives?" she asks. "And how much of it is because of your guilt over Oliver's death? Your guilt over abandoning your father?"

Finn knows this is not a question in need of an answer. They both know their shared guilt is tying them to this place. Eva flying out here in Martin Macauley's shadow only makes that far more glaring.

That guilt has always been there in the background. But not until tonight has it led them to such foolish, rash decisions. How much longer are they to let the past define their future?

"Maybe we've done enough," he says. The words make something tighten in his chest. "Maybe we've paid our penance."

Eva sits up in bed, staring down at him. Wet hair falls long and dark over her cheeks. There's a cut on her jawline that he hadn't noticed before. He reaches up and brushes away a bead of blood with his thumb.

He's struck, suddenly, by memories of all they have been through together out here. Nights of watching the sea; of waiting, of fearing. Nights of holding each other in the firelight; of living so much of their lives with a dark sky above their heads. Impulsively, he closes a hand over hers.

"What are you saying?" Eva's voice is soft.

He lets out a breath. "Keeping the light, it ought to be Trinity House's responsibility. Not ours. It never ought to have been ours. Or my father's. Da never ought to have sacrificed as much as he did."

"Trinity House failed to put a light out here."

"The last petition was more than fifty years ago. And they've never needed another because we've always been here. Surely, if we weren't, they'd have to at least consider putting a lightkeeper out here. Especially after what happened to the *Cygnus*."

Eva nods faintly, noncommittal. Finn can barely believe he has spoken the words, but now they are out, he allows himself to imagine a life without this weighty responsibility in it. A life of dry land and unbroken sleep and a future for their children without lightkeeping in it. Is that the life he wants? It feels so hazy, so unformed he can barely tell. "Us being out here isn't going to change what happened to Oliver, or Donald Macauley, or my father." His words come out husky. He is only half aware of having spoken them aloud. "And I don't want Noah to go running off like I did because he can't stand the life he's living."

"What?" Eva leans forward, meeting his eyes. "How long have you been worried about this?"

He doesn't know. Supposes some part of him has been afraid of it since that very first night Noah had spent beneath the firelight. Maybe even before that. "A while," he says.

"Noah is not going anywhere," Eva says firmly. A smile flickers at the corner of her lips. "Not until he's thirty-five at least. Besides," her smile fades, "you've seen what he's been like since the wreck. He's thrown himself into keeping the light."

"I'm not sure I want that for him anymore than I want him leaving." Finn lets out a breath. Scrubs a hand across his eyes. "Christ, I sound like a madman."

Eva smiles. "You sound like a father who cares deeply for his son." She lies back down, twining her legs with his again, their clasped hands held against his chest.

For a long time, neither of them speak. Rain throws itself against the windows, shutters thumping wildly. The rhythmic plink of water in the pot becomes a steady stream. Finn hears the sharp crack of roof tiles splintering against rock. Water drizzles down the chimney, dimming the fire. He pulls the blankets up higher.

"Perhaps you're right," Eva says finally, into the thickening darkness. "Perhaps we have done enough." Her voice wavers. "I don't want to carry this guilt anymore, Finn. I don't want to spend the rest of my life trying to make up for my mistakes." She presses her head hard against his shoulder. "And I don't want to die for them either."

Finn pulls her tighter against him. Holds his lips to hers. Listens to the steady drumming of the rain besieging their cottage. Their last night here, he thinks distantly. This must be their last night here. Let the roof blow to pieces and water flood the chimney and the sea wear away the solid stones of the walls.

Let them break free from the mistakes of the past before the need for redemption consumes them.

CHAPTER FORTY-ONE

Nathan trudges towards the house in the blue haze of dawn. High above his head, the first snow of the season is falling silently, melting into mist before it touches the earth. The air smells fresh and clean; of cold, of sea, of fragrant soil.

He lets himself inside, exhausted, his head aching. After he had prised himself from Julia's bed, he had waited out the storm and the darkness in some regretful corner of the Rose Tavern, bolstering himself with whisky to keep his thoughts from swallowing him whole.

A thick cold has settled into the stone walls of the house; he suspects Mrs Brodie has not yet laid the fires. He makes his way to the parlour. Finds Theodora asleep in an armchair, a cloak pulled to her chin. Thomas and Noah are sprawled out across the settle, legs entangled, their blanket in a pile on the floor.

As though sensing her father's presence, Thea's eyes flutter open. She leaps to her feet and flies at him. Holds him tightly for the briefest of moments, before pulling away. "Where have you been? I was so worried."

Nathan pulls her back in. Folds his arms around her and kisses the top of her head. "I'm so sorry. I was caught out at Bamburgh. It didn't feel safe to return."

"You took the *boat*, Papa! Without telling me! If *I* ever did that, you would lose your *mind!*"

Nathan nods, chastened. "I know." Can't help a faint smile at her violent punctuations.

"What were you thinking?" she demands.

"I wasn't." It feels like the only appropriate answer.

Theodora eyes him for a moment and Nathan steels himself for her questions. But all she asks is, "Are you all right?"

He is sure the ache of leaving Julia is showing in his eyes. Sure he has not managed to hide his concern for her, about what she will face when her husband returns home. But he does not want Thea to carry any of that. "I'm all right," he says. It's the truth, in some small way. He does not have Julia, but he has never had Julia. And he has his daughter with him, at least for now. And that is enough. Has always been enough.

Nathan glances over at the two boys, chests rising and falling steadily. He picks the blanket off the floor and tosses it over their sleeping bodies. "Are your aunt and uncle here?" he asks Theodora.

"No. They're out on Longstone." She pulls her cloak from the armchair and wraps it around her shoulders. "We've had quite the night."

Nathan feels a pull of regret. "What happened? Is everything all right?"

"Noah and Tom got out of the house when I wasn't looking. Went running about out there in the middle of the storm. They came back raving about how they saw the Lady in the Dunes."

Nathan smiles faintly, putting a hand to her shoulder. "Perhaps you ought to be more careful about who you tell your stories to," he says gently. He ushers her out of the room so as not to wake the boys. "Why don't you go upstairs and get a little more sleep? Sounds as though you've not had much."

Theodora nods wearily. Trudges up to her bedchamber.

Nathan moves quietly through the house, lighting the fires in the bedrooms, the dining room, the parlour. Trying not to think about Julia. How many hours of his life has he spent trying not to think about Julia? He hears Mrs Brodie stirring, heading for the kitchen. Finds more of Eva's children in one of the downstairs bedrooms.

The knock at the door yanks him from his thoughts. Eva and Finn, no doubt, come to wrangle their family.

Nathan goes to the foyer. Pulls open the door, covering a yawn.

The man on the doorstep is a stranger. He's tall, round-shouldered and bulky, the beginnings of a beard darkening his cheeks and chin.

A stranger, yes, but Nathan has no doubt as to who this man is. Because Julia is standing behind him, eyes full of expectant dread.

A thousand thoughts clatter through Nathan's mind as he stands on the doorstep, eye to eye with Julia's husband. He knows how gravely he has wronged this man. And, yes, how gravely he has wronged Julia.

"Are you Nathan Blake?" says Calum.

"Yes." He looks the man in the eye. Braces himself. For what? The blow, the brandished pistol, the declaration of a duel—Nathan knows he would deserve all of it. His fingers clench around the edge of the door.

"You laid with my wife. You brought her to stay under your roof."

Nathan swallows heavily. Forces himself to hold Calum's gaze. "Yes."

Calum's dark eyes flash and Nathan grits his teeth, waiting for the fist to the jaw. It doesn't come.

"It was all my doing," Nathan says quickly. "Not Julia's. She's not the one who ought to be punished."

"I know what Julia is like," Calum says thickly. "I know who she is. And I'll not be shamed by her any longer." He reaches into the pocket of his coat for a folded sheet of paper. Shoves it into Nathan's hand.

Nathan opens it with a faint pull of dread. *Bill for the sale of a wife…*

His stomach turns over. He thinks of the wife selling he has seen in the markets and public houses across the country. The halter at the woman's neck, the money changing hands, the gathered crowds. Has Julia not faced enough shame in her life? He dares a glance at her. Her eyes are fixed to the ground. Her chest is rising and falling rapidly, cheeks blazing. "Please don't do this to her."

Calum snorts. "Save me the trouble of taking her to market. She's yours if you wish it."

Nathan feels heat prickle the back of his neck. Feels his heart pound. To do this, to accept Calum's bill and take another man's wife as his own, it undoes every step he has made to regain his family's good standing. He'd make himself the topic of fresh gossip, of whispers, rumours. Shame would hang over his family name again. And this scrawled bill that Calum has clearly cobbled together in his anger, it has not a scrap of legal weight. He could come back at any moment. Reclaim Julia as easily as he is giving her up.

But somehow, Nathan knows that he won't.

In his old life, before Julia, when he was a coffee house frequenter and a Cambridge graduate, and a starched and stilted businessman, he would have been horrified at himself for even considering this. But his old life feels distant. Nathan knows he is not seeing through the eyes of that rigid Cambridge businessman any longer. Now he is stargazer, sailor, lightkeeper's brother—and *before Julia* seems a lifetime ago.

He says, "I do wish it."

Julia says nothing. Just stands with her eyes down, unable to look at either of them.

Calum doesn't speak to her. Doesn't speak to Nathan. Just marches to the wagon waiting outside the house. He pulls out a trunk and dumps it on the wet earth. Scoops Minerva off the bench seat and tosses her out after Julia's luggage. She stalks indignantly across the grass, tail in the air, then disappears inside the house.

Calum leaps into the box seat and grabs the reins. The horse begins to trudge across the wet embankment towards the coast path. Wheels sigh through the grass and Calum is gone.

Julia stands outside the house, breathing hard, watching her husband disappear. For long moments, neither of them speak.

"I'm so sorry," Nathan says finally. "Whatever I did that caused him to find out you and I were together, I…"

Finally, Julia dares to look up at him. Snow settles in her hair and vanishes. "You didn't do anything, Nathan." She keeps her distance from him. Knots her hands together. "I told him."

He swallows. "Why?"

"Because I wanted him to know. I wanted him to rid himself of me." She lowers her eyes. "I'm sorry. He forced me to tell him how to find you. I didn't know he was going to come here. Or ask you to… rid him of me."

Nathan is silent, thoughts rattling. Having Julia here, with him, doesn't feel real. Doesn't feel possible. Feels like it will all evaporate if he tries to believe it. Finally, he says, "There's no need to stay if you don't wish it. If you wish to go to North Sunderland with Bobby, or look for your brother in London…"

Julia takes a tiny step towards him. "Nathan," she says, voice trapped in her throat, "I told Calum you and I were together because I wanted another chance to have you in my life." She draws in a breath. "However… imperfectly."

Nathan feels a smile on his lips. Imperfectly, yes. But hasn't it always been this? He thinks of all the lies and secrets and moments of distrust that had once passed between them. But there has been none of that, this time around. Now they are free from the shadow of the Rising, there has only been openness and honesty. "I want that too," he says. "So much."

Julia dares to reach for his hand. Keeps her fingers loose around his. "I know I'm asking a lot," she says. "I've abandoned the thieving ring. Calum may tell them where I am. He's angry enough to do so. They may come after me."

Nathan tightens his grip on her hand. Brings their clasped fingers to the place his heart is beating. Warmth spreads through his chest.

He thinks of the letter his mother had written to Henry Ward. Thinks of her confession that she had been coerced by the anti-Jacobite thieves. Thinks of her tearing into the ocean with her children in her arms, leaving this house, this island behind.

The Bamburgh thieving ring has changed the course of his life once before, and he has no intention of letting it happen a second time. No intention of relinquishing this impossible, unlikely life on Lindisfarne with Julia. "Let them come," he says. He's fought for Highfield House in the past. Will do it a second time if it comes to that. He pulls her close, so she might never disappear from his life again. Presses his lips to hers. "I'll not be forced from my home by thieves."

CHAPTER FORTY-TWO

When Finn opens his eyes, he's surprised to find bright white daylight spearing the gaps in the shutters. He can't remember the last time he slept through the night. Can hardly believe he's done so, with the shutters rattling like the gates of Hell. Beside him, Eva is still sleeping deeply. The roof has stopped leaking, but there's a small ocean on top of the sideboard drizzling onto the floor, pools of water in several places around the living area. The rug is soaked through, the ash in the fireplace turned to muck. Finn doesn't quite have the will to inspect the damage to the children's room right now.

A thick chill is seeping into the cottage and he shifts instinctively to light the fire. Stops himself. Are they not to leave this life behind? Leave the fireplace cold and the roof full of leaks, and an ocean rising and falling atop their sideboard?

He sits up, untangling himself from Eva, and wincing at the pain roaring down his side. In the morning light, his torso is dark with bruising, palms flecked with crimson—it feels like an outcome to be grateful for after all they had faced last night. He slides out of bed gingerly. Pulls on a dry shirt and tugs on his wet boots. His coat is still soaked through from the rain last night—he'd flung it aside before he'd dived into the water after Eva—and he makes his way outside in his shirtsleeves. The morning is white and bracing, the sea glassy. The first snow is dusting the sky, disappearing as it reaches the ocean.

He sits on the bottom step for a long time, inhaling the place. Listens to the soft sigh of the sea lapping at the black castles of the archipelago. A faint bloom of sunlight tries to push through the clouds. He can hear the chaotic squall of birdsong coming from the top end of Longstone.

Pieces of the broken skiff are knocking against the edge of the island. One has made it into the rockpool not far from their door and is floating listlessly above the nine-pins ball. Finn sees several more pieces bobbing out on the grey water beyond the firebasket. Mercifully, the longboat is still knocking against the jetty, though he imagines there'll be a lagoon to bail out of her before they leave. Roof tiles lie in pieces across the island.

There's a stillness here that has not existed for years. Those years when he had been alone on the island usually feel impossibly distant. But right now, that alternative life feels so close to hand. Finn is certain that, had Eva not come crashing onto Longstone the night of Donald Macauley's death, he would never have married. Never become a father. And never confronted the memories of Oliver Blake's death. This silent, unpeopled island would have been the rest of his silent, unpeopled life.

He turns at the sound of the door clicking open. Eva is wrapped in a shawl and thick quilted skirts, dark hair hanging loose down her back. He stands, pulls her close, inhaling the scent of her; sea salt and warmth and familiarity.

She looks down at the shattered tiles, then up at the roof. "Well," she says, "at least the house is still standing." Her eyes drift to the broken pieces of the skiff drifting on the surface of the rockpool. "I'm sorry," she says. "I'm so sorry."

He shakes his head. He doesn't want apologies. He is just grateful they are both still here. Both still standing. Both still breathing.

Neither of them speak as Finn pulls the longboat away from the jetty. Duffel bags crammed with pieces of their lives are sitting at their feet. They've emptied the sideboard of potted meats and jam jars and candles. Flung waterlogged bags of flour and oats into the sea. Cleared the mantel of its candlesticks and quadrant and twine; of all the rocks and shells and driftwood Archie has excavated from the rockpools. Will come back soon to collect the rest of their clothing, and the children's toys, and the furniture that's dry enough to be saved.

There's a heaviness to the thought of leaving that was not here last night. After the storm—and half a century of being pounded by wind and sea—their cottage is still standing. And in the bright light of morning, Finn is not seeing the confined life he had tried to escape as a boy. Is not seeing the frustration and anger of yet another fight with his father. He is seeing the cottage where he had fallen asleep listening to his mother tell stories about selkies and sea spirits. The coal shed where he had first stumbled across Eva. And when he looks at that unassuming plane of rock this morning, he is not seeing the place his father had died, but the place his wife had lived.

He lifts the oars from the water and lets the boat drift. The snowflakes have given way to thick beams of sunlight breaking through the clouds, lifting the water from grey to blue. Finn feels Eva's eyes on him.

"You don't wish to leave, do you."

He tries to read beneath her words. Is she disappointed by the realisation? Relieved? Her voice feels deliberately empty, as though trying not to guide him to a response.

She squints into the sunlight, taking in the silhouette of their cottage on its high stone foundations. The firebasket swaying in the breeze. The creak of the chain reaches them from across the water.

"This is the life I chose, Finn," Eva says, after a long silence. "This is the life I would choose a thousand times over. I've never seen that more clearly." She slides forward on the bench and laces her fingers through his. "But," she says carefully, "if we are to stay, it cannot be out of guilt. Not anymore. It must be because we want it."

He is so desperately ready to release his guilt. Over Oliver. Over his father. So desperately ready for Eva to release her guilt too.

And yes, he realises. He does want it. This life, this island; it has been what he wants for a long time. Who is he without this place? Without the sleepless nights, the sea on the doorstep, the blazing light in the sky. And perhaps the next time he lights the beacon, he might do it out of pride, rather than out of a desperate search for absolution. Because when he takes a step back from his father, and Oliver, and Donald Macauley, Finn can see that yes, he is proud of all he and his family have done out here. He is proud to carry the responsibility of lighting these dark islands. And if this is the life his children choose, well, then he will be proud of that too.

"That roof's going to be a real bastard to fix," he says.

A smile flickers on Eva's lips. "I'm sure Nathan will have us at the house for as long as it takes to make the repairs." She shifts on the bench seat, looking over her shoulder at their home. "And Longstone will always be here waiting for us."

Eva cannot remember the house ever being so full, this creaking and shadowed fisherman's cottage grown wild. Full as perhaps it was always supposed to be.

It's a different place to what it had been in those months after her brother had died, when she and Nathan and their mother had been dwarfed and drowned by the enormous silence of the house. A time whose memories have been steadily filtering back to her over the years she has been back in Northumberland.

The parlour is full of voices; the children clinging to her and Finn and talking all at once; Nathan and Julia tucked beside each other on the settle; Theodora, Tom, the golden-eyed cat.

But Eva goes to the bottom of the stairs. Looks up, hesitating. Then she returns to the parlour.

"Where is Harriet?" she asks Thea.

On the journey back to Lindisfarne, Eva had steeled herself against the thought of seeing her sister again. Had convinced herself they could find some path through the bitterness. They had to, didn't they? Especially now, that she has sworn to herself she will let her guilt over Macauley's death fall away. But at the look of confusion in Theodora's eyes, the unease lodged deep in Eva's stomach shifts into something else.

"What do you mean?" Thea asks. "Aunt Harriet never came to the house."

"Yes, she…" Eva feels panic flickering inside her. "She was with me when I went looking for Noah and Tom. I told her to take the boys back inside. I told her to come in and warm herself. She was shivering…"

"The boys came back to the house alone," Theodora says. "They told me you had to go to Longstone. They…" She sucks in a breath. Covers her mouth with her hand. "They were raving about seeing the Lady in the Dunes."

And, *The Lady in the Dunes*, Eva says to Tom and Noah. *Tell me about the Lady in the Dunes. Where did she go?*

The boys go to the window, pointing out onto the embankment, eyes shining with the thrill of the story. "She told us to go inside the house," says Noah.

"She said she couldn't come in."

"We came to the window and watched her from here."

"Watched her do what?" Eva pushes.

"Watched her walk into the water."

Her stomach dives. She thinks of the wrecked ship, of Harriet's story of the bearded man, and the crewmen who had pulled her back from jumping into the sea. She is racing towards the front door as Tom says, "And then the boat came."

Eva whirls around. "Whose boat? Did she get aboard?"

The boys eye each other. "I don't know," Noah says finally. "It was too dark to see."

Eva rushes from the house. Hurries over the wet rocks of the embankment. Silver pools of the low tide are shining in the pale morning sun. A heron swoops low, wings outstretched.

She is not alone, Eva realises. Finn is just behind her, Nathan and Julia too.

"She's not…" Finn puts a hand to her shoulder. Starts again. "We'd have found her in the low tide if she…"

Eva hears the uncertainty in his voice. Feels a pull of too-familiar fear. The fear of what might lie beneath the surface of her lost and complicated sister. Disappeared into the fabric of this island as she has so many times before.

CHAPTER FORTY-THREE

She wakes to creaks and rattles and that constant unseen hiss of the sea. She is curled up on a sleeping pallet on the floor of the cabin, a scratchy blanket thrown over her shoulders. Eva's storm-cloud grey skirts hang drying over the table. Harriet has dim memories of wrangling herself out of them, trying to shake away the cold, the sluggishness, the haze.

Her gaze is drawn to a shard of glass on the floor, a few inches from her eyes. She thinks of ramming the telescope into the side of Lawler's head. Thinks of the glass exploding across the cabin. Hears the dull thud as he had slumped to the floor. She has not yet found the courage to ask her father what has happened to him. Is afraid of the answer.

The brass box is still on the table. Ward must have seen it, surely. He had helped her down here to the cabin last night after finding her on the edge of the embankment close to Highfield House, dazed by cold, her thoughts tangled. This box that had once been so precious to him—that surely must be still, given what is inside it—there is no way he would have missed it, even in the dark, the chaos, the noise and danger of the storm.

Harriet does not know what had caused her to walk into the water last night. To walk out towards the boat she could see careening over the swell. Confusion, wrought by cold? Perhaps. Somehow, out there in the water had felt like where she belonged. But Harriet can't quite tell if it was a sense of belonging on Henry Ward's boat, or belonging in the dark and silent depths of the sea.

She stands, steadying her legs against the rhythmic tilt of the boat. She climbs into her skirts and laces her bodice, both still far more wet than dry. Takes the box from the table and slips it into her pocket. Then she draws in a breath and climbs the ladder.

Her father is sitting on the bench by the tiller, eyes glassy as he looks out over slate-grey water. He turns as she steps through the hatch. Gives her a faint smile. "How are you?"

It's a complicated question; too complicated for an answer right now. She hands him the box. Ward stares down at it for a long time, running a finger over its tarnished surface.

"Where did you find it?" he asks finally. "When?"

"My brother found it several days ago in Bamburgh. Among thieves." She swallows heavily. Steels herself. "Have you read…"

"Yes," says Ward. "I have." When he finally looks up at her, the expression in his eyes is impossibly weighted. He opens the lid of the box. Peers inside it before closing it again quickly. "I went back for your mother," he says. "A few months after Oliver died, I went back to Lindisfarne for her. I planned to tell her I wanted to make a life with her. I planned to tell her I was leaving the sea."

Harriet sits on the bench beside him. Nods at him to continue.

"The night we arrived on Holy Island, I told my crew I was planning to leave the ship. When they realised that meant cutting their articles of agreement short, they began rioting. I sent one of my crewmen to the house to tell Abigail what was happening. To tell her I'd be there as soon as I could. When Mr Graveney came back, he told me the house was empty."

"Mr Graveney," Harriet repeats. "The man who tried to take the house from Nathan."

Her father nods. He toys with the broken lock on top of the box. "Once it was safe for me to leave the ship, I went to the house for myself, just to make sure. It was dark. Empty. Your mother and siblings were gone."

"They were running from thieves," Harriet says.

Ward nods. "Yes." His voice feels deliberately empty, as though he is doing his best to keep his emotion at bay.

Harriet curls a hand around the gunwale, watching the grey shape of the mainland drift by on their right. Her mind is racing, thinking of that other life that might have been. The life that might have unfolded if Abigail's letter had landed in her father's hands. It's the most pointless of thoughts, she knows. But it is hard to avoid.

She stares at her feet. Can hardly bear the weight of what the revelations in this letter mean for her and her father. But she will not run, she tells herself. Not this time. The life that might have been has fallen away. But she will find the courage to catch hold of this one.

"Mother's letter," she says, "it changes things." Her words come out strained, and suddenly she can't look at her father. "She did not run to keep you from me."

On the edge of her vision, she sees a hint of a smile lighten Ward's face. "No. It would not seem that she did."

Right now, she can go no further than this. Cannot invite him into her life, or discuss what the future might look like. Not yet. The vulnerability already has her heart pounding. Right now, this feels like enough. Feels like everything. "Are you all right?" she asks finally.

Her father passes the box back to her, covering her hand with his for the briefest of moments. "I hardly know." There's a look of bewilderment in his eyes Harriet can tell is reflected in her own.

They sit in silence for a long time. The sea sighs rhythmically against the hull of the cutter, wind piercing Harriet's damp clothes. "Where is Lawler?" she dares to ask. "Did I…"

"No. You didn't. He was like a caged lion when I came back to the ship and found him locked below."

She releases a breath of relief. Swallows heavily. "Do I need to be concerned about him?"

"No."

And she will let this be enough too. She will not pry for answers she does not want. She will give herself permission not to hide a pistol in her pocket. Will let her father carry this for her. She will give herself permission not to go through every inch of life alone.

"Where are we going?" she asks.

"South. Back to London if you wish it. Unless you intend to return to Northumberland?"

She shakes her head. "No. There's nothing for me there." She thinks of her sister, her brother, her son. Thinks of all the memories that hurt to remember. "Rather," she says, pain striking her throat, "there's too much for me there."

Her father gives a her a faint, weighted smile that doesn't quite reach his eyes. "Yes, my girl," he says, glancing over his shoulder to the island disappearing behind a wall of cloud. "I know exactly how you feel."

The low tide has given up its secrets: stepping stones and fishing hooks and stolen jewels from a discarded Bamburgh box safe. It has not given up her sister.

Eva has walked the rim of the island; past the rockpools and embankment beyond the windows of Highfield House. Past Saint Cuthbert's Island and the broken shards of the priory, where her eldest brother had dreamed of Viking raids. Past the Pilgrims' Way, where she had fled Lindisfarne in her nightgown, wrapped in her mother's arms.

Searching the island for her sister feels like a piece of both the past and the future—something she is destined to keep repeating. She has been here before. And Eva tells herself she will be here again.

She will choose to believe the best. Will choose to believe Harriet has found her way back to London, to a life that makes her happy. Will choose to believe the boat has finally come for Thea's Lady in the Dunes.

And perhaps in another ten years, Harriet will reappear.

Are you happy? Eva will ask her. *Are your paintings hung in palaces and Parisian salons?*

Yes, she has no choice but to believe in this. To trust there is some part of Harriet that feels, like the rest of them, the tidal pull of these islands; of this silver-black sea that reshapes and scours; that takes and spares lives. To trust that a part of her might be drawn back here by the ghost of that life that might have been. A life that never was, but that somehow, someway, has always been guiding them, starlike, right back to this.

ACKNOWLEDGEMENTS

A very big thank you to everyone who has helped me put together this series: "vibe consultant" extraordinaire Sam Fiorani; beta readers Leanne, Annette and the team at AJC Publishing; and my wonderful cover designer Tim Barber.

Thank you to the National Trust team at Lindisfarne Castle and the Northumbrian Jacobite Society for a wealth of incredible information, and to Dave Isom and Denise Yeung for imparting your boat-handling (Dave) and child-handling (Denise) skills.

A big thank you to my wonderful readers' group for coming up with the perfect names for those characters (and cats) I just could not find the right names for; and to Irene Laing—quite possibly the world's biggest fan of these characters—for all your story suggestions (or should that be "demands"?)!

ABOUT THE AUTHOR

A lover of old stuff, folk music and ghost stories, Johanna Craven bases her books around little-known true events from the past. She divides her time between the UK and Australia, and can be very easily persuaded to tell you about the time she accidently swam with seals on Holy Island.

Find out more at www.johannacraven.com.